LIVING DOGS AND DEAD LIONS

A

NOVEL

BY

R. LANNY HUNTER

LIVING DOGS and DEAD LIONS

AND VICTOR L. HUNTER

VIKING

VIKING

Viking Penguin Inc., 40 West 23rd Street,
New York, New York 10010, U.S.A.
Penguin Books Ltd, Harmondsworth, Middlesex, England
Penguin Books Australia Ltd, Ringwood, Victoria, Australia
Penguin Books Canada Limited, 2801 John Street,
Markham, Ontario, Canada L3R 1B4
Penguin Books (N.Z.) Ltd, 182–190 Wairau Road,
Auckland 10, New Zealand

First published in 1986 by Viking Penguin Inc.
Published simultaneously in Canada

Excerpt from "To an Athlete Dying Young," from "A Shropshire
Lad"—Authorized Edition. From *The Collected Poems of
A. E. Housman*. Copyright, 1939, 1940, © 1965 by Holt, Rinehart
and Winston, copyright © 1967, 1968 by Robert E. Symons.
Reprinted by permission of Holt, Rinehart and Winston,
Publishers, and The Society of Authors as the literary
representative of the Estate of A. E. Housman and Jonathan
Cape Ltd., publishers of A. E. Housman's *Collected Poems*.

LIBRARY OF CONGRESS CATALOGING IN PUBLICATION DATA
Hunter, R. Lanny.
Living dogs and dead lions.
I. Hunter, Victor L.   II. Title.
PS3558.U488L58   1986   813'.54   85-40564
ISBN 0-670-80901-2

Printed in the United States of America by
The Book Press, Brattleboro, Vermont
Set in Caledonia and News Gothic
Design by David Connolly

For
Russell and Gwen,
who started the journey,
and
Carolyn and Lynette,
who continue it

This is an evil

in all that is done under the sun,

that there is one fate for all men.

Yea, the hearts of men are full of evil,

and madness fills their hearts

throughout all their lives.

And after that they go down to join the dead.

But to him that is counted among the living,

there is still hope.

For a living dog

is better than

a dead lion.

Ecclesiastes 9:3–4

LIVING DOGS AND DEAD LIONS

CHAPTER ONE

The truck maneuvered carefully up the narrow forest service road. The grade steepened and the engine strained, chassis shuddering, as the deuce and a half bucked against the slope. The driver downshifted and gunned it. The men in the rear of the truck gripped the plank seats and lurched against each other as the vehicle clawed its way up the rutted track.

Joshua Scott shifted his feet amid the tangle of gear and equipment piled in the center of the truck bed. He clung to his seat as desperately as he clung to the fragile structure of his life, and braced himself against the kidney-jarring blows. The truck jounced the last few hundred yards to the top of the ridge where the road dead-ended, and jolted to a stop in a swelter of dust. Joshua stood up slowly, long frame uncoiling like a whip. He was tall and lean and dark. Dark eyes, dark hair, and thick dark mustache. His face had an ill-defined tautness about it, the look of a man who had been out in a high wind too long. Joshua swept his tongue across the enamel of his front teeth, wetting the film of Virginia dirt that coated them, and stared back down the mountain. A pall of smoke and ash hung over the valley like a festering fog. Over one hundred thousand acres of the Monongahela had already burned.

It was the best view he'd had of the fire in the six days they'd been fighting it. Until now he'd felt like one of the blind men grappling with his particular piece of the elephant. Joshua watched the flames, captivated by them. He began to tremble, an almost imperceptible shaking that was both agitation and anticipation. Now he sensed the danger of this big, sprawling fire and felt the adrenaline begin to pump. He felt alive again. But also pushed toward the brink of total disintegration.

A thick red slab of a man stood at Joshua's shoulder. "Bewitchin', ain't it?" A folksy up-hollow twang.

Joshua nodded. Destruction. Graceful and beautiful. Terrifying. Fascinating. He pursed his lips in a subtle grimace. He had never learned to live with ambiguity.

Joshua's squad boss, a West Virginian named Jethro Carley, gestured toward the valley. "Wonder if that thunderhead's gonna help us or hurt us?"

Joshua followed Carley's gaze. A bank of clouds was building up in the southeast. They boiled up twenty thousand feet into the sky, a purple rack of cumulus, shifting and violent. "A good rain wouldn't hurt us," Joshua said, "but the winds can do funny things to a fire." His voice was tinged with the soft accents of the Virginia tidewater country, but it was emotionless, flat and hard. Everything about Joshua seemed flat and hard. Like an ax embedded in a chopping block.

"Well, we're supposed to try and tie it off here in case it starts up this canyon." Carley clambered over the side of the truck and went around and lowered the tailgate.

Joshua and a few other men dropped to the ground while the remainder began to hand down equipment. Shovels, Pulaskis, axes, brush hooks, chain saws. They laid the equipment out on the ground, sorting it by black-stenciled letters. MNF for the Monongahela National Forest, and SWF for the Southwest Forest. Lunch buckets, bedrolls, and water coolers stayed on the truck. Joshua watched the men off-load. Ten of them worked with him in the Monongahela fire-fighting squad. The remainder of the men on the truck were Navajos. Ten in all. The Southwest Forest squad was one of more than a dozen Navajo fire-fighting crews. They had all been flown in from Arizona in the past two days to try to help control the fire. Joshua was glad to see them. They were supposed to be the best in the business.

Another truck, engine grinding, labored up the mountain road. Joshua turned to watch the second deuce and a half negotiate the last fifty yards of the steep grade. It rocked from side to side over the ruts, rolling like a ship in a rough sea, stirring up clouds of dust. It ground to a stop just behind him. Two additional squads of

Navajos unloaded. Twenty men. They were greeted by the Navajo squad that had ridden up in Joshua's truck. The stocky mahogany-colored men moved among each other with a limber, rolling swagger. They shook hands with exaggerated pumping motions, almost ceremonially. *"Yah-te-hay! Yah-te-hay!"*

Joshua watched them sort out their equipment and saddle up. He hadn't seen a Navajo since Jimmy Smallcanyon. Not in twelve years.

The flare burst high above the compound, a phosphorescent flower painted against a black canvas.

Joshua's stomach constricted and he could taste the acrid, brassy styptic of fear on his palate. He glanced down the perimeter. His platoon of Chinese Nungs crouched in the trench on either side of him. A few yards away one of them grinned, flashing gold, and clicked the safety on his carbine on and off, on and off, in nervous rhythm. Joshua grinned back and thumbs-upped with a bravado he did not feel. On the far left of the perimeter he could see Tom Bishop with his platoon of Nungs. To his far right he could see Jimmy Smallcanyon with his.

"Here they come!" Bishop's voice was shrill, and affected a certain bizarre gaiety.

Joshua peered over the rim of the trench. The North Vietnamese were sprinting across the open ground between the jungle and the concertina wire. Hundreds of mustard-colored uniforms flickered jerkily in the cold, sputtering light of the flare. They looked like an old black-and-white newsreel.

"Fire!" Bishop screamed. "Fire!"

Joshua flipped his M-16 on fully automatic and squeezed the trigger, firing short, three-round bursts. The North Vietnamese attackers fell in front of him, sprawling in convulsive heaps, but others swarmed out of the night and took their place. Incoming rounds slapped viciously into the perimeter and the Nung next to Joshua stumbled backward, twitching violently. He saw a team of sappers fling themselves down near the concertina wire. With controlled haste they began to assemble Bangalore torpedoes and slide them forward under the wire. Joshua concentrated on the sappers and picked them off one by one. Out of the corner of his eye he saw another team of sappers setting a charge at the compound gate. He swung his M-16 toward them but was unable to get the angle for enfilading fire. Jesus, he thought, if they blow the gate . . .

Joshua ducked away from the firing line and started running down the trench. By the light of another flickering flare he saw Jimmy Smallcanyon haul himself up out of the trench from his position at the far end of the perimeter and start sprinting across the open ground toward the gate. He made ten meters before a round caught him under his swinging left arm, lifted him up, and spun him to the ground. He pulled himself to his knees and sighted on the Vietnamese trying to insert wires into the charge. Fired and missed. His second round exploded in the sapper's chest. He crawled toward the gate, dragging his M-16. Another sapper took the place of the first. Smallcanyon shot him.

Joshua reached Smallcanyon just as he shot the last Vietnamese trying to detonate the charge. He rolled Smallcanyon over on his back. His tiger suit was sticky with blood. A pink froth bubbled on his lips. He was restless and sweaty.

"Fuckin' Anglos," Smallcanyon muttered.

Joshua slowly began to pull together his own fire-fighting gear. What did it mean, he wondered. Fuckin' Anglos. Was it for him? The team? Or just a Navajo epithet for the way of things?

Jethro Carley called the men around him. He was standing on the edge of the canyon. It was narrow, with sloping, timbered walls, and it tied into the valley below them. "Okay, you men, listen up." He knelt on the ground and brushed away the pine needles with a big freckled hand. He picked up a stick and drew a long V. "This here's the canyon." He placed an X at the open end of the V. "The slurry bombers are going to make their drops along here to try and keep the fire from turning up this canyon and breaking out up here on the plateau." He drew a line parallel to one limb of the V. "This is the forest service road we just came up. We'll use it as a natural fire line on this side of the canyon." Carley looked around the circle of faces. "My squad will work on the rim here." He looked at the foreman of the Southwest Forest squads. "The SWIF squads will tie it off on the other rim and at the end of the canyon."

The Navajo nodded, his face expressionless.

"Send two squads across to the other rim to cut a fire line there." Carley stood, moved over to the edge of the canyon, and pointed down into the narrow end. It was filled mostly with standing snags. About two acres of trees, dead from lightning strikes and bark beetles or some other blight. "Your other squad should clear that snag patch. I'll be your lookout from up here on the rim in case there's trouble." Carley turned around. He lifted his hard hat and swept a broad hand across a balding crew cut. "Any questions?"

"How far down the rim do you want us to work, Jethro?" It was one of the men in the Monongahela crew. A college student from the University of Virginia who had just joined the crew for the summer.

"As soon as we get to where the walls fall off too steep for tree growth so a fire can't climb out of the canyon, we can stop." Carley scratched at a week's growth of dirty red stubble on his chin. "We'll cut for burnout at this end where the ravine's shallow enough that trees grow up the walls right to the rim." He stared down at the valley. As the day heated up, the fire had gathered momentum. The smoke and ash, fanned by the gathering thunderstorm into roiling banks of gray scum, almost obscured the far side of the mountain range. The fire crept steadily toward the mouth of the canyon. "We've got maybe five, six hours. Let's get to it."

The Navajo squads moved off. They retrieved their lunch buckets from the trucks, knowing they wouldn't come back for lunch break. Joshua slipped his safety goggles off the front of his hard hat and settled them over his eyes. He tugged at the cuffs of his leather gloves, snugging them on his hands, making fists as he did so. He slung his brush hook from the spacer on his belt, then picked up his double-bitted ax. He removed the leather case from the head and tested the blades carefully with his thumb. Satisfied, he started toward the canyon rim. He was stopped by a brief guttural exchange between two Navajos. He turned back. He didn't understand a word of it, but from the gestures he could tell they weren't too happy about working in the bottom of a dead-end ravine trying to build a fire line downhill toward a fire with thunderheads in the background. He couldn't blame them. It was a combination of the worst factors for fire safety. He watched them shoulder their chain saws and scramble down the sides of the ravine, breaking their descent against trees and rock outcroppings. One headed toward the snag patch and the other started up the other side to the opposite rim.

Carley's squad went to work. They spaced themselves along the canyon on the narrow strip between the service road and the canyon rim, where loblolly pines towered skyward like sentinels. Joshua and seven of the crew limbed up the pines to a height of about four or five feet. Carley and the remaining three crewmen used chain saws to fell the occasional snags and thin the timber where it made for closely spaced fuel. All other sounds were drowned out by the harsh rasp of the chain saws.

Joshua worked with a measured rhythm. He used his ax with practiced skill, shearing off the lower hanging branches of the pines, moving from tree to tree. After he'd worked an area he would go back with his brush hook and drag the tree limbs and ground combustibles into piles along the edge of the canyon. If it became necessary they could set backfires along the rim. Joshua paused. Sweat poured from his face and stung his eyes. His yellow fire shirt was soaked. He took off his hard hat, placed it on the ground, and dropped his goggles and gloves into it. He removed a red bandanna from the pocket of his trousers and wiped his face. He rolled it up and tied it low around his forehead as a sweatband. He peeled open the Velcro tabs on the first aid kit hanging from his belt and removed two salt tablets. He washed them down with two sips of lukewarm water from his canteen. He took one more mouthful, carefully swished it back and forth, letting it seep into the parched crevices of his mouth and throat, savoring it, then swallowed. He was thirsty, but he deliberately capped the canteen and replaced it on his belt. Despite the fact that there were two twenty-five-gallon water coolers on the truck, he still practiced water discipline. It was pointless, he knew.

Joshua moved over to the canyon rim. He could feel the dry wind as it funneled up the canyon. Even against his sweat-soaked fire shirt, the wind felt hot. He looked down toward the valley. The fire was moving closer to the mouth of the canyon. Through the drifting smoke and ash he could see the flames move slowly along the ground cover. When the fire reached a stand of timber it would slowly ascend a tree and devour it. Sometimes showers of sparks would scatter ahead of the main fire and start spot fires. They'd better get those slurry bombers busy, he thought. Thunderheads continued to mass in the southeast and seemed to be stalking the head of the fire as it moved up the valley. He glanced down into the dead end of the ravine. The SWIF squad was working in two-man crews felling the snags. They were making good progress. He could hear the stuttering rasp of their chain saws echoing off the canyon walls.

Joshua retrieved his hard hat, goggles, and gloves, and went back to work. The crew began to link up their individual work areas, creating a strip between the forest service road and the canyon rim which was cleared of ground cover, snags, and closely spaced timber. The combustible material was dragged to the edge of the rim, and a long backfire line was slowly taking shape. At midday, with the sun partially blocked by the accumulated haze from the fire, they broke for lunch.

Joshua found his lunch bucket on the truck and moved off by himself. He settled down against the trunk of a pine and opened the battered black bucket. A paperback book, *The Structure of Genre Forms*, rested on top of two plastic-wrapped bologna sandwiches. What do you do with a degree in comparative literature? he wondered. Make interesting conversation? He laid the book aside. He always brought something to read in case things got slack or they got caught out overnight. It wasn't just the relaxation and the enjoyment. The books were a means of avoiding involvement with the rest of the crew. He began to eat, ignoring the grime on his hands and face, and watched the crew as they tilted the water coolers for each other and washed up. He still couldn't waste water.

The crew ranged along the ground near the truck and broke out their lunches. Joshua watched them and listened to their small talk. Felt their masculine presence. He half smiled. I'm still in uniform, he thought. Yellow fire shirt and green pants. Of all the odd jobs he had done in the last eleven or twelve years, he liked the fire-crew work the best. This was his third season. He liked the sense of camaraderie, even though he held himself aloof from it. He liked the hard work. Sweat and substance. He liked the visible, useful, definable accomplishment. A fire line established by the end of the day. And he liked the danger. Life under threat, but with vitality.

He finished his lunch, allowed himself four swallows of water from his canteen, considered the last two a luxury, and placed his

lunch bucket back on the truck. He ambled over to the canyon rim
and peered into the ravine. The SWIF squad had continued to
clear the snag patch. The snags had been bucked into smaller
sections and rolled or towed downhill into the timber to clear the
end of the canyon of combustibles. Half of the crew was still working, their chain saws creating a monotonous rasp, the sound rising
and falling as the teeth chewed into the timber. The remaining
crew members had broken for lunch and were sitting in the shade
of a stone outcropping near the opposite canyon wall. Joshua saw
the SWIF foreman clambering down from the far rim. He made his
way over to the outcropping and hunkered down to talk with his
men.

Joshua gradually became aware of the aircraft. He could hear its
engine above the rumble of the chain saws. He raised a hand to
shade his eyes and searched the murky pall that hung over the
valley until he spotted the plane. It was the first of the slurry
bombers making its run. The bomber was a converted Air Force
C-119. He watched the plane lumbering along a few hundred feet
above the floor of the valley. The wings tilted a few degrees as final
adjustments in the flight path were made. When the aircraft
reached the mouth of the canyon it released the slurry. Twenty-
four hundred gallons of fire retardant fell away from the fuselage.
Bright pink, it plunged toward the forest like pastel rain. The old
C-119 was a familiar aircraft, and Joshua was surprised to see the
slurry dropped through some bay cut into the bottom of the fuselage. They had always exited from side doors. He watched the C-119
bank away from the mouth of the canyon, peeling away to the
northeast so it wouldn't have to cut across the smoke-filled valley.
A second C-119 began its approach from the southeast to unload its
slurry. Joshua watched the plane buck and shudder as it skirted the
thunderheads. He knew the winds could be perilous around the
edge of a storm, often gusting to gale force.

Jethro Carley joined Joshua on the rim. They watched the aircraft make its drop, lunging upward as it suddenly lightened. "If
them thunderheads move in any closer, they ain't gonna be able
to make any more drops."

"That C-119 was feeling the weather," Joshua agreed.

Carley leaned forward and blew his nose forcefully at the ground
between his thumb and forefinger. As he wiped his hands on his

trousers, he said, "Josh, you get the crew back to work. I'm going to check in with the line boss on the CB." He moved off toward the truck.

Joshua started down along the edge of the canyon. The other men in Carley's crew had finished their lunches and were already drifting back to work. He ignored Carley's instructions that he get them back to work. He wasn't giving any orders to anybody. The crew knew what to do anyway. Joshua walked over to the stump where he had left his ax. He grasped the handle with his right hand and with an abrupt cocking motion levered the blade free from the stump. He removed a whetstone and a tin of oil from his kit and honed the blades on the ax with deft strokes. Then he went to work.

An hour later the weather had changed. As Joshua limbed up the pines and raked the limbs to the backfire line, he kept an eye on the valley below. The thunderheads had moved in, blocking off the far mountain range. A C-119 had made one more slurry drop, fighting the winds on the edge of the storm; then the weather cut the planes off from their target. The thunderclouds had not blocked out the afternoon sun, but the temperature had dropped. Cool winds funneled up the canyon and gusted over the rim onto the plateau. At first Joshua and the rest of Carley's crew worked faster, as though driven by the increasing force of the winds, racing the storm. Then the pace slowed. They were more and more absorbed by what was happening below them. The forest fire was being driven by the thunderstorm. It followed an erratic course dictated by the gusting winds on the fringes of the storm, and several heads developed. The flames spread more rapidly through the ground cover, gathering momentum. Trees ignited in fiery bursts, like incendiary torches, and the flames leapt from tree to tree. Fanned by the shifting winds, one head of the fire veered toward the mouth of the canyon.

Joshua moved toward the canyon rim. He was joined by Jethro Carley and the rest of the crew. They watched in silent fascination as the flames approached the canyon, spilling forward in fiery waves. When the fire reached the area of the slurry drop, the blaze faltered, deprived of easy fuel. But the intense heat and the wind defeated the fire retardant. Thin fingers of fire crept along the ground, feeling their way forward, finding a combustible path across the mouth of the canyon. Then the fire blazed up between the canyon walls. The inexorable laws of thermodynamics took over. As the wind poured into the narrow canyon it increased in velocity. The rising wind delivered more oxygen to the fire. More intense burning caused convected heat waves to rise, driving the fire uphill at an ever-accelerating rate and lifting it into the tops of the trees. The blaze became an inferno, a fire storm, a raging funnel of fire feeding on itself and racing up the canyon as if it were a chimney.

"She's gonna torch out, Jethro!" Joshua said, an edge to his voice.

Carley watched, broad hands resting on his thick hips, not saying anything. The flames climbed into the tops of the pines and then skipped from tree to tree with explosive force. The crowns of the trees simply ignited in a furious flash of fire. Even at that distance Joshua could feel the heat. And hear the fire storm. It sounded like a runaway freight train rushing toward them.

Joshua watched the fire race through the tops of the trees. "It's a crown fire, Jethro!"

"Where the fuck is the SWIF foreman?" Carley muttered.

One of Carley's crew, a huge black regular with the Forest Service, pointed into the floor of the canyon. "He's still down there workin' with them snags."

Carley pulled the portable radio from his belt and extended the antenna. He lifted it to his lips and pressed the mike button. "SWIF Seven, this is Monongahela Fifteen. Come in. Over." Carley waited a few seconds, then repeated the call signs.

A moment later a voice sheathed in static answered. "Monongahela Fifteen, this is SWIF Seven. Over."

Carley stared into the canyon and spotted the foreman looking back at him with his own radio to his lips. "SWIF Seven, we've got a crown fire in the canyon. You've got to get your boys out fast."

The SWIF foreman didn't bother to acknowledge Carley's transmission. He hung his radio on his belt and started moving through the snag patch spreading the word to his crew. It was a footrace against the rampaging fire.

Joshua and the rest of Carley's squad watched from the canyon rim. The Navajos scattered, picked up their equipment, and sprinted heavily toward safety. Some were closer to the far rim and moved in that direction. Others ran to the near rim and started

scrambling up the canyon walls. A few made their way to the far
end of the canyon and up the narrow end of the gorge toward the
plateau. The SWIF foreman took a last look around to satisfy himself that all of his crew was on the move. He was just ready to make
his run for it when he spotted a chain saw left embedded in the
trunk of a towering snag. He turned back to retrieve the saw, but
the cut was halfway through the trunk and the bar and chain were
caught in a bind. The foreman pulled on the handlebars, trying to
rock the blade free. It wouldn't budge.

"Leave it," Carley muttered under his breath.

The foreman glanced down the canyon, trying to gauge the rate
of the fire.

"You can't see it, you son of a bitch," Carley said, louder. "Leave
it!"

The foreman threw the switch and pulled the starter rope. He
engaged the chain and revved the throttle, bracing himself against
the torque as the teeth bit into the wood. The weight of the tree
continued to settle on the bar and he was unable to back the blade
out of the cut. The foreman took one last glance down the canyon
and then pivoted the blade into the trunk to finish the cut and fell
the tree.

"What the hell's the matter with him?" the black man growled,
as much in wonder as irritation.

"He can still make it," Joshua said, "if he gets with it."

The foreman worked swiftly and skillfully, forcing the cut
through the trunk. Slowly the snag began to tilt, the remaining
wood beyond the cut splintering as the tree toppled. The foreman
jerked the saw free and stepped away in case the tree kicked back
off the stump. As the snag fell, dead limbs crashing through nearby
trees, it jarred loose a big freestanding snag that leaned heavily into
the other trees. As it lost its precarious support, the snag plunged
toward the unsuspecting foreman, who stood off to the side.

"He don't see the widow-maker," the black man said.

"Watch out!" It was the college kid from Virginia. He screamed
again involuntarily, knowing that the distance and the roar of the
fire drowned out his words. "Watch out!"

The snag struck the foreman a glancing blow. He was flung
sideways to the ground, rolled once, and lay still. Carley's crew
stood transfixed on the rim.

Joshua looked for the other SWIF crewmen. They were running for their lives, scrambling up out of the canyon. None were aware of what had happened below them. He looked down the canyon. The fire was at most fifteen minutes away, howling with destructive fury as it exploded from treetop to treetop. A crown fire would parboil an unprotected man beneath it as it flashed over him.

"Let the Yah-te-hays save him!"

Joshua looked for the voice. It was Zeller, a thin stick of a man he had crewed with for two seasons. Zeller was quiet, pleasant, dependable, and hard-working. He was married, had five kids. No trouble on or off the job.

"Fuckin' Anglos."

Joshua wheeled and sprinted to the truck. Scrambling up into the bed, he jerked three blankets from the bedrolls and overturned a water cooler on them, soaking them completely. He wadded them up, tucked them under an arm, and headed back for the canyon rim.

Jethro Carley met him halfway. "Don't do it, Josh!" He clutched at Joshua's arm.

Joshua shook him off and started over the rim.

"He may already be dead!"

Joshua ignored Carley. He bounded from rock to rock, crashing down the steep slope, breaking his headlong rush by grabbing at the pine trees speared into the ground. He slipped on some shale, head-over-heeled for a dozen yards and came up running, a laceration over one eye and bloody abrasions on his leg and wrist. A few moments later he was on the floor of the canyon. To his left he saw the fire racing toward him through the tops of the trees, shrieking like a monstrous turbine engine. It was less than a hundred yards away. The conflagration created a vacuum, sucking in air like a blast furnace. It pulled at him with increasing force. The heat seared his face. Joshua whipped the blankets over him like a shroud, peeked through a fold and got his bearings, and stumbled toward the SWIF foreman. He spread the wet blankets on the ground beside the injured man and then lay on top of him. He clung to the Navajo with one hand and the edges of the blankets with the other, rolled over and over, and wrapped the blankets around them. They lay together, bundled in the wet blankets like a cocoon.

Joshua's ragged breathing slowed. In the dark of their dripping sanctuary he could barely make out the features of the foreman. But he was alive. He could feel the movement of his chest as the man breathed, and could hear an incoherent moaning, an occasional Navajo word. Pressed against the semiconscious Indian, Joshua lay there, and listened to the fire bear down on them. It became a continuous roar, a caterwaul of crackling and snapping. The wind buffeted them, drawing at the blankets like the vortex of a tornado. Whipped them from side to side with ferocious gusts. The fire was on top of them, trees and snags ignited in lofty blazing torches. The wet blankets began to simmer. Joshua was suffocating. He gulped hungrily for air and sucked steam into his lungs. His heart pounded and he thought his lungs would burst. The blankets began to smolder. He could smell the scorching wool. The water in the blankets evaporated. He could feel the heat searing his back and legs. Joshua fought his rising panic. The urge to break free and run. To flee the heat. To breathe. The impulse was almost overpowering. The functioning fragment of his rational mind told him that cremation awaited him beyond the feeble protection of the blankets. He endured the heat and the suffocation with failing consciousness.

The fire storm raged past them. Consuming all fuel. Leaving behind a smoking wasteland.

Jethro Carley, kneeling on the canyon rim, watched in horror as the fire flashed over the blankets that protected Joshua and the SWIF foreman. There was a good chance they would live, perhaps virtually unharmed. But very few men had ever tried to survive a crown fire by ducking under it. At any rate, Carley knew there was nothing he could do. He watched the fire climb out of the canyon, darting up the trees along the steep walls toward the rim. He stood up and yelled to his crew above the roar of the fire. "Spread out! And be ready!"

The crew scrambled down the long backfire line: brush, dead

snags, tree limbs—everything that had been cleared between the forest service road and the canyon rim. It had been doused with starter so it would go up easy. The men kept their eyes on Carley. Timing was critical.

Carley watched the flames leap up the canyon walls, scaling the trees as though it were ascending a ladder rung by rung. He shielded his face against the intense heat with a gloved hand. Carley felt the fire pull at him as it sucked in oxygen to support combustion, gradually at first, but then increasing until he had to brace himself against its almost irresistible power. He put a match to the backfire line, turned, and raced toward the road. The men in his crew, ranged down the line, did the same.

The backfire line blazed up. Then, fed by the sucking winds created at the head of the fire, the line ignited in an instantaneous sheet of flame that flashed toward the forest fire as though drawn by a magnet. It fused with the forest fire in a searing conflagration, burned furiously a few minutes, and then just as suddenly died down. All the fuel had been burned. Like cellophane that ignites, blazes up, consumes itself, and is gone.

Joshua squatted on the ground in the midst of the burned-out snag patch. His eyes smarted and teared from the wisping smoke. Ash drifted in the air and settled on him. His skin was tender and he felt like he had a sunburn, but other than the laceration over his eye and the abrasions on his leg and wrist he was all right. The injured SWIF foreman, still semiconscious, lay stretched out beside him, covered neatly with the folded blankets. Joshua reached out a hand to smooth them across his chest and tried to control the shakes. He could suppress the trembling by a determined act of will, but only for a moment. Then the tremors would start again. He cursed himself and watched Carley and several of his squad, plus some of the SWIF crewmen, pick their way down the canyon walls through the burned-out trees. He was still shaking when they reached him, but he stood up, fighting the paroxysms that swept over him. The men met him with rowdy admiration, but it soon gave way to embarrassment as he tried in vain to control the shakes. Assured that he was all right, they slung the blankets like a stretcher and carried the foreman to the canyon rim.

Carley got on the CB and called in a helicopter to evacuate the Navajo. Joshua got fresh water for his canteen from the water cooler on the truck and then moved off alone. He nursed the canteen and began to pull himself together. He heard the familiar thudding of a chopper, sound waves pulsing against his eardrums, long before he saw it.

Joshua watched the Dust Off contour over the ridge line, rotors slashing, and pound toward the compound. He plucked a smoke canister from his web gear, pulled the pin, and rolled it out on the flat ground in front of the bunker. A festering cloud of yellow smoke billowed up. The Huey zeroed in on the smoke, red cross on the nose gleaming against its white background in the early morning sun. It flared prior to touchdown, whipping yellow smoke and red dust into spiraling ribbons.

Joshua and Bishop and a squad of Nungs picked up the casualties waiting on the floor of the bunker and scurried toward the Dust Off. They jammed nine wounded on the chopper. Smallcanyon, Laszlo, Hendersen, and six Nungs. Then they dived back into the bunker for cover and turned to watch. Shuddering violently, turboprop whining, the helicopter lifted slightly and then settled heavily back to the ground. The pilot revved the engine again, driving the manifold into the red, but the straining helicopter still couldn't get enough lift.

Joshua watched the overloaded helicopter. He expected to see a couple of Nungs ejected to lighten the load, but the pilot tried again. Joshua thought the vibrating Huey would come apart. As the rotors pounded the air savagely, the pilot bounced the chopper along the ground, substituting forward speed for lift. Gradually the helicopter gained airspeed and the distance between bounces lengthened until finally it stayed airborne. It groaned sluggishly away from the compound, slowly picking up speed and altitude.

The full fury of the North Vietnamese gunners on the ridge was unleashed against the single helicopter. Bullets stitched it from chin bubble to tail boom. The chopper shimmied as though caught in a violent windstorm. A moment later a bullet stabbed into the

engine and set it to howling with a hideous mechanical screech.
The Huey stuttered out of control. Moving at over fifty knots, the
nose tilted downward at an ever-increasing angle until the rotors
struck the ground. The chopper cartwheeled, shedding aluminum
panels, hatch doors, rotors, tail fin, and bodies, and then ignited
in a magnesium flash.

The Forest Service helicopter landed in a clearing beyond the
truck. Two men exited from the open hatch. One carried a
stretcher. They ducked low under the idling rotors and were met
by Jethro Carley. He led them over to where the SWIF foreman
lay tucked in blankets. Joshua watched them confer. He was
gripped by a foreboding of impending disaster and the trembling
started again. The men with the stretcher placed it on the ground
beside the foreman and began to bundle him onto it. Joshua hurried over to Carley.

"Jethro," Joshua said, "let's take him down in the truck."

"What the hell are you talking about?"

"Let's take the foreman down in the truck." It was not a sugges-
tion. Joshua's voice was pleading.

"That's crazy, Josh. It's a long, rough ride. The helicopter's here.
He'll be in a hospital in thirty minutes."

"Please, Jethro. It's safer."

Carley looked at Joshua. His arms were clutched to his chest. He
was shaking as though he were suffering a chill. Carley was not a
man given to subtlety or sentimentality. "Knock off the horseshit,
Josh." He turned. The two men stared at Joshua with a mixture of
disbelief and scorn. Carley gestured with a brief jerk of his head.
They lifted the stretcher and started toward the helicopter. "Put
him down!" Joshua commanded. The two men ignored him. "Put
him down, dammit!" There was a note of desperation in his voice.
The men half crouched as they moved under the rotors of the
helicopter. Joshua trailed along beside them. "Please," he begged.
They slid the stretcher through the open hatch onto the metal deck
plate and scrambled on board. The pilot engaged the rotors. A
rising whine accompanied the increasing rpm's and the helicopter
vibrated prior to getting lift.

Joshua watched, helpless. Tears rolled down his cheeks. Tears of frustration, rage, humiliation. He turned and pushed through the watching circle of men. He didn't look as the helicopter lifted off, hovered, rotated on its axis, and then, tail up, sped down the mountain toward the valley. He removed his gear and slowly loaded it onto the truck.

CHAPTER TWO

Joshua walked off the job. After the fire had been tied off in the canyon, the trucks hauled Carley's squad and the SWIF crew down the mountain to put them into the line at another location. They stopped at the ranger station to touch base with the fire boss, and Joshua's Toyota Land Cruiser was there. He left his fire-fighting gear on the truck, loaded his lunch bucket, bedroll, and duffel in the back of his vehicle, and drove away.

Jethro Carley had tried to stop him. Reasoned with him at first. Told him he had just been through a shit storm. Anybody could get a little crazy. Come unstuck. Told him he was a good hand. Instinctive leader. Knew fires. If he stayed on he could probably get a job with the Forest Service full time. Not just the seasonal work. Joshua was indifferent. Put the Toyota in gear. Then Carley tried threats. If Joshua walked off the job in the middle of a fire he would never work for the Forest Service again. Anywhere.

Joshua left Carley standing in a cloud of dust at the base of the flagpole in front of the ranger station. He pointed the Land Cruiser in the general direction of Richmond. He could have taken the Interstate, but he didn't feel like it. Didn't want the four-lane technological efficiency. Most especially he didn't want the speed. There was no hurry. He was going nowhere. He drove across the Appalachians and through the Shenandoah Valley. He took the back roads, winding among the peaks and through the gaps. The evening haze settled in. A blue mist touched the valleys with delicate fingers and mingled with the smoke that came from the cabins nestled in the hollows. He stopped at a service station and gassed up the Toyota. It was a caricature of hardscrabble Appalachia. Two old-fashioned glass-bell pumps, gummy with oil and dirt, stood under a dilapidated awning. The service station was clapboard, peeling paint and weathered driftwood gray. It appeared to be in terminal disrepair. The grease rack was off to one side of the station and consisted of wide timbers braced up over a flash-flood gulley. Beyond it was an outhouse, serving both employees and customers.

Joshua watched an old man with a three-day growth of whiskers, lips working in and out over edentulous gums, pump the gas. The amber liquid percolated through the glass bell, turning the float and tallying up the gallons. Gasoline. The smell was Vietnam. Napalm. Helicopters. Firebombs. Flamethrowers. Burning flesh. And Vietnam was not a word or a place. It was an emotion. And he responded like a Pavlovian dog. Except the mouth was not wet. It was dry. The palms were wet. It was like a chain reaction. Lightning quick and irreversible.

Joshua wiped his palms on his pants and stepped onto a sagging stoop. He opened a screen door that was slightly askew on its hinges. The service station also sold groceries and sundries. He drifted between flyblown counters that displayed a hodgepodge of products ranging from motor oil to oatmeal. He saw the proprietress, a clone of the old man pumping gas, eyeing him suspiciously. He thought at first it was simply an inbred mistrust of strangers, but then realized he was all soot and grime and red dirt and beard stubble and singed hair and blood-encrusted eyebrow. He rummaged through a cooler for a Heineken. Settled for a Schlitz. He picked up a tin of aspirin from a counter, wiping off the dust. He paid for the items and the gas with cash and settled in behind the wheel of the Toyota. He downed four aspirin tablets, pulled back onto the blacktop, and wound his way along the narrow road. Wooded banks rose up sharply on either side, devoured by the headlight beams. He drove into the gathering night, alternately drinking the beer and holding the cool bottle against his forehead.

An hour later, pumping the brakes as he approached a four-way stop sign, he saw the church. It was set back in a clearing. A neat white frame single-story building. Unadorned by steeple or belfry or columns or stained glass. It was a rectangular structure, elevated a foot off the bare ground by piles of stacked bricks. His headlights picked up a hand-painted sign that announced, THE CHURCH OF CHRIST MEETS HERE. Joshua, almost against his own volition, turned off into the gravel parking area that surrounded the building. He coasted to a stop near the front door and swung his legs out of the Toyota. The night air was warm and humid and smelled of damp earth and dogwood and pine. Crickets clacked in the trees. Two birds echoed each other's night song. He stood, hands in pockets, and stared at the simple building. The language of architecture proclaimed a no-frills church, the church of his youth.

"Religion spoken here," Joshua muttered aloud, "not theology."

He mounted the one step to the front door and turned the handle. It was locked. Just as he knew it would be. "Sorry, Lord," he murmured, "I know you're only here on Sunday morning, Sunday evening, and midweek prayer meeting." He rattled the door. "But I'm a little needy now." Joshua walked around to the side of the building and moved along peering in the windows. The interior was dark, so he could barely make it out. He walked back to the front door, boots crunching on the gravel in the quiet night. He tried the handle again, then in exasperation raised a booted foot, drew back, and kicked. The jamb splintered and the door crashed open. It slammed back against the wall and the noise echoed hollowly in the empty building. Joshua walked down the center aisle, flanked on either side by simple wooden pews. He took a pew midway down the aisle and sat quietly, pensively, in the darkened church. There were no adornments, paintings, sculptures, or crucifixes. No choir loft, piano, or organ. There was a small table at the front for the communion bread and grape juice. Not wine. Beyond it was a low podium with a pulpit. Behind it the large baptistry.

Joshua shook his head. It seemed a thousand years ago, but it was only 1956. The summer revival had come to Pine Mountain, Virginia. Brother Jim Bob Duncan, storm trooper for the Lord, had come to launch his attack on the evils of drinking, dancing, and denominationalism. Some of his most eloquent sermonizing on those hot August nights focused on *lasciviousness*—what the King James version of the Bible called the *superfluity of naughtiness.* Jim Bob Duncan could make the phrase last about fifteen seconds. Young Josh Scott didn't know what it was, but he knew he wanted to try it. Even though he was absolutely convinced that some dread apocalyptic beast would capture his soul forever if he did. In that summer of his thirteenth year, when the preacher described the sins of the flesh and the lusts of the heart, Joshua knew he was guilty.

Puberty had come upon him with the warm spring winds that swept across the Virginia countryside. The mountains and valleys had suddenly turned into breasts and buttocks. When the preacher delighted the congregation with a vision of the fires of lust being consumed by the fires of hell, Joshua would slide down just a little lower in the hard wooden pew. At which point his eyes would fall on the softly turned calves of Linda Jean West. In one particular frenzy of castigating oratory Brother Jim Bob's false teeth had spurted halfway out of his mouth. It gave the appearance of a grotesque, cackling death mask. Linda Jean's calves, Brother Duncan's unhinged teeth, and Joshua's slowly rising erection joined in an unholy alliance of lust and death in the fevered imagination of his conscience. Then the congregation sang an invitation hymn about being washed in the blood of the lamb. Brother Jim Bob appealed above the singing for the sinners to come forward and be buried in the watery grave. "You know who you are," he cried. And Joshua did, too. So down the aisle he went, carrying his images of blood and lust and death to the cool and soothing waters of baptism. The next morning he awoke to the life of regeneration with a throbbing erection.

Joshua shook himself free of his reveries. I wonder which comes first, he mused, loss of innocence or loss of faith? Or did credibility merely diminish with age? Or experience? Or knowledge? Or could faith simply not survive the absurdity of eternal truths declaimed through the unhinged false teeth of a man who thought God handed down the Bible through a hole in the sky, while Linda Jean's postpubescent calves interposed themselves on the whole preposterous scene?

Joshua pushed himself out of the pew and went to the communion table. Underneath it he found what he was looking for. Two flat nickel-plated trays. He removed a twenty-dollar bill from his billfold and dropped it in a collection plate. It would probably pay for the door. He slowly made his way back down the aisle. On the rear wall was a tract rack. The neat wooden rack held a dozen different pamphlets. He took several of them at random and left the building, pulling the door closed after him. He climbed wearily into the Toyota and scanned the titles on the tracts by the overhead

light. "The Heresy of Instrumental Music." "God's Plan of Salva-
tion." "The Sin of Divorce." "How to Convert a Baptist." "How to
Convert a Methodist." "How to Convert a Catholic." Joshua tossed
the tracts on the right front seat and slammed the door. "God," he
murmured, "I hope you're not as stupid as the church makes you
out to be." He turned the key in the ignition and pulled out onto
the county road. The blacktop disappeared into the darkness behind him like the faith of his adolescence.

It was nearly eleven that night when Joshua reached the out-
skirts of Richmond. He drove along darkened streets to a deteri-
orating residential neighborhood on the west side. The homes
were two-story turn-of-the-century structures that had fallen into
disrepair. He stopped in front of a large house, gray in the moonlight, and streaked with shadows from large weeping willows in the
front yard. Joshua removed his bedroll, lunch bucket, and duffel
from the rear of the Land Cruiser. He pushed through a gate on
a fading picket fence, from which a third of the staves were missing, and walked around the side of the house. The lawn had gone
to seed except for the worn path to the rear of the house. He made
his way up a rickety flight of stairs that skirted a back veranda and
let himself into his upstairs apartment.

Joshua stepped into a small entryway, and dropped his bedroll
by a washer and dryer. He unlaced his boots, pulled them off, and
set them against the wall. He stripped and left his clothes in a dirty
heap by the bedroll. He unzipped the small duffel and dumped out
his spare clothing, folded the bag and placed it on a shelf above the
dryer. He carried his lunch bucket into a small kitchen, feet padding on the worn linoleum. He removed the book from the bucket,
put the thermos in the sink and the remains of his lunch in a
plastic-lined wastebasket, wiped out the bucket and placed it on
top of an old refrigerator. He walked through a sparsely furnished
living room into his bedroom. Along one wall were a series of cheap
metal bookcases, four in all, with shelves from floor to ceiling. They
were filled with books. Mostly paperbacks. He placed *The Structure
of Genre Forms* in its empty slot with the rest of his comparative
literature selection, and went into the bathroom.

Joshua leaned against the sink and stared at his reflection in the
mirror. No wonder he made that old woman nervous at the gas
station. His hair was matted, and where the lining of his hard hat

had fit, it was pressed into creases. He had a week's growth of beard, grimy with dust and soot and ash. Oddly, there were streaks down his cheeks washed by his tears that afternoon. He shook his head. How many times had he destroyed his credibility? He could add the Forest Service fire-fighting crew to his drifter's résumé of underachiever jobs. Poor Jethro Carley. Carley liked him. Was beginning to depend on him. Had wanted him to boss a crew this fire. It was just as well. He turned to a tub enclosed by a mildewed plastic shower curtain. He adjusted the water, diverted it through the shower head, then stepped in and pulled the curtain around him. He stayed under the hot, stinging spray a long time.

Joshua slowly toweled off, moseying through the apartment as he did so. A clock on a bedside table glowed a green midnight. He opened the refrigerator. He could scramble some eggs. Instead he opened a Heineken, wrapped the towel around his waist, and went back to his bedroom. He switched on a lamp on the bedside table and went over to the bookcases. Pulled out a copy of Muggeridge's *Chronicles of Wasted Time,* thumbed a few pages, then restlessly put it back on the shelf. He went to the living room and perused his record collection, but thought better of it as he considered the late hour and his landlady downstairs. He drifted over to the window that looked out on the street, pushed aside a chintz curtain, and leaned against the frame. The enamel, smooth from decades of repainting, felt cool on his arm. He looked out absently on the dark, deserted street. A mongrel dog moved dispiritedly along. Joshua thought about the day and finished his beer. Abruptly he turned, leaving the empty Heineken bottle on the windowsill, and went to his bedroom. He knelt in front of a chifforobe and opened one of the drawers at its base. He removed a small metal chest no bigger than a shoe box. The metal was heavy, durable. The type used to protect valuable papers. He returned to the living room and sank into a worn overstuffed chair. Reached up and pulled the chain on a floor lamp. He balanced the box on his knees in the dim yellow light and slowly lifted the lid.

Joshua stared at the contents for a moment. He pushed aside a small rolled cardboard cylinder and withdrew a faded color snapshot. There were two men in the picture. One was himself, about a dozen pounds lighter and as many years younger. The other was Tom Bishop. He was about Joshua's height, but where Joshua was

lean, almost lanky, Bishop was powerfully built, broad-shouldered
and muscular. Both had close-cropped crew cuts and wore camouflage tiger suits. They stood in front of a single-story unpainted
frame building with a corrugated tin roof. Sandbags were stacked
protectively against the building's exterior walls to a height of four
feet. Bishop sported a wide grin and held a small hand-painted sign
in front of his chest. The block letters were red, white, and blue,
and spelled out FUCK COMMUNISM. The middle finger of his right
hand was crooked under the sign, surreptitiously flashing a bird at
the camera.

Joshua picked up a small flat rectangular case of soft blue leather
and opened it. A bronze cross with an eagle with outstretched
wings superimposed on it, and suspended from a red, white, and
blue silk ribbon, rested on the gold velvet lining of the case. He
read the two words engraved on the bronze scrollwork beneath
the arms of the Distinguished Service Cross: For Valor. He snapped
the case shut and replaced it in the metal box.

Joshua sorted through the contents again and removed two letters. One, addressed to Captain Tom Bishop with a San Francisco
APO, was open, the smudged envelope slit along the narrow end.
He reached in, ignored the letter, bits and pieces of life at home
which he knew by heart, and withdrew a snapshot. A young
woman stood by the side of a two-story white house shaded by large
cottonwood trees. She held a small boy wearing a plaid shirt, jeans,
and tiny cowboy boots, who stared somberly at the camera. The
woman was of medium height, slender, with a look of determined
strength in her open, smiling face. Her brown hair was tousled by
a breeze, and she had reached up to pluck a few strands back from
the side of her face. It had a look of easy grace. Joshua studied the
picture, then slipped it back in the envelope.

The second letter was unopened. It was addressed to Mrs.
Claudia Bishop, Rural Route 2, Plains, Kansas. The return address
was Tom Bishop at the San Francisco APO. Joshua turned the letter
in his hand a moment. In all of the intervening years he had never
had an urge to open it, but the impulse struck him now. He paused,
then resolutely placed both letters back in the box.

After a moment he removed the final item from the box. It was
a small stack of white business cards, held together by a doubled

rubber band, now brittle and cracked with age. He slipped the top card from under the rubber band, dropped the remainder back in the box, and held the card up to the floor lamp. It was dog-eared and faintly yellowed. Embossed in black in the center of the card was a miter-shaped chess piece, the bishop. Above the chess piece, engraved in boldface type, were the words **HAVE NUNGS WILL TRAVEL**. At the bottom, in regular type, the card read: Wire Captain Tom Bishop, Detachment A-219, Fifth Special Forces Group (Airborne). Joshua turned the card in his hands, reread it, and passed his fingers over the embossed chess piece.

"Air strike, Lieutenant!" The chopper pilot pointed.

Joshua pushed himself up on one knee behind the cockpit and looked through the forward windscreen. In the distance he could see Thang Duc. The compound had been gouged out of the jungle's millennia-old domination of the earth. The red clay contrasted sharply with the jungle, like an ugly crimson scar. As though the earth itself had been wounded. Yellow gouts of flame erupted from the jungle edge as two F-104's whipped away from their bombing runs in spiraling turns.

"We'll set you down when the fours pull out!"

Joshua scooted across the vibrating deck plate to the open hatch, easing past one of the Nungs in his squad. He gripped the fuselage frame and leaned through the hatch. Strung out behind them were more than a score of Hueys, thrashing through the air like mechanical birds of prey. He shifted his weight and looked forward at their objective again. The compound was shaped like a triangle, no bigger than a city block, and pointed west toward Laos like an arrowhead. A smoky pall hung over the camp and obscured much of it, but Joshua could make out the perimeter, a zigzag trench interrupted by heavily sandbagged bunkers. The jungle had been cleared away on all three sides, leaving open fields of fire strewn with concertina wire. Despite the heavy North Vietnamese assault, Joshua thought, it looked defensible. Another hot spot for A-two-one-niner and the Nungs. Joshua pulled back in and glanced over his squad. The stocky yellow men stared back impassively. Was it the strain, or oriental inscrutability? He had no idea what they really thought of him. But it mattered little. The Chinese merce-naries were tough. Very hard-dying men. He had no misgivings about serving with them.

The crew chief tapped Joshua on the shoulder. "Captain Bishop wants to talk to you." He offered him his helmet.

Joshua stripped off his camouflage hat, jammed it between his legs, and slipped on the helmet. The sponge padding was wet with the crew chief's sweat. He found it repugnant. The pilot changed frequencies and tuned past an Armed Forces Radio station. Eerily, rock music filtered through the headset. Then Joshua heard Bishop's voice.

"Do you read me, Josh?"

Joshua moved his lips against the carbon mike. "Five-by."

"Change of plans. There's a lot of heavy ground fire. If we go in in staggered lifts, they'll shoot the shit out of the last sections. We'll go in all at once. Swarm 'em. They'll set us down all over the compound. Wherever they can find a spot." Bishop paused. "Sort of a controlled crash." Even over the electronic distortion of the radio, Joshua could hear the irony in Bishop's voice. "Get out fast. Meet me at the teamhouse."

"That's a rog." Joshua tugged off the helmet and handed it back to the crew chief.

The pilot turned and shouted over his shoulder. "We're going in! It's a hot LZ, Lieutenant!" He autorotated the helicopter toward the ground in a stomach-wrenching drop and leveled off just above the jungle floor. The Huey sped toward the compound, contouring five feet off the jungle canopy at one hundred and forty knots. The trees whipped past the open hatches in a green blur. The door gunners cleared their M-60's and sprayed the tree lines on either side of the chopper. Joshua looked through the forward chin bub-bles and saw streams of tracers boring toward them. The tracers seemed to pick up speed as they zipped closer to the Huey. The pilot ignored the bullets and took the chopper right through them. Rounds slashed through the skin of the helicopter, leaving jagged tears in the aluminum. The plexiglass in front of the copilot splin-tered into an opaque cobweb of plastic.

The catch bags on the door gunners' M-60's filled with ejected shell casings. The gunners ripped them off so they wouldn't jam their weapons and continued firing. Smoking brass cascaded to the deck and piled up around Joshua's boots. He was afraid he would fall trying to get out of the chopper and began brushing the shell casings away from his feet. Suddenly the door gunner next to him was slammed back against the rear bulkhead, his body jerking spastically as he pitched through the open hatch and dangled there, held by his safety belt.

The green jungle abruptly disappeared, and the chopper was over the red clay of Thang Duc. The pilot wedged the rotor pitch sharply, and the helicopter was thrown into a shuddering hover. Joshua stared through the open hatch at the ground, which pitched crazily as the pilot maneuvered the helicopter violently toward touchdown. Concertina wire and bunkers were replaced by a patch of yellow sky. Wood-frame buildings jerked in and out of his line of sight. Sandbagged mortar pits suddenly slid under the helicopter, and then Joshua's vision was blocked by a cloud of red dust. The helicopter slammed against the ground. Joshua's right knee was jammed into the metal deck plate and a pain stabbed along his leg into his foot.

"Go!" Joshua croaked. He piled through the open hatch followed by the Nungs, and sprinted toward a slit trench visible a dozen yards away. Small-arms fire slashed at them. A Nung off to his right stumbled to the ground in an awkward sprawl, and lay crumpled by a bunker. Joshua dived into the trench, blinded by the whipping dust as the Hueys pounded back into the air and bolted away from the compound. As the dust settled, he got his bearings. He was in one of the interior trenches of the compound. It looked like they had made it in in pretty good shape. There were some casualties scattered about. He couldn't see any team members, just Nungs. A few rounds of harassment fire pinged erratically into the camp; otherwise it was quiet.

Joshua climbed out of the trench and moved along a log and earthen breastwork toward the center of the compound to find Bishop. He saw him sauntering across the open ground, an M-79 grenade launcher balanced over his shoulder like an oversized shotgun. They made their way toward a low wooden building protected by a log and sandbag barricade. As they approached the teamhouse a man in a dirty tiger suit came out to meet them. A

pressure dressing encrusted with dried blood was tied around his
right arm. A powder burn blackened his left cheek and the skin
was denuded at its center, leaving a raw pink, oozing surface.

The man stuck out his hand. "I'm Ed Wittenhauer," he said,
"team sergeant."

Bishop shook his hand. "I'm Tom Bishop. This is my exec, Josh
Scott." He reached in the front pocket of his tiger suit and handed
Wittenhauer one of his business cards. "Hear you fairy piss ants
are on the way to gettin' your asses whipped."

Joshua returned the business card to the stack and closed the metal
case. He tugged the chain on the floor lamp and sat in the dark. He
began to tremble. Slowly at first, imperceptibly, then with greater
force until his whole body shook. He gripped the arms of the chair,
knuckles white, and hung on. Gradually the shaking diminished,
winding down until he sat limp and exhausted in the overstuffed
chair. Finally he got up, moved through the darkened house to the
bedroom, and returned the box to the drawer. He opened the
doors on the chifforobe and removed a T-shirt, faded jeans, and
denim jacket. He dressed and slipped on sneakers without socks.
He pocketed his billfold and picked up the Toyota keys.

It took Joshua twenty-five minutes to drive to downtown Richmond. The area was run down. Tenements. Crumbling apartment
buildings. Pawnshops with heavy metal grillwork over flyblown
windows. A few all-night bars. He parked the Land Cruiser and got
out. Joshua shoved his hands deep in the pockets of his jeans,
hunched his shoulders against the cool night air, and stared up at
the Gothic facade of the All Souls Catholic Church. It was lighted,
somewhat garishly, by spotlights, and the stone was dark with a
century of grime. He crossed the street, mounted a dozen worn
marble steps, and entered the dimly lit foyer. He passed on into the
nave. To his left were several confessionals, with doors with ornamental wooden grilles. To his right a painted and chipped statue
of Saint Jude. The air was heavy with incense, and guttering candles cast flickering shadows on old, ornate columns.

Even after three A.M. there were two dozen people scattered
among the pews. Kneeling, heads bowed. Weeping, rosaries in
hand. Asleep, a refuge from the streets. Joshua stepped past a laver

and a locked metal box labeled "Intentions, Offerings, Poor Box" and took a rear pew. He didn't pray or meditate. He didn't wrestle with his conscience, ponder his past, or contemplate his future. He simply identified with the fellow members of his transitory congregation. All those driven to their knees because they had no place else to go. Not necessarily driven to their knees to pray, but just to rest. Sitting among them was the closest Joshua ever came to peace.

After an hour Joshua stood and moved across the aisle to a votive stand with tiers of vigil lights. The stand was placed beside a life-size crucifix. A woman stooped with age and carrying a paper shopping bag bent to kiss Christ's feet, and shuffled on. Joshua glanced up at the face of Christ. Above his head was a scroll with the inscription INRI. Joshua contemplated it, puzzled. Were the letters initials, or a word? He knew the etymology of the Greek word *baptizo* backward and forward, but he had no idea what INRI meant. Somehow at that moment it seemed important that he know. He turned back to the votive stand, picked up a candle, lit it, and placed it in the rack. He stared at the yellow flame.

Thang Duc exploded in sheets of fire and steel as recoilless rifle rounds slammed into the compound. The defenders cowered in their bunkers and rifle pits as the earth rocked beneath them. The shelling seemed to have an interminable, mind-numbing life of its own. Then abruptly it stopped. A mortar coughed from the center of the compound, and seconds later the night sky glowed with an eerie dull white light that bathed the ground below in a phosphorescent sheen. As the parachute flare swung to and fro, its glare outlined scores of North Vietnamese running at a rapid crouch toward the barbed wire.

Joshua reared up out of the trench, the dirt from the barrage spilling off his tiger suit. He flicked his M-16 on automatic and began to spray short bursts at the sprinting attackers. Suddenly it was dark. The flare drifting above them had sputtered out and was not replaced by another. Joshua fired blind. Panic gripped his mind as he fumbled for another M-16 clip and slapped it into the magazine well. Incoming rounds whipped past him with vicious sucking sounds. Another flare popped above them as Pete Franklin

*alternated flares and explosives. Two or three mortar rounds would
explode among the North Vietnamese massed at the barbed wire
apron, and then as darkness closed down, another flare would
illuminate the perimeter. Joshua depressed the muzzle of his M-16
and began to fire frantically at the North Vietnamese crawling
toward him. The flare sputtered out and it was midnight black.*

*"Keep the lights on! Keep the lights on!" Joshua babbled over
and over in a half-crazed prayer. "Oh, Christ, Pete, keep the lights
on!" Joshua squeezed the trigger. A long burst chewed into the
North Vietnamese closing in on him. Suddenly the fear was replaced by exhilaration. And power!*

The terrifying vision faded to black, as though a projector playing
in Joshua's mind had been switched off. He stood silently and
watched the candle burn down. He had haunted dozens of
churches like All Souls in the past twelve years in as many cities.
And he had lighted hundreds of candles for Tom Bishop. Why, he
wondered. It was absolutely foreign to his religious heritage, an
uncompromising brand of fundamentalism devoid of ceremony,
liturgy, sacraments, or ritual. It was a religion of tradition and
ordinance, but without beauty or power. It offered Truth that was
pitiless. It was not to be understood, only believed. Facts but no
comprehension. Revelation but no insight. Guilt but no grace.
Judgment without justification. Accusation but no absolution. Wor-
ship without healing. It was a system where religious thoughtless-
ness conspired to trivialize God. Proclaiming a religion that was
simple for a life that was complex. Preaching a gospel that was not
good news, but bad. A hell that was real, and a heaven that was
vacuous.

I bought it all, Joshua told himself. I bought it all. He held another candle to the cathedral candle, lit it, and placed it in the rack.
"For Tom Bishop," he said aloud. Then on impulse he began to
light additional candles, one after another, and set them in a line
beside Bishop's candle. As he did so he softly called the names.
"Tim Colfax. Miklos Laszlo. Manny Almendarez. Joe Finelli. Karl
Wirtz. Jimmy Smallcanyon. Ted Hendersen. Dick Tate." When he
had finished, he lit two more and added them to the row. "For
Wyatt Porter and Eddie DuBoise, wherever they are tonight." As

the eleven flames flickered side by side in the rack, Joshua removed his billfold and withdrew one of Bishop's cards, which he always carried with him. He pressed it into the melting wax at the base of Tom Bishop's candle.

Joshua watched the candle burn down. He decided he would go see Tom Bishop's widow.

CHAPTER THREE

J oshua drove his Toyota across the rectangle that was Kansas, angling toward the south-west corner of the state. The day had started in the northeastern urban center, and by midmorning he had passed through the rolling Flinthill country out into the broad rangelands. As he faced the afternoon sun he left the interstate for the state highways, and finally, the county roads. The roads became narrower, the communities smaller, the prairie flatter, and the farms larger. Vast wheat fields stretched away in all directions as far as the eye could see. The limitless expanse of grain rippled in the wind like waves. Here and there combines were in the fields, starting an early harvest.

The narrow blacktop cut through the ocean of wheat as though a meridian on a map of the globe had actually been banded across southwestern Kansas. The heat caused everything to quaver, out of focus, like looking through wrinkled cellophane. Joshua chased roadbed water mirages all afternoon and watched them evaporate away to dry blacktop under his tires. The wide bar ditches were filled with sunflowers. Their brilliant yellow heads slowly turned to trace the sun's path across the sky. Joshua felt that ten thousand eyes watched him all day long and observed his journey across the state to Plains. By late afternoon the sun-fired landscape was a panorama of shimmering gold. The western sky was burnished brass. The monochromatic vista was broken only by a complex of gleaming white cylinders that gradually appeared on the horizon. The cylinders grew larger, took shape and form, and became mas-sive concrete skyscrapers. The huge grain elevators of Plains, Kan-sas, dominated the countryside.

Joshua slowed as he approached the farming community. A series of small road signs proclaimed that Plains, Kansas, had a population of 1,892, was a garden club community, and possessed the world's deepest hand-dug well. The county road that led into Plains widened at the city limits into four lanes and became its main street. On the edge of town the outside lane was blocked by about a dozen trucks stacked up bumper to tailgate in front of the grain elevators. Filled to overflowing with harvested wheat, they waited for the Plains Cooperative to claim the grain. As Joshua drove slowly past the line of trucks, he was conscious that he was being scrutinized by the sunburned men in dusty, sweat-stained dungarees who lounged in the truck cabs or clustered with other drivers by the edge of the street. Their gaze was not unkind, just idle curiosity about the out-of-place.

Main Street was bordered by large Chinese elms and cottonwoods that shaded the street and houses. Joshua turned off the air conditioner and rolled down the window. The shade was deceptive. It was hot and the air was dry. Set back from the street were one- and two-story frame houses with wide front porches. They all had a neat, well-maintained, fifty-year-old look. There was an occasional brick home, but very plain, as though apologetic for venturing into a different architectural style. The older frame houses had unattached garages set off to the side or at the rear. The newer brick homes had attached garages, but only for a single car—an apparent commitment to a certain austerity. The front lawns of Bermuda grass appeared dry, despite the lawn sprinklers. Children played in the spray, shrieking at playmates who bicycled in the street or roller-skated and maneuvered skateboards on the sidewalk.

The houses gave way to a business district limited to one side of two city blocks on Main. The businesses were utilitarian. John Deere Farm Implements, Southwest Kansas Feed and Grain, IGA Food Town, Dowler's Hardware, Moody's Drug and Sundries, Moffett's Dry Goods and Clothing, the Main Street Café, Kansas Power and Light Company, Woolworth's, the Farmers and Merchants Bank, and the Billiard Parlor Bar and Packaged Goods. Traffic was light. Mostly pickups. The trucks were utilitarian, too. Not toys with oversized tires, chrome roll bars, and fog lamps mounted on the cab.

On the other side of Main Street, across from the business district, was a modest city park. One corner of the park held the Cimarron County Courthouse. It was a square dun-colored structure, old, but in good repair, built of native stone. The quiet park had large shade trees, brick walkways, a few park benches, a collection of swings and teeter-totters, and a band shell. A sign pointed toward the world's deepest hand-dug well. A large white banner, affixed to street lamps, was stretched across Main Street. It announced the Harvest Street Dance, nine days away, and in smaller letters underneath, the Annual Rattlesnake Roundup.

Joshua drove past the park and business district and Main Street again became residential, a mirror image of the opposite side of town. There were a few cross streets. To Joshua's relief, for some unknown reason, he was glad that Plains was a community of greater size than a single street. On the edge of town was the Wheatlands Motel and Restaurant. Opposite it was a Kerr-McGee gas station. The blacktop narrowed to two lanes again at the city limits. A highway marker reestablished the road's identity as County Road 11. A sign said that Jackfork, Oklahoma, was fifty-seven miles away. Joshua felt the urge to keep on driving. Plains, Kansas, had trees, lawns, flowers, gardens, kids, bicycles, skateboards, pickup trucks, the world's deepest hand-dug well, wheat, a city park, and an Annual Harvest Street Dance and Rattlesnake Roundup. It also had Mrs. Tom Bishop.

A few hundred yards past the city limits was a pullout into a small roadside rest area. Joshua turned into it. It was barren sand and gravel and contained only a wooden picnic table with a fifty-gallon drum chained to it for trash. Apparently, Joshua thought, the Plains Garden Club activities didn't extend to the rest area just beyond their city limits. He got out of the Toyota and stretched, pausing by the picnic table. The top was solid with names, dates, and places carved into it. He turned away. Giant thunderheads had banked up in the west and the sunset fired the clouds a brilliant crimson. The entire horizon appeared to be ablaze, like a vast prairie fire. At the far edge of the rest area was a historical marker. Joshua, stiff from the day's drive, hobbled over to it. A bronze plaque was set in a stone frame. Done in bas-relief was a covered wagon pulled by a team of oxen. The plaque declared that a half mile away was the Cimarron River crossing, where settlers forded the Cimarron on their pilgrimage west a century ago. Joshua contemplated hiking over and finding the river, but decided instead to find a place to spend the night.

He drove back to the Kerr-McGee station, an old-fashioned white stucco structure. A kid with a greasy Kansas City Chiefs T-shirt and a Kansas City Royals baseball cap pumped the gas. He didn't offer to clean the accumulated western Kansas insect population off the Toyota's windshield. Joshua glanced at his watch. Six-forty. A big metal thermometer hanging from a nail on the front of the station, and stamped with a Milagro Feed logo, registered ninety-eight degrees. Joshua went over to a battered soft-drink cooler, an old horizontal metal box with sliding doors in the top. He slid back a door, studied the selection, and plucked a bottle of Grapette from the crushed ice. He found the opener on the end of the cooler and snapped the cap off. Joshua drained about half of it in one long draft.

Joshua sat on an ammunition crate in a rifle pit. The sun was well up. A flat white disc in a copper sky. The heat had wrung the water out of him and his tiger suit was streaked white with the salt of evaporated sweat. His throat was as dry as dust. He forced himself to swallow. His tongue undulated backward in a convulsive spasm and rasped against his palate. It felt like a sandbag stuck against the roof of his mouth. He removed his canteen from his web belt and sloshed it. Over half full. He unscrewed the cap, fingers shaking. I'm like a damn wino, he thought. He took a long gulp and held the water in his mouth, letting it seep into every parched fold and crevice. The warm, pungent water was incredibly delicious. He would have to conserve it. The C-119's and Caribous were dropping jerry cans with supplies, but the thirsty garrison soaked it up almost immediately. He allowed himself another swallow and then began to replace the cap.

"Hey, buddy, can you spare a thirsty man a drink?"

Joshua turned. Bishop had come up behind him in the trench. Bishop smiled, and it seemed to erase some of the harsh lines of fatigue that were chiseled in his face. "Sure." Joshua passed him the canteen.

Bishop leaned his M-16 against the sandbagged trench and

hunkered down beside Joshua. He tilted the canteen to his lips, took a measured sip, swished it back and forth in his mouth, and slowly swallowed. He let out a long, satisfied sigh. "Better than a Budweiser," he said as he handed the canteen back to Joshua.

"Whiskey sour," Joshua replied softly.

"Strawberry daiquiri," Bishop responded without hesitation.

"Cool green Heineken."

"Tequila sunrise."

"Root beer in a frosty mug," Joshua said, "from the Toot 'n' Tell 'Em in Pine Mountain."

"Grapette from the crushed ice cooler at the Kerr-McGee station in Plains."

"Ice cold milk."

"Fresh lemonade with the rinds in the glass," Bishop said.

"Water," Joshua replied, and raised the canteen to his fissured lips.

"Goddamn right," Bishop agreed, and motioned for the canteen.

Joshua watched the kid pump the gas. He could smell the gasoline and see the fumes as they quavered at the tank outlet. He licked his lips and wiped his palms on his jeans. "Is the Wheatlands the only motel in town?" he asked the boy.

"That's it," the attendant said in a flat, expressionless twang.

"Is there a hotel?"

"In Plains?" the boy asked, incredulous.

"Any place else to stay?"

"Some people rent rooms during the harvest." The boy looked Joshua up and down. "You a cutter?" The tone of his voice made the question a statement with an implied answer.

"A cutter?"

"Custom cutter. Follows the harvest from Texas to Canada."

Joshua shook his head and tilted the Grapette to his lips.

"Covering the roundup?"

"No."

The boy cocked his ear at the open gas tank. The nozzle didn't have an automatic shutoff valve and he expertly gauged how full the tank was by the audible gurgle of the gasoline. He deftly stopped the flow just as the tank was full, without a drop of overflow. Joshua paid for the gas and the Grapette with cash. The station didn't take any plastic.

The Wheatlands Motel did, though, and Joshua let them make an imprint of his MasterCard and checked in. He was told he was lucky to get a room. The motel was filling up with custom cutters. And in fact the gravel parking lot was nearly filled with pickups. The Wheatlands didn't cater to extravagant whims. It was simply a bed and bathroom motel. The room did have a window-unit air conditioner, which rattled and wheezed, and a phone. Joshua picked up the phone book. It was about an eighth of an inch thick, and it still combined about fifteen communities in the southwest corner of the state. He looked in the white pages for Claudia Bishop. She was listed under C. Bishop, with her address given as Rural Route 2. Apparently she was still on the farm. He had written her almost three weeks ago at the address on the letters in his metal case, telling her who he was, and that he would be traveling through Plains and wondered if he could give her a call. She had answered with a cryptic note, saying only that if he wanted to stop by she would see him. Joshua ran his finger along the line to her phone number and picked up the receiver. He held it for a moment and then replaced it. Now that he was here, he really didn't want to talk to Claudia Bishop. At least not tonight.

Joshua unpacked. There was an open closet along the rear wall of the room with a few shelves that substituted for a dresser. He placed some of his clothing on hangers and the rest of it on the shelves. He put his dop kit in the bathroom by the sink where a sign admonished, "Please Don't Clean Pheasants in Sink or Tub." Then, leaving the metal box containing the Vietnam mementos in the suitcase, he closed it and shoved it under the bed. Satisfied, he put on his jogging gear and went out into the gravel parking lot. The sun had set and the wind had died down. The evening was quiet, but hot. He stretched and limbered up in the parking lot under the curious gaze of the desk clerk, an elderly man who peered at him through the plate-glass window of the office.

Joshua stepped onto the blacktop county road and jogged toward the city limits. He glanced at his watch. He didn't have a measured course here, so he thought he'd jog about forty minutes. At the edge of town he took the first side road so he wouldn't have to jog on the main highway. He doubted if it was like Richmond, where pimply-faced kids in Plymouth Dusters with jacked-up rear ends swerved to run you off the road, but he still didn't like traffic. The dirt road ran straight as an arrow between two wheat fields. It was bordered on either side by wide bar ditches and barbed wire fences. Sunflowers, some chest-high, grew in the ditches, and large tumbleweeds were hung up in the fencing. A row of telephone poles stretched away into the distance. The poles didn't have a crosspiece. A single strand of wire was fastened to the poles on glass insulators. Somehow the single strand of wire made Joshua feel incredibly desolate. He swung along easily, but the evening air was close and the heat was oppressive. He began to perspire. The sweat stung his eyes and he reached up to wipe it away. After about six or seven minutes he reached a crossroad, and spotted another jogger about twenty yards down the road. The jogger speeded up and turned the corner and caught up with him.

"Mind if I join you?" the man asked. His words were a little breathless as he pounded along.

Joshua preferred to jog alone. Especially tonight in Plains, Kansas. "Okay," he grunted.

They jogged in silence for a while. The man was shorter than Joshua. Stocky, short brown hair, slightly balding. He wore tortoise-shell glasses held in place with an elastic band. "Never seen you before," he puffed. "Not too many joggers in Plains. People here work, they don't jog."

"I'm just here overnight," Joshua lied. He didn't ask the man why he didn't work. His attitude was friendly enough, but Joshua wanted as few personal contacts in Plains as possible.

The man stuck out his hand. "I'm Charlie Wilson."

Joshua shook it. "Josh Scott."

They jogged in silence past another crossroad.

"Jog a lot?" Wilson asked.

"Pretty regular."

"What's your distance?"

"Usually about seven miles a night." Joshua glanced at his watch. "Thought I'd just do it by time tonight."

"No need. Every crossroad is a section line. You're two miles now from the county road."

Joshua nodded. "Makes it simple." There's not a road in Virginia that runs straight for even one mile, he thought.

Charlie Wilson appraised Joshua out of the corner of his eyes. Finally he said, "If you'd rather jog alone, I'll turn back."

Joshua felt a twinge of embarrassment. "No, that's fine. Sorry I seem unfriendly."

"That's okay. I hate to jog alone. Boring as hell."

"I like it. Turn everything off but the alpha waves."

"At least in the city you occasionally get harassed by a dog," Wilson said.

"Or run down by a driver."

Wilson raised his eyebrows behind his tortoiseshell glasses. "New York," he said.

Joshua began to regret the entanglement again. "I'm from all over," he replied. He picked up the pace a little, hoping it would abort the conversation. He felt a stitch in his right side. He hadn't jogged in the five days it had taken him to reach Plains. He pressed his hand against his side where it hurt and pushed on in silence. Wilson stayed right with him. A few hundred yards further on they approached the third crossroad.

"Three miles," Wilson said. "Want to turn around?"

Joshua nodded. They headed back the way they had come. The twilight deepened into a purple dusk. They jogged in silence, experiencing the evening, the peace, and a delicious sense of fatigue that seemed to provide energy instead of sap it. When they reached the paved county road they slowed to a walk and turned toward town. Within fifty yards they had recovered their wind. Joshua felt loose. It was like some neurophysiologic pathway had been short-circuited and he had broken into a sphere where the brain controlled the body but didn't generate emotions. It was the only time he really felt good, other than on haunted late-night visits to churches.

Charlie Wilson intuitively respected Joshua's silence. When they drew abreast of the Wheatlands Motel, Joshua pointed in that direction. "Here's where I get off."

Wilson stuck out his hand. "Thanks for the company."

Joshua shook it. "You're welcome."

"Have a good trip." As Wilson walked on into town he turned and called over his shoulder, "Peace!"

Joshua showered, had a chicken-fried steak with mashed potatoes and gravy at the Wheatlands Restaurant, and then drove slowly around Plains. All of the streets except Main were paved with brick. The Land Cruiser's tires thrummed on the uneven edges as Joshua drove along the turn-of-the-century paving. Street lamps cast soft pools of light on every corner. Gypsy moths fluttered erratically around each lamp. A few residents sat in lawn chairs or swings on their porches, taking the night air. On one block the kids had a game of kick the can going. A few blocks farther on they were playing green ghost. At one house a basketball goal had been mounted over a detached garage. It was lit by a floodlamp and some teenagers were playing one-on-one. Joshua recognized the man he had jogged with earlier, Charlie Wilson, mixing it up with them. He had a hell of a fadeaway jump shot.

He passed the Dwight D. Eisenhower Post Office a couple of blocks off Main, and identified a number of churches that served the community's religious needs. The little tour did nothing to change his first impression of Plains. On the east edge of town he ran across the Cimarron County Consolidated High School. Beside it was a football field. Tiers of wooden bleachers flanked the far sideline marker. Joshua nosed the Toyota into the curb and parked. He walked across the school grounds until he reached the field. He crossed it, feet rustling in the dry grass, and climbed into the bleachers. He took a seat on a splintery weathered board and stared down on the darkened field. He sat for a long time without moving.

Joshua rested against a log barricade in the center of the compound. Bishop sat beside him. Nearby were Finelli, Colfax, and Porter. They formed a mobile squad, prepared to move to the most threatened area of the perimeter with the next assault. He looked at his watch. After midnight. The compound had not been mortared for almost two hours, and the unaccustomed quiet seemed threatening. Eyes and ears strained against the black night. Occasionally, driven by a mounting obsession that something was happening in front of their positions on the perimeter, Tate or Laszlo or Wittenhauer would radio Franklin to send up a flare. In the stillness of the night Joshua could hear the slick metallic whisper of the flare as it slid down the four-deuce barrel; then it would bound skyward with a hollow whump. A few seconds later the flare would pop, swaying gently to and fro, bathing the terrain with a ghostly white glare. For a few moments the handful of defenders manning the perimeter would breathe more easily, reassured that the wire apron was not being infiltrated. As the flare fizzled out, the struggle with fear and the dark and the imagination would begin again, finally mounting to an intolerable level, when another flare would be requested.

Joshua and Tom Bishop sat together in silence, with the ease of friends who need not make small talk. Bishop cupped his cigarette in his hands to shield the glowing tip and took a long drag. "Tom," Joshua finally said, "they can stroll in here and take us with a troop of Girl Scouts."

"Hell, Josh, we can whip these dinks. We got the sonsabitches cornered on all three sides of us."

Joshua grinned in the dark. "The old all-American spirit," he said wryly. "Let's win this one for the Gipper."

"Piss off," Bishop said. They sat in silence for a while; then Bishop spoke in a soft, reflective voice. "My junior year in high school we had the shittiest football team that ever pulled on jockstraps." He took another drag on his cigarette. "I was the only guy on it who could do anything."

Joshua laughed quietly.

"No, no kidding." Bishop brightened. "I was really good," he said without a trace of egotism. "I always was. But everyone else that year was terrible. Our little consolidated high school played a big school from Wichita. They weren't in our league, but they were in our end of the state, so we played them to round out our schedule."

"What happened?" Joshua asked, fascinated.

"They stuck it right down our gizzle is what happened. It was fucking awful. Seventy-seven to six. Our defense was so bad even a white boy scored on us." Bishop chuckled. "We finally scored on their third team. Missed the extra point. I played every play of the game, both offense and defense, and carried the ball every goddamned offensive play."

"I don't believe that," Joshua scoffed.

"It's true." Bishop cupped his left hand to his crotch and raised his right hand. "I swear it on the pride of Cimarron County. After the first few minutes, every time the ball was snapped, eleven *fucking guys ran at me."* Bishop *paused and then said quietly, with the wistful tone of one who is far away,* "It was the best game I ever played. And that includes my all-American year at KU and two years with the Forty-niners."

Another flare burst above them. Their eyes followed its slow descent and the conversation died. A distant rumble could be heard, crescendoing into a wailing screech.

"INCOMING!" *Bishop yelled.*

Joshua slid away from the log barricade and dove into an adjacent slit trench. The others piled in on top of him. An explosion shook the ground with a deafening roar and orange flames shot skyward. Dirt, bits of sandbags, and splintered logs rained down on them. They cowered on the floor of the trench, arms shielding their heads.

"What is that?" *Colfax screamed.*

"One twenties," *yelled Bishop.*

Salvo after salvo of Russian-made 120-millimeter rockets whooshed into the compound. Log barricades, sandbags, concertina wire, perforated steel plate, and buildings were pulverized by the flashing concussions. As suddenly as it had begun, the rocket barrage stopped.

Joshua raised his head cautiously out of the slit trench. The camp was a smoking shambles, lit like some rendering pit by a flickering fire from the dispensary. A flare popped above them. On all three sides of the camp, North Vietnamese Infantry crept steadily forward into the quavering phosphorescent light.

Bishop climbed out of the trench and stood up, observing the attack. "East wall! East wall!" *he shrieked, and sprinted toward the perimeter, cradling an M-60.*

Joshua and the others in the mobile squad clambered out of the trench and followed him.

Joshua pushed himself up from the hard wooden seat and stiffly made his way down from the bleachers. He slowly crossed the football field where Bishop had carried the ball every offensive play when Plains had been shellacked by Wichita. He paused in the middle of the field and glanced around. "East wall, east wall," he called softly. "Hut, hut, hut."

CHAPTER FOUR

The next morning Joshua ate breakfast at the Main Street Café. He took the lone stool remaining at the counter and judged the food better than at the Wheatlands, an opinion apparently shared by custom cutters who crowded every booth and table. He paid, took a toothpick from a dispenser by the cash register, and walked down to the grain elevators. Wheat trucks were stacked up along Main for two blocks. He cut across the coop yard, used to park mobile nitrogen fertilizer tanks, and made his way to the office. A man in a green visor gave him directions to the Bishop farm.

Joshua didn't call Claudia. He wanted to go out and get the lay of the land. He drove slowly, windows down, absorbing the morning heat. Dust from the dirt road drifted in a small cloud behind the Toyota. The road was flanked by wheat fields. There was an occasional combine at work. He passed several farmhouses, most set well back from the road, all surrounded by large shade trees. Each house seemed like a green island in the ocean of wheat. Joshua watched the names on the mailboxes as he passed. Eleven miles out of town he passed a black box with the name C. BISHOP stenciled on its side in small white letters. Joshua drove on to the next section line, made a U-turn, and came back. He pulled over before he got to the drive and observed Bishop's house from a distance. He sat behind the wheel, felt the heat, and studied the house. Maybe I should send over a recon, he thought.

Bishop passed Joshua the field glasses. "What do you think?"
Joshua leaned against the lip of the trench. The red clay still

radiated warmth from the blistering heat of the day. He slowly swept the ridge that dominated the eastern perimeter. "I don't see anything, but that doesn't mean a diddly." He lowered the glasses. "Why don't we send over a recon? Small. Two men."

Bishop shook his head. "We'd just give ourselves away."

"SFOB says the ARVN may break through tomorrow."

"Josh, ole buddy, we ain't gonna be here tomorrow."

"Where's all that 'we can whip these dinks' bullshit?"

"That was two days ago. How many Nungs we got left?"

"Maybe fifty."

"Right. And there's Tate, Porter, and DuBoise left from our team, besides you and me. And Wittenhauer and Haskell from Thang Duc. We're stretched so thin on the perimeter we can hardly see each other."

Joshua wearily rubbed the dirty stubble on his face. "We can keep air cover over us all night long," he said.

"Might work," Bishop agreed. "But if they get inside this compound we're dead."

"We haven't been mortared much today," Joshua said. "Maybe they're pulling out."

"Why the hell should they mortar us? It would only pulverize the wreckage."

"They've taken a hell of a beating, too, Tom."

"They'll attack or they wouldn't have ambushed the ARVN relief column again."

Joshua was silent, knowing Bishop was right.

"There are only two kinds of people in this camp, Josh." Bishop fumbled in his tiger suit for his Winston pack and lit up. "Them that's dead. And them that's going to get dead." He exhaled slowly. "We've got to get ourselves a new game plan. E and E tonight."

"Sneak through the North Vietnamese," Joshua murmured. "Just like that."

"They sure as hell won't be looking for us to come straight at them."

"That's true," Joshua conceded.

"Besides," Bishop said, "Charlie thinks the jungle's his at night."

"Yeah, well," Joshua said dubiously, "the reason Charlie thinks that is because it's true. I think we ought to hang tough right here.

Get the whole damn Air Force over us and try to last one more night."

"You may be right, Josh." Bishop took one last drag on his cigarette and ground the butt out against a sandbag. "We don't have to decide now. I'll see what I can do to get us ready for another assault. Hope today's air drop included the claymores. You stay here and watch for any activity." He moved off down the trench.

Joshua turned back to the ridge and raised the field glasses to his eyes.

Bishop's house looked just like it did in the snapshot. Two stories, white frame. Well-maintained. Lots of shade trees. Somehow Joshua expected it to be different after twelve years. He observed the farm a while longer, saw no one, then drove slowly back to town. He ate a grilled ham and cheese with a Coke at the Wheatlands Café. Then he went to his motel room and called Claudia Bishop. She offered to meet him at the Main Street Café at four o'clock for coffee.

Joshua sat on a wooden bench in front of the Main Street Café. There were two benches on the sidewalk, one on either side of the café's entrance. Joshua discovered that Plains didn't have a bus depot. Tickets were sold in the café. In bad weather the proprietor would let people wait inside. In good weather they waited outside on the benches. Joshua didn't know if the unbearable heat qualified as good or bad weather, but he was the only person on either bench. Despite the late-afternoon hour, the scorching heat of midday still gripped the little farming community. The oiled blacktop of Main Street looked liquid, and he could smell the hot tar surface. He settled back to wait for Claudia.

His gaze wandered up and down the street. Saturday-afternoon traffic was heavy. Pickups and wheat trucks mostly, with a sprinkling of automobiles and farm implements, and a steady flow of pedestrians socializing and shopping and conducting business at the county seat. Plains' citizens mingled in the park. Several picnics were spread out under the trees. People clustered around the world's deepest hand-dug well. Four old men pitched horseshoes while their wives chatted on a nearby park bench. The dull chink of metal on metal as the horseshoes struck the stakes reached Joshua's ears on the gusting wind. He leaned forward and peeled his shirt, wet with sweat, away from his skin. As he waited for Claudia, the uneasiness that had been with him all day persisted. A sense of reluctance to confront the inevitable gnawed at him now that it was upon him. Apparently Claudia felt the same. At any rate, there had been no outpouring of Jayhawker hospitality with an invitation to dinner at the farm. A cup of coffee at the Main Street Café sounded distant and cautious to Joshua. Well, that was all right with him. He wasn't sure he wanted to get too close to Mrs. Tom Bishop, either.

A late-model Fairlane cruised slowly down Main and nosed into the curb in front of Joshua. The woman behind the wheel remained in the vehicle a moment, studying Joshua, face expressionless, then got out. She wore faded Levi's and a plaid shirt. The wind whipped her brown hair around her face and she raised a hand to push it back. It was the woman in the snapshot. Very little changed after twelve years. She came forward and stepped up on the curb as Joshua rose to meet her.

"Joshua Scott?" the woman asked. Her voice was reserved, neither cordial nor unfriendly.

"That's right." He extended his hand.

"I'm Claudia Bishop." She shook his hand firmly, without smiling.

Joshua felt like he had just concluded a business transaction in which he was the loser. He stepped back. "I'll buy the coffee," he offered, essaying a smile.

Claudia moved toward the door to the café and pushed on through as Joshua followed her. The air conditioning was a pleasant shock to his sweat-damp skin. There were a few customers, and Claudia led the way to the rear and took an isolated booth. He slid onto the worn green vinyl seat and looked at the woman opposite him. Her manner was cool and distant, almost defiant. She was pretty, though, no doubt about that, with regular features and a rather wide mouth. She wore no makeup. Her fine skin was sunburned and her nose was peeling. There were tiny wrinkles at the corners of her eyes. They were probably from squinting into the

Kansas sun rather than smiling, Joshua thought wryly. Her brown hair, bleached lighter in places by the sun, showed a few strands of gray. She stared back at Joshua out of uncompromising hazel eyes. The impasse was broken by the waitress, a heavyset woman in a loud print dress that accentuated her size. She called Claudia by name, gazed at Joshua with frank curiosity, and took their order.

As the waitress retreated, Claudia broke the silence. "Well, tell me about yourself, Mr. Scott."

Joshua had the feeling it was the opening line from a Dale Carnegie course on "How to Win Friends and Influence People." He hesitated a moment. "Are you really Claudia Bishop?"

"Of course. Why do you ask?"

"You're not quite what I expected, I guess." Joshua shrugged imperceptibly. "Somehow not the way I saw you through Tom."

"What did you expect, a cheerleader?" Claudia looked away. "That was a long time ago."

Joshua glanced down at his hands. There was still an angry-looking scab across the back of his right wrist from his nose-dive down the canyon in the Monongahela. "It was a long time ago for both of us," he ventured, "but I guess I thought that Tom was a common link between us that might make it easier." He studied Claudia's face. "Are you mad at me about something?" He paused while the waitress served them. "We've barely met."

Claudia looked at Joshua soberly. "I know you," she said quietly. "I heard about you in almost every letter I got from Tom for nearly a year."

"I thought Tom liked me," Joshua murmured with a deprecatory grin.

Claudia was discomfited by the fact that when Joshua smiled, only the lips smiled. Not the face, and especially not the eyes. "Tom did," she said, "but, Mr. Scott, let's get one thing straight. . . ."

"Please call me Joshua," he interrupted. It was an appeal that carried more urgency than he had intended.

Claudia stared at the table. Joshua's request struck her as a proposal for instant friendship, an intimacy she did not need or want. His very presence intruded on her privacy. More than a decade of changing Kansas seasons had moved her beyond the painful past. And now this stranger from that past appears and says, "Call me Joshua." Claudia raised her eyes to look directly at him. "Mr. Scott,

Tom liked you." She shook her head as if warding off the memory.
"God, it was clear from his letters that he liked you. But he knew
you. I don't want to know you, and I don't want to like you."

Joshua lifted the coffee cup to his lips. "Well, that's straight
enough."

"There are twelve years between me and Tom's death. They
haven't been all bad, but they've been hard." Claudia stirred some
Sweet 'n' Low into her iced tea while she went on. "It's behind me
now, and I don't want to rake it all up."

"Why did you agree to see me when I wrote?"

Her face softened a fraction. "A momentary weakness." She
sipped her tea. "Why did you come here?"

"To see you."

"What for?"

Joshua hesitated a moment, uncertain of his own motives. "To
talk about Tom," he said finally. "Apparently we're working at
cross-purposes, though. It's all the things you don't want to talk
about."

"Not after twelve years," Claudia murmured. "You can't live in
the past."

"I do."

"Why?"

"I'm stuck to it like a tar baby."

"Put it behind you."

"That's why I came."

"What has it got to do with me?"

"You're my link with Tom."

Claudia pushed her glass away from her with a gesture of impatience. "I don't want to be your link with Tom. I don't want to be
anybody's link with Tom. Tom is gone."

"Don't you have any feelings for him? Nothing left at all?"

"You don't know me well enough to ask that."

Joshua decided to press ahead. "No pride? No loyalty?" He
paused. "No curiosity?"

"Just who do you think you are?" Claudia bristled.

"I was with him when he died."

Claudia paled. "That's not fair," she said at last. "What do you
want from me?"

"I'm not sure," Joshua said slowly.

An uncomfortable silence settled between them. Finally Claudia spoke. "What have you been doing since the Army?" Her voice sounded less hostile.

"There's not much to tell. My college major was comparative literature. When I got back from Nam I went to graduate school and got a master's. God knows why," he muttered, almost as an aside. "Then I taught a year in high school, but I couldn't stick with it. Mostly I do odd jobs."

"Odd jobs?"

Joshua nodded. "One thing and another."

Claudia waited.

"Last thing I did was fire fighter with the Forest Service."

"How did you like it?"

"Fire fighting or the Forest Service?"

"Either."

"I liked it less than I thought I would."

"Why was that?"

Joshua shrugged. "I like everything less than I thought I would."

Claudia arched neat eyebrows. "Including me," she observed, allowing herself a small smile.

For an instant Joshua saw before him a different woman. "That's correct," he said slowly, "but I don't have to like you. I just want to talk to you."

The smile faded and the momentary warmth evaporated. "That depends on what you want to talk about."

Joshua finished his coffee and pushed the cup and saucer away. "Well," he said, "for starters, tell me about yourself. What have you been doing the past twelve years?"

Claudia took a deep breath. "Raising Todd and running the farm."

"Todd is your son?" Joshua asked, picturing the little boy in the snapshot, squinting seriously at the camera.

"Yes."

"How old is he?" Joshua said, trying to make small talk, buying time, hoping to find some way to break through Claudia's reserve.

"Sixteen. He'll be a junior next year at Consolidated."

"I'd like to meet him."

Claudia hesitated. "I'm not sure that's a good idea. Besides, he's away at football camp at KU. That's Tom's old alma mater," she explained.

"I know."

Claudia studied Joshua. "I know you knew Tom very well," she said thoughtfully, "but you can't pick up his life here. He's not here anymore. And anyway," she added, "I don't want you to."

Joshua sat quietly a moment, deliberating with himself. "A few weeks ago I walked off another job," he said slowly. "I went back to my rented apartment in Richmond. It was empty. There was nothing in it that belonged to me but my clothes, some books and records, and a few odds and ends. I was alone. I was angry. I was frightened." He hesitated a moment. "I was sort of thinking about the past. I had no one to talk to and no place to go. I wound up in an old Catholic church at four o'clock in the morning. I realized that the only difference between me and the other derelicts there was that I shaved." He glanced up at Claudia. "My life began to come apart when Tom was killed. I want to try and put it back together. I thought I might start here."

"I can't help you."

"Can't or won't?"

"Perhaps both."

"Why not?"

"You're twelve years too late. My life is settled now. Going back will only complicate it."

"I can see that it might." Joshua nodded. "I was thinking primarily of myself."

"Is that what you were doing twelve years ago?" Claudia said, the bitterness apparent in her voice.

Joshua looked up sharply, a sinking feeling sucking at his insides. "What do you mean?"

"I heard from every surviving member of Tom's team but you. I can't remember their names, but—"

"Eddie DuBoise and Wyatt Porter."

"Yes, DuBoise wrote, and so did Porter. But not you."

Joshua nodded numbly. "I couldn't then."

"Well, I can't now." Her face was implacable and her voice hard. "Twelve years ago we might have helped each other. God knows

I needed it then." She paused, and her voice softened. "You see, I really do know you, Mr. Scott. Or at least I did then. Through Tom. Of all the men on his team, you were the one." Her face twisted in anger and frustration. "You were *the* one! Where the hell were you?"

Joshua didn't respond.

Claudia went on, slowly and deliberately. "Things are settled here now. I won't say that I've made a perfect adjustment to Tom's death, but I'm reconciled to it. Todd never really knew his father and it's hard to miss what you never knew. I have structured our lives pretty carefully and it works reasonably well for both of us."

"I'm glad for you."

"You're nothing but grief. I don't want to deal with you and I don't want to like you."

"I think you've succeeded," Joshua said wryly, and signaled the waitress for the check.

"How long are you going to be here?" Claudia asked abruptly.

Joshua shrugged. "I thought I might stay a few days. Whatever it took."

Claudia slid out of the booth and gestured to Joshua to remain seated. "Don't show me out," she said brusquely as she stared down at him, a perplexed look clouding her face. She paused a moment. "Where are you staying?"

"The Wheatlands."

"I may call you tomorrow." The anger was back in her voice as she turned and left.

Joshua ordered another cup of coffee and slowly drank it while he thought about Mrs. Tom Bishop.

Claudia couldn't sleep. The conversation with Joshua that afternoon simmered in her mind, fueled by the stifling midnight heat. The curtains beside the open window of her second-floor bedroom hung absolutely motionless. Her skin, damp with perspiration, seemed feverish rather than hot. Abandoning her efforts to defeat both mind and heat by force of will, she swung her feet to the floor and padded down the darkened hall to the bathroom. She switched on the overhead light, squinting in the sudden brightness, and opened the medicine cabinet. She removed a Valium from the half-empty bottle, filled a glass next to the sink, and washed down the yellow tablet.

Claudia stared at her reflection in the mirror, not something she did very often. What did Joshua Scott see there? she wondered. The few strands of gray in her hair were not unbecoming. But the crow's-feet around the eyes betrayed the years of unhappiness and hard work. Turning her head she could see the irregular splotches of pigmentation along the sides of her neck, deposited there years ago when she had first taken the pill. It looks like I need to scrub my neck, she thought. With a little grunt of resignation she unbuttoned the pajama top, slid it from her shoulders, and let it drop to the floor. She stepped out of her panties and turned to view her body in the full-length mirror on the door. Her breasts, never large, but full, sagged slightly now. She was a little thick-waisted, and her abdomen bulged slightly. One pregnancy was all it took, she mused. Her hips and legs, always her best features, seemed to have withstood the years. Well, she thought, as I said this afternoon, my cheerleading days were a long time ago. Thank God.

Claudia turned on the shower and adjusted the water until it was cool and soothing. She let it flow over her skin a long time. After she toweled off, she returned to her bedroom and found fresh nightclothes. Her rumpled bed looked totally uninviting. Wide awake now, and still filled with thoughts of the afternoon's disquieting meeting with Joshua, she retraced her steps down the hall and pushed open the door to Todd's bedroom. She seldom entered his room. It was more than respecting the privacy of a sixteen-year-old son. She found his room unsettling. It interfered with her controlled detachment from the past.

She stood in the middle of the room and scanned the walls by the dim moonlight filtering through the windows. A new Styx poster had been added since she last had been there. She noted that the life-size poster of Christie Brinkley was still thumbtacked to the ceiling above his bed. But the rock groups and the girls didn't bother her. It was the other items that kept her from the room. Claudia looked at the wall beside Todd's bed. There were two framed photographs. One of Tom Bishop in a formal team portrait of the Cimarron County Consolidated High School Mustangs. The other a glossy eight-by-ten of Tom Bishop in Jayhawker powder blue, kneeling on the turf of War Memorial Stadium. And finally, a large, slick poster of Tom Bishop in a 49er uniform, a running back all stretched out in full stride.

Claudia raised a hand to her throat and turned to look at the opposite wall. Bric-a-brac shelves held memorabilia Todd had collected about his father's tour of duty in Vietnam. Her eyes picked over the mix of snapshots, medals, citations, and other items. Her pulse quickened. All of the old, repressed emotions surged through her. Revulsion, fear, resentment, anger. And yet? What had Joshua said? *"No curiosity?"* Claudia moved closer to the shelves. She and Todd had quarreled repeatedly over his persistent accumulation of these mementos from his father's military past. It represented everything she hated. Hated for what it symbolized, and for what it did to her. She bit her lower lip as the thought took shape in her mind. Did to me, she mused. Is that what I think? Tom did something to me? Yes. Oh, yes! He got himself killed and he left me alone! Frightened and alone.

Claudia picked up a snapshot. She peered closely at it in the darkened shadows, then replaced it. I am beyond it, she thought. Or have I simply put distance between me and the past? What about the present? Have I also put distance between myself and the present?

Claudia softly closed the door to Todd's room and made her way downstairs. She had the front closet open and the mattress from the rollaway bed out of its folded metal frame before she realized what she was doing. She hadn't slept on the front porch since she and Tom were first married and he came back summers and off-seasons to work on the farm. After a moment's hesitation, she dragged it through the front door and dropped it on the porch. She found a pillow and sheet, then stretched out on the mattress.

Claudia listened to the drone of the locusts and absorbed the night smells of earth and wheat. It was a long time ago. On this mattress on this porch she had learned about her sensual nature. Oh, she knew about sex, and was not without experience before she married Tom. But here, and with him, she had discovered her sexuality. Her hunger. Her profanity in heat. Exploring the parameters of her erotic potential. And Tom's. They brought words to bed which they had found in a dictionary, words to which they had assigned salacious meanings, and required the other partner to perform them or act them out. Among others, Tom had come up with "filiation" and "pedantic," and Claudia had contributed "philologist" and "sacculate." They had also invented a game called Titillate, an acronym for Tell Incidents Truthfully Involving Lascivious Libidinous Acts, Thoughts, Expectations. In this game each would ask questions about the other's sexuality, and the response had to be completely truthful.

Claudia, one of three sisters, learned about male sexuality from Tom. Long-repressed memories flooded back. She smiled at one that touched present as well as past. Tom had revealed that as an adolescent he used to masturbate in bed into a sock to conceal the practice from his mother. Now she found stiff socks in Todd's laundry. And once, playing Titillate, they had agreed to make love with one partner remaining passive while the active partner played out a fantasy in their own mind. Tom, in the throes of his orgasm, cried out, "Sock! Oh, sock!" and they had rolled apart convulsed by laughter.

Claudia tasted the salt of tears on her lips. Don't tinker with the past, she told herself. Then she remembered an old adage: The first law of tinkering is to save all the parts. "I'm afraid I haven't saved all the parts," she whispered.

Joshua stood in the open door of his motel room, hands jammed deep in his jeans pockets, and stared into the night. He was filled with a morbid discontent. He had played the meeting with Claudia Bishop over in his mind a hundred times on the trip to Plains, but no scenario had matched the reality. She was distant and cold, and wanted nothing to do with him. Her reluctance to deal with the past seemed even greater than his own. Should he force the issue, or flee?

He turned back into the room. The bedside lamp cast a dim glow on the flimsy sheets of fake walnut paneling. The air conditioner wheezed and gasped with death-rattle exhaustion. It was dreadful. He jerked his suitcase out from under the bed, opened it, and tossed it on top of the mattress. He went to the closet shelves and began to collect his clothes. After a moment he paused, turned, and hurled them at the open suitcase. He snatched the Toyota keys off the bedside table and left the room, slamming the door behind him. He drove down Main to the Billiard Parlor Bar and pulled the Land Cruiser up against the curb. He stared through the lighted windows. The bar was filled with men nursing beers. Looked like a collection of hard hats and cowboys. Maybe custom cutters. He put a hand on the door handle, then stopped. He didn't really want a drink. And he knew he didn't want to talk to anyone in a bar that fed on loneliness.

Joshua backed away from the curb. He drove to the Catholic church he had seen the previous night. On the edge of town, it was situated on almost an acre of ground. Wind-whipped elms were massed on the west side to shield it from the afternoon sun. Beyond the buildings were the endless wheat fields. The structure was unpretentious, almost severe in appearance. Native stone. Very narrow, with a steep roof and a high steeple. Light reflected through small stained-glass windows. Joshua walked toward the front entrance. A carved wooden sign at the steps read, "St. Mary's of the Plains." He mounted the steps and pressed the thumb latch of a heavy brass fixture, and the wooden door swung open. The church was empty, silent, and air-conditioned cool. Heavy brass light fixtures hung from the high ceiling on long chains, casting soft rheostated shadows on dark oak pews. Beyond the altar rail the chancel was dark, except for the red glow of the candle above the sacrament on the high altar. A wooden crucifix on the wall behind the altar was dimly visible. At the front of the nave, off to the side, stood a rack of votive candles, unlit except for the lighted parish candle. It guttered fitfully under a recessed alcove containing the icon of the Madonna.

Joshua slumped into a pew midway down the center aisle. He pressed his fingers against his eyes for a long moment. Maybe I can keep on going, he thought wearily, but I will always look back.

Joshua and Bishop sat at the table in the teamhouse. It was so dark they could barely see, but they finished taping their M-16 magazines butt-to-butt with army-green tape for faster reloading.

"Plains, Kansas, and Pine Mountain, Virginia," Bishop murmured almost to himself.

"What's that?" Joshua asked.

*"Plains, Kansas, and Pine Mountain, Virginia," Bishop repeated
as he picked up his M-16 clips and started for the door.*

*Joshua swept the remainder of the magazines off the table,
crammed them in his cargo pockets, and followed him out. They
stood behind the log barricade in the gathering darkness and
stared out across the shattered compound. Smoke from burning
buildings smudged the terrain and stung the eyes. Here and there
parachute silk—gaudy colors of red and blue and yellow—lay in
brightly colored swatches where the cargo chutes had landed on
resupply drops. It gave the compound a bizarre and festive appearance. Like a carnival on the fringes of hell.*

*"We're a long way from home tonight," Bishop concluded. He
looked at Joshua and grinned, but the expression had an ache in
it that seemed spun out to infinity. He touched Joshua's arm, settled
his web gear more comfortably on his shoulders, and moved off
toward the northwest wall.*

*Joshua watched him go for a moment, then turned and started
for the east wall.*

The words echoed in Joshua's mind. The next time he saw Bishop,
he was crawling along the bottom of a trench, mortally wounded.
Joshua passed his hands over his face and pulled himself out of the
pew. He made his way to the front of the nave and crossed over
to the votive candles. He removed a candle from the rack, held the
wick to the parish candle, watched the black smoke curl upward
as it caught, and replaced it in the rack.

"You're out late tonight, Josh."

Joshua swung around toward the voice, startled, half expecting
to see Tom Bishop. The priest stood in front of the altar rail.

"I'm afraid I have you at a disadvantage," the priest said, smiling.
"I'm Charlie Wilson. Your jogging partner."

Joshua nodded slowly as the pudgy face and tortoiseshell glasses
became recognizable through the concealing facade of clerical
collar and black cassock.

"I thought you were just passing through," Wilson said.

"I lied."

"When the front door opens it rings a bell in the rectory," Wilson
explained. "I thought I'd come see what was happening. Wednes-

day-night bingo is reasonably popular in Plains, but we almost never get late-night piety."

"I was just going," Joshua said.

"There's no need, if you'd like to stay. I can leave."

Joshua felt vaguely embarrassed. I can shoulder him aside on the road, he thought. But hardly in his own church. "No, I just stopped by briefly. On impulse."

Wilson nodded. "Good reason." He sat down in the front pew and propped his feet up on the altar rail.

"It's of no importance," Joshua said. "I'm not really religious."

"You believe in lighting candles."

Joshua was silent a moment, lips pursed in thought. "Superstition," he finally said, as he leaned back against the altar rail and faced Wilson.

"If superstition isn't religion," Wilson mused, "it's the next thing to it."

"That's a hell of a thing for a priest to say."

Wilson shrugged deferentially. "Both deal with the unknown and the nonrational." He watched Joshua for a moment, then asked, "What brings you to Plains?"

"Personal business."

"In Plains?"

"Butt out, Charlie."

Wilson nodded, not unsympathetic, and stood up to leave. "I can see you're a private man, Josh."

Joshua studied Charlie Wilson. His face was smooth and round. His eyes were great brown disks magnified behind thick lenses. Like pennies in a wishing well. "Do you know Claudia Bishop?" he ventured.

Wilson reflected a moment. Sat back down. "Yes. Pretty well, actually. For one thing, she's a Catholic, but we're also friends."

"How friends?"

"We worked together on a committee in western Kansas to end the war in Vietnam."

"When was that?"

"After her husband was killed. Late sixties, early seventies."

"Were you here when he was killed?"

"No. He was killed in 1967, and I didn't come here 'til about two years later."

Joshua mulled over the priest's words, trying to gain some insight into the woman he had come to see. "So Claudia worked in the peace movement," he murmured.

"Yes. She wasn't a fruitcake peacenik, mind you. She just thought the whole Vietnam War was senseless. A mistake. She and her husband apparently differed on that. I gather he was a believer."

"Part believer. Part adventurer."

"You knew Tom Bishop," Wilson said matter-of-factly.

"We served together in Nam."

"And that's your personal business in Plains."

Joshua nodded. "I talked to Claudia this afternoon, but I'm considering moving on."

"Why?"

Joshua shrugged. "As Claudia pointedly told me, the past is past and it's best left there."

"The past holds the key to the future," Wilson said. "Somebody smart said that. I forget who. Jimmy the Greek, maybe."

Joshua didn't smile. "I'm not sure I want to stay anyway. I think it will just make trouble."

"For you or for Claudia?"

I'm already in trouble, Joshua thought. Aloud, he said, "For Claudia."

"Well, Claudia's certainly had enough trouble."

"That's why I'm thinking of moving on."

"You never told me where you were from," Wilson said.

"Virginia."

"Where would you go?"

"Someplace else."

Wilson shook his head. "You've come two thousand miles after twelve years to see a woman you've never met about her dead husband."

"That's right."

"That's a lot of unfinished business."

Joshua didn't respond.

"Maybe you need a psychiatrist." Wilson smiled.

"I've had a psychiatrist."

"Maybe you need a priest."

"I don't need a priest."

"Everyone needs a priest," Wilson replied easily.

Joshua and Wilson sat in silence for a while, each lost in his own thoughts. The candle Joshua had lit burned down to a guttering pool of hot wax and flickered out. The nave seemed a lot darker somehow.

Wilson broke the silence. "So you were in Vietnam with Tom Bishop in 1967?" It was half statement, half question, as though he were picking through the pieces to put a puzzle together.

"That's right."

"Why?"

Joshua looked up sharply. "Hell, I was drafted."

"There were other options."

Joshua slowly shook his head. "Not for me there weren't."

"But, if you served with Tom Bishop, you were in the Special Forces. All-volunteer outfit, Airborne."

"All The Way," Joshua muttered, his voice self-mocking.

"Why?"

"Southern boys always volunteer."

"Come on, Josh."

Joshua shifted his eyes around the nave and thought a moment. Why should I open up to this Catholic priest? But in the darkened sanctuary in the middle of the vast Kansas prairie, Tom Bishop's words came back again. And they seemed as haunting as the night Bishop had uttered them. *"We're a long way from home tonight."* He looked at Wilson, and wiped his thumb and forefinger down across his mustache. "What was I doing in Nam with the Special Forces?" he repeated. "I was a True Believer, Charlie. Paying any price, bearing any burden, torch passed to a new generation."

"Truth?"

"Well, the words are tinged with cynicism now. But it came easily to me in the mid-sixties." Joshua shook his head. "I *believed.* I believed in myself. I believed in my church. I believed in my country. I believed you shouldn't ask what your country could do for you, but what you could do for your country. I believed in the vertical theory of geography with countries standing on end like dominoes. I believed I could help keep them from toppling."

"That is all to your credit."

Joshua stretched his long legs out in front of him. "It was all naive and gullible and an absolute waste."

Wilson watched Joshua for a moment, and listened to the cynicism and bitterness in his voice. "We were all pretty naive, Josh," he said. He removed his glasses, held them up to the muted light of a brass chandelier, then withdrew a linen handkerchief from an inside pocket of his cassock and began to clean the lenses. "But I'll tell you what, Josh. Naiveté isn't such a bad thing." He folded the handkerchief and replaced it in his pocket. "We all lose it, of course, like we lose our innocence. But without some kind of naiveté there's no wonder, no openness to mystery, no surprises, no possibilities." Wilson shrugged in a gesture of finality. "No life."

"Are you making this up as you go along, or is this your Sunday sermon?"

"It's what I believe."

"So what's your solution, Charlie?"

"There aren't any solutions, Josh, if you mean how can we fix life. There are no solutions to life but living it. But my hunch is we need a second naiveté. We've lost the first. The second gives us some place to stand to catch our breath. Less certitude, more trust. Less bravado, more courage. Maybe it's just something or someone to open up the closed circle. I guess we need a hand to hold without thinking we've got to earn it." Wilson fell silent, pudgy hands folded in his lap.

They sat together in the darkened nave, lost in their own thoughts. After a few moments Wilson turned to Joshua. "Would you like a drink?"

Joshua hesitated an instant, then nodded.

The priest led Joshua through a door behind the lectern into a book-lined study and then the rectory. Wilson removed his cassock, tossed it over a stick-back chair, and went to an old liquor cabinet. "What'll you have?"

"Whatever you're drinking's fine."

"I'm drinking an Episcopalian."

Joshua looked at the priest with a blank expression.

Wilson grinned. "It's a drink my father mixed. He used two mixers, ginger ale and soda, and called it an Episcopalian because he said it was neither Catholic nor Protestant."

Joshua nodded in appreciation. "Maybe you should fix me a Church of Christ," he said dryly. "Just give me an empty glass."

Wilson chuckled. "How about some Bushmills?"

"Fine."

Wilson poured a glass a third full and handed it to Joshua. He took the drink and settled into a wing chair. Joshua took a sip of the whiskey, felt it warm him. "Good sippin' whiskey," he murmured.

Wilson sank into a sofa across from Joshua, propped his feet up on a coffee table, and stirred his drink with a swizzle stick. "I used to drink too much," he said, "but in recent years I've almost stopped."

Joshua gazed at the priest without comment.

"What did you expect?" Wilson asked quietly. "Bing Crosby in *Going My Way*?"

"I've never known a priest."

Wilson shrugged. "Most people have never known a priest." He discarded the swizzle stick and sipped the Episcopalian. "I never had either," he went on, "so I had all the stereotypes, too. But when I got to the Church of the Epiphany the other priest there was shit-faced by nine o'clock every morning."

"Where was that?"

"New York City," Wilson replied. "Little Italy."

"How did you get to Plains, Kansas?"

"I like to pheasant hunt."

"Are you telling me to butt out now, Charlie?"

Wilson exhaled a long sigh. "Not really," he said. "But people usually don't ask priests personal questions. We're nonpersons." He tugged at his clerical collar. "This one-inch strip of celluloid takes away my face." He looked intently at Joshua. "You didn't even recognize me in the sanctuary tonight. All you saw was my function." He waved a hand in dismissal. "Few people see past the function to the man."

Joshua sensed the regret in the priest's words. "Who is the man, Charlie?"

"He's hard to find. I've always been Father Wilson the parish priest, or a cleric among clerics, but not Charlie Wilson the kid from the Bronx."

"Why did a kid from the Bronx become a priest?"

Wilson hesitated. "I'd like to say it was a calling," he said, "but that puts a slant on it that's a little too sublime." Wilson smiled. "The only calling I got was when the police called at the front door looking for the kid who'd stolen the milk truck and given away all the milk."

Joshua laughed. "The Bronx Robin Hood."

"Juvenile court didn't think it was very funny. But I was only fifteen and Gold Seal Dairy didn't press charges." Wilson sipped his Episcopalian. "I'll tell you what, Josh. I drank Gold Seal for a long time after that." He shook his head. "That's when my mom's parish priest took me in tow. Before I knew it, I was enrolled in Cathedral College."

"At fifteen?"

"Cathedral was a prep school for the priesthood. It was a revelation. I discovered I had a brain. After Cathedral I went to St. Joseph's Seminary in Yonkers." Wilson settled deeper into the sofa and rested his head back and contemplated the ceiling. "It was like Marine boot camp for priests. It created an incredible esprit de corps. And a hunger in the soul." He was quiet a moment as he gave himself to the memory. "Vespers with two hundred and fifty men singing a Gregorian chant would make Jehovah God himself weep. I loved it." He looked back at Joshua. "Then I got blind-sided."

"What happened?"

Wilson stood up. "If we're going to keep on like this, I'm going to need a real drink." He went to the liquor cabinet and poured himself a Bushmills. He gestured with the bottle toward Joshua. "Want a refill?" Joshua moved over to the cabinet and let Wilson refresh his drink. "They wanted me to become a canon lawyer for the church," Wilson continued.

"What does that mean?"

"Canon law is pure, pettifogging legalism." Wilson held out his hands and started ticking off points like a debater. "The law recognizes mortal and venial sins. Mortal sins send a sinner straight to hell. Venial sins condemn one to purgatory. The nature of the sin determines how long one is consigned to purgatory. That's *the law!*" Wilson shook his head sadly. "It stopped me dead in my tracks. Religion could be reduced to a first-degree misdemeanor, second-degree misdemeanor, third-degree misdemeanor, right on up to a felony with vehicular homicide, manslaughter, and murder one." Wilson took a drink and grimaced as the Bushmills stung his throat. "Might as well convene church in municipal court."

"So what did you do?"

"I knew I didn't want a career in the bureaucracy of the church. I wanted to be a priest. So when I was tonsured I asked for a parish and they sent me to the Church of the Epiphany in Little Italy. I was back on the streets." Wilson swirled his glass and stared into the amber liquid. "It was there I learned that God weeps for other things than Gregorian chants." He looked at Joshua. "And it all had faces. Little Mario DiMatteo, who was afraid to leave his apartment for the street. Mrs. Montanelli, who had seven children and needed to have her tubes tied. Tony Farris, out of work at forty-three. Maria Sanchez, whose marriage bed was a place of rape. Skeeter, the junkie, whose eyes died at eighteen and who waited for his body to follow. Gina Cianchetti, sensual and all too willing. Albert Salvoni, slum lord and loan shark."

Wilson paused. "Everyone had a face but me. I was just a function. I was supposed to fulfill the function and disappear into the rectory." He lifted his glass and drank. "There was no one to talk to. There was no companionship, no warmth, and no human presence, let alone another human touch. No friends. Not one first-name friend who really gave a damn about Charlie Wilson."

"What about the other priests?"

"Half of them are assholes, and the other half are alcoholics."

"I guess a priest can talk to God, huh, Charlie?"

"Prayer is not conversation, Josh. When a man talks to God, that's prayer. When God talks to a man, that's schizophrenia."

Joshua laughed. "But what about 'What a Friend We Have in Jesus'?"

"Try and hug Jesus." Wilson shook his head. "Loneliness," he muttered. "I mean being *alone* lonely. It became *the fact* of my life. And then"—he nodded his head—"then I felt the fear. The fear that it would never change. That it would never be any different." Wilson glanced around the room. "I sat in the rectory one night and realized I was in exactly the same position as the Orthodox Jew who waits for a Messiah he knows deep in his heart is never going to come." He drained the Bushmills. "And I hated the self-pity."

"So what does a priest do, Charlie?"

Wilson shrugged, "Oh, there are about three alternatives. Reach for the Bushmills." He turned the empty glass in his hand and contemplated it. "The universal panacea that comes eighty-six proof. Or get desperately busy stage-managing the affairs of the parish. Or call Gina Cianchetti and see if you can come over for a cup of coffee."

"Which alternative did you choose?"

"Hell, I tried all three. But I wasn't a very good drinker. And while I was running around like a crazed social worker, I found out you couldn't hug a cause either." Wilson smiled, almost to himself. "So I hugged Gina Cianchetti."

Joshua chuckled and shook his head sympathetically.

"About that time I got a summons from the bishop. He told me to get back to Epiphany and do it by the book." Wilson set his glass on the coffee table so hard Joshua thought it might shatter. "I wanted to be a *priest*. They wanted me to be a *function*. It got so I couldn't fart in Little Italy without the bishop smelling it in midtown Manhattan."

"What happened?"

"I asked to be allowed to transfer, and a bishop in Kansas agreed to take me on."

"How's it gone in Plains?"

"Do you know how many people have been in this apartment?" Joshua shook his head.

"Two. You and Claudia Bishop."

"The loneliness hasn't changed."

"Do I seem desperate?"

"No," Joshua replied, "you don't." He thought back to the moment earlier in the evening when he refused to go in the Billiard Parlor Bar and substitute a drink and an hour's conversation for loneliness and call it friendship. Maybe, he mused, I just found another bar. But he knew this was something different. With Charlie Wilson it was something more. He stood, feeling the old wariness closing in. "Better call it a night, Charlie."

Wilson nodded. He picked up his and Joshua's glass and carried them over to the liquor cabinet, then followed Joshua back into the nave. "Finish your business with Claudia, Josh," he admonished. "I think she may need it. And you need it, or you wouldn't be here."

Joshua didn't acknowledge the priest's comment. "Thanks for the drink." He turned to go.

Wilson watched Joshua walk up the aisle of the darkened sanctuary. When he reached the baptismal font, Wilson called after him. "Who's the candle for, Josh?"

Joshua stopped, then slowly turned to face the priest. After a moment's hesitation, he said, "Tom Bishop."

Wilson went over to the votive candles. He selected one, lit it, and placed it in the rack. "This is for Tom Bishop," he said. Then he took a second candle, lit it, and placed it in the rack beside the first. "And this one's for you."

Wilson turned back in time to see Joshua hurry from the sanctuary.

CHAPTER FIVE

Joshua ate breakfast at the restaurant adjoining the Wheatlands Motel, and then puttered around his room for a while. He left while a Spanish-speaking maid cleaned his room, and walked to town. He stopped at Moody's Drug and Sundries. From their limited selection of westerns and housewife porn, he selected *Cowboy Lore of the Great Plains*. Back in his room, he read, listened to the clatter of the air conditioner, and waited to see if Claudia would call. He was contemplating what he would do if she did not when the phone rang. She asked him to come to the farm for supper that evening. The conversation was brief and unambiguously cool. Other than the invitation, it included only directions to the farm, which Joshua allowed her to give him rather than trying to explain that he knew where it was. She already had reservations about seeing him. If she knew he had reconnoitered the farm, in addition to whatever else she thought, she would probably think she was dealing with a demented vet.

Joshua rested in his darkened room until midafternoon. Then he jogged. The same course he had run the night before. Six miles. It was hot. He pushed hard. By the time he returned to the motel, the sweat and dust had covered his skin with a thin layer of congealed grime. He took a long time in the shower.

At six o'clock he turned up the drive to the Bishop house. The drive ended at a rambling outbuilding off to the side of the house. It served as both garage and toolshed. Claudia's Fairlane was parked in one side of the shed. In the other was a Case tractor. Beyond the shed were three metal silos. Beside them was the well-house. Joshua circled around so the Toyota was pointed back down the drive, wondering as he did so if he was preparing for a quick getaway. He got out and started hesitantly toward the side of the house. There was a small stoop at a side door, but he wondered if he should walk around to the front porch. While he was making up his mind, the side door opened and Claudia stepped onto the stoop, drying her hands on a dish towel. She wore faded Levi's and a soft yellow blouse. She stepped off the stoop to meet him.

Joshua held out a hand. "Thanks for calling," he said simply.

"I almost didn't." Claudia's hand was still damp from the towel. She turned toward the house, mounted the stoop, and opened the screen door. "You don't mind going in the kitchen, do you?" The kitchen was large and high-ceilinged. Countertops were cluttered with kitchen utensils and pots and pans. "I'm a messy cook," Claudia apologized.

"That's all right, I'm a messy eater. Hope you didn't go to too much trouble."

"No, I just use a lot of dishes to cook a little meal." Claudia left the dish towel on the sink and beckoned with a nod of her head. "Let's go in the living room." She led him through a large dining room with a heavy oak table and chairs, and then through wide French doors into the living room. She pointed without comment to a big overstuffed chair, and moved a high-backed rocker so she could sit facing him.

Joshua hesitated a moment, gauging her sober manner. "I appreciate you asking me out," he offered. "Maybe we'll get along better than we did yesterday."

Claudia paused before she replied. "Look," she said, "when you wrote telling me you were going to be coming through, I thought I could see you. But I've had increasing doubts about the wisdom of it. And when I met you yesterday, I knew I couldn't go through with it."

"What made you change your mind?"

"I haven't yet. You said yesterday you wanted to talk about Tom. I thought I would at least see you again and find out exactly what you wanted."

Joshua shifted uncomfortably in his chair. "I don't know, exactly." He paused. "Tom was probably the best friend I ever had." He glanced at Claudia. "We'd have been good friends had we met back in the world, but in Nam everything got compressed. Heightened."

Claudia nodded in understanding.

"When Tom was killed . . ." Joshua stopped, struggling with his thoughts. "Everything about it . . ." He searched for the words, feeling the anxiety build. "I couldn't let it go, and I couldn't deal with it." Joshua studied Claudia's face. "I thought it might help if I could talk to you."

Claudia stood up and moved across the room to the front door. She folded her arms and leaned against the jamb and stared through the screen. The land she farmed stretched away in front of her. It ran in straight lines, neatly divided into acres, quarters, and sections. Fenced, flat, predictable, and secure. She had struggled to make it so. Just as she had with her life. Claudia turned back to face him. "My life works now, Josh," she said softly.

Joshua looked up at the mention of his name and caught Claudia's eyes. "That's a start," he said. "It sure as hell beats 'Mr. Scott.' "

Claudia paused, held Joshua's gaze a moment, then looked away. "No," she said with finality. "Everything in my life is in order. But I have to hang on real tight. If I talk to you, I'm afraid it might not work anymore. See someone else. Maybe the other two men on your team, DuBoise or Porter."

Joshua shook his head. "I don't even know where they are. Besides," he added, "I wanted to talk to someone it mattered to. Someone who knew Tom, and it really mattered."

Claudia shook her head slowly, almost sadly. "I'm sorry, I don't think I can."

"Well," Joshua said with resignation, "I'm sorry, too. I think it has to be you."

Claudia returned to the rocker and perched on the edge of the seat. "Why, dammit? Why just me?"

Joshua tried to think. Why? Why just Claudia? Because she's the one who must know. "You're the next of kin," he replied.

"My God!" she cried. "The next of kin?" Her voice had a note of hysteria in it. "The next of kin! Do you want me to have to do it all again?" She leaned back in the rocker, huddled there, it seemed, as far away from Joshua as she could get. "You don't know what it was like then. When Tom went to Vietnam, we were estranged. I don't mean separated or anything like that. We differed about the war. It ran deep and put a barrier between us that we never broke through. Never! Not before he left, and not after." She paused, a little breathless. "And of course there was never anything else, no 'ever after.'" Claudia paused a moment, then went on dully. "Tom didn't have to go. He could have farmed. He left me for you and the likes of you. You stand for what Tom stood for, and what I stood against. And you come to me from where Tom came from and say, 'Let's talk about it.'"

Joshua stared at his hands in his lap. He felt sorry, truly sorry for Claudia Bishop. The thing he needed most was anathema to her.

"The next of kin," Claudia repeated quietly, composed. "Do you know what that's like? Tom went away all eager and strong and full of life. He came home in a casket, his remains marked 'Unfit for Viewing.' An Army officer and two enlisted men came out from Fort Riley for the funeral. They folded an American flag and gave it to me."

Joshua and Porter and Bishop sat at the table in the teamhouse. Joshua made himself a peanut butter and jelly sandwich while Wyatt Porter, a muscular black, determinedly worked his way through a C ration can of ham and lima beans. Bishop wearily stubbed out his cigarette in a Kerr lid. "Wyatt, later this afternoon I want you and DuBoise to get some more claymores out on the perimeter."

"It's going to take more than claymores to save our asses," Porter said. "We got the shit kicked out of us again last night."

"There are only six of us left, Tom," Joshua said. "Wittenhauer's not too bad off, but Hendersen's on his last legs."

"And there ain't no more than a hundred Nungs on the perimeter," Porter added.

"Half of them are wounded," Joshua said as he tilted his canteen to his lips.

Bishop sat, chin in his hands, staring at the bulletin board on the wall above the single-sideband radio. A few messages were thumbtacked to the board. An enlargement of an aerial reconnaissance photograph showed nothing but solid banks of clouds. Lettered in grease pencil across the bottom of the picture were the

words "Twenty-percent cloud cover, color VC huts red." A hand-
lettered sign read, "Tet—Year of the Horse's Ass." A souvenir
American flag was also tacked to the board. No more than twelve
inches long, it had a glossy satin sheen and a gold-braid fringe.

"Hell," Bishop drawled as he contemplated the board, "we're
elite troops. We're in-fucking-vincible." He got to his feet and
walked over to the bulletin board, removed the souvenir American
flag, and flung the thumbtacks into a corner of the room. He
pushed through the door of the teamhouse into the midday sun.
Joshua and Porter followed him curiously, joined by DuBoise, who
was stacking cases of mortar shells in the nearby four-deuce pit.
They stopped behind the log barricade and watched while Bishop
strode resolutely across the open ground to the camp's flagpole.
Snipers on the surrounding ridges noted the lone figure standing
completely exposed in the center of the compound, adjusted their
sights, and began to fire.

Bishop released the halyard and lowered the large saffron-and-
maroon flag of the Republic of Vietnam. He unsnapped it and
draped it over his shoulder, scarcely pausing as a near miss sent
splinters of flagpole flying a few inches in front of his face. Bishop
tied the small American flag to the rope and ran it briskly up the
flagpole, where it caught a faint breeze and unfurled with a slight
flutter. Tying off the halyard, he stepped back and snapped off a
parade-ground salute. He spun on his heel in a crisp about-face
and marched smartly back to the protection of the log barricade.

Bishop sauntered over to where he had left the others and joined
them as they stared up at the tiny flag audaciously whipping in
the breeze. "What do you think?" he asked casually.

"You dumb piss-on-the-campfire son of a bitch," Joshua said.

"Tonight," Porter said, "those NVA mother-fuckers are going to
nail your white ass."

"If we're going to get killed," DuBoise said, "we might as well
get killed under our own flag."

"Have you ever seen DuBoise or Porter?" Claudia asked.

Joshua looked up and shook his head. "No, never."

"Never have looked them up in all these years?" Her voice had
a note of incredulity in it.

"No."

"Why not?"

"It's not much of a war for reunions." Joshua saw Claudia's perplexed look. "Anyway, what would I say to them?"

"Tell them the things you want to talk about with me."

Joshua shook his head with annoyance. "You still don't understand," he said. "The only thing I could ask Wyatt Porter is if anybody ever turned out the light at the end of the tunnel."

Resigned to the impasse with Claudia, Joshua looked away and glanced around the living room. On the mantel of a gas-log fireplace was a formal portrait of an elderly couple, a picture of a young girl, and a portrait of Tom Bishop. Joshua pushed out of the easy chair and went over to the mantel. He reached up and took the framed portrait of Bishop in his hands. It was taken in his Class A tans. His green beret was squared resolutely on his head. The familiar crooked Bishop smile was there, half amusement, half devilment, but the complexion was airbrushed to perfection. Artificial. Flawless. It wasn't Tom Bishop. "Doesn't look like Tom," Joshua said. His tone was disapproving. "Too slick." He replaced the portrait on the mantel. Somehow the single studio photograph of Tom Bishop on the mantel seemed a mere deferential courtesy to his memory. Almost disrespectful. He wasn't sure what he expected, though. An elaborate memorial? A shrine? "Not much here to remind you of Tom."

"No." Claudia passed over Joshua's comment and pointed to the portrait of the elderly couple. "That's Tom's folks. Clarence and Martha. Todd and I lived on the farm with them when Tom went to Vietnam. After he was killed, we stayed on. I got along very well with them and I felt safe here." She tucked a sneakered foot up under one thigh and gave the rocker a little push with her other foot. "They both died eight years ago. Mom first, and then Pop six months later. He just died in his sleep. I don't think he could bear to live without her. They had been married for forty-six years," she said, her voice tinged with wonder and envy.

Joshua picked up the final photograph on the mantel. "Who's the little girl?"

"That's Kathryn Bishop, Tom's older sister."

"I didn't know he had a sister."

"She was killed when she was eleven in a tractor accident. Tom never really knew her. He was only six when she died."

Joshua replaced the photograph on the mantel and returned to the overstuffed chair.

"When Tom was killed," Claudia went on, "his folks left the farm to me and Todd."

"Are you a farm girl?"

Claudia smiled, but it was an expression of irony, not humor. "I am now," she said. "I was a big-city girl. Kansas City. But after Mom and Pop Bishop died, I decided to stay on the farm, at least for a while. And I've been here ever since. Besides," she continued, "it's a good life for Todd. The only one he really knows. The thought of going back to Kansas City now and putting Todd in an urban high school really scares me."

"Do you farm this place?"

"Yes."

"There's no Mr. Claudia Bishop?"

"No." Claudia dismissed the question with a wave of her hand. "How about you?" she countered. "Is there a Mrs. Joshua Scott?"

"There was," Joshua said.

"What happened?"

Joshua shrugged. "It was my fault. Nothing worked. I'd been home about eight or ten months. One morning I left home on my way to the university. I just kept going and didn't go back."

"What did you do?"

"Kept driving. I called her about two weeks later and told her we just couldn't go on. She knew it, too." Joshua shook his head. "After Nam, nothing worked." He stopped suddenly and looked at Claudia. "We're talking."

Claudia nodded with a look of resignation.

"You know, Claudia," Joshua went on, "there are things about Tom you think you don't need to talk about, and refuse to. There are things about Tom I've never talked about, and want to." He paused. "Maybe we could meet each other half-way."

"You make it sound so simple."

"I don't think it would be simple, but I think it could be done. Maybe even needs to be done. After all, if you refuse to talk about something that happened twelve years ago, maybe something's wrong. And if I can't put away what happened twelve years ago, obviously something's wrong."

Claudia was silent for a long moment. "I couldn't do it all at once," she finally said. "And maybe I couldn't do it at all. It would have to be slow."

Joshua nodded. "That's all right by me. I'll take the time."

Claudia studied Joshua a moment. She may not have been what he had expected, but he certainly was not what she had expected. "Well," she said, "we could start with supper."

"That sounds fine."

"Let me change clothes first. You caught me before I had a chance to clean up." Claudia stood up and went to the screen door and held it open. "Wait out on the front porch. I'll bring you something to drink."

Joshua stepped onto the porch. The wind had died down. It was a quiet, blue-twilight evening. Still warm, but the heat had lost its intensity. He walked along the porch. A planter and several flower-pots set on the rail were filled with well-tended flowers. At the corner of the porch a trellis reached from the ground to the porch roof. It was covered with climbing roses. Apparently the city girl had a green thumb. He leaned against a post by the steps and studied the front yard. The house and yard appeared to have been carved out of a wheat field. And the cultivated ground was stingy, begrudging the land something as nonproductive as grass. The wheat came right up to the edge of the lawn. The heads of grain were virtually motionless in the still evening air. Off to the side of the porch was a large cottonwood, which in the afternoons shaded the entire porch from the western sun.

Claudia came out on the porch and saw Joshua contemplating the tree. "That cottonwood is thirty-nine years old," she said. "Pop Bishop planted it the day Tom was born. He called it Tom's tree." She handed Joshua a tall glass. "I'll be down in a little while and we'll eat."

Joshua took the glass, wet with condensation, and sipped it. He was expecting something alcoholic. It was lemonade. He stared at the lemon rinds immersed in the icy drink.

Claudia returned a half hour later. She had a fresh-scrubbed look and wore no makeup except for lipstick, a little eye shadow, and mascara. Her nose was peeling slightly from sunburn. Her Levi's and sneakers had been replaced by Gloria Vanderbilt's and heels. She wore a silk wrap blouse, open at the throat. "Ready for supper?" Claudia really smiled for the first time, exposing even white teeth.

The meal was served on china. Tossed salad, pot roast, home-baked bread, garden peas, iced tea, and molasses cookies for dessert. Joshua helped with the dishes. Afterwards, they went out on the darkened porch and sat on the swing. Light from the living room cast patterned rectangles of yellow on the boards of the porch as it filtered through the screen door and front window. June bugs flung themselves at the screens with a mindless, instinctive determination to reach the light. Sometimes they fell to the porch, landing on their backs, and buzzed incessantly as they flailed away with their stubby wings in attempts to right themselves. The porch swing creaked on its chains. The delicate scent from the roses touched the night air. It was altogether peaceful. The conversation died as polite trivialities became exhausted. Finally Claudia said tentatively, "Tell me a little about Tom, Josh."

"Where do you want me to start?"

"I don't know. Something safe. Tell me how you met him."

Joshua tilted his head back and studied the enameled rafters of the roof over the porch. "Well," he reflected, "I'd been in Nam about three months. I was the exec on an A-Team at a camp called Peng Lem up along the Laotian border. Word came down from SFOB that they wanted volunteers for an A-Team for a special combat assignment. Volunteers were to forward copies of their 201 file to a Captain Tom Bishop at the SFOB at Nha Trang. So I did."

"What happened?"

"Tom reviewed the 201's of the volunteers and wanted to talk to me and a couple of other guys before he made the selection for exec. A chopper picked me up and took me to Nha Trang. We met, visited, went out and had a drink that night. We just hit it off from the start. I went back to camp and he interviewed the other two guys, then sent me a TWX telling me I had the job. They replaced me with some fresh meat from Bragg and I went to work with Tom."

"What was Tom like? There, I mean."

Joshua kicked the porch swing into gentle motion. "Tom was a good officer. He knew what he was doing. Before we got the Nungs, he commanded an A-Team that acted as advisers to an ARVN Ranger battalion. Tom said it was a lousy job. All you could do was advise and the Rangers did what they damn well pleased. Tom was aggressive. He wanted to win the war. If not for the good of it, then just for the hell of it."

"That's a Tom I knew."

"So SFOB decided to recruit two companies of Nung mercenaries. The Nungs were ethnic Chinese who lived in South Vietnam. They gave us an independent strike force. Before that, when a camp got in trouble or we needed additional combat troops, we had to rely on the ARVN. If they thought the operation was a bad idea or looked too risky, or they felt it was the wrong phase of the moon, or whatever else, they wouldn't do it. We had no fallback position. It was their war. When SFOB recruited the Nungs, they assigned a special A-Team to command them. That was Tom's team. Detachment A-219. We were used on search-and-destroy missions, special assaults, to reinforce other camps, recon, things like that."

"Tom wrote about what he was doing some," Claudia said, "but not a lot." She paused. "I did know he was high on the team."

Joshua half turned toward Claudia. "Oh, Claudia," he said, "we were good." He held up a hand defensively. "I know. Every A-Team commander in Nam probably thought he had the best. But damn, we were *good.*"

Claudia smiled. "That's the first time you've said anything with enthusiasm since I met you yesterday."

"A-two-one-niner was probably the last thing I had any enthusiasm for," Joshua admitted. "Of the ten enlisted men, six of them were Regular Army. They had about seventy years of service among them, most of it with Special Forces. The Nungs were professionals. Very tough. Half of them had fought with the French at Dien Bien Phu." Joshua shook his head in wonder. "It took some doing," he said softly. "We bailed out Plei Djereng from a major Victor Charlie assault. We cleared a tunnel complex near Duc Co. We raided a POW camp in Laos and rescued three Americans. We ambushed an NVA unit in the Ia Drang Valley and whipped their ass." Joshua grinned. "We beat the shit out of some ARVN Rangers in Pleiku."

"Tom never wrote about any of that," Claudia said. "He wrote news and personal items and funny stories. He wrote explicit erotic letters that I had to burn so they wouldn't ever fall into anyone's hands." She paused a moment, reflecting. "Because of our differences, I think Tom sort of closed the war off when he wrote to protect me. Or to spare my feelings, maybe."

"Well, most of what we were doing was classified," Joshua said, trying to gloss it over. "We were supposed to act like we'd never heard of Laos, let alone stage a raid there."

"Well, Tom shared your enthusiasm for the team," Claudia said. "That much was clear from his letters."

"Did he ever send you one of his business cards?" Joshua asked.

"No. What business card?"

Joshua withdrew his billfold and handed her one of Bishop's cards. Claudia turned the card to the light coming through the screen. " 'Have Nungs Will Travel,' " she read aloud. " 'Wire Captain Tom Bishop.' " Her voice caught. " 'Detachment A-219. Fifth Special Forces Group.' " She knew instinctively where it belonged. Todd's room. "Could I have it?" she asked.

"Sure." Joshua was about to say he had more, then thought better of it.

Suddenly Claudia realized she was much more vulnerable than she wanted to be. "Maybe you'd better go now, Josh."

Joshua looked at his watch. "Yes," he said, "I didn't realize it was so late."

"Perhaps you could come again tomorrow."

"I'd like that. What time?"

"Come after lunch. I'll show you the farm."

"Don't you have to work?"

"There's not too much doing right now till the harvest starts. Besides, I have a couple of hands who take care of the chores."

"Can I take you to dinner tomorrow night?"

"Maybe," Claudia hedged. "There are only two restaurants in town."

"Where do you go for a big night out?"

"Wichita, but that's a three-hour drive."

"Where do you go for a little night out?"

"Jackfork, Oklahoma. That's an hour away. We'll decide tomorrow." Claudia pushed out of the swing and made her way across the porch. When she reached the steps, she gripped a short metal flagpole affixed at an angle to the corner post and swung to the ground.

Joshua took in the flagpole, complete with an ornamental eagle mounted on the tip. "Do you fly the flag much?" he asked dryly.

"Not now, but Pop Bishop flew it every holiday without fail." Claudia turned back. "Do you disapprove?"

Joshua shrugged. "I don't fly the flag."

Claudia led the way around the side of the house. They walked in silence through the warm evening air, feet whispering in the Bermuda grass. Joshua opened the door to the Toyota, got in, and inclined his head toward the open window. "Thanks for having me out. I enjoyed it." He started the Land Cruiser. "And thanks for talking to me. I think it's going to be okay."

Claudia stepped back. "We'll see," she said, as she brushed her hair away from the side of her face in the self-conscious gesture that now seemed quite familiar to Joshua. "If it doesn't feel right, I'll stop."

Joshua put the Toyota in gear and pulled away. As he turned onto the section line road, a sense of dread and misgiving swept over him. I've pressured her into talking to me, he thought grimly. Now will I be able to go through with it?

CHAPTER SIX

Joshua pulled up the dirt drive to the Bishop farm just after noon. The sun glared down out of a cloudless sky, pushing the temperature over a hundred degrees. The wind blew dry and hot from the southwest. Explosive gusts set the cottonwoods surrounding the farmhouse to shuddering, leaves whipped to a rustling frenzy.

Claudia held open the side screen door and called out to him to come in. The big, high-ceilinged kitchen, shaded from direct sun by surrounding trees, seemed cool by comparison with the outdoors. "I'm almost ready," she said. Claudia crossed the linoleum floor to the refrigerator, removed a thermos, and placed it in a wicker picnic basket on the kitchen counter. "You can take me out to eat some other time," she said. "Let's just relax today." She picked up the picnic basket and led the way out the door. As she crossed the yard to the shed, she spoke over her shoulder. "You get the grand tour today." She placed the picnic basket under the seat of the Case tractor and climbed aboard. Claudia turned the key in the ignition, and the engine coughed to life. "Climb on," she said.

Joshua pulled himself onto the tractor and leaned against the molded fender that covered the huge, cleated wheels. Claudia backed the tractor out of the shed. Joshua spread his feet to brace himself, and hung on to the open rim of the fender. Claudia revved the engine and circled around the shed. She maneuvered past a single gasoline pump and picked up a rutted track that ran down between two wheat fields. "We have four sections," she explained as they jounced slowly along, talking above the grinding engine. "Two are irrigated, and two are dryland."

"Why the difference?"

"Expense. Tom's folks were dryland farmers. Six years ago I decided to irrigate one section. Then three years ago I did another section. There's no doubt production is higher on the irrigated land, but the wells and the irrigation equipment cost a fortune." She swung a hand in an arc taking in the fields on either side of the track. "This is all dry land." Claudia stopped the tractor and meshed the gears into neutral. She hopped down and went over to the wheat, broke off a couple of stalks and stripped the grain from the heads. She climbed back onto the tractor and sifted the grain from her hand into Joshua's. "Hang on to it," she said. "I'll show you in a little while." The tractor lurched on down the track between the two fields. In another ten minutes they came to a cross track and Claudia turned off to the right. She stopped and killed the engine.

"Come on." Claudia jumped down and waded into the next wheat field. The wheat stretched away in a curving arc, the corners of the field not cultivated. "This is irrigated land," she said. "The irrigation equipment pivots from wells in the center of the fields and makes a huge circle. You lose the corners, but the increased bushels per acre more than make up for the loss." She stripped a couple of heads of grain and sifted the wheat into Joshua's other hand for comparison. He rolled the grain in his hands. The grain from the irrigated land was larger, more plump, firmer. Claudia scooped some of the grain from Joshua's hand, popped it into her mouth, and began to chew. "Go on," she said, mumbling, "try it."

Joshua put the grain in his mouth and chewed. It turned into a congealed wad with gumlike consistency that was sweet and moist and fragrant.

Claudia put a hand up to shield her eyes from the sun and studied Joshua's face. "Beats spearmint," she said.

Joshua looked at Claudia. Hazel eyes clear. Hair blowing. Freckles darkened by summer sun on her peeling nose. Somehow she seemed different today. She was obviously delighted with the day and the outing. Relished showing him the farm. Joshua nodded. The grain was good.

Claudia motioned for Joshua to follow and plunged deeper into the wheat field. Joshua turned slowly on his heel, making a full 360-degree circle. The wheat fields stretched from horizon to horizon. An endless vista of golden grain.

He hurried to catch up with Claudia. She had reached the irrigation equipment. The center-pivot system with its wheels and pipes and struts and sprinklers extended across the field like a giant Tinkertoy. "Why isn't it on?" Joshua asked.

"It's time for harvest. The wheat has to be dry. We pray for rain the rest of the year, but not now. The custom cutters will be here in two days."

"They show up"—Joshua snapped his fingers—"just like that."

Claudia smiled. "I have a contract. I've used the same man for ten years. Jake Vanlandingham from Seminole, Texas. He brings his crew, combines, and trucks, and comes through on the way north." She returned to the tractor and they rode on down the track to the next field and stopped behind a pickup. Two men were at work in the field. One of them waved and started for the tractor.

"That's Jess Walters," Claudia said. "He works for me full-time. The other man works during high season. They're doing some maintenance on the irrigation equipment." She climbed off the tractor and walked to meet her farmhand. Joshua followed, wending his way through the stalks of wheat, feeling the sun and the sweat and the dry, hot wind.

In his mid-fifties, Jess Walters was of medium build and a little stoop-shouldered. Despite a straw hat his face was sunburned. He wore coveralls and a work shirt. "Afternoon, Claudia." Walters' voice was soft, his manner warm.

"Hi, Jess." Claudia introduced Joshua, and Joshua shook the rough, callused hand. "Vanlandingham called me this morning, Jess," Claudia said. "He expects to be here, ready to cut, on Wednesday."

"That's about when we thought," Walters replied.

"He thought he might be here tomorrow, but they had a breakdown on a combine and lost a day."

"Doesn't make any difference, I guess."

"Well, it might," Claudia said. "The long-range weather report says there could be rain by the end of the week." The wind whipped her hair around her face. She swept it back with both hands, took an elastic tie from her jeans, and fixed it in a ponytail. "He's got a crew of twenty this year. They'll stay in town or in campers at the RV park."

Walters removed his straw hat and patted his bald scalp with a handkerchief. "Do you want Clara to fix the noon meals again this year?"

"If she'll do it."

"She likes to. I'll ask her when I go home tonight."

"Todd will be back from Kansas City on Wednesday evening, so he'll miss the first day. I'd like for him to drive a truck this year."

"All right." Walters settled the straw hat on his head.

Claudia glanced around the field. "How's the irrigation equipment?"

"Have to replace a couple of sprinkler heads."

Claudia nodded. "Anything else today?"

"I don't think so."

"Okay. Josh and I are just going to look around this afternoon. I'll be at the house this evening if you need me."

Joshua and Walters shook hands again, and he and Claudia headed back to the tractor. "Jess is a dear," she said. "He managed the farm implement dealership in Plains. After Tom's folks died and I took over the farm, I persuaded him to come to work for me." She shook her head. "I couldn't have made it without him. He taught me how to farm." Joshua nodded his agreement and Claudia went on. "He lives in town with his wife. Their kids are grown and moved away." They climbed up on the tractor and Claudia turned the engine over. "If Todd doesn't want to farm the place," she said, "I suppose I might sell it to Jess. I don't know though." Her voice was wistful. "This place has been farmed by Bishops since it was homesteaded by Todd's great-great-grandfather." They drove along the track between the wheat fields until they came to a barbed wire fence. "This is our property line," Claudia explained.

On the other side of the fence was another wheat field. "How large did you say your farm was?" Joshua asked.

Claudia turned to the left and started down a rutted track beside the barbed wire fence. "Almost four sections."

"A section is one square mile?"

Claudia nodded. "Six hundred and forty acres."

Joshua pondered that a moment. "Is this a big farm?"

"Bigger than average." Claudia pointed a finger across the fence. "Bob Johnson farms ten sections. But four of those are leased from an absentee landlord."

Joshua nodded.

"Want to know who?"

"Who what?"

"Who the absentee landlord is."

"Sure."

"Saudi Arabia. They own quite a bit of land out here."

Somehow it troubled Joshua that Saudi Arabia owned a chunk of Middle America.

The track stopped at a fence that paralleled a dirt road. Claudia idled the tractor and pointed at a portion of the fence. "Would you open the gate?"

Joshua jumped down and went over to the fence. The gate consisted of the three strands of barbed wire that was the fence, except the last fence post wasn't embedded in the ground. It hung suspended from an adjacent post by a loop of barbed wire. Joshua put some pressure on the suspended post to stretch the fencing, took advantage of the slack, and lifted the barbed wire loop off the top of the post. He dropped the fence to the ground and Claudia drove over it and pulled up on the road. Joshua refastened the fence gate and climbed back up on the tractor.

"How'd I do?"

"You're hired." Claudia smiled. She pointed to the wheat fields on either side of the road. "These are our other two sections." A wheat truck rumbled toward them. They squinted against the dust, held their breath, and waited till the wind whipped it away from them. They reached the end of the cultivated land on their left, and the wheat gave way to pasture. Claudia turned across the bar ditch and Joshua jumped down and unfastened another gate. She pointed toward the corner of the pasture where they were headed. "That is Todd and Jess's hobby."

Joshua followed her pointing finger. In a corner of the pasture by a clump of trees was a cluster of metal tanks and silos and about a dozen head of cattle. The Case tractor jounced toward them, rolling over foot-tall prairie grass that was brown and dry. Claudia skirted a draw and pulled up and stopped in front of the small herd. She killed the engine and leaned both elbows on the wheel.

"Todd and Jess want to build a prize herd of polled Herefords. That bull"—Claudia pointed toward a massive red animal—"cost twenty-five thousand dollars. We got four calves this spring."

Joshua observed the calves, skinny creatures on spindly legs, moving among the cows, nuzzling at udders.

Claudia climbed down from the tractor. "Want a drink?" She led him to the windmill. The fan spun in the wind, clattering with functional efficiency, its galvanized blades a blur. A one-inch pipe ran from the pump housing to a metal stock tank a few feet away, filled to overflowing with water. Claudia stepped onto the wooden flooring at the base of the scaffolding, took a tin cup from a wire hook, and turned a spigot on the pump housing. Water gushed from the spigot. She rinsed the cup and dashed the water downwind, then filled it and handed it to Joshua. He drank in long, thirst-quenching drafts. The water was cool and sweet.

Joshua handed the cup to Claudia. "Hit me again." She refilled the cup and Joshua drained it. He wiped his lips with the back of his hand and gave it back. Claudia filled it and drank greedily, tilting her head back. Joshua observed her neck where it curved gracefully into the folds of her blouse. The wind molded the blouse against her breasts, outlining the full globes. Claudia lowered the cup and shook out the last few drops. She turned to Joshua, caught his stare. There was a brief moment of silence as their eyes met.

Claudia hung the cup back on the wire hook. "I love this old windmill," she said. "It's been here for sixty years. Jess wanted to replace it with an electric pump, but I said 'nothing doing.' He gets the cows, I get the windmill."

Claudia moved away. A cow came up and nudged her. She scratched it on the bristly white hair of its square face. "The big, dumb things are more like pets." She shoved the cow aside and made her way along a wooden trough to a series of silos, metal tanks, gauges, and connecting hoses. She reached a hand in the trough and picked up some feed, letting it sift through her fingers. "I think we ought to be wheat farmers, not gentlemen ranchers. But Todd and Jess like it. Todd's had Big Ben there"—she nodded toward the huge bull—"at the Kansas City Royal and the Fort Worth Stock Show. He's won a few ribbons."

Claudia returned to the tractor, glancing at her watch. "Almost four. How about the picnic?"

"Fine."

She pulled the wicker basket from under the tractor seat and handed it to Joshua. "Come on."

"Where to?"

"The best part of the farm." Claudia led him toward the fence at the back of the pasture. They sprung the two top strands of barbed wire apart for each other and carefully snaked through to the other side. He followed her along a worn path that led through prairie grass and sage till they came to a barren, windswept rise. They climbed it, sweating in the heat. When they reached the top they stood on a bluff. Claudia rested her hands on her hips and nodded below her. "There it is," she said.

A muddy brown ribbon of water curved around in a great arc beneath the bluff and stretched away into the wheat fields to the southwest. The current moved sluggishly between two wide, sandy banks. Here and there the sunlight reflected off a ripple. Off to the right were some hard sandstone flats eroded smooth by perennial spring floods. Large trees, cottonwoods and elms mostly, lined the banks. Tamaracks and berry bushes flourished. The sight held Joshua suspended a moment.

Claudia watched Joshua's reaction. "It does that to me every time I come up here," she said. "I think it's the surprise. There are a lot more impressive rivers than the Cimarron, but it cuts right through this big dry prairie like a miracle. A cool, wet green miracle." She started down the bluff, working her way over the rocks and ledges with Joshua following.

"Do you own this part of the river?" Joshua asked.

"Nobody owns the Cimarron. A century ago people thought they did. There were some bloody range wars here then. Access to the river meant life or death for both cattleman and farmer."

They scrambled the rest of the way down the bluff in silence until they reached the sandy banks. Claudia picked her way along, skirting bushes, downed cottonwoods turned to gray driftwood, and here and there the tangled brush and debris of flood tide. She stopped at a soft, sandy flat a few yards from the river's edge. It was surrounded by tamarack that blocked the wind, and shaded by overarching cottonwoods. She removed a blanket from the picnic basket and Joshua helped her spread it on the ground. He sprawled across it and gazed up through the canopy of cottonwood leaves.

A few cottonwood pods had burst and wisps of cotton floated on the breeze. The glare of the sun was diffused to a golden flush by the green leaves. Claudia sat on the blanket and folded her legs under her.

They were silent a while, resting lazily in the heat and absorbing the sensual experience of river, earth, and sky. Finally Joshua rolled up on his side, cocked an elbow, and placed his head in his hand. "Do you feel okay about our conversation last night?" he asked.

Claudia didn't reply for a moment. "I think so." She hesitated. "You remember saying that if I couldn't talk about something that happened twelve years ago, something was wrong?"

"Yes."

"Well, I thought about that last night. That's right, of course, and I tried to figure out what was wrong."

"Did you succeed?"

Claudia waggled her hand in equivocation. "Some of it's simple, and some of it's complex."

"Do you want to start with the simple part?"

"For one thing, I don't want to dredge up events that were a heartache." Joshua nodded as Claudia went on. "But I think it's more than sadness. I feel guilty. Tom and I never resolved our differences about the war. It was a bitterness between us. Then he was killed, and we never had a chance to understand or heal."

Claudia leaned toward Joshua earnestly. "And this is where it gets complex. I knew in my heart it was not basically a philosophical difference about the morality of it all. There was that, too, but I believe the deeper issue for me was rejection. I felt that Tom rejected me and our life together just for his goddamn macho adventuring!" Claudia realized her voice had become strident and paused, embarrassed; after a moment she continued with quiet intensity. "And I'm angry. I'm angry at Tom." Claudia doubled her fist and shook it in exasperation. "We had it so good, and he threw it all away."

Joshua sat up and locked his arms around his knees. He watched Claudia sympathetically as she struggled to recover her equanimity.

Claudia took a deep breath and forged ahead. "But that's not all.

Last night I realized that I had simply papered over everything where Tom and I were concerned. That part of my life is unfinished." She paused. "There was no conclusion to my life with Tom. It ended without an ending. Now you come back and want to resurrect the dead. Maybe I'll let you." Claudia hesitated. "Maybe." She looked steadily at Joshua. "You were with Tom at the last. You knew him in a way I never knew him, and in a place where I have never been." She smoothed the blanket on the sand in front of her. "Maybe you can help me write the ending to my life with Tom."

There was a long silence. Finally Joshua said softly, "I'm very touched. Truly. If there is some way I can help you, I want to, but I find it ironic. I really came to Plains for you to help me."

"How?"

Joshua felt the flush of adrenaline, but was uncertain if it was anticipation or apprehension. "Vietnam comes back on me."

"What do you mean?"

"There's rarely a day goes by that some sight or smell or sound or incident doesn't trigger flashbacks. Sometimes I'm there. Like it was all real. Sometimes it's just memories. Sometimes there's just a feeling, a dread, that pulls at me. I feel like I'm being sucked under."

Claudia nodded in sympathy and encouragement.

"My life seems hung on the hinge that was Vietnam," Joshua went on. "There's Before Vietnam and After Vietnam. After Vietnam nothing has ever worked."

"In what way?"

Joshua crossed his legs under him. "You said you thought you were angry at Tom. Well, I know I'm angry. I'm angry all the time."

"What at?"

"You name it, I'm angry at it. The country, people, work, play, life."

"At yourself?"

"That, too."

"At me?"

"No," Joshua said quietly, "I'm afraid of you."

"Why?"

"I don't know if you're destruction or deliverance."

Claudia studied Joshua, puzzled, then asked, "Have you ever gotten help?"

"I saw a psychiatrist for a while several years ago."

"Did it help?"

"I wasn't very cooperative. I really didn't want to pick at the scab."

"Then let it heal."

"I've been waiting twelve years."

"Somewhat like me," Claudia said. "Except I haven't been waiting, I've been hiding."

Joshua smiled sardonically. "It is strange," he said. "We may be more alike than I thought. We both have spent twelve years looking at the same event through a telescope, only through opposite ends. For me it is magnified, close up, terrifying, and overwhelming. For you it is distant, remote, untouchable. You remember the first afternoon in the café," Joshua went on, "when I said you were my link with Tom?"

"Yes."

"You weren't too happy about that, but Tom *is* a link between us. I knew that and tried to exploit it. You knew it and recoiled from it." Joshua shook his head. "When I first came to Plains, I thought you would be anxious to see me. You know, to fill you in on some of the details about Tom's life. Nostalgia for the past. Something like that. And I had a lot of reservations about opening myself up to you and trying to sort it all out. But when I arrived, it was clear that you wanted no part of it and I found myself in the peculiar position of having to convince you to talk to me." Joshua paused and looked at Claudia. "Now that you seem to want to, I feel all the old anxieties and reluctance again."

"We're sort of out of sync," Claudia murmured.

"So now *I'm* not sure that talking is such a good idea."

"What's changed?"

"You're a real person now, not some backdrop to bounce my life off of. I may only hurt you and complicate your life."

"I don't think so," Claudia said. "I'm almost beginning to be glad you came." She tilted her head toward the setting sun. "How about supper?"

Claudia opened the picnic basket. There were sandwiches from the previous night's roast. Whole tomatoes, red and plump and vine-ripened. A thermos of iced tea. And molasses cookies. They ate and watched the sun disappear beyond the far bank of the muddy Cimarron. It balanced for a long while on the horizon, then melted like hot wax and dissolved below the plain.

CHAPTER SEVEN

Adozen workmen were busy in the city park. The pace was slow because of the midday heat. But they worked steadily, and progress was made as they prepared the park for the Harvest Street Dance. A large square dance floor was being constructed out of plywood sheeting in front of the band shell. Colored lights were being strung between the antique lampposts skirting the brick walkways. Along one side of the park a crew was putting up a long row of booths. Wire mesh cages were being stacked at the rear of the park near the world's largest hand-dug well. And on the other side of the park a large barbecue pit was taking shape, flanked by rows of tables and folding chairs.

Joshua watched from a secluded park bench. A man moved among the workmen, kidding, giving advice, occasionally lending a hand, and, Joshua decided, politicking a lot. From the interplay Joshua deduced that Big Ed was the mayor of Plains. Big Ed deserved the adjective big. Joshua estimated he was a good six feet tall, and maybe four feet around. His huge girth was circled with blue serge slacks of tentlike proportions, the wide cuffs flapping in the breeze. His white shirt was dark with sweat at the armpits, and his broad pink forehead glistened with oily perspiration. Joshua felt a bead of sweat trickle down the side of his neck, was glad he didn't weigh three hundred pounds, and vowed to keep on jogging. He glanced at his watch. Charlie Wilson was late. He removed a sealed envelope from his shirt pocket, turned it over, and read the address: Mrs. Tom Bishop, Rural Route 2, Plains, Kansas. He had removed it that morning from the metal box in the suitcase under his bed. The envelope was a little dirty, the edges worn, but it had survived the twelve years in his safekeeping quite well.

Joshua saw the Caribou. He nudged Bishop and pointed. "Here it comes."

The cargo plane roared in at low level, flaps down. The North Vietnamese gunners on the ridges opened up. Streams of blue-green tracers flicked out of the jungle and wove a tapestry of steel around the lumbering aircraft. The pilot was in the glide pattern for the drop, so he took the Caribou straight through the hail of bullets. When the aircraft was over the compound the supplies came tumbling out the ramp. Huge multicolored cargo chutes barely had time to deploy before the wooden pallets crashed to the ground.

"I'll check on the munitions," Bishop said. "You look for the replacement barrels for the fifties."

Bishop scrambled out of the trench and headed for the red cargo chutes. Joshua scurried toward the yellow. Thirty minutes later Bishop found Joshua in the corner bunker on the east wall, replacing the burned-out barrel on a .50-caliber machine gun.

"Mail call," Bishop sang out. He handed Joshua a letter and kept one for himself.

"Where'd you get that?"

"A good mail clerk will scrounge mail," Bishop cracked. He sat down in the bunker beside Joshua, and eased back against a sandbag. "SFOB stuck our mail in with the M-79 rounds," he explained. Bishop pulled a razor-sharp knife from a scabbard taped to his boot, and slit the end of the envelope. He turned it up and tapped it against the palm of his hand, coaxing the letter out. He unfolded the single page and a snapshot dropped to the floor of the bunker. He reached between his knees and retrieved it, holding it up and blowing the fine red dust from the surface. Bishop studied the snapshot a moment and then handed it to Joshua. "Would you look at that little piss ant," Bishop said, a note of quiet pride resonating in his voice.

Joshua took the snapshot. A woman holding a little boy stood in the side yard of a white frame house. Her hair was blowing in the wind and she had reached up a hand to pluck some strands from her face. The boy was solemn. There was a lot of Tom Bishop in the set of his jaw. "Good-looking kid," Joshua said.

"Yeah. And his mom ain't bad either." Bishop unfolded the letter and settled back to read.

Joshua opened his letter. It was from his wife. He read it rapidly, eyes scanning for information. Then he read it more slowly a second time, filling in the details. He perused it a third time, savoring the intimacy of a touch from home, the warmth of words written in love. At that moment he realized how desperately he wanted to survive. He was overwhelmed with a profound sense of regret that life might very well be over. Life, after all, was all he had. It was the only reality in an eternity of nothingness. There did not seem to be a thing or a cause or a person worth dying for. Well, he thought, there will be no miracles for this Joshua. No walls will tumble down. The sun will not stand still. I will lead no one into the promised land. There is no promised land. There is only now.

Bishop stirred, interrupting Joshua's thoughts. He replaced the letter and snapshot in the envelope and tucked it away in the breast pocket of his tiger suit. "You know, Josh," he said quietly, "I think I'll go write Claudia."

"Last will and testament?"

"I'll be in the teamhouse."

Joshua replaced the envelope in his shirt pocket as he saw Charlie Wilson making his way along the brick walkway, carrying a paper sack. His clerical collar was wilted in the heat and the damp edges pressed into the flesh of his pudgy neck. He stopped to pass a few words with Big Ed and some of the workmen, laughed easily, then sauntered on down to join Joshua on the park bench. He pulled a six-pack of Miller Lite out of the paper sack and set it on the park bench between them.

"Here's my contribution to lunch." Wilson popped the tabs on two cans.

Joshua picked up a carry-out lunch box from beside him on the park bench, and opened it. He passed Wilson a napkin-wrapped cheeseburger and took the other one for himself. He placed the box between them so they could both reach the fries.

Wilson took a big bite of the burger and talked as he chewed.

"Sorry I'm late. I had to go see one of my parishioners. Mildred Glaab." He shook his head. "Poor Mildred."

Joshua removed the cheeseburger patty from the bun. He picked up some extra napkins and pressed them against the patty and the bun, absorbing the excess grease. Satisfied, he rebuilt the cheeseburger and began to eat.

"Mildred is eighty-three," Wilson went on. "She was happily married for sixty-two years, then her husband died about eight years ago. Mildred is healthy as a horse but has gotten more senile the past few years. For about the past two years she has gotten up every morning thinking that her husband just died the night before, and that she has to make the arrangements for the funeral. Can you imagine that? Every day for two years she relives the worst day of her life." Wilson tilted the Miller and drained a quarter of the can. "Her neighbors kind of help her through the days, but occasionally she gets too distraught and they call me to come comfort her."

Joshua shook his head. Part disbelief, part wonder. "Every day she relives the worst day of her life," he mused. "The shrink I saw had a word for it."

"What's that?"

"Delayed stress syndrome."

"What's that mean?"

"Lots of things, I guess. For me it means flashbacks, nightmares, rages, anxiety, melancholy. The shrink said it was the lingering, incapacitating effects of overwhelming stress."

"Religion has a word for it, too. Guilt."

"We're great at naming things," Joshua stuffed the last bite of cheeseburger in his mouth. "Rumplestiltskin," he mumbled. "Name the myth and it becomes impotent." He washed down the cheeseburger with the last of his Miller. "What do you do for Mildred Glaab, Charlie?"

"Well, I said the mass for Emery at his funeral, so usually I do part of the mass. I sit her down and say, 'This is how it was, Mildred. You were there.' And I repeat the mass. It usually gets through to her and she settles down for a while."

"Reality therapy."

Wilson popped the tab on another Miller. "What would you do?"

Joshua helped himself to the fries and thought a moment. "She does that every day? Gets up to make the 'arrangements.' "

"Yep."

"Hold a pillow over her face. You can live too long."

Wilson looked sideways at Joshua. "Send her on to her reward?"

"There is no heaven, Charlie."

"What about hell?"

Joshua nodded grimly. "Oh, yes, there's a hell." Then he grinned. "For Mildred, a mercy killing. Never solve anything philosophically that you can settle with violence."

Wilson studied Joshua's face a moment. In the silence the lazy drone of locusts swelled to an almost palpable hum. "What's the matter with you?"

Joshua looked at Wilson and thought a moment, the old protective reserve closing in. It wasn't a lonely midnight in the sanctuary of St. Mary's of the Plains. It was broad daylight in the city park. He watched Wilson as he took a long, hearty pull on the beer. Rumpled. Sweaty and relaxed. Nonjudgmental, sympathetic, approachable. Maybe, Joshua thought. Just maybe. Why else did I call him to meet me here? Suck it up!

"Several years ago," Joshua said, "a psychiatrist told me I suffered from delayed stress syndrome. Only naming the myth didn't help." He opened another Miller. The carbonation sprayed his hand with a refreshing mist. "Since Vietnam, I've had a lot of trouble. I can't seem to get my life on track. I tried both religion and psychiatry. Useless." He fingered the letter in his shirt pocket. Looked again at Wilson. "I carry my delayed stress syndrome around with me in a metal box. Here's part of it." He removed the letter from his shirt pocket and handed it to the priest.

Wilson read the address on the envelope, puzzled. "What is it?"

Joshua studied Bishop's face. His features were already congealed into a waxen death mask. A fly settled onto an open, sightless eye and crawled indifferently across it. Joshua brushed it away. He leaned over Bishop and broke the chain on his dog tags. They were taped together with army-green tape. He peeled away the tape, stuffed the dog tags in Bishop's mouth, and placed the tape over his lips. Then he went through Bishop's pockets. In his breast pocket he found the opened letter from Claudia. With it was a

second, sealed envelope addressed to her. There were also two
dozen of Bishop's business cards. Joshua pocketed the two letters
and the cards. The rest of the personal effects were inconsequential.
He laid them aside.

Joshua glanced up at Finelli and Porter as he unfolded the body
bag. He unzipped it and stretched it out beside Bishop. While he
held the heavy vinyl bag open, Finelli and Porter manhandled
Bishop's big frame into it. Joshua zippered the bag, pausing momentarily before he closed it over Bishop's face. "Let's put him in
the command bunker," Joshua said.

They grabbed the body bag by its handles, slung it up between
them, and wrestled its awkward dead weight along the trench.
Suddenly, out of Joshua's past, a past he felt alienated from, a past
of seminars and discussion groups and essays, a past composed of
the seemingly useless trivia of comparative literature, came the
lines of A. E. Housman's poem "To an Athlete Dying Young." They
snapped into his mind with stunning force.

> Today, the road all runners come,
> Shoulder high we bring you home,
> And set you at your threshold down,
> Townsman of a stiller town . . .
> And silence sounds no worse than cheers
> After earth has stopped the ears.

Joshua and Finelli and Porter gently lowered the body bag to the
red clay dust on the floor of the bunker.

"After Tom was killed," Joshua said, "I found the letter on him. I
never mailed it."

"Why not?"

Joshua pursed his lips in a gesture of uncertainty and equivocation. "It seemed wrong, somehow, to send her a letter from a dead
man."

"Why did you keep it all these years?"

Joshua ignored the question. "I'm thinking of giving it to
Claudia."

Wilson said nothing, but balanced his two empty Miller cans

neatly on top of each other on the edge of the park bench. He opened the third can and sipped it.

"Claudia thinks she wants to know about Tom now," Joshua said. "About his life there. What he was like. What happened. She says she wants to write the ending to the story and close it out."

"Can you help her do that?"

"I don't know. If I could close Nam out, I'd do it for me."

"Is that why you're in Plains?"

Joshua was silent a long moment. "Yes," he said. "Yes, that's why." He shook his head. "But I'm really afraid, Charlie."

"That's understandable."

"Before I came I was just afraid for me. Now I'm afraid for her, too."

"Perhaps with Claudia you can do more than name the myth. Maybe you can demythologize it."

Joshua smiled. "Charlie, myths are powerful magic. There may be no way to break their spell."

Wilson raised his hand to Joshua and made the sign of the cross. *"Experimento enim scitur multa per daemones fieri,"* he intoned.

"What the hell's that?" Joshua asked.

Wilson grinned. "Just some old Latin magic." Then he poured the last of his Miller on his fingertips and sprinkled the beer on Joshua's forehead.

"Charlie, you pious fraud," Joshua said. They both laughed. "Come on," Joshua badgered, "tell me what it means."

"Roughly translated, it means that our darkest and most inexplicable experiences teach us that a great deal is done by demons."

Joshua pondered the priest's comments. He knew nothing of demons. But he was well acquainted with the night terrors and the cold sweats and the flashbacks and the shakes that had invaded his life since Vietnam. And he didn't know if Charlie Wilson was serious about demons. The priest held his faith with a light hand, responding openly to life with a kind of Christian nonchalance. What appeared to be complacency was the deepest sort of commitment. He looked back at Wilson. "Do you have any magic for my demons?" he asked.

Wilson laughed. "Hell, Josh, you don't want magic for your demons. You want a confrontation. Freedom! That's why you're in Plains." The priest turned the sealed envelope in his hands, then held it up to the sun and squinted at it. "What's in the letter, Josh?"

"I haven't the faintest notion. It was written the afternoon before Tom was killed. At a time when we all thought we wouldn't
live through the night."

Wilson handed the envelope back to Joshua. "Give it to Claudia.
It's a start."

"Start to what?"

"A confrontation with the demons."

Joshua stood up. "You may be right. Thanks, Charlie." He turned
and walked toward Main Street.

Joshua drove up the drive to the Bishop farm after dark. He had
talked to Claudia after his visit with Wilson. The conversation had
been brief. She had work to do. Jake Vanlandingham's custom cutting crew was arriving that afternoon. He declined an invitation to
supper and arranged to come later. The farmyard was lit by a bulb
over the door to the shed, and one on a pole near the drive at the
front of the house. But the farmhouse was dark except for a light in
the dining room. The effect was strangely muted. It deepened
Joshua's somber mood. He parked and went to the front door. He
could see Claudia through the screen. She sat in a circle of light at
the oak table in the dining room. Granny glasses perched on her nose,
she was hunched over a ledger, making entries. Joshua knocked
on the screen door. It rattled against the frame in the still night.

Claudia finished her entry, then removed her glasses and left
them on the open ledger. She walked across the darkened living
room, her figure backlighted through the French doors. She
moved with a fluid grace. In the measured lilt of her hips there was
functional purpose, not provocation. But Joshua felt the stirrings of
desire. He recognized the curious juxtaposition of emotions from
past experience. It was not just Claudia. For him, fear and eroticism were conjoined emotions.

Claudia opened the screen. "Hello, Josh." Her voice was warm
with welcome.

Joshua stepped into the living room. He felt like before a jump.
Not afraid, but careful, tightly controlled. No mistakes.

Claudia cast a thoughtful, appraising eye on Joshua, then turned and went to the dining room. "Bookkeeping tonight," she said, indicating the ledger. "I'm trying to get everything current before we start cutting."

Joshua followed her into the room. "Will they start tomorrow?"

Claudia nodded. "As early as possible. How about a drink?" she asked.

"Fine."

She went to the kitchen. Joshua lounged against the door and watched her by the light from the refrigerator as she poured two glasses of white wine from a carafe. They returned to the darkened living room, illuminated only by spillover from the dining room. Joshua took the easy chair. Claudia faced him in the rocker.

Joshua looked around the room where they had met for supper just two days ago. "Seems like old times," he said.

"To old times." Claudia inclined her glass toward him and drank.

Joshua lifted his glass in return. He sipped the wine and studied Claudia. Was there an easy way? Probably not. He chose his words carefully. "I have something for you from Tom."

Claudia's wineglass stopped midway to her lips. "What?" Her voice seemed to come from far away.

"A letter."

Claudia lowered the glass to her lap and clutched it with both hands. "What do you mean, a letter from Tom?"

Joshua removed the envelope from his shirt pocket. "It's Tom's last letter. He wrote it the afternoon before he was killed. I went through his things." He left the sentence hanging.

Claudia's features were frozen, white, stretched taut like flesh over ice. "You've had it all these years?"

"Yes."

"My God, Josh." Claudia put her hand to her throat. "Why?"

"Just because."

"Not good enough." Her voice rose in a pinched cry. "You ghoulish bastard! Ghosts! Relics from the dead!"

Joshua felt his gut constrict. He silently cursed himself for being a fool. It wasn't going to work. Another miscalculation in his life. "You said you wanted to finish out your life with Tom." His voice was part challenge, part despair. "To finalize the past and put it to rest."

"Not this way. Oh, Josh, why didn't you either send it back then or get rid of it?"

"Damn you, Claudia. I'm trying to put the past to rest, too."

Claudia's voice was a forced whisper. "I don't want it, Josh." She shook her head. "I can't. Not now."

Joshua waited, feeling the anger. At himself. At Claudia. Then it diffused into the old vague unfocused resentment. Nothing works. His trip to Plains, Kansas, was at its end. He replaced the letter in his pocket and wearily pushed himself up out of the chair. He took his wineglass to the kitchen and set it on the countertop by the sink. As he passed through the living room on his way out, he stopped momentarily behind Claudia's rocker, laid a tentative, apologetic hand on her shoulder, then left. He was halfway across the front yard when he heard Claudia's cry from the living room.

"Josh!"

He turned back and saw her dim silhouette at the screen.

"Give it to me." Claudia pushed open the screen door and held out a hand. There was a brittle note in her voice.

Joshua made his way back across the lawn, dappled with moonlit shadows by the giant cottonwood. He climbed the steps to the porch as though he were mounting a scaffold, and handed her the letter.

"Wait for me." Claudia retreated from the screen door, turned, and left the room.

Joshua resumed his seat in the easy chair and listened to her climb the stairs to the second story. Her tread was measured and slow, forced, as though each step required an inordinate amount of energy. He sat in the dimly illuminated room, hands folded in his lap. The house became as quiet as death. Even the ever-present June bugs and night locusts were silent, as if they had vanished from the face of the earth. Joshua raised his eyes and found himself staring into the face of Tom Bishop, who gazed down on him from the portrait on the fireplace mantel.

Joshua heard Claudia moving around on the second floor. Steps descending the stairs. She came into the living room, the letter dangling limply from her hand. Face tear-streaked, she paused a moment at the rocker, then dropped the letter in his lap. She went to the screen door, leaned against the jamb, and stared into the night. Joshua picked up the letter and turned it toward the light from the dining room. It was written on the lined paper TWX's were copied on. He squinted at the ragged scrawl.

Dear Claudia,

I received the letter today with the picture of you and Todd. It made me terribly homesick for the both of you, and the old farm. I've got it bad this evening, Claudia. Things I want to say. Things I want to do. I want to walk the section line with you. I want to swim in the Cimarron. I want to lie on the rock ledge above its banks and look up through those cottonwoods at the blue Kansas sky. I want to sit on the porch swing with you and talk half the night away, and tell you things I never had words for before. I want to talk about Todd, and tell you things he ought to know. And then I want to crawl in between some clean, crisp white sheets and hold you and love you and show you, after I've said all I'm able to say, what I still don't have words for.

It's funny, you know. It was so dark on the perimeter last night, I couldn't make out where the concertina wire ended and the jungle began. But I think I could see further than I ever had before. It was like I could see all the way to the end. When you live on the edge of extinction, it erodes the body, but it concentrates the mind. And I know what counts and what doesn't now. And I realize I learned most of it from you. It seems this evening that all the lines of my life intersect, and have always intersected, at you. Remember that. Remember it always. Remember it for me. For both of us. And for Todd.

I know the war came between us in the same way that the distance separates us now. I regret that. It's not who was right and who was wrong. I doubt if there is a right and wrong. I just regret the dissension. It's of no consequence now, of course. The plain fact is, I chose to be here. Perhaps was even driven to be here. Not by any overripe ideological bullshit, there was enough of that on both sides of the war question, but just by who I was. I don't assign a value to that as either weakness or strength. It was simply my nature fitted against the opportunities of life.

Josh asked me, kiddingly, if this letter was going to be my last will and testament. I hope not. But it seems I want to say some-

thing lasting to you. To affirm what we've had, and to say I have
no regrets there. In a strange way, I don't even have any regrets
for being here now. Only the regret that there may be no more.

The Coonskin has virtually destroyed A-219. It's crazy beyond
explaining, so I won't even try. I've lost Laszlo, Colfax, Almendarez, and Wirtz. Tate, Hendersen, and Smallcanyon were killed
when we tried to med-evac them. God, I had a good team. Last
night Josh went into Indian country to try and pick up a downed
Skyraider pilot. It was unbelievable. I'm going to put him in for
the DSC. As though that means a damn. Everyone deserves a
medal. Porter, Smallcanyon, DuBoise. Especially me. Hell, I de-
serve the Congressional Medal of Honor. We're stretched a little
thin right now. But I think we're going to make it. If sheer human
endurance has anything to do with it, we will. And if you haven't
heard from Uncle Sam by the time you get this, then start counting those days and getting ready for those nights, because the
second thing I'm going to do when I get home is put my suitcase
down.

I miss you, Claudia. I love you. I remember our times together.
Especially those last days before I left. They haunt my memory
like a fever dream. The look of you. The smell of you. The taste,
the touch . . . I've got to quit and go jerk off.

Love,

Tom

Joshua lowered the letter to his lap and glanced at Claudia. She
still stood at the screen door with her back to him. He got up and
went to the fireplace mantel, folded the letter and slid it under the
corner of Bishop's picture, then walked over to Claudia and laid a
hand on her shoulder. "Oh, Josh, Josh." She turned and clung to
him, face pressed against his shoulder. Her grip was tight, tinged
with desperation, almost fierce. She shuddered with silent, convulsive sobs. Joshua held her. Gently. Tentative. He reached up with
a hand and stroked her hair. Say something, he thought. Say something comforting and reassuring. Something hopeful. He could
think of nothing. He held her. Felt the supple strength of her body.
Felt the heat and the tears and the sweat on the back of her neck.

Finally Claudia released him and stepped back. Her hand went to her hair and plucked wisps away from the side of her face. "I'm getting you wet," she said. She stripped the tears from her cheeks with her fingers and wiped them on her jeans. She took a deep, tremulous breath; then her eyes filled again and tears spilled across her face. She pressed her fingertips against both temples. "I've got to stop crying," Claudia moaned. She stepped past him and went out on the porch. Joshua followed her. She paused at the steps, arms clutched to her chest. "Let's go for a ride," she said, voice choked with tears. Claudia led him to his Toyota and held out her hands for the keys. "I'm driving."

Claudia turned the Land Cruiser in the drive and drove down to the section line road. She took a right and gunned it, accelerating with the reckless determination of a drag racer. Joshua glanced over at Claudia. Her face was set, both hands gripping the wheel, hair whipped by the wind. He felt like they weren't driving, but fleeing. Telephone poles threw shadows at the vehicle as it sped down the road. Section lines flashed past. Claudia braked hard, careened around a corner, dropped a front wheel off the shoulder of the road, then recovered. Joshua clutched the hand rest, feet braced against the floorboard. Claudia made two more section lines, skidded around another corner, fishtailing wildly, then floored it. The Toyota gathered speed, hurtling down the narrow road between two wheat fields. Telephone poles streaked by in a blur. Fence posts seemed to unravel in their wake.

Joshua looked at Claudia. Her facial expression had not changed since she had turned onto the road in front of the farm. He leaned over toward her, voice raised above the wind noise. "Think we ought to come in for a landing?"

Claudia, eyes fixed unwaveringly on the road, didn't acknowledge his comment.

"Claudia!" Joshua waited for a sign of recognition. *"Claudia!"* The word exploded from his lips with the force of a rifle shot. Abruptly she lifted her foot from the gas pedal and looked at him. He pumped his palm toward her in a braking motion. "How about it?" he sung out. "Could we set her down somewhere along here?"

A glimmer of awareness softened Claudia's features. A sleeper awakened from a dream. She let the car coast, touched the foot feed at a safe speed, and drove back along the checkerboard system of section line roads. They rode in silence until they reached the farmhouse. Claudia turned off the engine. Her hand gripped his momentarily as she handed him the car keys. "Would you stay for a while?" she asked. Her voice was quiet, calm again. Features serene and composed.

"Sure. If you like."

They got out of the Toyota and Claudia took his arm and walked him across the yard. When they mounted the steps to the front porch, she guided him to the porch swing. The chain creaked under their weight. The night moon on the ripened wheat caused the fields to shimmer like cream-colored silk.

"Are you"—Joshua paused, groping for words—"feeling better?"

Claudia took his hand in both of hers. "Yes, I am."

"You scared the shit out of me!"

Claudia laughed quietly, a muted ripple with the timbre of a wind chime. "I'm sorry. I felt like if I stayed here I might cry forever."

Joshua nodded.

"But I wouldn't have killed us."

"You could have fooled me." Joshua set the swing in motion. He felt her soft fingers warm against the back of his hand.

"Tell me about Thang Duc," Claudia said quietly.

Joshua reflected a moment, lips pursed. Where to begin? How to begin? "Thang Duc was an isolated little camp up near the Cambodian and Laotian borders. There was a Special Forces A-Team there, plus about three hundred Montagnard troops. It was on a North Vietnamese infiltration route into the South, and they decided to take it prior to their Tet offensive. SFOB thought it was just a VC probe at first, but it developed into a major attack and the camp was nearly lost the first night. They decided to send us in with the Nungs and ferried us in by helicopter the next morning. What they sat us down in was the middle of a major assault by two regiments of North Vietnamese regulars—maybe five thousand men." Joshua paused a moment. "During the day they shelled us from the ridges around the camp. Mortars, recoilless rifles, 120-millimeter rockets. At night they tried to overrun us. This went on for seven days and nights. We were in trouble right from the start. A relief column of ARVN Rangers was sent out from Pleiku. The

North Vietnamese ambushed them and they never got to us. We just hung on."

"Sheer determination?"

Joshua nodded, thinking of Bishop's words in the letter. "We had no choice. There was no place else to go. We talked about E and E. Escape and evasion. Get into the jungle and wait to be picked up. But we decided against it. The last night, I think that if they had mounted one more determined assault, they would have over-run us. We had taken so many casualties and were so used up, we couldn't have fought off my unarmed grandmother. They just quit before we did."

Joshua looked at Claudia. "When you sit here and talk about it twelve years later, and you know the outcome, there is a certain sense of inevitability about it. You know, I would live, the others would die, Thang Duc would hold. But then"—Joshua shrugged—"we thought we were all dead. We actually did. There seemed no way we could hold the camp."

Claudia gripped Joshua's hand.

"There were twenty-four Americans in Thang Duc," Joshua went on, "counting the original A-Team and us. And there were about four hundred and fifty 'Yards and Nungs. On the morning of the eighth day, when the siege was lifted, there were three Americans alive out of our team. DuBoise, Porter, and me. DuBoise and I were wounded. Everyone else was dead. And of the other team, two survived and both of them were wounded. There were about seventy-five 'Yards and Nungs left. Hung up in the wire around Thang Duc were some six hundred NVA. No way to know how many dead and wounded were carried away." Joshua paused a moment, removed his hand from Claudia's, wiped it down across his mustache, then went on. "On the morning of the eighth day, the First Air Cav set down three companies just outside our wire. God, it was impressive. The all-time for-real-life war movie. Directed by Cecil B. De Mille. Starred John Wayne and Audie Murphy. The cavalry to the rescue." Joshua pressed the thumb and forefinger of his right hand against his eyes. "Where the hell were they three days before? Or even one?"

"What happened?"

"They swept the ridges around the camp. Not a shot was fired. The NVA had melted back into Cambodia. The battle didn't end,"

Joshua said as he passed a hand in front of his face, "it simply disappeared. A shadow war with a shadow army." He allowed the swing to creak to a stop. They sat in the still dark of the night. Lost in their thoughts.

Claudia finally broke the silence. "Tell me about the Skyraider pilot Tom mentioned."

Joshua shifted his weight in the swing. "The third or fourth night, I forget which, we were getting air support from two Navy Skyraiders. One of them got hit and pancaked into the jungle about four hundred meters beyond our wire. His wingman said he saw his strobe, so he was alive. He wanted someone to go out and pick him up. So I tried."

"Why you?"

"Why not me? I felt like we owed them. The night before a couple of Skyraiders, probably not even the same guys, had circled the jungle twenty klicks away, trying to wait until the NVA made their assault so they could give us the most help. Catch them out in the open instead of just bombing the ridges. Anyway, they held off and waited till the attack. Saved our asses. But one of them ran out of fuel on the way home and crashed. Anyway, I went out to get the pilot."

"What happened?"

Joshua shrugged. "The NVA got to him first."

"Did you get the Distinguished Service Cross?"

"Yes. But not for that."

"Why not?"

"Tom didn't live to do the paperwork."

"What did you get it for?"

"For staying alive, Claudia."

"Tom was awarded the DSC, too."

"I know."

"The citation said—"

"He got it for dying."

"But the citation—"

"They make up the citations, Claudia." Joshua waved a hand in dismissal. "Oh, he deserved it. For any number of things. For everything. But I got mine for staying alive. And Tom got his for dying. Laszlo and Smallcanyon and Finelli and the rest only got

Silver Stars. They were enlisted men. When enlisted men stay alive or die, it's not worth as much."

"Joshua, please." There was a note of pleading in Claudia's voice.

"Give a country ten yards of ribbon and they can build an army."

"What's the use of all the bitterness?"

"You're going to hate the ending to this movie, Claudia. When the Cav landed and didn't make any contact, they were airlifted back to Division at An Khe. Then MACV decided that they didn't want Thang Duc. It was of no strategic value. They abandoned the camp and pulled everybody out. They sent the 'Yards who were left to other camps in South Vietnam. The Nungs were paid off and discharged. Both of the A-Teams had been destroyed. The wounded were sent home. The survivors were assigned other duties. It didn't mean a damn."

Claudia didn't say anything. She reached out again and took one of Joshua's hands. Stroked it gently. "How did Tom die?"

Joshua could feel his stomach constrict. A nauseous churning that seemed to flood his system with bile. It set his teeth on edge.

"Josh," Claudia urged quietly, "I want you to tell me how Tom died."

Joshua looked at her. "Are you sure?"

Claudia nodded slowly. "Yes."

Joshua took a deep breath. "The last night everything broke down. All of us—the Americans that were left—were positioned alone at different points on the perimeter to help rally the Nungs and 'Yards. Tom's position got overrun. I tried to get to him to help him, but I was too late." Joshua sat unmoving in the swing. "I was too late." His voice was a barely audible whisper.

Claudia watched Joshua for a few moments. He was only a foot away, but she knew it was a distance she would never cross. It was in the eyes. They seemed to say, "If I show you what I've seen, or tell you what I know, you won't ever stop falling." She squeezed his hand. "Thanks, Josh," she said. "And thanks for bringing the letter. I didn't want it at first. But I'm glad I have it now." She smiled ruefully and shook her head, her voice tinged with regret and wonder and admiration. "Wasn't it like Tom?"

Joshua allowed himself a smile. "A hell of an exit line. An epitaph maybe for the whole war. Not 'Send us more Japs.' Not 'Damn the torpedoes, full speed ahead.' But 'I've got to quit and go jerk off'!"

Late that night Joshua lay awake, sweating and trembling in his bed. "I had the chance to tell her," he groaned through clenched teeth. "Why didn't I? Tomorrow. I'll go out and tell her tomorrow."

CHAPTER EIGHT

The early-morning sunlight cut obliquely across the wheat field. It promised another blistering day. Claudia moved deeper into the field, followed by Jake Vanlandingham. She paused and stripped the grain from several heads of wheat. She sifted the grain in her hands and rolled the kernels between thumb and forefinger, gauging the dew-damp, then moved farther on and repeated the process. After a few moments she turned back and gave some of the grain to Vanlandingham. "I think it's dry enough for us to start," she said.

Jake Vanlandingham, a taciturn man with a long face who looked more like a mortician than a ramrod for a custom cutting crew, rolled the wheat in his hand and nodded in agreement.

Claudia looked across the field toward the house where Vanlandingham's custom cutters were gearing up for the first day's harvest. Combines and wheat trucks were strung out along the drive to the house, and pickups and four-wheelers choked the side yard. Near the kitchen stoop was a turquoise Ford XLT Ranger. She had hoped that Travis Rawlins wouldn't be with Vanlandingham this year, but that was his pickup. Claudia felt a moment of apprehension, then shrugged it off and turned back to the custom cutter. She prodded the ground with the toe of her boot, turning up clods of rich dirt between the furrows. "Let's start in the first dryland section," she said. "We'll work there mornings and then move into the dryland section bordering the river in the afternoons."

Vanlandingham lifted his hat, a black fedora which only added to his funereal appearance, and shaded his eyes as he scanned the broad expanse of wheat. "What about the irrigated sections?" he asked.

"We'll cut them last. We've had the water on within the last week. Let's give the ground a little more time to dry out." Claudia looked at Vanlandingham. "Anything else?" Vanlandingham shook his head. "Well, let's get the men moving," she said.

Claudia led the way back through the waist-high wheat. When she reached the drive she moved easily among the custom cutters. Most of Vanlandingham's crew had worked for him for several seasons, and she knew them personally. They greeted her with high-spirited warmth, like vacationers seeing family. The talk was of the wheat crop (good), the weather (hot), the economy (middlin'), Texas (dry), Oklahoma (wet), the oil boom in the panhandle (petering out), the rodeo circuit (tough), a bar in Chilliocothe (mean), the Dallas Cowboys (plastic), and the Harvest Street Dance (best damn shindig this side of Fort Worth).

There were a few new hands and Claudia stopped to meet them. Then she left Vanlandingham and walked on toward the kitchen stoop. She saw Travis Rawlins close the tailgate on his pickup and move to intercept her. He left three men idling at the rear of his truck. They were new men, and Claudia thought they watched her with more than passing interest. Seeing that she could not avoid Rawlins, Claudia stopped and waited for him to confront her.

Rawlins was big and rawboned. He raised rodeo livestock on a small spread in the mesquite country of West Texas, and made the rodeo circuit in season. During the summer he drove a combine for Jake Vanlandingham. Rawlins swept a sweat-stained Stetson off his head. The skin protected by the Stetson was milk white. Below it his face was the color of a saddle. "Howdy, Claudia." The voice was a flat drawl.

"Hello, Travis."

Rawlins hooked his thumbs in a worn, hand-tooled leather belt and gazed languidly at Claudia. "How's the Widow Bishop?"

"Don't start, Travis," Claudia said, her voice level.

"It's just a friendly question, ma'am." His eyes, the color of a tornado cloud bank, mocked her.

Claudia glanced over toward Rawlins' pickup. One of the men, big and paunchy, grinned openly at her. She stepped deliberately past Rawlins and mounted the stoop, feeling Rawlins' and his friends' eyes on her. She forced herself to look down at them. Rawlins stared at her with hungry insolence, and the big man with the paunch was still grinning as he wedged a large pinch of Skoal in his cheek. Claudia maintained eye contact with the big man until his grin faded into uncertainty. Then she put two fingers between her lips and called the crew to attention with a shrill whistle. The chatter died out and the men turned toward Claudia.

"Welcome to the Bishop farm," Claudia called out. "We've got a bumper crop this year. I can promise you three things—hard work, good food, and a swift kick in the butt if I catch you sitting on it!" The men laughed. "We'll cut the dryland sections first," she continued. "In the mornings we'll work in the near section. In the afternoons we'll work in the sections bordering the Cimarron. The river damp makes it harder to cut there mornings. We'll cut the irrigated sections last." She glanced around at the faces of the men. "I want to drive a wheat truck this morning. I'll take the first load to the coop to set up the account and check for quality." She turned to Vanlandingham. "Whose truck shall I use?"

Vanlandingham pointed at a man from Nacogdoches. "Carlos, let Claudia use your truck. You troubleshoot for the combines this morning."

Carlos pulled a key ring from his Levi's. "It's the red GMC," he said, and tossed the keys toward Claudia with an underhand throw.

Claudia fielded the keys with a nod of thanks in Carlos' direction. "Mrs. Walters will be fixing dinner here each day," she said.

"Mighty *fine,*" a man in greasy coveralls interrupted. "Ain't no flies on *her* back!"

Claudia smiled. "We'll eat in two shifts," she went on. "Work it out among yourselves and the first shift come in at noon." She looked around. "Any questions?"

"Can you get Jake to air condition his combine cabs?" It was an old hand from Monahans.

Claudia shook her head. "Jake's idea of comfort is a seat cushion."

When the laughter quieted another man called out, "How about a dance Saturday night?" He was tall and loose-jointed, with a full red beard split by a toothy grin, and had been crewing with Van-landingham for years.

"Sorry, Dowdy. My feet haven't recovered from last year." The men guffawed again. "Now listen," Claudia broke in, "there's a rain forecast for later this week. I want the wheat in before it hits."

"Hell, Claudia," the combiner from Monahans cracked, "we cut wheat like Carlos eats beans."

"You mess with this bean," Carlos shot back, "and I make you eat the whole burrito."

Claudia let the banter subside, then glanced down at her custom cutter from Seminole. "Are the cutting platforms assembled on all the combines?"

Vanlandingham turned to his maintenance ramrod. "How about it?"

The man removed an unlit, half-chewed cigar from his mouth. "Does the Pope shit in the woods?"

Vanlandingham turned back to Claudia with a grin. "I think he means yes."

"All right," Claudia said, "you truck drivers listen to me. Pay attention to the combines in the fields. Off-load them as soon as they stop. I don't want John Deeres with their guts full and their blades in neutral." Claudia removed her hat and wiped a sleeve across her forehead. "And another thing. When you go into the coop, watch the turnaround time. There's no use standing in line. If it gets stacked up, I can take ten thousand bushels in my silos." She thought a moment. "Anything else, Jake?"

"I'd like to top off the drums on my refueling truck."

Claudia pointed at the pump by the side of the shed. "Use mine for now, but I don't have an unlimited supply. Your gofer will have to fill up at the coop every morning." She waited. The crew watched her expectantly. "Okay, let's move! I want eight combines in the fields in half an hour!"

The men fanned out to their equipment. Travis Rawlins motioned to his three buddies as he walked toward his combine. He threw a mock punch at Norton's belly and grinned. "Well, good buddy, what do you think?"

"Shee-it!" Norton drawled in admiration. He spat a thin stream of tobacco juice at the ground. "When you gonna see her?"

"Well, let's put it this way. You boys are gonna be drinkin' alone tonight."

"She didn't seem none too friendly to me, Travis." The challenge came from a man as stringy as a range-starved longhorn, balding and gaunt, who looked like he had all his brains down in his neck.

"Farrell, you dumb peckerwood, you don't know shit about women."

"I don't know, Travis, I think Farrell may be right." The baiting came from a man who was thick-necked and heavyset with a build like a wrestler, but about thirty pounds over his fighting weight. "I kinda figured you been passin' gas about this woman."

Rawlins' face flushed with anger. "I'm tellin' you, J.W., I been watchin' this widow-woman. She's ripe for the pickin', and I'm the man with the cherry picker."

"Talk's cheap," J.W. grunted.

"If you don't piss me off," Rawlins said as he climbed up into the cab of the John Deere, "I might cut y'all in on the action."

J.W. moved off toward a wheat truck. "Well, I wouldn't kick it out of bed. She's all I been hearin' about all winter."

The morning calm was broken by the roar of engines. An occasional backfire ripped through the rumble of the combines and trucks as drivers revved the motors. Diesel fumes and shouts filled the air. Claudia watched the flurry of activity a moment, then jumped off the stoop and headed for the red GMC. She pulled the Jimmy out of the drive, skirting the other vehicles, eased past the refueling truck that was topping off a dozen fifty-gallon drums at her pump, and stopped just beyond the shed. She put the truck in neutral and stomped on the emergency brake, then hauled herself up into the truck bed.

Claudia squinted into the sun and watched the combiners jockey their monstrous machines into line behind her. She waited till the remaining trucks and pickups got unsnarled, then clambered back into the cab. She noticed that Carlos had installed an airhorn in the truck. She reached for the handle next to his plastic Jesus and fired three long blasts. Claudia led the column down the track between the two fields. She checked the side mirror and smiled. She never tired of the sight. Eight combines, four wheat trucks, one flatbed with the diesel drums, a half-dozen pickups with mechanics, wheat scoopers, gofers, and troubleshooters. Twenty men. And over two thousand acres of wheat to cut in the next four days.

Claudia braked the GMC to a stop and got out and kicked loose the barbed wire gates. Four giant combines peeled off into each field, moving up either side of the track like feathers on the shaft of an arrow. They churned forward, four abreast, maneuvered by their drivers in a staggered line with the precision of a drill team. The John Deeres, glinting brilliant green in the sun, rolled across a plain of gold set against an immense blue summer sky. Together, their thirty-foot cutting platforms devoured a swath of wheat nearly two hundred and forty feet wide. Eighteen hundred bushels of grain every hour.

Claudia tasted the dust and felt the heat. The wind blew damp against her sweat-soaked shirt and whipped her hair in tangles around her face. She felt the exhilaration. The start of the harvest never failed to electrify her.

She turned into a field and drove slowly across the newly cut stubble in the wake of the four combines. The wind blew the dust and wheat chaff in a choking cloud toward the Jimmy. She chose suffocating heat over suffocating dust and rolled up the windows. Claudia trailed the John Deeres into their first turn at the quarter-section fence line. When the lead combine stopped, she eased the truck up to the chute beneath the holding bin to collect the harvested wheat. The grain poured into the truck bed like a sluice of gold. As the last of the wheat trickled from the spout, the combiner engaged the cutting platform and moved ahead.

Claudia collected the wheat from the next two combines. As the third John Deere disgorged its grain, she piled into the rear of the truck, grabbed a wheat scoop, and leveled out the load. She estimated there was enough room for the fourth combine's wheat, and pulled beneath the idling John Deere's holding bin. She climbed into the truck bed, plunging thigh-deep through the wheat, and scooped the cascading grain away from the spout to prevent spillage.

When the bin was empty, Claudia pulled herself free of the grain and dropped to the ground on the far side of the Jimmy. She sank to the running board, breathing hard from the exertion, and tugged the boots from her feet. She dumped out the wheat and put her boots back on. Claudia stood up, feeling the prickling itch of the wheat dust. She leaned forward from the waist, pulled her hair forward over her head, and wiped the sweat and grime from the back of her neck. She straightened up and flung her hair free of her collar with a toss of her head. Her denim shirt, wet with perspiration, clung to her body. Removing a handkerchief from her Levi's,

Claudia reached inside the throat of her blouse and wiped her skin. Suddenly she stopped. The combine had not pulled on in line with the others. She turned slowly toward the rear of the truck and saw Travis Rawlins.

He was leaning against the truck watching her. "You are one hankerin' woman."

Claudia folded the damp handkerchief and shoved it in the hip pocket of her Levi's. "Your break's over, Travis. Get back to work."

Claudia climbed into the cab of the GMC and headed back across the field to the gate. As she pulled up on the track, she signaled the next wheat truck to tail the combines. She slowly picked up speed, double-clutching the heavily loaded Jimmy. As she rolled past the farmhouse, she passed Rawlins' turquoise Ranger, which was still parked by the kitchen stoop. She glanced in the side mirror. The last thing she saw as the dust drifted in to obscure the pickup was Rawlins' Winchester .30-30 slung on a rifle rack in the rear window of the cab.

The pinpricks of the cool shower pelted Claudia's skin, washing the day's accumulated grime from her body. Aside from the brief incident with Travis Rawlins, it had been a good day. Everything had gone without a hitch, and she had called Joshua and asked him to meet her for supper and go with her to meet Todd's bus.

She finished her shower and slipped into a white sundress, tying the sash at the back. She brushed her hair and applied a minimum of makeup. She was looking forward to Todd's return, having decided that it could be a good thing for him to meet Joshua. He was not the kind of man she had feared he might be, and perhaps he could help Todd put his father's service in Vietnam in some kind of perspective. God knows, I've never been able to help him, she thought.

The bedroom melted into shadows as dusk enveloped the farmhouse. In the half-light Claudia walked down the stairs, groping in her handbag for the car keys. Preoccupied with thoughts of Joshua and Todd's meeting, she turned toward the kitchen door. She stopped, startled, and stifled an involuntary cry. Travis Rawlins leaned nonchalantly against the doorjamb, a wooden match protruding from the corner of his mouth.

"Good God, Travis, you gave me a fright!" As soon as Claudia uttered the words, she regretted them.

Rawlins smiled, his eyes brazenly wandering over her body, white dress against tanned skin. "There ain't no cause to be frightened, Claudia."

Claudia turned away and began to walk toward the front door. "I was just leaving," she said.

Rawlins reached out and grasped Claudia's sash. The bow slipped open and the sash came away in his hand. "I do appreciate you prettyin' up for me."

Claudia turned, eyes flashing. "Stop it, Travis!" She reached for the sash and Rawlins teased it away.

"You ought to be more friendly," he drawled. "The only reason I'm cutting this year is to finish up our business."

"All of our business is finished. It was finished last summer."

Rawlins stepped in front of Claudia as she tried again to move to the door. He lifted his hand to the side of her face, and as Claudia slowly retreated, he slid his fingers down her neck and hooked them through the shoulder strap of her dress. "Come on, now. You know you want it."

Claudia felt her stomach turn and brushed his hand aside. "Take your adolescent fantasies somewhere else."

"You ain't been cinched up against somebody else's snubbin' post, have you?"

"I'm not one of your mares to be broken and rode."

"Rode," Rawlins smirked, "not broke."

"I'm warning you," Claudia said, "don't try anything."

"Like hell," Rawlins growled. "Plains is the high point of my summer."

Claudia suppressed her rising fear and decided to humor him. "Come on, Travis, you've got a lady friend in every town from Muleshoe, Texas, to Kamsack, Canada."

"That don't make me no never mind." Rawlins' drawl was laced with threat. "I want you." He backed Claudia against the dining room table, pressed against her, and kissed her. She stiffened, then forced her body to go limp, passive, her lips slack. Rawlins held the kiss. His tongue probed her mouth. His left hand slipped to her breast, drawing the nipple up between thumb and forefinger through the cloth. His right hand trailed down her back to her buttocks, gripped them, and pushed her hips forward against him. Claudia remained inert, her body indifferent.

Rawlins released her. "Damn you," he snarled.

Claudia pushed past him, retrieved her sash from the floor, and then turned on him. "You're finished, Travis. Fired. Stay off my farm!" She stormed out the kitchen door, slamming the screen behind her.

Rawlins hesitated, confused. It hadn't turned out at all like he had played it out in his mind the past year. He rushed out on the kitchen stoop. "You can't fire me," he blustered.

"The hell I can't," Claudia shouted back. She gunned the Fairlane around Rawlins' pickup and roared down the drive.

Joshua and Claudia finished supper in the Main Street Café. They occupied the same booth they had the previous Saturday when they had first met for coffee. As they spooned deep-dish apple cobbler from the same bowl, Joshua eyed Claudia. "You seem upset tonight," he observed.

Claudia hesitated a moment. "There was an incident at the farm this evening."

"Good," Joshua said. "I was afraid it was me again."

Claudia smiled briefly. "I fired one of Jake's hands."

"What happened?"

Claudia shrugged. "Oh, this combiner gave me some trouble."

"Is everything okay?"

"It worries me a little bit," Claudia admitted. "He has a violent side." She grinned. "I don't think his silo's quite full."

They finished their coffee and settled up at the cash register. They walked across Main toward the city park, skirting the Cimarron County Courthouse, which occupied one corner of the park. Joshua led Claudia toward the four monuments that had been erected on the courthouse lawn. He paused at the nearest monument.

It was a gray granite obelisk about six feet tall in memory of the boys from Cimarron County who had died in what the commemorators called "The Great War: 1914–1918." There were two names carved in the granite face. A little distance from the obelisk was a rectangular slab of marble like a large gravestone which listed the names of Cimarron County boys who died in World War II. Joshua counted eleven names. They walked across the lawn toward the third monument. It was built of grayish-brown native stone, like the courthouse, and had a metal casting of a Confederate flag affixed to its face. Under it was a plaque that read, "In honor of William C. Quantrill's band of irregulars who fought for The Cause on the frontier, 1861–1865. Judson Slade of the settlement of Plains rode with the raiders."

"Wasn't Quantrill just an outlaw?" Joshua asked.

"Depends on whose side you were on," Claudia replied. "He tied up a lot of Union troops in the border states, and that was good for the South."

Joshua shook his head. "Somebody will think you're a hero no matter what you do."

They wandered over to the last monument. It was another rectangular slab of marble standing upright on a marble base. It commemorated the men from Cimarron County who had died in the Korean conflict. Four names were carved on its flecked and flinty face. Joshua read the names aloud. Slowly. Softly. Savoring the syllables and absorbing the sounds. For a fleeting moment he felt as though he were reciting the names from his own team. Curiously, it gave him a sense of solace. As though all war dead were interchangeable. From Thermopylae to South Africa. Regardless of country or cause, victory or defeat. He turned and glanced around the courthouse lawn at the four monuments. The feeling left him. "I would bet more than I'm worth that more Cimarron County boys besides Tom died in Vietnam between 1960 and 1975."

Claudia took him by the arm. "Put it behind you, Josh."

"Yeah, why not," he muttered.

They crossed the courthouse lawn to the park and ambled along one of the brick walkways, enjoying the solitude. By unspoken assent they made their way toward the hand-dug well. A stone wall, the same stone used on the courthouse, rimmed the circumference of the well. The wall was about waist-high, and continued into the well as the casing. Joshua and Claudia leaned against it.

Joshua peered into the black depths of the well. The bottom was invisible. "How deep is this thing?" he asked.

"A little over a hundred feet."

"Did they really dig it by hand?"

Claudia nodded. "Back in the 1880's. The Santa Fe Railroad had it dug to provide water for the railhead. The town used it for its water supply until the middle of the 1930's."

Joshua ran his hands along the top of the wall, still warm from the day's heat. "Where did they get all of this stone? All I've ever seen here is dirt."

"They quarried it from the banks of the Cimarron."

Joshua shook his head. On impulse he reached into his jeans and pulled out some change. He selected a penny and held it over the well. "Make a wish," he said.

"Out loud?" she asked.

"Sure."

Claudia cocked her head thoughtfully to one side. "I wish for tall wheat and fast combines," she laughed.

Joshua dropped the penny. They waited expectantly, staring at each other. After what seemed forever, they heard a faint splash from far below. Claudia walked over to a nearby park bench and sat down. Joshua leaned against the wall. The wind had died down. He felt the heat and the stillness of the evening. He tilted his head back and looked at the sky. The western horizon was tinted with a watercolor wash of magenta. The hush seemed to dominate and possess him. His senses were so acute he felt like he could hear the earth turning on its axis and feel the pull of gravity. Like the night they had evacuated Thang Duc.

When the first Dust Offs began to hover, Joshua had the uneasy feeling that at any moment the ridges would erupt with gunfire. But the jungle was quiet. The Dust Offs took the wounded Nungs to the Vietnamese Hospital in Pleiku. The wounded Montagnards went to the C-Team. DuBoise and the two survivors from the Thang Duc A-Team were evacuated to the Eighth Field Hospital in Qui Nhon. Joshua accompanied them to the Huey and watched them aboard. The helicopter lifted slowly, carefully, it seemed, hovered a few feet in the air, and then tilted into forward flight. The men disappeared in a swirling cloud of red dust and he never saw them again.

Two Chinooks, giant cargo helicopters with huge twin rotors fore and aft, settled onto the shell-scarred dirt airstrip just outside the compound. The surviving Montagnards collected their meager belongings and boarded one of the Chinooks for the C-Team. The surviving Nungs stacked gear and supplies and all salvageable equipment on the second Chinook. As the last rays of the evening sun were refracted into soft ribbons of light by the haze of blue smoke layered over the valley, the Nungs climbed wearily aboard. The Chinook pounded into the air to ferry them back to SFOB.

At dusk the last three helicopters touched down inside Thang Duc. Joshua supervised the crew chiefs and gunners as they removed the American dead from several bunkers and loaded them on two of the choppers. Heavily loaded with body bags, they lumbered into the air to deliver their cargo to Graves Registration in Nha Trang, the first leg on their escorted journey home. Joshua watched them out of sight, then turned back toward the remaining helicopter and sliced his index finger across his neck. The pilot cut the engine and the rotors pumped to a halt and drooped in a graceful parabola. The silence in Thang Duc was absolute. Only one of the American dead remained to be ferried out. Joshua had waited till the very last. He wanted Tom Bishop to go out with him. He led the crew chief and one of the gunners toward the command bunker. It unnerved Joshua to walk exposed across the open compound. He walked slowly. Tense. Wary. Prepared to dive for cover. It's over, he assured himself.

The helicopter crewmen, intimidated, kept a quiet, respectful distance from the apparition who staggered in front of them. Joshua's face was covered with dirty stubble and flushed with fever. His eyes, deep-set in hollow sockets, glinted dully. His lips were peeling and fissured. His tiger suit was encrusted with blood and sweat and red dust. He paused on the lip of the trench above the entrance to the command bunker. "In there," he croaked, nodding at the army blanket that still hung over the bunker entrance. The two crewmen dropped to the bottom of the trench and entered the bunker. They reappeared a moment later with the body bag slung between them. Joshua grabbed a handle and gave them an assist as they hauled Bishop's remains to the top of the trench. He followed as they struggled awkwardly across the blasted ground to the helicopter. The other noncom riding shotgun on the chopper jumped down as they approached, and the three of them manhandled the body bag through the open hatch.

Joshua leaned in through the hatch and called out to the pilot, "Be back in a minute."

"Okay, buddy, but make it snappy. We're all alone out here, you know."

Joshua nodded and turned back toward the teamhouse. Weariness overwhelmed him as he pushed open the door. He had never noticed before that a hinge squeaked.

Wyatt Porter sat on a chair with his feet up on the table, a can of Budweiser, brought in on the first relief choppers, in his hand. There were three empties on the table in front of him which he had slammed down in about as many minutes. On his lap in a bulky manila envelope were all the classified documents he had collected from the team safe. He let out a horrendous belch and lifted the Budweiser toward Joshua in a toast. "You can't kill a blue-gummed nigger from Philadelphia," he said.

Joshua didn't have the energy to smile. "Ready to go?"

"Been ready for a week." His black face glistened as he tilted the Budweiser and chugalugged it, losing some down his shirt front.

Joshua took a last look around. Now that it was time to go, he almost hated to leave. Twenty-four hours earlier he had wanted out of Thang Duc more than he had ever wanted anything in his life. But my God! They had won! He wanted to claim it some way. He glanced around the room, everything in disarray. Light filtered through a hole in the roof from a recoilless rifle round. His eyes strayed to the bulletin board. There was one item on it—the TWX ordering them to close down Thang Duc and evacuate it. Across the message, scrawled in bold print, was a single word: INSANE! Joshua reached in the shirt pocket of his tiger suit. He withdrew one of Bishop's cards. The miter-shaped chess piece gleamed black and shiny against the white background. He thumbtacked the card to the board just above the TWX.

Joshua turned and walked outside into the long shadows. He gazed up at the wooden flagpole. The tiny souvenir flag still stirred in the breeze atop the pole. Unconsciously he pulled him-

*self erect and buttoned the two remaining buttons on his cam-
ouflage shirt. He squared his shoulders and strode resolutely to the
base of the flagpole, untied the halyard, and slowly lowered the
flag. As the flag fluttered to the bottom of the pole, a hand suddenly reached in front of Joshua and caught the flag in its grasp.
Joshua turned.*

*Wyatt Porter, hand still clutching the flag, stared intently at
Joshua. Then he drew his knife from his boot scabbard and cut the
cords where Bishop had tied the flag to the halyard. Joshua noticed
a thin seam of blood along the shank of the blade, reflecting crimson in the last twilight glow of the sun. Porter sheathed his knife,
faced Joshua, and handed him the end of the flag with the blue
field. Holding the four corners of the flag, they pulled it taut
between them and snapped it to whip it wrinkle-free. They folded
the width of the flag twice and stretched it tight. Then, meticulously, with immense concentration and great care, Porter turned
the striped end on itself in a small triangle. He worked his way
up the red and white stripes with repetitive triangular folds until
only the end of the blue field was exposed. He tucked the free edge
of the blue field carefully into the pocket of the triangle, and
smoothed the remaining wrinkles out of the small bundle. Porter
took a small step backward and extended both arms, elbows
locked, and handed the flag to Joshua.*

*Joshua took the flag without a word and tucked it inside his shirt.
He looked at Porter and their eyes locked briefly. Porter moved his
head slightly and tightened his lips. The gesture was half shrug,
half smile, all regret.*

*Joshua and Porter turned and walked toward the waiting heli-
copter.*

Joshua looked at Claudia where she sat on the bench. She glanced
up, reached a hand to her hair, and drew it away from the side of
her face. Smiled. I think I can tell her, Joshua thought. He didn't
know why. But he thought he could do it and perhaps it would be
all right. Tonight he would tell her about Tom. He went over and
took a seat beside her. She sat up suddenly and looked toward Main
Street. A turquoise pickup slowed, then turned in and parked at

the curb. A man got out and stared at them as he slowly closed the door of the truck. He stepped up on the curb, turned back, looked again. He lifted his hat, settled it more comfortably on his head, and entered the Billiard Parlor Bar.

"I figured you turned heads, Claudia," Joshua said, "but that guy's almost two blocks away."

Claudia didn't smile. "That's Travis Rawlins." Her voice was strained. "He's the man I fired tonight."

"It will be all right," Joshua said reassuringly. He glanced at his watch. "Come on. Let's go meet the bus."

They walked back across the park to Main Street and settled on one of the benches in front of the café. After about five minutes, only a few minutes late, a silver and red Continental Trailways bus rolled up. It stopped in the middle of the wide street, air brakes hissing. The door opened and one passenger stepped off, canvas duffel in hand. The door levered shut, the gears meshed, and the bus pulled away in a cloud of diesel fumes.

The young man was tall and broad-shouldered. Muscular, but still with the slimness of youth. A big frame waiting to be fleshed out. He had deep-set eyes and a square face, and his jaw was set. Determined, bordering on stubborn. A quick, easy grin creased his face the minute he saw his mother. He walked swiftly to her, with the pelvic-thrust-cantilevered-hip stride of a sprinter. He grabbed Claudia with a loud whoop and crushed her in a bear hug.

Joshua stepped back. Stunned. Transported back twelve years. It was Tom Bishop. A young Tom Bishop. Alive, standing before him in the flesh. Joshua started to tremble. A faint tremor of the fingers at first, then his hands began to shake. He clenched his fists tight. They still shook. He felt the shudder in his legs. Stop it, he told himself. Stop it. You're going to come apart right here on Main Street in Plains, Kansas. With a tremendous concentration of effort he willed the trembling to stop. Gradually it slowed. He breathed deeply, focusing his mind, allowing the conscious control of his nervous system to saturate every muscle fiber in his body. The spasm passed. But the sense of déjà vu remained.

Claudia turned to Joshua and introduced Todd, explaining that Joshua had served with his father in Vietnam. Joshua shook Todd's eagerly outstretched hand. His grip was firm. His smile was spontaneous and infectious. A mischievous grin that sprawled crookedly across his face lit his eyes, and animated his entire face.

"Josh, we got these slope-headed sonsabitches cornered on all three sides of us."

They turned toward the curb. Travis Rawlins stood watching them, leaning against the rough stone front of the Main Street Café. After a brief moment he sauntered toward them, ignoring Claudia and Joshua.

"Howdy, Todd." Rawlins extended a large, callused hand.

"Hey, Travis." Todd's voice was pitched in the bass register, but it still had the timbre of adolescence. He shook Rawlins' hand.

"Boy, you get better-lookin' every year," Rawlins said. "Just like your momma." Todd didn't reply and Rawlins went on: "You want to be the gofer on my combine tomorrow?"

"You won't be driving a combine tomorrow," Claudia interrupted.

Rawlins turned to Claudia and smiled engagingly. "I'm willin' to let all that pass. Let's just say we both made a mistake," he cajoled.

"You made a mistake," Claudia said flatly. "See Jake and settle up tonight. I'll give him a call."

Rawlins' eyes narrowed; then he said expansively, "Well, let me buy y'all a drink." He cocked a thumb toward the Billiard Parlor Bar. "Just to show there's no hard feelin's."

"We'll be going on home with Todd," Claudia said.

Rawlins fixed Joshua with an insolent stare. "How 'bout I buy you a drink?" His voice was low, a conspiratorial whisper. "A minute ago you sure looked like you could 'ave used one." He smiled, but the smile was so severe it served only to bare his lips.

"Get your bag, Todd," Joshua said, without taking his eyes off Rawlins. "Mr. Rawlins is the kind of man who drinks alone."

Joshua rode home with Claudia and Todd. The encounter with Rawlins was ignored. They talked of football camp, Claudia's mother in Kansas City, a girl who lived down the street from her, harvest, the dance on Saturday, and the Annual Rattlesnake Roundup. Todd enthusiastically explained rattlesnake hunting to Joshua. He asked Claudia if she would let him off the next day so he and Joshua could go hunting. Claudia assented, determined that Todd should get to know Joshua.

Joshua left that night without any further conversation with Claudia. Todd drove him back to the motel and dropped him off. He tried to get Joshua to buy a couple of six-packs for him at the Billiard Parlor Bar. Joshua, somewhat taken aback, refused, and watched Todd drive away.

CHAPTER NINE

Joshua squatted in the dust of the shed. It was early morning, just light. Still cool. The dawn had a luminous quality about it. The shed was suffused with silver light that seemed to gather intensity as it fused with the first pink flush of the impending sunrise. He watched Todd, crouched motionless before a crack in a wood partition, behind which bulging feedbags were stacked. Todd concentrated with unwavering intensity on the crack, muscles tensed, an empty tin can poised a few inches off the floor. Bits of cheese were scattered on the ground. Joshua watched with a wonder that was tinged with longing. A longing for the past. A past that was simple, ordered, predictable, perfectable. A past he controlled, rather than a past that controlled him. Todd Bishop, bursting with youthful energy, seemed almost a carbon copy of his father. The feeling that had settled on him the night before when he had first met Todd, which had troubled him through a fitful sleep, had not abated with the new day.

At that moment, two eyes, twin beads of midnight, appeared at the crack. Cautiously, whiskers twitching, the mouse poked its head through the crack. Does it sense danger, Joshua wondered. Is it, like us, drawn by the danger, instead of repelled by it? The mouse crept forward toward the cheese. Todd slammed the tin can down with lightning speed, trapping it. He let out a holler and swept the can upward in a single fluid motion, at the same time slipping a hand over the mouth of the can. Joshua removed a fitted cover from a green plastic wastebasket and Todd dumped the mouse in. They watched it scurry around the bottom of the basket a moment before Joshua snapped the lid in place. "One should be all we need," Todd said.

Todd picked up the wastebasket and left the shed. He walked across the yard toward the kitchen and paused by a cellar door beside the stoop. He set the wastebasket down on the grass and turned to Joshua. "Wait here a second. I'll open the cellar." He disappeared into the house and a moment later Joshua heard the locking brace slide away from the cellar door. Todd pushed the heavy metal door open and let it drop back against the stoop.

Joshua followed him down the stone steps into the cellar. It was a small damp subterranean room with a dirt floor, dug out under the kitchen. The joists of the kitchen floor were just above his head. The walls were lined with stone. A long workbench was situated against the outside wall. Wooden shelves had been placed against the inside wall, and were filled with home-canned fruits and vegetables. Beyond the shelves were crude wooden steps leading up to a door that opened into the kitchen.

Todd walked to the workbench. He pushed aside a Coleman lantern and a red metal can labeled "Kerosene." "I've spent many an hour down here," he said as he grasped a fishing tackle box by the handle and pulled it toward him.

"Claudia lock you in the cellar if you were a bad boy?" Joshua asked.

"Tornadoes," Todd explained. "Mom keeps a sharp eye out in the spring." He glanced up at a small window no more than a foot square. It was built into the stone of the outside wall just beneath the kitchen subflooring, and provided the only light in the room other than the cellar door. Todd slid the tackle box to the far end of the workbench until he was beneath the window, and opened the box under its meager light. He rummaged through it, checking the contents. He removed a small hand mirror, a glass medical thermometer, heavy twine, large nails, a pocketknife, a couple of pairs of leather work gloves, and a snakebite kit. He replaced them in the box and glanced up at the wall. Hanging from nails in the stone above the workbench were two implements, both handcrafted. Todd took down the first, a long-handled pair of tongs. It was made of a pair of pliers with a four-inch flat steel blade welded as an extension to each jaw, and with a three-foot golf-club shaft welded to each grip of the pliers' handles. Todd grasped the handles of the golf clubs and worked the pliers, opening and closing the flat steel blades on the jaws. "We'll pick 'em up with this," he said, "and we'll hook 'em out of the rocks with this if we need to." He took the second implement off the wall. It was a five-foot length of three-quarter-inch pipe, with a metal hook welded to one end, and a Y-fork welded to the other. He handed both tools to Joshua.

Joshua took them and studied Todd's eager face and crooked grin. "Done this much?"

"I've been hunting rattlers about five years. Jess Walters taught me. He's Mom's farmhand," he explained.

Joshua nodded. "I've met him."

Todd closed the tackle box and picked it up. He started toward the cellar door. "You should never hunt alone."

Joshua couldn't resist. "Have you ever?"

Todd grinned. "Some." Then he added as a sober afterthought, "But it's stupid."

Bishop found Joshua and Porter on the northwest perimeter. They were wiring claymores just over the rim of the trench. Bishop watched them a moment and then said, "Josh, did you talk to a captain at Danang this morning about the flamethrowers we wanted from the Marines?"

Joshua pursed his lips and inserted a wire into the receptacle on the back of a claymore. "Yeah, on the single sideband."

"Did you call him a chickenshit son of a bitch and ask him which side he was on?"

Joshua turned the thumbscrew to anchor the wire in place. "That's pretty accurate. The son of a bitch said we couldn't have them. Hell, they gave 'em to us at Duc Co when we cleaned out that NVA tunnel complex."

Bishop removed a TWX from his shirt pocket and handed it to Joshua. "This is an official complaint to SFOB. He wants to put your ass in a sling."

"What for?" Joshua stopped working and read the TWX.

"That was a Navy captain, Josh," Bishop said dryly, "not a Marine captain."

Joshua pondered the difference in rank a moment and then grinned. "One of the dumber things I have done."

"Swung at 'Man Mountain' Masowiecki," Bishop countered, "while he still had his helmet on."

"Built an entry for the soapbox derby made with an orange crate."

"Hooked my dick up to Dad's milking machine."

"Mailed a dog turd to my seventh-grade homeroom teacher with a return address."

"Watered a plant for a week while Claudia was gone and then found out it was plastic."

"Preached a sermon on the scientific proof of God," Joshua said.

"Tried to clear a jammed combine without shutting it off."

Joshua looked at the TWX again, wadded it up, and dropped it on the floor of the trench. "One of the stupider things that Navy captain could do is come get me."

They returned to the shed. Joshua placed a lunch bucket and the snake-hunting gear on the Case tractor, while Todd got a five-gallon can from beside the gasoline pump and topped off the tank. They climbed on and Todd turned over the engine and backed the tractor out of the shed. They bounced down the drive just as the sun was spreading heat and light from the eastern horizon.

"You've got to hunt rattlers before it gets too hot," Todd explained. "They hunt at night and get in their dens during the day. They can't take the summer heat." Turning onto the section line road, he shifted gears smoothly and the tractor gathered speed. For a moment Joshua recalled his midnight ride with Claudia. Maybe all of the Bishops like speed, he thought. Ten minutes later Todd turned onto a rutted track. After a five-minute bone-jarring ride, during which Todd didn't slacken the speed, he stopped the Case on a low rise by the Cimarron. "There's some good dens along the river here," Todd said, scrambling off the tractor. He took the tackle box and his tongs, and Joshua carried the lunch bucket, wastebasket, and forked pipe. Fingers of light from the early morning sun reached out and touched the rocky terrain by the river.

"Why do you hunt rattlesnakes, Todd?" Joshua asked as he made his way down a rocky defile.

Todd shrugged diffidently. "They give prize money. Biggest snake, smallest snake, most rattles, sidewinders, and total catch."

"How much could you win if you won them all?"

Todd calculated a moment. "Maybe fifty bucks."

"I'll give you fifty bucks right now. Let's go for a swim."

Todd stopped and looked at Joshua. Then a grin creased his wide face. "I like it," he said.

"That's what I thought."

They reached the river. Joshua placed the lunch bucket by the trunk of a large cottonwood that arched out over the muddy water, and then Todd led the way along the bank. He worked his way toward a low rock bluff back from the river. It was a tangle of stone slabs and slide rocks. As they approached it, Todd opened the tackle box. He drew on a pair of the leather gloves and gave Joshua the other pair. Then he removed the hand mirror and squatted in front of the bluff. He angled the mirror toward the sun and sent a brilliant beam of reflected light toward the rocky slabs. He focused the light on the dark crevices formed by the stones and boulders. They peered into the tangled rock pile.

"Don't see anything," Todd muttered. "Do you?"

"Don't think so."

"It's better if you see 'em before you hear 'em." Todd continued to traverse the face of the rock pile with the reflected beam from the mirror. "Sometimes they'll strike and never rattle," he added, shaking his head. "And just because they rattle it doesn't mean they're going to strike. It's hard to figure." Finally he pocketed the mirror and walked up to the bluff. He knelt beside some stone slabs and studied the ground around the crevices.

"Snakes leave sign just like deer or rabbits," Todd said. "They smooth down the sand and pack it flat where they crawl in and out of a hole or under a rock."

Joshua watched Todd closely. A mixture of snake-smart caution and eagerness. He had seen it before.

Todd crept along the rock face. "Don't see any sign," he said. He removed the thermometer from the tackle box, shook it down, and pressed the red tip about a half inch into the sand. After a minute he withdrew it, held it up, and squinted at the mercury. "Ground temperature is already eighty-four." He replaced the thermometer in the tackle box. "Snakes prefer temperatures of sixty-five to seventy-five degrees. It's already too hot here." Todd stood. "There's another good place about a hundred yards from here. Faces west and has some tree shade. Shouldn't be as hot."

Joshua followed Todd along the wide riverbank. Some areas were barren sand. At other places they pressed through tamarack and huckleberry and stepped over tangled driftwood. They reached an area where a stand of cottonwoods shaded a rocky ledge. Todd pulled the mirror out of his pocket and angled a beam of light along the shadow-dappled ledge. He moved closer and handed the mirror to Joshua. As Joshua directed the light at the rock slabs, Todd squatted to peer into the darkened crevices. "Look at that!" he suddenly blurted.

Joshua moved up beside him and repositioned the mirror to illuminate the crevice. Todd pointed. Deep beneath a stone slab that jutted out from the pile of rock, a nest of rattlesnakes lay twisted like spaghetti. They lay absolutely motionless. He felt a spasm of revulsion at the sight and his pulse quickened.

"Mostly we have prairie rattlers here," Todd said, "but there are a few diamondbacks. Sidewinders are rare." Todd contemplated the snakes. "Can you smell 'em?" he asked in a hushed voice.

Joshua inhaled a tentative sniff.

"I think they smell a little like rotten squash."

Joshua nodded, unconvinced. "Now what?"

"They're too far back to hook." Todd got up and went over to the tackle box. He took the pocketknife and cut a length of twine about three feet long. He picked up a nail and gave both the nail and length of twine to Joshua. He went over to the plastic wastebasket, removed the lid, reached in and trapped the mouse with a gloved hand. Todd gripped the mouse between both hands by its tail and neck skin. The small gray rodent twitched and struggled violently for a moment, then lay shivering in Todd's grasp. "Tie the string around his middle," Todd said.

Joshua looped one end of the twine around the mouse's body just behind the front legs.

"Tie it tight so he can't slip out."

Joshua cinched it down and knotted the twine.

"Tie the other end to the nail."

Joshua did so, and then Todd took the nail and carried the mouse back to the rock ledge. He drove the nail deep into the ground about six feet in front of the crevice where the rattlers rested in their rocky den, and released the mouse. "Mice are natural food for rattlers," Todd explained. "One of 'em will come out." He positioned himself on one side of the crevice and waved Joshua off to the other side. "Most hunters spray gasoline from a garden sprayer in places like that to drive the snakes out." His tone of voice indicated his disdain. "That's a chickenshit way to hunt rattlers."

The mouse scurried around the ground, exploring the extent of its tethered world. It moved at a frantic pace, emitting sharp squeaks. Was it just the string, Joshua wondered, or did it sense danger? Perhaps it could smell the snakes. Rotten squash, Joshua mused.

"When one comes out," Todd said, "I'll try to tong him. If I can't get a grip I'll fling him out in the open away from the rocks. He'll head back toward his hole and we'll pick him off." They waited for a minute. Two minutes. The mouse squeaked and darted about at the end of the string. Three minutes. Joshua looked at Todd. Todd nodded and winked. "Always works," he said. Cocky, confident.

Joshua's stomach constricted with a sudden hollow rush. The likeness to Tom Bishop was uncanny. Don't do that, he thought, gritting his teeth. He feared the words would be involuntarily wrenched from him, audible.

They waited five more minutes. Joshua shifted his weight, muscles cramping. Then a wedge-shaped head, desert brown and glistening, appeared at the crevice. Eyes narrow slits, tongue quavering in pulsing thrusts. The rattler raised its head a few inches from the ground, swaying back and forth. Hypnotic, graceful, and menacing. The mouse squeaked in terror. The snake slithered forward, its diamond markings etched in geometric patterns of brown and gray.

Todd lunged with the tongs and gripped the diamondback just behind the head. He lifted it into the air, writhing and thrashing. It twisted free of the metal blades and dropped to the ground. Todd immediately thrust the tongs under the rattler's thick midsection and flipped it onto the sand about fifteen feet from the rocky ledge. The snake struck the ground in a twisted heap and instantly gathered itself into a tight coil, head up, sinuous, undulating, malevolent. Its tail rose, a vibrating blur, and emitted a prolonged dry rattle, like castanets.

Todd crouched and faced the rattler. "I think we made him mad."

Joshua moved away from the rocky ledge. "What do you want me to do?"

"Just work at him from both sides. If he tries to head for the brush or the rocks, just toss him back out here in the open. If you can, fork him against the ground. But be careful."

"You've never even seen careful," Joshua said. "Careful is what I do when I'm asleep."

Todd and Joshua moved warily toward the diamondback. It remained coiled, its rattle a deadly buzz. Todd lunged with the tongs. The rattler struck, a lightning slash that hit the tongs a glancing blow. Todd drew back. A few drops of faintly milky liquid, the rattler's venom, glistened on the shank of one of the golf-club handles. Todd never took his eyes off the snake, coiled again, fangs exposed. "Be real careful, Josh. He's a high striker."

They edged toward the diamondback again. Out of the corner of his eye Joshua saw a second rattler glide from the rock crevice. It stopped and lifted its head, oscillating from side to side, tongue flicking in and out. "Looks like one of his buddies is going to join in," Joshua said.

Todd glanced over his shoulder. "He may have come out for the mouse. But sometimes another snake's rattle draws 'em out. Curious, I guess." Todd continued to move toward the first diamondback. "They never work together. Just ignore him for now."

Joshua wet his lips and inched toward their quarry. He felt a bead of sweat form between his shoulder blades and trickle down his back. He wasn't sure if it was the increasing heat of the day, the exertion, or fear. He eyed the second snake furtively. To him the reptile was totally inscrutable. Despite Todd's confidence, he wasn't sure if the boy knew what snakes thought or how they behaved.

Todd grabbed for the diamondback with the tongs. The snake struck, missed. Todd grabbed it about a foot behind the head and lifted it into the air. The snake coiled its body around the tongs, writhing and hissing. "It's a climber," Todd said as he held it at arm's length and walked over to the plastic wastebasket. Joshua removed the lid and Todd tried to place the snake in it. He slowly opened the steel-bladed jaws, but the snake wouldn't drop. It continued to wrap itself around the tongs, and when it felt the jaws release, it jerked its head, fangs bared, and struck again. Todd slammed the rattler to the ground beside the basket. "Fork him!" he yelled.

Joshua stepped closer, took aim with the forked end of the pipe, and pinned the body of the snake against the ground. He had the rattler about eighteen inches behind the head and it twisted and struck the pipe. The pipe shuddered from the force of the hit.

Todd grasped the snake with the tongs again, just behind the head, and held it against the ground. "Fork him just behind the head!" Joshua did so and Todd released his grip. The rattler thrashed violently for a moment, its body whipping and undulating, then lay still. Todd laid aside his tongs and tugged on the cuffs of his gloves. "This is the tricky part," he said. Joshua pressed the forked pipe more forcibly against the snake's neck. "Don't break its neck," Todd cautioned. From his tone Joshua realized that dead snakes were only good for sneers.

Todd knelt beside the snake, reached out with his left hand, and gripped it at midbody. With his right he grasped it just behind the head, closing thumb and forefinger tightly just back of the jaws. "Turn it loose," he said. Joshua removed the pipe and Todd stood up. He held his right hand high in the air, and slid his left down the body of the snake to the tail, stretching it full length. "Not bad," Todd said. "About a four-footer." He poised the snake tail first over the plastic wastebasket and lowered it into the basket as he released his grip on the tail. The snake stiffened its body as its tail touched the bottom. Todd paused, waiting. "If they stand on their tail, they can strike you when you let go." The snake opened its jaws wide, its mouth a cavern of white, velvet-soft flesh. Two glistening fangs curved downward from its upper jaw. Todd continued to wait. The snake slowly relaxed, and he gradually lowered it into the basket, then literally flung the head of the diamondback downward as he jerked his hand back.

Joshua clapped on the lid and snapped it firmly in place. They stared at each other over the basket, breathing hard. Todd smiled. "They got a million ways they can kill you." He picked up the basket and carried it into the heavy shade of some tamaracks near the base of the weathered cottonwood. They retrieved their snake-hunting tools and turned back to the rocky ledge. The second snake was a prairie rattler, much smaller. Maybe two feet in length. It bellied over the ground with quick movements, circling outside the area where the frantic mouse was staked. Joshua and Todd separated and moved to either side of the snake.

"The little ones are more dangerous," Todd cautioned. "They're faster and quicker, and drop for drop their venom's just as poisonous as the big ones."

"Why didn't he already eat the mouse?" Joshua asked.

"Dunno. Maybe he wanted a leisurely meal." Todd stalked the rattler, legs spread in a balanced stance. He made a stab with the tongs. The snake darted away, speeding back toward the rocks. "Head him off!" Todd yelled.

Joshua quickly moved between the snake and the ledge. He thrust the end of the pipe at the snake and it veered away. He tried to hook it and flip it back out on the sandbank, but the rattler tumbled forward over the hook in a coiling mass and lunged at Joshua's feet. Joshua backpedaled but the snake struck quickly. Two lightning thrusts, the second one hitting the toe of his work boot, fangs slashing at the leather. Joshua shook free from the strike, heart pounding, and stumbled backward out of reach. The snake sped toward the ledge and disappeared into the rocks.

"Damn," Todd said, "he got away."

Joshua looked at Todd, eyes wide with fear, not comprehending Todd's lack of concern. "He bit me!" he exclaimed, wondering why he felt no pain, waiting to die.

"A little snake like that can't strike through leather," Todd scoffed. "A big one hardly ever can."

Joshua stared at the toe of his boot. The leather appeared intact. It was wet with oily drops of venom. "*Now* you tell me."

"Didn't you know that?"

"How should I know it?" Joshua said, exasperated. "I've never hunted rattlesnakes."

"Why'd you think we wore the boots?"

Todd grinned and went over to where the mouse, either exhausted or resigned to its fate, crouched quietly at the end of its tether. He checked the knots on the mouse and determined that the nail was still firmly anchored in the ground. Then he retrieved his tongs and went back over to the stone ledge. Joshua slowly relaxed, but he could still feel his heart pounding against his rib cage. He had to grin at Todd's nonchalant attitude.

"Hell, Josh, we can whip these dinks."

Joshua picked up the metal pipe and joined Todd at the ledge. They waited several minutes for a rattler to appear. When nothing happened, Todd went over to the mouse and stirred him around with the toe of his boot. The mouse scurried around and squeaked a little, but its performance was lackluster. Todd removed the mirror from his pocket and backed off from the ledge, reflecting light into the crevices as he played it over the stone face. He got the thermometer from the tackle box, shook it down, and pressed the tip into the ground at the face of the ledge. After a minute he withdrew it, squinting. "Eight-two," he said. "Getting too hot even in the shade. They'll move back deeper into the rocks and not come out till night. Let's quit and have lunch." He drifted over to the tackle box and removed the pocketknife as he replaced the thermometer. He cut the mouse free, pocketing the knife, nail, and string.

They walked back along the riverbank to the place where they had left the lunch bucket. Joshua carried the plastic wastebasket. He could hear a sibilant whisper as the snake shifted on the bottom of the basket, and occasionally a muffled rattle penetrated the thick plastic.

"Is this a good one?" Joshua asked as they made their way along.

"It won't win anything," Todd said, a deprecating tone to his voice. "It'll take at least a six-footer to win length. It's not old enough to have a big rattle. Put up a good fight, though," he added, voice brightening.

They reached the cottonwood and settled down in the shade against the trunk, facing the river. Todd opened the lunch bucket and dispensed cold fried chicken, a Tupperware container full of cucumber slices, and fresh peaches. They shared the thermos of iced lemonade, passing it back and forth. After a lunch filled with small talk, filling in some details about each other's lives, they washed their hands in the river and then sat on the sandbank under the cottonwood. The ground was dappled with sunlight, and the mosaic pattern of shadows changed constantly as the wind shifted the small branches and the leaves shuddered. Wisps of cotton floated in the air. Occasionally a frog croaked from somewhere along the bank. They watched the river in silence. A never-ending sweep of brown water, the ebb and flow of merging currents, the occasional splash of a channel cat, the ripple of an undercurrent.

"I never knew my dad," Todd finally said. His tone was informational. The regret voiced was intellectual, not emotional.

"That's too bad." Joshua knew what was coming. Dreaded it. With Claudia he was almost there. Now with Todd there was this new dimension. Somehow he was more than Tom Bishop's son. It was as though a young Tom Bishop had materialized on the scene.

"All I know is pictures of him," Todd went on. "Things my grandfolks told me. Jess Walters and I have talked some. Lots of people in town knew Dad, but it's like talking about ancient history with them. And Mom, hell, she won't even talk about it." He glanced at Joshua. "She's talked more since I came home than she has since I can remember. She told me last night she thought you and Dad were a lot alike. She said you were twin sons of different mothers."

Joshua felt the fear graze the edges of his mind. Like the night after he went back to the motel and nearly packed up and left. My God, were he and Tom Bishop really twin sons of different mothers? Was Claudia abyss or sanctuary? She seemed to peel away his public self layer by layer and peer into his soul. To know his angels and his demons.

"Are you okay, Josh?"

Joshua turned. Todd was staring at him with puzzlement. "Sure, I'm okay. Your mother is very perceptive. Tom and I were alike at least in some ways."

"Were you and Dad good friends, or did you just know each other a little bit?"

"Good friends." Joshua nodded slightly for emphasis. "We hit it off as soon as we met."

"What was he like?" Todd asked. "What was my dad really like?"

Joshua thought a moment. Where to begin? Or to begin at all? Maybe just slough it off. Better for me. Better for Todd. Better for

Claudia. For everyone. Instead he said, "I think he was a lot like you."

"That's what Mom says."

"Well, two votes must make it unanimous."

"In what way am I like him?" Todd turned an eager, inquiring face to Joshua.

Joshua shrugged. "However you are, that's like him." He saw the disappointment in Todd's eyes. It wasn't enough. "You look like him," he added, "but it's more than that. The smile. The quickness. A hell-for-leather cheerfulness. An enthusiasm for life. A risk-taker." Joshua stopped, uneasy. Not sure if he was describing Tom Bishop the way he was, or the way he wanted him to be. It got fuzzy after all these years. At least some parts of it got fuzzy. Some of it remained with a dreadful clarity. Joshua picked up a smooth river stone from the sand, drew back, and tossed it to the middle of the river. He watched the splash.

"Did he ever talk about me?" Todd asked.

"Oh, yes. Lots of times."

"What'd he say?"

Bishop studied the snapshot a moment and then handed it to Joshua. "Would you look at that little piss ant."

"He said you were a really neat kid." Joshua paused. "You know, you said you knew your dad mostly through photographs. That's really the way he knew you. From your mom's letters and photographs."

"What was it like in Vietnam?" Todd asked. "The war, I mean."

Joshua looked away. Which war, he thought. It's like the ocean floor. A different war for every acre. The early war in the sixties, the late war in the seventies. The delta war, the highland war, the city war, the coastline war, the river war, the highway war, the naval war, the air war. Joshua half smiled to himself—psy war.

How could he explain it to Todd? Jungles, mountains, rice paddies. Army base camp with thirty thousand men, jungle outpost with twelve. West Point "ring knocker," regular army, two-year draftee. Infantry grunt, Marine rifleman, Special Forces trooper.

Point man for the LURPS, ARVN adviser, requisition officer for air conditioners in Saigon. Chopper pilot with his eye on the yellow smoke, Phantom pilot with his afterburner kicked in, B-52 pilot with his briefcase. Professional, serious citizen soldier, incompetent, hero, coward, killer, crazy, adrenaline freak, druggie. Short-timer with the dreadlies who crosses every single day off the calendar in his helmet liner, war junkie who extends his tour. What was the war like in Vietnam?

Joshua looked back at Todd. "Hard to say. Like all wars, I guess, mixed up."

"Did my dad want to be in Vietnam?"

Joshua smiled. "That's easy," he said. "Your dad definitely wanted to be in Nam."

Todd picked up a green cottonwood leaf that had drifted to the ground. He folded it in half, stretched it taut between his hands, held the end of it to his lips, and blew. The free edges vibrated together and screeched like a sour fiddle note. "How come? How come he wanted to be in Vietnam?"

Joshua studied Todd. All arms and legs and lean bulk. Face browned by the burning edge of the Kansas sun. Clear-eyed. Steady gaze. Untouched, really, by life. Tom Bishop, no doubt, at sixteen. Not Tom Bishop at twenty-six. "Do you know anything about Vietnam, Todd?"

"Not much."

Joshua tilted his head back and contemplated the sky. It arched overhead, a cloudless azure expanse. Beyond the far riverbank, a small kingbird, yellow breast flashing in the sun, dove on a large crow, driving it away from its territory. Joshua turned back to Todd. "Do you know what we were doing in Vietnam?"

"Not really."

"Do you know where it is?"

"Sort of."

Joshua nodded. Comprehension without comprehending. Todd Bishop's father was dead. And it was not that Todd didn't understand the complexities of the circumstances. He didn't even know the circumstances. And he didn't know them because everyone, from his mother to his government, contrived to foster the illusion that it was something that hadn't happened. That Vietnam didn't exist. Like a relative in the state asylum. A public embarrassment.

A private disgrace. This was no time for a history lesson. And no time for private cynicism. Is there such a thing as a simple explanation? A simple truth?

"Your dad was in Vietnam for two reasons, Todd," Joshua said slowly. "First, he was a patriot. Corny, right? Well, it's not a bad word, although it's not a part of our vocabulary anymore. The government decided it was important for America to be in Vietnam. They needed men to do it. Your dad was one of the men who did the job." Never mind, Joshua thought, that the government didn't know its ass from the Mekong Delta. "And second," Joshua went on, "your dad wanted to be where the action was." That at least is simple and true enough. Then an explanation occurred to him. "He probably went to Nam for the same reasons you hunt rattlesnakes." Not bad, Joshua congratulated himself. Besides, he thought sardonically, there are some similarities. They're both slant-eyed, slope-headed sonsabitches, *and I wish we'd whipped their ass!* The last was an inner silent, shrill scream. He was shocked at the vehemence of the emotion. The passion. After all these years. Is that the hook? The bitter, humiliating ignominy of defeat. Perhaps. That, and the utter uselessness of it.

"Speaking of snakes, look there!" Todd's voice was an exuberant, disbelieving cry.

For a moment Joshua felt disoriented. Jerked out of his own painful introspection, he realized that what was of vital importance to him was of only passing interest to Todd. He gathered his wits and looked where Todd was pointing. Down the bank near some sparse ground cover. He could see nothing.

"The sly, secretive son of a bitch." Todd jumped up and grabbed the forked rod. "Bring the tongs!"

Joshua followed him down the sandbank. Todd moved carefully into an area of scattered creeper vines and seedlings. He stopped and pointed. Joshua followed his finger, still not seeing what Todd was trying to point out.

"Sidewinder," Todd said. "Just the head."

Joshua squinted. He saw a narrow, wedge-shaped gray-brown head just poking up out of the dry sand.

"Sitting down over there on the bank," Todd explained, "I had just the right angle to see his head. Pure luck." He hefted the rod in his hand, fork angled toward the ground. "They burrow into the

sand where there's a little shade so they don't get too hot. They just
leave their head out, waiting for a mouse or something to come by.
'Course if a man comes by, they'll accommodate him." Todd slowly
circled the area where the snake lay buried. "They're dangerous
and fast," Todd muttered, "so be careful."

"What do you want me to do?"

"Let's stay on opposite sides of him so we can keep him headed
off if he breaks loose."

Joshua circled away from Todd, feeling a little foolish and uncertain. A novice. Greenhorn. Cherry. Fresh meat. FNG—fuckin' new
guy. Like before your first firefight. Todd leaned forward and
stretched his big frame toward the snake, aiming the pipe. He
lunged, thrusting the pipe at the snake, trying to fork it just behind
the head. The snake recoiled, snapping its head backward with
blurring speed. Todd missed and buried the end of the pipe six
inches in the soft sand. The ground quivered, an agitated shifting
of fine grains of sand as the sidewinder wriggled free from its
hiding place.

"Here he comes," Todd sang out, his voice shrill, a mix of eagerness and fear.

The snake was only about thirty inches long. Its slender body a
patchwork of gray and brown. It moved across the sand toward a
tangle of brush and driftwood cover. It didn't crawl, it walked,
throwing loops of its body forward one after another in a rapid
series of movements that propelled it swiftly across the sand. Its
forward motion was sideways, giving the illusion that it was moving
off at an angle to the direction it really intended to go. The total
effect was both fascinating and chilling.

Todd scurried around to cut off the snake, and slammed the rod
to the sand in front of it. The sidewinder lashed out, struck the rod
with a hiss, and then recoiled. It shrunk backward, then moved off
at a tangent, roiling over the sand with deadly grace. Joshua made
a grab with the tongs, came up empty. The sidewinder slashed at
the metal blades, a shuddering strike that Joshua felt with jarring
force in his forearms. Looping backward, the snake stopped in the
center of the sand bank, not coiled, but drawn together in a compact woven mass, like a compression spring. It waited, motionless.

"Watch it, Josh," Todd cautioned. "He can hit you at four or five
feet."

"How about we let this one go?" Joshua murmured.

"You kidding? This one's a winner."

They edged forward, crouched, leaning forward slightly, tense, wary, eyes riveted on the snake. Without warning, from its frozen reptilian stance the sidewinder struck at Joshua. A lightning thrust, straight as an arrow, a full foot longer than its outstretched length. Joshua flung himself backward, an instantaneous reaction as though it were without his own volition. A pure reflex for survival. The sidewinder missed, dropped to the ground, body compact, already poised for a second strike.

Todd lunged forward and forked the sidewinder about a foot behind the head, driving the fork into the sand. The snake turned, a writhing blur, scattering sand like ocean spray, and struck the rod. Joshua moved in quickly, grabbed the snake with the tongs a few inches behind the head, and slammed it to the ground. The snake thrashed savagely for a moment, then lay still, pinned between the two implements. Joshua and Todd maintained a tight grip on the snake, not daring to relax. Breathing hard, dripping sweat, they looked at each other across four feet of sun-baked sand. Todd grinned. Joshua stared back, haunted by the likeness of Tom Bishop. Slowly he smiled and nodded his head, not necessarily in agreement, but at least in understanding.

Suddenly the midday silence was shattered by the crack of a rifle. A crisp, sharp report that reverberated up and down the riverbed. The sidewinder was cut in half, back severed, bloody stumps writhing convulsively in a moment's death agony before they dropped, flaccid and still, to the sand.

Joshua flung himself sideways and hit the ground, elbows and knees working like pistons. He propelled himself toward the nearest cover, a fallen tree, the bare log a satiny driftwood gray from sun and wind and rain, and burrowed into the hot sand against it.

The bullet snapped past Joshua's ear with a vicious sucking sound. He ducked below the lip of the trench, ripped the taped clips out of the magazine well of his M-16, and reversed them. Nungs on either side of him were slammed backward against the far side of the trench. He reared up and fired point-blank. Saw the uniformed figures fall in front of him. But others swarmed out of the night

and took their place, clawing their way over the concertina wire.
They had faces now, contorted and harsh and twisted. Sensing a
line about to crack, the North Vietnamese hurled themselves
against his position.

"They're going to do it this time," Joshua grunted through
clenched teeth. "Oh, Jesus, they're going to do it." He emptied the
clip at them.

North Vietnamese assault troops began dropping into the trench
around him. A soldier lunged toward him, bayonet on his Russian
carbine leveled at his chest. Joshua stumbled backward, jerking
frantically at the .45 on his hip. With great clarity he saw he could
not clear the pistol in time.

Joshua heard Todd and Travis Rawlins arguing about the sidewinder. Todd was angrily protesting that Travis had shot the rattler out of spite.

"Hell, Todd," Rawlins said, voice a patronizing drawl, "I saved
you and your momma's friend's lives."

"You're not even supposed to be on our place!" Todd yelled.

"Your momma don't own this river!"

The conversation stopped. Joshua lifted his face from the sand to
see Todd and Rawlins staring at him. Todd, just now aware that
Joshua was pressed against the ground in the cover of the log,
stared in disbelief. Rawlins looked at him with mocking condescen-
sion.

Joshua felt his face flush crimson. He got to one knee and brushed
the sand from his face and arms and chest. The tremor started in
his right hand. He tried to suppress it, but failed, and the fine
trembling, barely perceptible, spread like the ague to the rest of
his body. It wasn't an uncontrollable shake, just a spasmodic quak-
ing, like shivering in the cold. He walked toward Todd and Rawlins. They stood a few feet apart on a barren sandbank about a
dozen yards from the river. Todd's stance was belligerent, feet
spread, fists clenched. Rawlins stood relaxed, Stetson back on his
head, Winchester resting on its stock by his foot, the muzzle held
loosely in his fingers. Joshua ignored Todd and stopped about a foot
in front of Rawlins, crowding him a little. He was still trembling,
although the spasm was passing.

Rawlins didn't move. He smiled, derision etched in every feature of his face. "You're about as nervous as a itty-bitty dawg."

Joshua flicked out his right hand and snatched the rifle from Rawlins' loose grasp. At the same time he drove a knee upward into his crotch. Rawlins fell backward, collapsing to his knees, hands clutching his groin, a nauseous moan forced from his lips. Joshua worked the lever action of the .30-30, ejecting the empty brass casing and snapping a shell into the firing chamber. He leveled the muzzle at Rawlins' chest.

Rawlins stared at Joshua, unblinking, hands still clutching his privates. His face was ashen and beaded with sweat but without a visible trace of fear.

Joshua swiveled the rifle a fraction of an inch and squeezed the trigger. The round whizzed past Rawlins' head and ricocheted with a receding whine into the distance. Rawlins didn't flinch. Joshua chambered another round.

"Josh . . ." Todd began.

Before he could finish, Joshua worked the lever action in a succession of rapid movements. He ejected all of the copper-jacketed bullets in a cascading arc. They fell to the sand, glinting gold in the bright sunlight. Joshua gripped the rifle barrel with both hands, lifted it high over his head like a club. He paused, then spun on his heel and hurled the Winchester into the middle of the Cimarron. It sailed end over end and dropped with a splash into the muddy current.

Joshua turned away and started up the rocky bluff out of the riverbed. When he reached the Case tractor he kept on going, cutting through the wheat fields until he reached the Bishop farmhouse.

Todd was sitting on the side stoop, waiting for him. He squinted his eyes in the bright sun and watched Joshua move between the rows of wheat in the field beyond the shed. He jumped off the stoop and met him where the field bordered the drive. Todd looked at Joshua a moment, a mixture of anxiety and curiosity. The anxiety took precedence. "You okay?"

Joshua's shirt was dark with perspiration. He was breathing a little heavily from his hike, and his face glistened with sweat and sunburn. "Yeah, I'm okay." They walked in silence toward the stoop. Joshua saw Claudia watching them through the screen door.

Todd's curiosity got the best of him. "What happened back there?"

"I got angry."

"No, before that."

"I got scared," Joshua said abruptly, "and then I got angry."

"How come?"

"Let's drop it, Todd."

Crestfallen, Todd stepped up on the stoop. Claudia swung the door open for them, and they trailed into the kitchen. Claudia handed Joshua a towel and washrag. In the bathroom he removed his shirt, soused his face and hair with cold water, and sponged his chest and shoulders. He toweled off slowly and studied his reflection in the mirror. His eyes were drawn to a jagged white four-inch scar along his right chest.

The Bangalore torpedoes exploded in a linear sheet of flame that ripped a wide hole in the concertina wire. The North Vietnamese plunged into the gap.

"Pop the claymores!" Bishop screamed.

Joshua waited. Nothing happened. What the hell was the matter with Manny? The North Vietnamese were through the wire. They leveled their AK-47's and opened up on the trench.

"The claymores!" Bishop screamed again. "Trigger the claymores!"

Joshua hauled himself out of the trench and scrambled across the shell-pocked ground toward the control bunker. Suddenly a searing blow to his chest spun him sideways and flung him to the ground. He gasped, trying to suck air into his lungs, but it was like breathing against the point of a dagger. A whirling black funnel threatened to engulf him. He fought against losing consciousness and sat up. Stared down at his chest, incredulous. A crimson stain slowly spread across the right side of his tiger shirt. He could hear the volume of fire crescendo on the eastern perimeter. He struggled to his feet and stumbled the remaining distance to the control bunker.

Manny Almendarez lay at the entrance to the bunker, his face sheared away by a mortar fragment. Joshua stepped over him and entered the bunker. He flipped the switches for the claymores on the eastern perimeter. A series of jarring explosions shook the ground up and down the line. The trench convulsed as though in the grip of an earthquake. Thousands of steel balls slashed into the North Vietnamese ranks. Shredded enemy bodies—heads, arms, legs, viscera—were hurled backwards into the concertina wire, forming a grisly montage.

Joshua leaned against the sandbagged bunker wall, breathing shallowly to minimize the fire in his side. Slowly he unbuttoned his shirt and exposed a ragged chest wound. Tentatively he placed a finger in the wound and explored it. A wave of pain cascaded over him and the black whirlpool threatened to suck him under again. He paused and waited for his head to clear. Again he probed the wound, forcing his finger into the torn flesh. A groan was forced from between clenched teeth. Smooth, curved, intact rib. Muscle bands resilient between the ribs. A glancing round. He did not have a penetrating chest wound. I'm not going to die, he thought giddily. I'm not going to die. Beads of sweat formed on his forehead. Nausea swept over him and he vomited in a foul rush across his shirt.

Joshua rummaged in a bathroom drawer, found a comb, and combed his hair. He slipped on his shirt and buttoned it as he went back to the kitchen. Claudia handed him a tall glass wet with condensation.

Joshua tilted the glass and took a long, sweet swallow of the lemonade. He drained the glass without taking it from his lips, let out a satisfied sigh, and handed it back. "Thanks." He wiped his lips as he ran his tongue across the bottom of his mustache, tasting the flavor of residual lemonade. "Show me a man with a mustache, and I'll show you what he's had for breakfast."

"More?" Claudia asked. Joshua shook his head and tucked his shirt in his jeans. Claudia leaned back against a kitchen counter and folded her arms across her chest. "Todd told me what happened. I can't believe Travis would even come out here. It worries me." She studied Joshua. "Are you all right?"

"Sure."

"Is that the way it works? The anger and the violence?"

"Yes. When Travis shot the snake, for a brief moment I was back in the Nam. Under fire."

"Would you have really hurt Travis? I mean, could you . . ."

"Have killed him?" Joshua finished.

"Yes."

Joshua shook his head noncommittally. "I don't know. I don't think so. When I went after Travis and took the thirty-thirty, I was right there on the riverbank."

"And?" Claudia asked.

"Well, I wasn't caught in the flashback. I'm not some schizophrenic veteran who believes himself to be under attack and wipes out his family."

"That's good."

Joshua smiled. "Yeah. I'm not a crazy son of a bitch. Just a hostile son of a bitch."

"Did you ever doubt it?"

"Sometimes." Joshua studied Claudia as she leaned against the counter. She reached up with her right hand and drew the hair from the side of her face. As he observed the gesture with a sense of familiarity, it sobered him. She was the first person he might consider a friend in more than a decade. She and Charlie Wilson. Is that what it's all about? To come ten thousand miles and twelve years to Plains, Kansas, to make two friends and put an end to Vietnam?

Suddenly the music crashed down the stairwell and echoed through the house. Piercing Moog synthesizer, strident lead guitar, driving bass, battering percussion. Joshua glanced up at the ceiling and imagined he could see it shake. He looked at Claudia and silently mouthed the word "Todd" as he pointed questioningly upstairs.

"In his room!" Claudia said, raising her voice above the hard rock. "You hurt his feelings."

"How so?" Joshua hollered.

"When you shut him out," Claudia explained loudly. "He didn't mean to pry. He only wanted to know if you were okay and what had happened at the river."

Joshua nodded. "I'm sorry. Let me talk to him."

Claudia went into the dining room and led the way upstairs.

Joshua followed her down a narrow hallway with wallpaper of tiny, red roses. She knocked sharply on a door at the end of the hall.

"It's open!" Todd yelled.

Claudia turned the handle and pushed open the door. The music blasted their eardrums. Joshua peered into the room. Todd was stretched out on a double bed covered by a quilt. He was in stocking feet, boots kicked off on a braided-rag throw rug beside the bed, and his long frame reached from headboard to footboard.

"Mind if I come in?" Joshua's voice was almost a bellow to defeat the amplified sound.

Todd waved him in.

Joshua stepped into the room. Not only the music but the heat overpowered him. Despite the fact that there were windows on two sides of the room, one that overlooked the side yard, and one that opened out over the roof of the front porch, it was still hot. Curtains fluttered in the afternoon breeze, but it seemed only to stir the heat. Joshua located the stereo and triggered the reject on the turntable. He put a finger in his ear and shook it. The quiet was like a release from pain. He turned back to Todd. "I thought maybe we could talk."

"You didn't much want to a while ago." Todd's voice was sullen.

"I've changed my mind," Joshua replied easily.

He walked to the foot of the bed and surveyed the room. The wallpaper had disappeared under posters. Styx, Kiss, Police, Mick Jagger, Farrah Fawcett-Majors, Morgan Fairchild, Loni Anderson, Christie Brinkley on the ceiling. "How do you sleep," Joshua muttered, to no one in particular. There was a poster of James Dean and a great poster of Clark Gable as Rhett Butler. Todd had affixed an Oly pin to his cutaway coat.

Joshua looked at Claudia. She was leaning against the doorjamb. Her facial expression didn't change, but her eyes said it all. Here was Tom Bishop's shrine. Joshua slowly turned on his heel. He took in the athletic photographs of Tom Bishop, as well as his 49er poster, which adorned the wall beside the bed. Then he turned to the bric-a-brac shelves on the opposite wall and moved closer to examine their contents. A plastic dime-store frame held a five-by-seven enlargement of a black and white snapshot. He picked up the frame. They were all there. Porter, Almendarez, Smallcanyon, DuBoise, Finelli. Bishop. All the rest. Everyone except Wirtz. He had snapped the picture with Bishop's camera. A-two-one-niner. Finest soldiers in a useless war. They were in jungle fatigues, crammed into Bishop's hootch at SFOB. All smiles except Small-canyon. Jimmy didn't smile much.

Joshua replaced the picture. He picked up a beret. The green cloth was faded and soiled. The leather headband stained with sweat. Silver captain's bars, dulled and scratched, were pinned to the flash of the Fifth Special Forces Group. He crumpled the beret lightly in his hand, then smoothed it out and returned it to its place on the shelf. Next to it was a square of corkboard. Affixed to it was the Special Forces shoulder patch, an upright dagger with the blade crossed by three lightning bolts, and a pair of jump wings, the rifle badge of a combat infantryman, and the Special Forces crest, crossed arrows on a scroll with the words *"De Oppresso Liber."* Beside the corkboard was a familiar blue leather case. Joshua opened it and gazed at the Distinguished Service Cross. He trailed his fingers across the bit of bronze and colored ribbon, and then snapped the case shut.

Next to the DSC was another plastic frame which held a Xeroxed copy of a typed sheet of paper. Joshua picked up the frame, angled it to screen out the glare, and read silently.

> Headquarters United States Army, Pacific
> General Orders Number 162
> The following award is announced.
> Bishop, Thomas T.   05412936   Captain
> Infantry United States Army
> Award of the Distinguished Service Cross

Joshua scanned the citation. It was all there. All the buzzwords and catchphrases of military prose: extraordinary heroism in connection with a military operation . . . armed hostile force . . . continually exposed himself to hostile fire . . . complete disregard for his own safety . . . courage under fire . . . example for many other heroic acts . . . source of inspiration to his comrades . . . extraordinary heroism and gallantry in action in keeping with the highest tradition of the United States Army . . . reflect great credit upon himself and the military service.

Well, Joshua thought, just because it's contrived doesn't mean it's

not true. He placed the framed citation back on the shelf. Next to
it was the final item. Another framed snapshot, this one in color,
showed Bishop standing outside his hootch with a spider monkey
perched on his shoulder. "Deros," Joshua said aloud as he turned
away from the shelf.

"What's that?" Todd asked.

"The monkey's name."

"That's a weird name."

"Weird to you. Not to anyone in the Nam." Joshua went over to
the window that looked out on the porch roof and sat on the edge
of the sill. "It's a word formed by joining together the first letters
of several words," he explained. "Deros stood for 'date estimated
return overseas.' Every man in Nam knew his Deros. That was the
day he rotated home. Back to the World. Mine was June twenty-
fifth."

Todd swung his feet over the side of the bed and sat up, intrigued
by this bit of trivia. He went to the shelf and picked up the picture.
"Was Deros my dad's monkey?" His sulkiness began to fade.

"Well, he was kind of a team monkey. Porter picked him up in
a Cholon market when he was down in Saigon for some slack time.
But your dad messed with him a lot." Joshua looked up at Claudia,
who still stood in the doorway. "He was the one who thought we
should get Deros jump-qualified."

Todd carried the picture back to the bed, laid it on the quilt, and
plopped down beside it. He studied it a moment, then looked up,
waiting.

"Your dad didn't think it was right that an Airborne outfit should
have a straight-leg monkey," Joshua went on. "So he planned to
jump him from a helicopter. He rigged up a little harness for Deros
and attached a flare parachute. I told him I thought the monkey
would panic, climb up the shroud lines to the canopy, and collapse
it." Joshua raised an index finger and rapidly plunged it toward the
oak floor. "Streamer in, and splat!" He paused. "Well, your dad said
he figured he could get around that. He went to the mailroom and
borrowed a little canvas mail pouch. We put Deros in the harness,
then slipped him in the mail pouch and tightened it up around his
neck. We went over to the unit helipads and got a guy we'd flown
with a lot to take us up. Your dad dropped Deros out the hatch at
about a thousand feet."

"What happened?" Todd asked.

"Well, it was a long time before that monkey would let your dad close to him. And the next time they used that mail pouch they delivered somebody some monkey shit."

Todd and Claudia laughed. Todd bounded off the bed and returned the photograph to its place on the shelf. "Is that really a true story?" he asked, skeptical, but wanting it to be true.

"Word of honor," Joshua said solemnly. He glanced at Claudia. Her eyes were sympathetic. "Claudia," he said, standing and slipping his hands in the pockets of his jeans, "why don't you let us be alone for a while." As Claudia pulled the bedroom door closed behind her, Joshua crossed the room to the side window. He drew the fluttering curtain aside and stared at the endless Kansas prairie. There was a softness to the gold expanse of wheat as it shone in the afternoon sun. A pair of hawks wheeled effortlessly in the cloudless sky beyond the section line road. Four of Vanlandingham's combines were in the near field. They churned through the wheat, trailing dust and wheat chaff. A wheat truck followed slowly in their wake, waiting to collect the grain.

"Every October," Joshua began slowly, "I have an anxiety attack." He turned away from the window and looked at Todd, who still stood by the bric-a-brac shelves. "I have a diffuse, vague, unfocused fear. My pulse races. I feel short of breath. Light-headed. My palms sweat." Joshua unconsciously wiped his palms on his jeans. "I can't sleep. Or eat. I'm sick to my stomach."

Todd stared soberly at Joshua.

Joshua walked over to the shelf and picked up the photograph of the team in Bishop's hootch. "That was the month we went in with the Nungs to hold Thang Duc. We lost the entire team except for me and Wyatt Porter and Eddie DuBoise." Joshua pointed to Porter and DuBoise in the photograph. "Everyone else on your dad's team was killed. We also lost almost all of another team that was at Thang Duc. And most of the 'Yards and Nungs."

"Did you hold that place?"

"Oh, yes. That's why your dad got this." Joshua picked up the case with the DSC and opened it.

"What did he do exactly?"

Joshua nodded at the framed citation. "Everything it says there. And more. Your dad was the heart and soul of A-two-one-niner."

He looked at Todd. "Just like the captain of a football team." He placed the leather case with the DSC back on the shelf, and went over and sat in a straight-backed chair near a small wooden writing desk. "I somehow feel that pressure every October. Like a Canada goose whose biological clock tells it when to migrate, I feel the pull of Thang Duc every October."

Todd returned to the bed and sat on the edge. He nodded at Joshua sympathetically, not fully understanding.

"Sometimes I relive it, or remember it, in little bits and pieces. And that's what happened today."

"At the river?"

"Yes. When Rawlins shot the sidewinder, I was back in Nam. Looking for cover. Scared to death."

"But it didn't last very long," Todd said.

"No," Joshua replied. "You think in milliseconds. But you feel in eons." He paused a moment. "I didn't mean to shut you out. I was embarrassed. Angry. Frightened."

"That's all right. It just sort of hurt my feelings." Todd shuffled his feet on the floor. "Like I was a dumb kid or something."

"Well, it wasn't a put-down. I just turn in on myself. I stopped reaching out to people years ago." They sat in silence for a moment or two. A bird could be heard in one of the huge cottonwood trees outside the window. Insects hummed.

Finally Todd spoke. "But, Josh, what about Mom and me?"

Joshua studied Todd with wonder and regret. He was big and young and energetic. Spirit not yet crushed by adversity. Will not yet diminished by defeat. Hope not yet eroded by fear. Optimism not dimmed by apathy. Joshua shook his head. "Yes," he said, "I have reached out to you and your mother. Let's go find her. I'll take you both out to supper."

"Take Mom," Todd replied. "I'm going to meet some guys in Plains and go snorkeling."

"In Plains?"

Todd grinned. "Come on, Josh," he said with sixteen-year-old leering insouciance. "Girls! When I come home tonight, my face is going to look like a glazed doughnut."

CHAPTER TEN

Joshua and Claudia drove to Jackfork. They took the Toyota and Joshua insisted that he drive. They angled southwest toward the Oklahoma panhandle, driving out of the Kansas wheat country and leaving the vast grain fields behind. When they crossed the state line the landscape changed. Fields were barren and the black topsoil gave way to red dirt. The incessant sweep of the wind scoured knolls down to hardpan and sifted the dirt into finely scalloped drifts. Occasionally a ravine was gouged out of the ground by flash-flood runoff, and the earth's crust appeared cracked. Arthritic mesquite trees clung desperately to the soil and mistletoe parasitized their gnarled limbs. Occasionally a wasted and weathered house squatted on a played-out farm and defied extinction. Joshua expected at any moment to see Tom Joad materialize by the side of the road.

Suddenly, as though God had lifted a curse, they drove out of the badlands and the earth was green. Small farms and ranches appeared. They were, if not flourishing, at least not suffering the calamitous ruin of their neighbors just to the north. Jackfork was the trade center for this agricultural area. It was about three times the size of Plains, but about a third as prosperous, with half the style and none of the charm. A community of five thousand people, it was built around a town square. The square was stark. It appeared to be the geometric center of Jackfork, but beyond that utilitarian function served neither to beautify the town nor provide a focus of community life.

Joshua pulled the Toyota up against the curb on the near side of the square. They got out. The sun had set and the western sky had the rose flush that preceded twilight, but the day's heat lingered. Joshua looked around, taking in the storefronts facing the square. "Where do we eat?" he asked. "Picnic in the park here?" He nodded at the town square, devoid of trees and flowers, with the Johnson grass fighting for its life against the crab grass.

Claudia smiled and pointed across the square. "The Cattleman," she said. "It's in the Slater Hotel."

Joshua followed her to a two-story porticoed building of salmon-colored sandstone. Affixed to the balcony railing that rimmed the portico was a fading sign: THE SLATER HOTEL, EST. 1882, PROPRIE-TOR HORACE SLATER. Joshua nodded appreciatively.

"Tom loved the steaks here."

"I know."

Joshua went over to where the C rations were stacked in the corner of the teamhouse. He rummaged through a case until he found a can of fruit cocktail. He returned to the table, turned a chair back-ward, and sat down. He cut the lid away from the can and, being careful of the ragged metal edges, slowly drank off the thick, sweet syrup. He picked up a spoon, examined it in the dim light to see if it was passably clean, and then began to dip out the maraschino cherries. He discarded them into a chipped coffee cup.

Bishop sat across the table from Joshua. He put a lump of C-4 in a Kerr lid, lit it with his lighter, and then placed an open can of beans and mother-fuckers on top of the lid. In a few moments the contents of the can were bubbling. He skimmed the grease off the top with his spoon and began to eat. "This shit's awful. Even heated it's awful."

Joshua looked up. The heavy syrup dribbled down his chin, eroding a path in the red dirt ground into his beard. He wiped his chin with the back of his hand. "C rats or gourmet delicacies," he said, "it all looks the same twenty-four hours later."

Bishop paused, spoon halfway to his mouth. "Pot roast, baked potatoes, and pickled peaches."

"Pork loin roast, parsleyed new potatoes, and orange-cranberry sauce," Joshua replied.

"Fried chicken, pan gravy on homemade bread, corn on the cob, and buttermilk pie."

"Filet, rare, with mushroom caps, at Lindy's in Richmond."

"Porterhouse steak, home fries, beans with salsa, and Texas toast at the Cattleman in Jackfork," Bishop said.

"Barbecue ribs from Dickies in Pine Mountain," Joshua countered.

"Corned beef on dark rye with Monterey jack cheese at Alfredo's Deli in San Francisco."

"Peanut butter on waffles with maple syrup, sausage, and ice-cold milk."

"Homemade doughnuts hot out of the deep-fat fryer, with cinnamon and sugar," Bishop replied.

"Tacos and sour cream enchiladas, sopaipillas with honey, and sangria from El Torro in Fayetteville."

"Bacon cheeseburger and a Budweiser from the Jayhawker Bar in Lawrence."

Joshua thought a moment. *"Pistachio nuts,"* he said, *in mock seriousness.*

Bishop spread his hands expansively in front of him. *"Clean, round-eyed pussy,"* he said. *"Table stuff."*

Joshua and Claudia entered the lobby. It was clotted with the smell of linseed oil and cigar smoke. They passed a dark oak registration desk that was served by a wrinkled octogenarian with glasses propped up on a bald head mottled with liver spots. To the left was the entrance to the hotel bar, the Remuda. To the right was the Cattleman. They were shown to a linen-covered table situated in front of one of the large plate-glass windows. As Joshua studied the menu, he looked around the dining room and was agreeably surprised. Someone with taste had restored the room to its 1880's decor. Antique cut-glass chandeliers, wainscoted walls in dark oak, fretwork bordering the ceiling.

Claudia ordered the prime rib, lady's cut. Joshua ordered Tom Bishop's favorite. What the hell. Porterhouse steak, home fries, beans and salsa, and Texas toast. Tom was right. It had to be about the best meal Joshua had ever eaten. They lingered over coffee and pecan pie.

"Thank you for talking to Todd today," Claudia said. "I know it meant a lot to him."

"I was glad to. He was probably owed an explanation after the incident on the river."

"Well, he wasn't owed it, but it was a friendly thing to do."

"That's quite a room he has," Joshua said. "The Tom Bishop Hall of Fame."

Claudia's voice was like stone. "I don't like it," she said. "It brings up all the bad memories." She looked at Joshua across the rim of her coffee cup. "And it glorifies war."

"Claudia," Joshua murmured, "war may be hell, but you might as well accept the fact that there are people who want to go there." He paused, letting his words sink in. "You won't get me in an argument over the morality of war or its place as an instrument of national policy, but in a world of meat-eaters there are times when force is necessary."

"You'll never convince me."

"I'm not trying to." Joshua sipped his coffee. "Besides, Todd may need to remember his daddy like that. After all, it's really all he ever had of him."

"Perhaps," Claudia replied. "But another thing that worries me about it is that Tom is bigger than life to Todd. It's tough to follow in the footsteps of a legend."

"Well," Joshua mused, "maybe it's more like if you found out you were related to Abraham Lincoln. It's a source of pride, not pressure." Claudia nodded. "The one trouble with legends," Joshua went on, "is that they're well protected."

"What do you mean?"

"It's disillusioning to find out your idols have feet of clay. Todd will never see, or know, Tom's failures. He'll never feel his bite. The ordinary things every child must learn about a parent. The temper, pettiness, anger, impatience, poor judgment. Tom's protected from all of that."

"Yes, that. But better for Todd to have seen Tom's feet of clay than never to have seen him at all."

Joshua was silent a moment. "I guess I expected *you* to have the shrine. Not Todd."

"I know you did. I felt it Sunday evening. When you saw the single picture of Tom on the fireplace mantel."

Joshua pushed aside the empty dessert plate and motioned to the waitress for more coffee. "Don't you have a memorial for Tom?"

"Yes, I do. Every Memorial Day I go to Tom's grave at the Maple Grove Cemetery and remember. Todd remembers him alive. That's his need. I remember him dead. That's my need." Claudia stirred some sugar in her coffee. "After Tom was killed I grieved. God, I didn't think it would ever stop. It crushed me. Then came the depression, a never-ending weariness and fatigue. After that, the frustration and the anger. Well," Claudia added, jaw set, "I learned to cope. I worked hard. I learned to farm. I raised Todd. Life goes on." Suddenly, unexpectedly, Claudia's eyes brimmed bright with tears.

Joshua felt like he was privy to some hidden grief. "Does it really, Claudia?" He searched her eyes, glistening with tears that wouldn't fall.

Claudia regained her composure, took a sip of coffee, then carefully replaced the china cup on the saucer. "No," she said, "in some ways it doesn't. There has been a great void in my life since Tom was killed. I know I have laughter to give, thoughts to share, secrets to tell, a body to be touched." Claudia swept her hair back from her face. "But that means someone has to be there. And no one is. I've not allowed it. I tried to make the farm and Todd enough. But there's always an emptiness, an ache." She looked at Joshua and studied his face. "What do you do with the empty places in your life?"

Joshua looked away from Claudia's gaze and stared at the town square. It was illuminated now by old street lamps. It looked much better at night. Quaint. Not as barren and forbidding. He felt the longing return for something more, but knew it couldn't happen. He looked back at Claudia. "Stuff old newspapers in the cracks," he said.

Claudia reached out a hand and touched Joshua's where it rested on the tablecloth. "Josh, let's both put to rest whatever has crippled us from the past."

Joshua withdrew his hand. Claudia's touch didn't bring closeness, it emphasized the distance. He knew that he could free Claudia from her past. Her life with Tom would have its conclusion. But it would close off the future he felt her hinting at. "Tom is dead, Claudia," he said firmly. "Your life with Tom didn't vanish. It ended with him permanently and forever dead. I saw him die."

They left the dining room and went across the lobby to the Remuda. The bar was not large, but had been decorated to equal the style and taste of the Cattleman. It was finished in dark oak, polished brass, cut glass, and wall-mounted gaslights. A large original Remington oil was mounted over the bar. The only other concessions to the twentieth century were a jukebox and a small wood parquet dance floor. Joshua and Claudia took chairs at a table, ordered a Heineken and a vodka collins with a twist. Joshua scanned the patrons. The crowd was small. Cowboys, farmhands, town folk. Quiet and well behaved. The dance floor was empty, but Claudia said she wanted to dance. Joshua said yes, but only slow dancing to sad songs full of heartache and desire. Virtually the entire selection on the jukebox was country and western. They fed it a handful of quarters.

Joshua followed Claudia to the dance floor as the first record began to play. She turned to face him. He stopped, discomfited, full of both misgiving and longing. Claudia stood there, waiting, neither threat nor promise. They studied each other in the reflected shadows of the gaslights. Finally Claudia smiled. Not the dazzling thousand-watter. Tentative. She lifted her arms. Joshua slowly stepped into them. He gently drew her close and they danced.

Lady, Could I Have This Dance? There's a Quarter Moon over a Ten-Cent Town. Here Comes the Hurt Again, but We're Too Far Gone. We could Love the World Away, if we could keep Time in a Bottle, just For the Good Times, it would be Easy from Now On. It's No Good to Watch Those Bridges That We're Burning. Take My Hand for a While, and Help Me Make It Through the Night, but Please Don't Tell Me How the Story Ends.

Joshua and Claudia remained silent during the drive back from Jackfork. Across the moonlit badlands of the Oklahoma panhandle, which might have been a barren planet in the night sky of a distant galaxy, and on into the Kansas wheat country. Much of the grain had been harvested now and the stubble shimmered like white gold, as level as a neatly trimmed lawn. The silence had been one of consensus. They reached the section line road in front of the Bishop farm before Claudia spoke. "I don't want to go home just yet."

"What do you want to do?"

"Go to the river."

Ten minutes later they were standing on the bluff overlooking the bend of the Cimarron. The light from the moon poured down like honey on the river. They made their way down to its banks, felt the river-damp, and inhaled its musky aroma. They stood and listened to the wash and ripple of the current.

Suddenly Claudia began to undress. With impulsive abandon she peeled off her clothes and left them in a heap beside her on the sand. She plunged into the current, wading out a few yards, then turned back to Joshua. "Come on in," she cried. He hesitated. "Come on!" Claudia drew back both hands and flung water at him. "You may have been a hero in Vietnam," she laughed, "but you're a coward here."

Joshua stripped and followed her into the river. The water was cool, but didn't take much getting used to. The riverbed was muddy and he felt silt ooze up between his toes and suck at his feet. They waded out to the middle of the river. It never got more than chest-deep. The sluggish current tugged at them. Claudia settled into the water up to her neck. "Go with it," she said. She let her feet skim the riverbed for balance and let the current sweep her slowly downstream. Joshua sank into the water and followed her along. Cool, buoyant, drifting, weightless, relaxed. The water pulled Claudia along faster. She dug in her heels, let Joshua drift up beside her, and reached out a hand. "Stay with me," she said.

Joshua grasped her hand and the current pulled them along together. Eddies caught them and turned them slowly in the water. Lazy, spinning circles. Feet touched, thighs brushed. Claudia reached out and found Joshua's other hand. They floated facing each other in the current, hands linked. Drifting with the ebb and flow of the river, circling aimlessly, propelled slowly and gently by the cool Cimarron. Claudia drifted in close to Joshua.

"You and Tom did this," Joshua said. It was not a question.

"Yes." They looked at each other, faces damp from ripples and splashes in the current. Sober, reflecting, measuring.

Joshua broke the silence. "Then you know how to get back."
"We walk."

They wedged against the current and drifted in toward the bank.
The warm night air struck their skin as they scrambled out of the
water. Shivering, they made their way in silence along the sandy
riverbank to their clothes. They dressed and climbed the bluff to
the Land Cruiser.

Claudia asked Joshua to come in when he stopped at the farmhouse. He declined.

Joshua drove back along the section line roads toward Plains. Having declined Claudia's invitation, he now regretted it. Desires
grown cold were being rekindled into life. Hopes once safely ban-
ished into emotional exile reappeared. Longings sufficiently repressed, resurfaced. As he drove through the luminous night, his
agitation increased. He pulled the Toyota into the shallow bar
ditch, killed the engine, and sat in silence. The events of the evening spiraled through his mind.

Joshua knew he wanted Claudia. Sexually, of course. But more
than that. He wanted *her.* He wanted the relationship, the
warmth, the sense of belonging and purpose. He was overwhelmed
by an urgent desire for tender connections and deeply planted
roots. Yet the expectancy that stirred within his soul terrified him.
He knew it was impossible to pursue. Nancy had been proof of that.
There had been others, but it had started with Nancy. He had met
her a year after his divorce. Full of life, she had the patience and
persistence to penetrate Joshua's protective shell. She accepted
Joshua's reluctance to share his past. She allowed the relationship
to develop cautiously, at Joshua's pace. As the weeks became
months, Joshua had slowly begun to come alive. They began to talk
of the future.

Six months after they had met they decided to spend the Thanks-
giving holiday at a lodge in the White Mountains in North Carolina.
They had spent their first day walking in the woods. They relished
the crisp bite of the autumn air and the pungent smell of the pine
smoke that hung in a soft haze over the valley. They strolled on a
carpet of red and yellow and orange leaves. They created great
piles of raucous color and buried each other in them, wrestling and

teasing and collapsing in an exhaustion of laughter. That night, full
of wine, their senses glutted on nature's stimuli, they began to
make love. But the more passionately Nancy caressed him, the
more panicky he became.

The intimacy became overpowering, loaded with threat and not
to be trusted. Indelible images of death swarmed over him. He was
tainted, a carrier, contagious. If he got too close he would endanger
ordinary people. Nancy reached up to him. If you feel nothing,
Joshua's atavistic instincts told him, then death will not take place.
She drew him toward her. He must resist the impulses of love, for
they carry within them the threat of annihilation. Joshua forcibly
pushed her away and fled. Weeks later, with Nancy patiently trying
to rebuild the tenuous relationship, the performance was repeated.
Shortly after that, Joshua vanished.

Joshua gripped the steering wheel with both hands and tried to
control the trembling. The years had taught him well. Sex without
connections worked. Relationships didn't. Eroticism had been cap-
tured by death. He slammed a fist against the steering wheel. He
could not, would not, inflict this on Claudia. The evening had been
a crack in time, an aberration. Like Vietnam. There was nothing
before it. And there would be nothing after it.

Joshua drove back to the Wheatlands Motel. It was late when he
pulled into the parking lot. He saw Travis Rawlins' turquoise
pickup on the edge of the lot. Joshua got out of his Toyota, leaned
back against it, and waited. Rawlins got out of his truck. He put
both hands against the door, and deliberately pressed it closed. The
only sound made was the latch as it clicked into place. Joshua could
barely hear it across the parking lot. Rawlins removed a pack of
Camels from his shirt pocket and shook one out. He stood, legs
spread, and deftly struck a wooden match with the edge of his
thumbnail. There was an audible hiss as the phosphorus flared
bright orange in the dark.

"INCOMING!"

———

Rawlins settled his Stetson on his head and stalked across the lot toward Joshua, flicking the match away with thumb and forefinger as he did so. He stopped just short of crowding him, rocked forward a little on his feet, and hooked his thumbs in his belt. There was a heavy moment of silence before Rawlins spoke. "I figure you owe me a rifle." His voice was quiet, but had an edge to it.

Joshua folded his arms. "Do you take MasterCard?"

"I'm gonna take it outta your hide."

Suddenly Joshua was aware of a noise behind him. Feet crunched on the gravel from the corner of the motel. He turned, and as he did so Rawlins threw a sinewy arm around his neck and clamped down like a vise. At the same instant three men rushed him from out of the darkness. Joshua raised his right foot chest-high and slammed it into the gut of the closest man. The man grunted, a sound like a bottle exploding, and collapsed to his knees. The blow toppled Joshua and Rawlins backwards to the ground, and in an instant the other two men were on him and pinned his arms at his sides. Joshua felt his world going black as Rawlins increased the pressure a minute longer, then let go, and the men heaved Joshua erect between them. Joshua's knees buckled. He gasped for air, choking and coughing, fighting the blackness and the head rush. Gradually he caught his breath. His head cleared and he could plant his feet without the parking lot slipping out from under him. His eyes focused on Travis Rawlins, standing just in front of him.

Rawlins had lost his Stetson. His forehead above his sunburn line was pale in the moonlight. The other man had recovered, a big man with a paunch that hung over a Skoal belt buckle, and he stood off to the side. Rawlins reached around behind Joshua and yanked his billfold out of his hip pocket. He opened it and withdrew the bills, counting them. "Two hundred and forty-seven dollars," he said as he stuffed the bills in his Levi's. "That oughta replace my Winchester." He riffled through the rest of the billfold, collected the contents, and tossed the billfold on the ground. Rawlins held a hand out to the man standing beside him. "Norton," he said, never taking his eyes off Joshua, "give me your knife." The man with the paunch shoved a thick hand into the front pocket of his jeans and laid a jackknife in Rawlins' palm. Rawlins extracted the blade. The steel, honed razor sharp, glinted cruelly.

Joshua tried to speak. It felt like he had a chicken bone lodged in his throat. "Be careful, Travis," he croaked. "I don't think you're stupid enough to kill me. And if you cut me up, I'll come find you. That's a promise."

Rawlins raised the knife to Joshua's neck. The two men on either side of him tightened their grip as they twisted his arms behind him. Rawlins pressed the flat of the blade against Joshua's throat and then tilted it slightly, just so he could feel the cutting edge. "Yeah," he sneered, "I take MasterCard." He pulled back the knife and shuffled the contents of Joshua's billfold in his hand. He held up the MasterCard and sliced it up, letting the plastic slivers fall to the ground. He snapped the blade back into the bone handle with a deft movement of his right hand, and handed the jackknife back to Norton.

Rawlins held up the remaining items from Joshua's billfold and squinted at them. "Joshua B. Scott," he read aloud from the driver's license. "State of Virginia." He ticked the head of a wooden match with his thumbnail and touched the flame to a corner of the license. He turned it between thumb and forefinger until it was nearly consumed and then dropped it to the ground. Rawlins produced another card. "Joshua B. Scott," he read. "Social Security number 310-36-9361." He struck another match and burned the Social Security card. Rawlins held up the last item. "Well, looky here. I do believe it's a souvenir from the war." He read from the card. " 'Have Nungs Will Travel. Wire Captain Tom Bishop.' Ain't that cute? How many babies you and Claudia's old man burn up? Huh? How many Momma-sans you big brave soldier boys kill in that two-bit war?" Rawlins struck another match. They seemed to appear in his big, callused hand as if by magic, and burst into flame. He set fire to the business card. When it caught, he turned it up and held the flame under Joshua's chin. Just close enough so the heat seared the flesh without doing any real harm. Joshua winced and drew back. Rawlins crowded him with the flame and slowly moved it back and forth. "Is this how you got inside that farmhouse and into Claudia's pants?" He looked at one of the men holding Joshua's arms. "What do you think, Farrell? Think he's a friend of the family?"

Farrell, thin and gaunt, guffawed. "Friend of the family," he echoed with a high-pitched whinny, as though the witticism beat anything he'd ever heard.

The card burned down to Rawlins' fingertips. He let go of it, and
the smoking ash floated to the ground. Suddenly Rawlins drove a
fist deep into Joshua's stomach. Joshua's breath was driven from
him with a grunt and he doubled up. Rawlins eyed him a moment,
features cold. "Turn him loose," he said at last. Farrell and the third
man released Joshua's arms and he sagged to his knees. They stood
around him and watched him where he fell, doubled over in the
gravel, recovering his breath in ragged gasps.

Slowly Joshua straightened up, hands still clutching his stomach.
"This ought to settle our account, Travis," he grunted.

"Not for Claudia." Rawlins turned. "Let's go," he said. They
started for the pickup.

"Travis," Joshua called after him, "you're dumb as a dog butt.
There's nothing between Claudia and me."

The men stopped and turned back toward Joshua. The third
man, thick and heavyset, walked back and knelt beside Joshua. He
twisted a hand in his hair and jerked his head back. "Hold it, J.W.,"
Rawlins said. He sauntered over to Joshua, a thin smile curling his
lips. "Let him go." J.W. released Joshua and stepped back. Rawlins
paused, caught J.W.'s eye, then drew back and aimed a kick at
Joshua's midsection. The toe of his cowboy boot, so pointed he
could kick a cockroach in a corner, buried itself in Joshua's gut,
lifted him up, and sent him sprawling on his back.

J.W. removed a crumpled cigarette from his shirt pocket and dug
a chrome lighter out of his jeans. He watched Joshua while he lit
up. "Finish him off," he said harshly, exhaling smoke through his
nostrils.

Joshua saw the boot coming again.

*Joshua stood in the rifle pit, leaned forward over the sandbags and
stared into the blackness beyond the perimeter. He stood stone-still
and held his breath. After a moment's silence the sound started up
against the far edge of the concertina wire. It rose in a sobbing
falsetto wail. Was joined by others. He shivered. It was as though
a contingent of crack-brained schoolchildren were raking their
fingernails across a blackboard that stretched all the way across
the length of the eastern perimeter.*

The moans rose and fell, burbling and shrieking. Grating, shrill, piercing screeches that carved a hole in Joshua's mind. He didn't understand the words, but the cries articulated an agony and terror and desperation and plea for help that transcended language. Joshua turned to look at Bishop standing a few feet away in the trench.

Bishop lifted the radio to his lips and pressed the mike button. "Give us some illumination, Pete." A few seconds later the flare drifted across the perimeter, casting a frozen glare on the blasted landscape. There was a little movement at the edge of the wire, but nothing beyond it. "They're not going to come in and pick them up," Bishop muttered.

Joshua nodded. The cries had been stifled when the flare burst above them, but as it fizzled out the ghastly refrain from the North Vietnamese wounded rose again. "We don't have to take that shit," Joshua whispered.

Bishop lifted the radio again. "Wyatt, you and Karl get the M-79's and some ammo." A few minutes later Porter and Wirtz struggled along the trench. They each had two grenade launchers slung over their shoulders and carried a case of ammunition between them. The four men each took a weapon, stuffed their cargo pockets with the huge rounds, and spread out along the trench. Joshua broke the breech on the bloated shotgun and inserted a shell. As he snapped the weapon closed, he heard Bishop radio Franklin.

"Light 'em up, Pete."

Joshua settled himself against the sandbags and sighted along the barrel. A moment later the flare burst in the night sky. Its white light quavered like a palsied moon. Joshua squeezed the trigger. An enormous orange flash detonated in the concertina wire seventy meters away.

They continued firing until the perimeter fell silent.

Joshua looked up to see the pickup roar out of the parking lot. As it passed Joshua it swerved toward him, a calculated miss of eighteen inches. Joshua didn't move. He lay on his side and watched it go, all four men crammed into the cab, silhouetted by the dashboard lights. Rawlins gunned it and the truck spun out onto the highway.

Joshua lay still until his breathing returned to normal. His mind probed his body, identifying the pain and cataloging the damage. He decided he was still in one piece. The worst problem seemed to be his right side. A few cracked ribs, or maybe just bruised. He sat up, the pain grabbing him as he did so. He remained seated for a moment, then stood up. A head rush made him a little woozy. He waited till it passed, then brushed himself off. Everything seemed to work. He looked around till he spotted his wallet, folded it, and put it in his hip pocket. No use losing that, too, he told himself. He paused a moment, catching his breath. He knew what he wanted to do.

Joshua made his way painfully over to the front office. There was only a night-light burning inside, and the door was locked. He rung the night bell and kept ringing it until the old man came. He was wrapping a plaid bathrobe around him, and his skinny feet, mottled purple, were stuck in house slippers with the worn backs turned under his heels. He shuffled to the door and switched on the outside light. His brows arched in surprise when he recognized Joshua. He fumbled with the dead bolt and turned it back.

"Mr. Scott," he wheezed. He didn't have his dentures in and his lips worked convulsively over atrophic gums. "What happened to you?"

"Mr. Lloyd," Joshua grunted, ignoring his question, "tell me how to get to the Maple Grove Cemetery."

"You're all mussed up. I can call Doc Rogers."

"I don't want a doctor, I want to go to the cemetery."

The old man's lips stopped moving. His watery eyes narrowed in suspicion.

"Mr. Lloyd," Joshua said, his voice patient but tinged with sarcasm, "I'm not a grave robber. Now if you don't tell me how to get to the cemetery I'm going to come in there and muss you up."

The Maple Grove Cemetery was on a windswept rise two miles north of Plains. County Road 27 skirted it, but you had to leave the blacktop and drive an eighth of a mile on a graded dirt road to reach it. Joshua parked the Toyota at the entrance and got out. A wrought iron fence kept the wheat fields at bay, and the name of the cemetery was worked in a wrought iron arch that curved across the narrow dirt road. The enigma of the name did not particularly trouble Joshua. There was not a tree in sight, let alone a grove of maples. But the arching sign caused his pulse to race. Unconsciously he reached a hand to his right side. His fingers probed his bruised ribs.

Joshua and Porter shuffled toward the waiting helicopter. Joshua pressed his hand against his side where a pressure bandage, stiff with dried blood, covered his gunshot wound. It hurt like a son of a bitch. He ducked under the drooping rotor of the Huey but stopped before he climbed aboard. He turned and took one last look around Thang Duc. It was a smoking shambles of burned-out buildings, blasted bunkers, smashed trenches, shell-pocked red clay, and twisted concertina wire. His eyes paused at the main entrance to the compound, caught by the sign that arched over the heavy barbed wire gate. Somehow the sign had remained untouched by the fury of the battle. It was hand-painted, and the carefully lettered proclamation was in Vietnamese. SOAT DUOC NHUNG VUNG HEO · LANH BU LAI SU TON · THAT LA KIEM. Beneath it, in smaller letters, was the English translation: The Risk of Loss Is Worth Control of Remote Areas.

Joshua turned back to the chopper. He motioned Porter aboard, then held out a hand. Porter gave him an assist onto the Huey. Joshua turned grimly to the open hatch, gripped the stock of the M-60, and swiveled it toward the sign over the compound gate. The Spec-four riding shotgun started to protest, but Joshua's manner stopped him cold. Joshua cleared the weapon, squeezed the trigger, and got the range on the sign. He fired a long, continuous burst. The bullets chewed into the wood as the hammering sound reverberated across the silent valley. When Joshua released the trigger, he was breathing heavily, as though from exertion, and the sign had been cut to pieces. The silence closed in again, even more profound in the aftermath of the staccato roar of the M-60.

Joshua swung the door-mounted machine gun back to the gunner and sank to the metal deck plate near the rear bulkhead. He reached out with his left hand and gripped a webbed handle on the body bag containing Tom Bishop's remains. He held on so tightly his knuckles turned white. The pilot glanced over his shoul-

*der at Joshua. Joshua nodded dumbly, lifted his right hand, and
twirled tight circles with his index finger. The Lycoming began to
whine and the rotors churned sluggishly, accelerating as the engine stuttered to life.*

Joshua walked slowly through the entrance to the cemetery, passing under the wrought iron sign. The night sky was cloudless, a
vaulted dome of black flecked with a million bits of light. A waning
moon spilled soft shadows from the gravestones.

He left the dirt road and roamed among the markers, shoes
stirring dust from the dry buffalo grass. He paused frequently, held
by an inscription or a date that annotated Cimarron County history
from the 1800's. It was an hour before he found what he was looking
for. It was a plot marked off with a white picket fence, and it
contained seven graves. Joshua pushed open the gate, hinges protesting the bare-metal friction, and moved carefully among the
graves. The oldest marker was a thin slash of weathered slate. Its
dark face was nicked and scarred, and the inscription worn by
more than a century of western Kansas wind and sleet and dust
storms. He stooped to read it, his fingers tracing the roughly chiseled lettering. "Rufus Polk Bishop," Joshua read aloud. "Born
March 29, 1849—Indian Territory. Killed July 14, 1877, in the
Homestead Wars."

Joshua stood and turned to the next two graves, placed side by
side with no more than six inches between the granite stones.
"Horace T. Bishop," he read. "Born September 17, 1874. Died May
25, 1951." He read the marker next to it. "Grace Bishop. Born July
12, 1881. Died January 19, 1904. Died in Childbirth and Mourned by
Loving Family and Friends."

Joshua inched his way along the foot of the graves, careful not
to step on them, until he reached the next pair of graves. The
stones were not much larger than the preceding ones, but were
polished marble. The first stone marked the grave of Clarence
Henry Bishop. Born January 19, 1904. Joshua's eyes slid back to
Grace Bishop's marker to compare dates. Grace Bishop died giving
birth to Tom's father. His gaze returned to Clarence Bishop's
gravestone. He died August 31, 1971. The adjacent stone of polished

marble identified the grave of Martha Mayo Bishop. Born November 20, 1906, and died six months before her husband, February 3, 1971.

Joshua moved on to the next grave. A bronze plaque was embedded flush with the ground. It bore the name of Kathryn Polk Bishop, Tom's sister. She was eleven years old when she was killed in March of 1946. Joshua contemplated the child's grave a moment before he turned to the last marker in the Bishop family plot. It was another rectangle of brass spiked to the earth. The name he had come to view had an unexpected twist that caught him unaware. "Thomas Todd Bishop. Born April 23, 1940. Died October 12, 1967." Joshua reread the inscription, contemplating it. Odd, what one knows and doesn't know about a close friend, he thought. He had never known Tom's middle name. That was a surprise. But the date of his death was burned into his memory forever. October 12, 1967.

The North Vietnamese lunged at Joshua, bayonet leveled at his chest. Joshua stumbled backward, jerking frantically at the .45 on his hip. Saw he couldn't clear his pistol in time. Suddenly the Vietnamese soldier was slammed to the far side of the trench as a bullet tore into his chest. Reprieved, Joshua jerked his .45 from the holster. The flare flickered out and the perimeter became pitch-black, illuminated only by muzzle flashes, explosions, and tracers. Shadows dropped into the trench around Joshua. He wheeled and fired frantically at the North Vietnamese. Point-blank. Spinning away from the plunging bodies, he emptied his pistol. Another flare burst above the compound. In its harsh glare Joshua saw Bishop dragging himself along the bottom of the trench. He flung aside his .45 and scrambled over the dead Vietnamese. He gripped Bishop by the shoulders and rolled him over on his back. Blood welled up from a black hole in his chest, pooled, and spilled across the front of his tiger suit. Joshua stared in horror. "Finelli!" he screamed. "Finelli!"

"How's it look?" Bishop's voice was a distant moan.

"Just a scratch."

"I been hurt worse when I got cleated." Bishop tried to grin, but

it was obliterated by a grimace as the pain slashed through him.

"We'll get a medic," Joshua said. He stood up and glanced around the compound. "Finelli!" he screamed again.

"One bullet can't bring down the Plains, Kansas, flash," Bishop mumbled.

"Hang on, Tom," Joshua pleaded. "I'm gonna go get Finelli." He started to get up.

Bishop reached out a hand and clutched feebly at his arm. "Don't go, don't leave me." His eyes glazed over and his breath rattled in his chest.

"Finelli!" Joshua screamed at the top of his lungs. He watched in agony, despairing at his helplessness, then crouched down beside Bishop and cradled his head in his lap. "Jesus, Tom." He rocked him back and forth, crooning, "Jesus, Jesus, Jesus."

Bishop muttered something, fading in and out. He coughed, and flecks of blood appeared on his lips.

"Don't die, Tom," Joshua sobbed. "Please don't die." He continued to hold Bishop in his arms, rocking back and forth. Back and forth.

Bishop exhaled in a gurgling rush. Joshua stopped rocking, watched, waited for him to breathe. Bishop lay still. Joshua scrambled up, frantic, and straddled Bishop's hips. He placed his hands beneath his rib cage and lifted his chest. "Don't die!" he begged. "Don't die!" He allowed Bishop's chest to collapse to the floor of the trench, and then lifted again. Up and down. He continued the rhythmic raising and lowering of the chest, as though Bishop's lungs were a bellows and he could keep him alive by the simple expedient of forcing air in and out. "Don't die!" Joshua whimpered, pleading. "Don't die!" Irrationally he continued to lift Bishop's rib cage. "Please don't die." Gradually he became aware of voices. He looked up. Finelli and Porter were there.

Finelli had a restraining hand on his shoulder. "Stop, Josh," Finelli urged quietly. "He's dead. You can stop now."

Slowly, like a windup toy running down, Joshua stopped his frantic, useless ministrations. Bishop lay silent and unresponsive beneath him. Eyes staring emptily.

Porter squatted beside Joshua, peering anxiously at him. "He's dead, Josh," he said, his voice soothing and reassuring. "You can stop now. It's all right to stop now."

Joshua slumped away from Bishop and dragged himself over to the side of the trench. He began to tremble.

Joshua lifted a hand to his face. It trembled as he touched his wet cheeks. He wiped the tears away. "Don't die," he said dully. "Please don't die."

His eyes swam as he swept them over the gravestones huddled together behind the rickety picket fence. Four generations, he thought. Four generations of Bishops had borne the pain and tasted the sweetness of life on this prairie. And found their final resting place on this hillock. It reminded Joshua that people have roots, just like trees. Like the cottonwood, now fifty feet tall, planted by Tom's father in the front yard the day Tom was born. Joshua looked again at the bronze plaque. Thomas Todd Bishop had come home. From putrid jungle to the Kansas earth.

"We're a long way from home tonight."

As Joshua stood at Bishop's grave, the memory was drawn from across the years as surely as the moon draws the tides. And the impulse could not be restrained any more than the tides can be checked. He began to recite aloud in a hushed voice.

> "Today, the road all runners come,
> Shoulder high we bring you home.
> And set you at your threshold down,
> Townsman of a stiller town . . .
> And silence sounds no worse than cheers
> After earth has stopped the ears."

Joshua stopped, breathless. Haunted. October 12, 1967. In the distance a dog barked. The sound carried across the prairie on the wind, a hollow echo of loneliness. Joshua turned and started back to the Toyota.

CHAPTER ELEVEN

"The blood of Christ keep you unto eternal life." Claudia Bishop made the sign of the cross and raised her lips to the chalice. The wine warmed her throat as she received the sacrament from the hands of Father Charles Wilson. She did not normally attend the early-morning Friday mass at St. Mary's of the Plains. This morning, however, she had awakened troubled from a fitful sleep. The trip to Jackfork with Joshua, the conversation, the dancing, and the moonlight swim had all left her in turmoil. She was filled with an uneasy mixture of disquietude and excitement, resistance and longing. How is it possible, she wondered, that in a few days this stranger from her husband's past could threaten to dismantle her carefully structured life? She needed to talk and knew there was only one person to whom she could turn. Charlie Wilson had been more than just her priest for the past decade; he had also been her friend.

Wilson pronounced the benediction and the small cluster of communicants began to disperse. Claudia waited alone in the silence of the church for the priest to return from the sacristy. "Good morning, Claudia," Wilson said. "You're not usually at morning mass. What's the occasion?"

"Charlie, I need to talk. Do you have some time?"

"Sure. Parish calls can always wait." He led the way into the rectory to his study. "What's up?"

Claudia plopped down in the chair in front of Wilson's desk. She threw her head back and pressed both palms against her temples. "Charlie, these last few days have been wild!"

"Well, harvest is always your busy time," Wilson responded, knowing it would take more than that to bring Claudia to his study. "How's it going?"

"Should be done late today. Hasn't been without its problems, though." Claudia hesitated a moment. "Do you remember me telling you last summer about one of Vanlandingham's custom cutters? A man named Travis Rawlins?"

"I do indeed," Wilson laughed. "He's the one with all the cowboy charm that got a little persistent when you weren't swept off your feet."

"It's no laughing matter, Charlie. He got more than persistent this year. I fired him."

"What happened?"

"He put some moves on me," Claudia said. "It was pretty ugly."

"Are you all right?"

"Yes. The man scares me a little." Claudia shook her head. "But that's not really why I came to see you."

"So what's on your mind?"

Claudia rolled her eyes. "Where to begin?"

"Why not start with Joshua Scott," Wilson prompted.

Claudia sat bolt upright in her chair. "How do you know about him?"

"We're jogging buddies," Wilson said with a smile. "I met him his first night in Plains. Since then we've talked some." Wilson pushed his glasses up on his nose. "I like him."

"That's the problem. So do I."

"Why is that a problem?"

"None of your pastoral counseling techniques, Charlie. We've been friends too long for that. You know why it's a problem. He represents a past I had closed off forever."

"Perhaps it should be opened up again."

"It may be a Pandora's box. The questions that couldn't be answered so long ago may have answers now." She stopped and looked steadily at the priest. "But I don't think I want to know them now. It frightens me."

"Cut the bullshit, Claudia. You're not afraid of answers, or the past." The priest leaned back in a squeaking swivel chair and put his feet up on the desk. "You're afraid of yourself."

"That's not true, Charlie."

"Tell me one single significant male relationship in your life," Wilson challenged.

"Todd."

"He doesn't count," Wilson said, brushing her response aside with a wave of his hand.

"You," Claudia shot back.

"Hah!" Wilson hooted. "Name someone else."

"There's been no time. I've had a son to raise. I've had to make a living."

Wilson swung his feet to the floor and leaned sharply across the desk toward Claudia. "That farm is four sections of excuse."

"That's not true."

"Oh, Claudia," Wilson scolded, "you've been the emotional iron maiden. Hell," he went on, "you've already admitted the only two significant relationships in your life are with your son and your priest." Wilson waved both hands at her in disgust. "That's pitiful. But with Joshua there are"—he paused and lingered over the word —"possibilities."

Claudia weighed the priest's words carefully. "Last night," she said, "I was so drawn to Joshua. But I don't want any more pain."

"Claudia," Wilson said quietly, "you always retreat from passion." He watched her carefully. "Passion isn't fundamentally sexual desire." The priest nodded toward the crucifix on the wall above the settee. "That's passion."

Claudia followed the priest's gaze to the crucifix. She had been a Catholic all her life. The ever-present crucifix had become part of the scenery. Whether at home or at Ward High in Kansas City or in church. But the thought that it might actually impinge on her life had never occurred to her. She studied the broken figure of Christ.

"That represents the human attempt to live a life of love." Wilson turned his gaze from the crucifix to Claudia. "Without suffering, without wounds and death, there is no life."

Joshua had slept in that morning. He had become accustomed to the asthmatic wheezing of the window air conditioner, so it no longer troubled his sleep. But when he rolled over, the pain in his right side woke him. He lay there a moment, eyes closed, contemplating his body before he raised a foot and kicked back the sheet. He opened his eyes, squinting in the dim light that filtered through the rift in the curtains where a hook was missing. He carefully propped himself up on his elbows and studied his belly. A purple bruise discolored his right side. The scar from his old gunshot wound stood out dead-white within it.

Joshua rolled out of bed and soaked in the bathtub for half an hour, then shaved. His chin was a little tender where Rawlins had scorched it. He dressed and drove over to St. Mary's. The nave was empty and cool and dark, lit only by refracted light from stained-glass windows and the parish candle flickering under the Madonna. He walked down the carpeted aisle between the polished, padded pews, and approached the open door of the rectory. He knocked softly on the door frame and glanced in.

Charlie Wilson had his feet up on his wooden desk and was reading a slick monthly, *The Runner.* He wore a T-shirt with his clerical collar and shirt front. He greeted Joshua, dropped his feet to the floor, and motioned him toward a chair.

Joshua settled into the chair, guarding his right side a little. "I came to buy you breakfast."

"Thanks, I've had breakfast."

"Lunch?"

Wilson glanced at his watch. "I usually don't eat lunch at eleven-fifteen."

"Okay, I'll have breakfast and buy you coffee."

"Fair enough." Wilson got up and went over to a closet, removed a black jacket and slipped it on.

"Can you help me cash a check?"

"Plains' night life a little too rich for you?" Wilson started for the door.

"I got rolled last night."

Wilson stopped. "In Plains?"

Joshua briefly covered the details of his confrontation with Rawlins the night before.

As Wilson listened, he filled in some of the blanks in the conversation he had had with Claudia early that morning. He was now genuinely concerned. "Do you want to report it to the sheriff?" he asked. "There's a little law in Plains. Not much, but we don't need much."

"What would I say? Some bullies beat me up?"

"Tell him you got robbed."

"Well, I did owe Rawlins. I threw his Winchester in the Cimarron."

"You neglected to mention that small item."

"Come on, I'm hungry," Joshua said. "I'll tell you while we cash my check." Joshua led the way to the Toyota and drove back to the business district. On the way he told Wilson about the snake hunt.

Wilson thought about the story a moment. "Even if you did toss his rifle in the river," he finally said, "there was no excuse for what he did last night."

"You won't get any argument from me about that," Joshua said. He pulled the Land Cruiser into the curb in front of the Farmers and Merchants Bank. "But I think it's over now."

"Don't count on it." The sentence hung between them, half challenge, half warning.

"What's that supposed to mean?"

Wilson got out of the Toyota. "Let's go cash your check, then we'll talk about it."

Wilson vouched for Joshua in the bank and he got two hundred dollars. As they left the air-conditioning, the heat hit them. Joshua paused on the sidewalk and glanced up and down Main Street, squinting in the glare of the sun. Heat shimmered off the blacktop in visible waves. Across the street, the park and the tall shade trees looked inviting. He decided he didn't want to eat. They ordered a beer in the bar off the billiard parlor. Joshua got a Heineken and Wilson a Miller Lite. Joshua paid and they started to leave.

The bartender spoke up. "It's against the law to take singles out of the bar, Father."

Wilson raised his Miller in a toast. "Parish business, my son." He followed Joshua through the door.

They crossed Main, dodging wheat trucks and business traffic. As they entered the park, several young boys approached Wilson. One bounce-passed a basketball to him as they pestered him to play. Wilson shifted the Miller to his left hand, fielded the ball with his right, spun and dribbled a few steps in a crisp demonstration

of ball-control, including a bounce between his legs, then fired the
ball behind his back to the oldest boy. "Later," he called over his
shoulder and walked on with Joshua.

"Not bad," Joshua said, admiring..

"In the Bronx the only way you could play was if you could get
the ball and keep it." Wilson smiled at the memory. "Street basketball was a combination of Knickerbocker razzle, keep away, dodge-
ball, football, and karate."

"Did you ever play in school?"

"Cathedral College."

"They had sports?"

"Only basketball." Wilson lifted the Miller to his lips. "Conse-
quently, we were very good." He grinned. "We took out our frustration over the lack of girls on the court. In practice we called a
foul only if we drew blood." He gave his belly a resounding slap.
"Ah, those were the days. The high point of the season was if we
beat Yeshiva." Wilson laughed. "Our coach Father Curry'd say,
'Play tough, kick ass, and by the grace of God we'll win this one for
Cathedral!' "

Joshua and Wilson made their way along a brick walkway. Everything had been completed for the festivities the next day. Colored
lights were strung between the old lampposts. Booths lined the
west side of the park. The barbecue pit and tables were grouped
along the east side, and the big dance floor had been completed in
front of the band shell. Dozens of fine wire mesh cages were scattered around the hand-dug well.

"Seems to me," Joshua said, as he looked around, "that Plains sort
of goes all out for this Street Dance thing."

Wilson nodded his head in agreement. "It's sort of like Yeshiva.
It's the high point of the season."

"You going to attend?"

"Would if I could, but I've got to go to Forty Hours Devotion."

Joshua looked at Wilson and lifted his eyebrows in silent question.

"It's a spiritual retreat. All the priests in the diocese go to the host
parish where it's held. This time it's in Great Bend."

"What do you do?"

"Well, I usually attend the solemn invocation, then get together
with a few buddies for some human companionship. The spiritual

renewal consists of saying 'Spades are trumps' and 'Pass the Bush-mills.'"

Joshua and Wilson found a park bench off to the side of the band shell. They sipped their beers and watched a half-dozen girls, maybe six or seven years old, roller-skating on the dance floor. A knot of small boys heckled from the sidelines and threw green cottonwood pods at them. A little sliver of a girl with pigtails, sailing along on her skates, called out gaily, "Fuck off, Billy!" Joshua grinned and shook his head. There was such a guileless glee about her.

Finally Joshua spoke. "Well, Charlie, what do you want to talk about?"

Wilson paused, thinking. He looked over at Joshua. "Be careful of Rawlins," he said. "He doesn't like you, and he doesn't like you with Claudia."

Joshua thought about Rawlins' final comment the night before. "No, probably not."

"He's got some kind of thing about Claudia. Fancies she's interested in him." The priest set his Miller on the bench, removed a linen handkerchief from his coat, and polished the sweat off his glasses. "Apparently he had his eye on Claudia for several summers. He can be quite a charmer in his down-home way."

"Then he's got a side I've never seen," Joshua muttered.

"He kept trying to get Claudia to go out with him, but she always put him off. She did dance a couple of times with him at the dance last summer." Wilson replaced his glasses and folded the linen handkerchief into his coat pocket. "Maybe Rawlins interpreted that as an expression of interest or something. I don't know. Anyway," Wilson went on, "something happened at the farm between them a couple of days ago."

"I know she fired him," Joshua said.

"And I know she didn't do it because he couldn't operate a combine." Wilson seemed to be lost in his own musings. "How much trouble are we sitting on here in Plains, Josh?"

"You mean Rawlins?" Joshua asked.

"Yes, but more than Rawlins. I mean you and whatever brought you to Plains. I mean Claudia and you. And Claudia and Rawlins. I mean ghosts and demons and all those things that aren't supposed to exist."

Joshua got up and stood facing the band shell, his back to Wilson. The chubby little man in black was getting close. Part of him wanted it. Wanted Wilson to flush out the hidden enemies and exorcise the demons. Wanted the Catholic magic of the confessional and the release of absolution. The Protestant part of him won out. Deal with it yourself. Figure it out. Go to work on it. Find the right answers.

Joshua turned back to face the priest. "How do you know all this?"

Wilson paused and drained his Miller. "Claudia came to see me this morning," he finally said. "But she didn't really come to talk about Rawlins. She came to talk about you."

"What about me?"

Wilson shook his head. "She feels on the verge of life again, and it's centered on you and why you came to Plains."

Joshua's unfinished Heineken grew warm in his hand. His emotions played leapfrog within him. Anger at Rawlins. Growing affection for Claudia. Guilt for the dead. Rage against life. Joy in survival. He wasn't sure which emotions he feared most. Suddenly Joshua felt like his whole life had backed up on him. For the first time in years he wanted to talk. To deal with it all. He looked at the priest. Eyes large behind his glasses, animated by both passion and compassion. Sympathetic, supportive, real. Brother Jim Bob Duncan, simulating idiocy for the Lord, had been supplanted by this rumpled, sweaty priest with a beer in his hand.

Joshua plunged ahead. "Last night was very strange."

"How so?" Wilson asked.

"Several things. First, Claudia and I drove down to Jackfork to eat. It was very good. Very easy between us." Joshua returned to the bench and placed the unfinished Heineken on the brick walkway beneath it. He hesitated a moment, glanced at Wilson, then went on. "The only women I've had since Nam, except for those first months at home until I divorced, have been one-night stands. No intimacy. No permanence. I didn't miss it. But last night I wanted Claudia." Joshua brushed a hand down across his mustache and went on. "Then I ran into Travis Rawlins and his buddies. I wanted that, too. It's a funny thing, Charlie, I'm ill at ease in the absence of enemies. I'm always on guard, vigilant, wary. Like walking point. Violence in the concrete, not the abstract, like with

Rawlins, gives me a focus. That can be a tremendous relief."

Joshua felt himself begin to tremble. He took a deep breath, held it, and then exhaled in a long, sustained sigh. The trembling subsided. "After Rawlins left," he went on, "I went out and found Tom Bishop's grave. Since Nam I have been tied to images of death. And not just the images. But sort of a"—he searched for the word—"thralldom to death itself. Like a death spell. I have a sense of having been there and returned, and I'm gripped by the power of death. I've lost my sense of invulnerability. I've learned the terrible lesson that death is real, and that I myself will one day die. And that reality has not always seemed so bad. It might be a relief to learn the final secret."

Joshua turned to look at Wilson. Wilson was regarding him with compassion and wonder. Joshua looked away and resumed his thoughts. "The sight of Tom's grave, surrounded by his family, and marked with a brass plaque, gave a certain reality to his death that it hadn't had before. Claudia said she feels that sometimes at his grave."

Wilson nodded in understanding.

"I mourned for Tom last night. I have been haunted by his death, and angry about it, and resented the premature absurdity of it. But last night I really mourned for the first time." Joshua stopped and pressed his fingers against his forehead. "But when I left, on the way home, I was glad. Glad that Tom died and I was alive."

"I think that's very natural," Wilson replied softly.

"No, Charlie. Not just glad that I survived. Not glad in the general sense, but in the specific. Because of Claudia."

"Josh, your feelings for Claudia are unrelated to Tom's death."

"Not really, Charlie. You remember what I said about feeling ill at ease in the absence of enemies. Before I went to sleep last night, I realized that memory is the enemy now."

Charlie Wilson sat at his desk with four commentaries open in front of him. To his right, his old battered typewriter held a sheet of paper. The paper held the sum total of his thoughts for his sermon. It was blank. He hated Friday afternoons with unfinished sermons, let alone unstarted ones. He had searched for some kind of inspiration for the sermon for the past hour, but Travis Rawlins' presence in Plains festered in his mind. Wilson's grim mood was momentarily broken by the recollection of an old Franciscan priest he knew who had given his philosophy of sermon preparation in one line: just stroke the text until it comes. Wilson stroked the text for another half hour. Nothing came.

Exasperated, he pushed away from the desk and paced back and forth in his study, surrendering to the problem that forced itself to the center of his attention. The stories Claudia and Joshua had told him about Travis Rawlins that morning put him on edge. His sixth sense needled him with the presentiment that Rawlins was more than a roughneck. He turned the problem over in his mind, gnawing at it like a dog with a bone. Except in this case the problem gnawed at him. Finally he went to his closet and dug out his jogging gear. He gave it a tentative sniff and then changed.

Wilson left the church and walked over to the courthouse on the edge of the park. The windows of the old stone structure reflected blankly in the sun's glare, giving the building an abandoned look. As he made his way down the sidewalk, the ripples in the ancient windowpanes, the result of imperfect craftsmanship, were easily apparent. Wilson didn't mount the steps to the main entrance, but took the walk that led around the building to the rear. He entered a door that had a window of frosted glass with stenciled black letters identifying the Cimarron County Sheriff's Office. A tiny brass bell, tipped by the opening door, announced his presence with a metallic jingle. Wilson was in an anteroom with an ancient rolltop desk, a bulletin board with a dozen federal-marshal wanted posters thumbtacked to it, a three-legged coat rack, and a wall-mounted gun rack holding two shotguns and a rifle. A padlocked chain ran through the trigger housings and secured the weapons to the wall.

Clancy Sturgeon had been sheriff of Cimarron County through eight Kansas governorships. He looked about as old as his desk. He tilted back in his chair and nodded at the priest, eyeing his jogging clothes. "Howdy, Padre," he said in a voice like gravel. "Lose your way?"

"Hi, Sturg, I need some help."

"Shoot."

"Can you find out if a man has ever been in trouble with the long arm of the law?"

The sheriff's expression didn't change, but before he replied his silence was pure skepticism. "Well, deputy," he drawled, "I probably could. It helps to have a date of birth."

Wilson shook his head. "Sorry."

"Driver's license ID?"

"Nope."

"Social Security number?" the sheriff prodded.

Again Wilson shook his head.

Sturgeon nodded slowly. "Figures." He turned back to his desk. "Wouldn't happen to know his name?"

"Travis Rawlins."

The sheriff scribbled on a scratch pad with a Mail Pouch tobacco advertisement on it. "It'd be nice to know where Mr. Rawlins hails from."

"Texas. Near Lubbock, I think."

Sturgeon jotted the information down on the scratch pad. "You havin' some trouble with this feller?"

"Not really." The sheriff raised one scraggy eyebrow. Wilson was beginning to regret his impulse to play detective.

"There's laws now about invasion of privacy, you know." Clancy Sturgeon slowly got up from his desk, putting a hand on his lower back to crab himself erect.

"You okay, Sturg?" Wilson asked solicitously.

"Yeah," the old man said, "it just takes some parts of me longer to stand up than others." He moved off toward the back room. "I'll put this on the Telex to TCIC." He observed Wilson's blank expression. "That's the Texas Criminal Information Center, deputy," he offered dryly. "If you want to wait I may have an answer for you in a few minutes."

Wilson read the wanted posters, cataloging the criminals and their crimes. In his profession he had dealt with virtually every nuance of perfidy, madness, meanness, and anguish the human story had to offer. He waited to see what the sheriff would turn up.

Fifteen minutes later Clancy Sturgeon returned with a printout in his hand. "Trouble with a custom cutter, huh, Padre?"

"You're a smart cop, Sturg."

"Hell, it don't take no smarts to figure that out." The old man lowered himself into his chair. "TCIC turned up three possibles with that name. This is the only one that fits." He glanced up at

Wilson, then looked at the paper in his hand. "Travis Rawlins, Caucasian male aged thirty-four," he read. "Owns a run-down ranch near Shallowater. Earns his livin' as a third-rate rodeo cowboy and a first-rate combiner." He looked again at Wilson. "He's had three arrests in the past five years. Once drunk and disorderly and resisting arrest, twice for aggravated assault. The last time he served ninety days of a six-month sentence." The sheriff paused and studied the priest. "Nearly beat a feller to death."

"You do good work, Sturg." Wilson turned to go.

"You goin' to tell me any more?"

"I don't really know any more."

"You ain't supposed to lie in your line of work, you know," Sturgeon grumbled. He turned back to his desk. "Amateurs," he muttered under his breath. "Geldings standin' stud."

Wilson began to jog, the sheriff's friendly accusation echoing in his ears. He's right, he thought. The only honorable vocation for a priest is to try not to lie about things that are significant. And he thought the information turned up by Sturgeon was significant. Enough so to make him feel less foolish about playing detective. Travis Rawlins had all the earmarks of a sociopath. Charming, convincing, unpredictable. Living by subterfuge and on the edge of violence, with a kind of mad design that is ordered by its own inner logic. Loving nothing more than to watch people squirm in whatever kind of mischief they can create. With any luck he'll be gone in a day, Wilson thought.

It was hot in the motel room. The air conditioner wheezed and rattled in its vain attempt to defeat the late afternoon sun. Joshua knew he could not put off the inevitable any longer. He pulled his suitcase from under the bed and removed the metal box. He rummaged through the contents and found the cardboard tube. It was about three quarters of an inch in diameter, about ten inches long, and closed at each end with brown tape. He slipped it partially into his front jeans pocket and left the motel. Joshua drove back through town and out Rural Route 2 toward the Bishop farm. It was like the first day. Reluctant, but drawn there by a job that had to be done. He drove carefully and methodically, and felt the detachment and control settle on him like a shroud.

Joshua reached the driveway and followed it to the farmhouse. Claudia's Fairlane was in the drive. Three wheat trucks were parked near the shed, the truck beds filled to overflowing with grain. A grain loader stood nearby, the long, galvanized steel tube glinting in the slanting rays of sunlight. Todd was in the garden at the rear of the house. When he heard the Toyota he turned and waved. Joshua left the Toyota near the Fairlane and walked across the yard to join Todd.

"Come on, Josh. You're just in time to give me a hand." He led the way between two rows of ripening corn, past staked tomato vines heavy with mostly green fruit, to a watermelon patch. The vines spread across the ground in a thick, raspy tangle. Joshua followed Todd as he picked his way through the patch. "Look at this," Todd said, and stooped and separated the leaves to expose a huge watermelon. "It's a mega-melon." He glanced up at Joshua. "Most melons don't get ripe here till August, but Jess showed me how to pot them early."

Joshua muttered an appropriate exclamation and nodded in appreciation.

"Thing must weigh eighty-five pounds. They just do that sometimes. Take off and grow like gangbusters." Todd removed a pocketknife from his Levi's and cut the stem.

"You'll be eating on that the rest of the summer."

"We ain't gonna eat it. We're gonna enter it in the contest at the dance tomorrow. I bet it's the biggest damn watermelon in Cimarron County." Todd searched around under the nearby vines, exposing other watermelons dwarfed by the mutant giant. He thumped several with a finger, listening with a critical ear to the dull sound. "We'll eat this one," he said. He cut the stem with his pocketknife and folded it away. Todd got a grip on the monster melon and heaved it into his arms. "You get the little one," he grunted. Joshua picked it up and followed Todd back through the garden to the side stoop. Claudia came out to greet them. She held her reading glasses in one hand, and brushed her hair away from her face with the other.

Todd placed the huge melon gingerly on the stoop. He looked up at Claudia. "I may have a little rattlesnake," he grinned, "but I got a big watermelon. I'm gonna weigh it." He disappeared through the screen door.

Joshua placed his watermelon down beside Todd's. "Do the big ones taste better than the little ones?" he asked.

"Not usually."

"Bigger but not better," Joshua said. "There must be a lesson there." He wiped some garden dirt from his hands and glanced around the yard. "Why the wheat trucks?" he asked, nodding in their direction.

"The coop is full and so are my storage bins. It happens sometimes with a bumper crop. We'll leave it here a couple of days till they ship some out on a train, then we'll take it in."

"Is Vanlandingham finished?"

"They're cutting in the last quarter this afternoon," Claudia said. "He'll stay over till he can unload his trucks and then move north."

Joshua nodded. "They'll be here tomorrow for the dance?"

"Yes. If the cutting's done, they often stay over that day anyway. It's a great party."

Todd came back through the door, the screen slamming behind him. He placed a bathroom scale on the stoop, manhandled the watermelon up on it, and waited for the dial to stop oscillating. "Ninety-two pounds," he crowed. "Think that will do it, Mom?"

"It might. Jessie Colter's eighty-six-pounder won last year."

Todd carefully rolled the melon off the scale and handed the scale to Claudia. He picked up the smaller melon. "Let's slice this one."

"Take it to the front porch," Claudia said. "It's shady there." Todd started up the side yard, and Joshua followed Claudia into the kitchen. She placed the scale on a counter and collected a butcher knife, plates, forks, napkins, and a salt shaker. They passed through the house to join Todd. As they went through the dining room, Claudia left her reading glasses beside several ledgers that were open on the oak table.

They knelt down on the gray boards of the porch and gathered around the watermelon. There was a curious air of excitement about it. Anticipation. Joshua felt it, and puzzled to explain it. There was a sense of reward. It was the end of a hot summer day, and the harvest was in. A bumper crop. There was satisfaction. Eating something grown and harvested by your own hands. There was the element of mystery. Was it a good watermelon, or a great one? There was a subtle party atmosphere. Food, a delicacy, was to be shared with friends and loved ones. There was a feeling of family.

Claudia plunged the knife into the watermelon and cut it in half. At the end of the cut the watermelon split open with a resonating crack. She circled the knife around the heart in half the melon, pried it out, and cut it in thirds. They each ate it with their fingers. Savoring the ripe red fruit, sweet juices dripping down chins and off fingertips. Claudia sliced the other half of the melon, placed the sections on plates, and they sat down on the steps to eat. Joshua felt the late afternoon heat, its edge blunted by the shade. He glanced up at the towering cottonwood tree. It was silhouetted against the setting sun with an aureole of diffuse golden light. Here and there the sun broke through its thick, leafy branches in dazzling shards of color. Joshua sat in the shade of Bishop's tree and ate watermelon. Making polite conversation with Bishop's wife and Bishop's son.

"There's something missing on this farm," he said lazily. "And I just figured out what it is."

"What's that?" Claudia asked.

"There's no dog."

"I used to have a dog," Todd said. He looked at Claudia. "How old was I, Mom? Six or seven?"

"About that," Claudia agreed. "Mom and Pop Bishop were still alive."

"What was his name?" Joshua asked.

"Dog," Todd replied.

"Just Dog?"

"He was generic," Todd grinned. He took a huge bite of melon and went on. "He was great. Dog only had three legs. He lost one of his front legs when he got hit by the cutting platform on a combine. After he got well, the first time he tried to piss he forgot he didn't have one of his front legs, and when he lifted his leg he fell over." Todd shook his head at the memory. "He learned to lift his leg and balance himself against a tree so he could take a leak."

Joshua chuckled. "What happened to him?"

"One of Grandma's friends drove out from town and ran over Dog in the drive." Todd pointed down where the front lawn met the wheat field. "The old biddy said if he was going to chase cars he deserved to get run over." He wiped his chin. "But I fixed her.

The next time she came out, I drove nails in her tires like she'd had a flat."

"Very crafty, too," Claudia said. "He drove nails in all *four* tires, and," she went on, "he drove them in the *sides* of the tires."

"Revenge is sweet," Joshua laughed, "but it sours if you get caught."

"The old biddy," Todd repeated. "Even Grandpa didn't like her." He took the last bite of his watermelon and pushed away the plate. "Anyway, after Dog I never wanted another dog."

They licked their sticky fingers, wiping their hands with the napkins. Joshua paused a moment, then slipped the cardboard tube from the pocket of his jeans and handed it to Todd. "I thought you might want this. It's something I've had for a long time, but you should probably have it."

Todd reached out, face animated by enthusiasm and curiosity. He shook the tube. It made no sound. "What is it?" Expecting no answer, he picked away the old dried brown tape covering one end. He lifted the tube to an eye, squinted, and peered into it. Then he held it up and tilted the open end toward his other palm. Nothing. He carefully slipped an index finger into the tube and coaxed out the contents. It was a tightly rolled piece of red-and-white-striped satin. Todd unrolled it and shook it free. It was the souvenir American flag. Faded now. About twelve inches long. The edges trimmed with gold fringe. And soiled in places with dirt and grime. Todd looked at Joshua, puzzled, the question on his face if not on his lips. What is it?

Joshua glanced at Claudia. Her eyes were riveted on the tiny flag. Her upper teeth bit into her lower lip. She raised a hand to her mouth, covered it, and turned to him. Her eyes a mixture of awareness and apprehension. Slowly Joshua told them the story of how, at the height of the siege of Thang Duc, Bishop had stood exposed at the foot of the sapling flagpole, with sniper fire cracking all around him, lowered the flag of the Republic of Vietnam, and raised this souvenir flag. "The last thing I did," Joshua concluded, "when we pulled out of Thang Duc was to lower this flag." He nodded at the flag in Todd's hands. "I've had it ever since."

Neither Claudia nor Todd spoke. The only sound was the hum of locusts. After a while Todd got up and went in the house. Joshua could hear him as he bounded up the stairs to the second story. He took them three at a time.

"Should you go up?" Joshua asked with quiet concern. "Or me?"

"No," Claudia said softly. "Later, maybe." They sat together on the steps. The sun had settled on the horizon, a gigantic flaming disk. Its rays began to touch the undersides of the clouds and impart the first faint tones of a fiery sunset. Claudia turned to Joshua. "It was very thoughtful of you, generous even, to give Todd the flag."

"Well, I think he should have it now. This is probably the place for it."

"It will mean a lot to him." Claudia laid a hand on his arm, her fingers cool on his skin. "It's a marvelous story about Tom."

"Yes, it is." The last marvelous story I'll tell you, Joshua thought. He withdrew his arm from Claudia's touch and turned to look at her. The broad, smooth forehead. The direct, unassuming gaze. Hazel eyes bright and clear. The sunburn highlighting her freckles. And all those even white teeth when she smiled. And the hair, even now brushed back by her right hand. It was too bad, he thought. Life has many regrets.

Claudia watched him, the uncertainty clouding her eyes. "What is it, Josh?"

"I'll be leaving soon, Claudia."

"What about last night?" she asked, hesitating.

"Last night was nice."

"Nice? Nice is when all the socks match when you finish the laundry. Last night was more than that. We've not known each other long, but there is something between us that is more than nice."

"It was very nice."

"You'll turn my head," she said wryly. Then her voice became quiet and intense. "I think, Josh, there could be something for us."

"Claudia, there's a ghost that stands between us."

Claudia looked at Joshua in consternation. "Damn you, Joshua Scott. I buried Tom twelve years ago. God knows I didn't deal with it very well. But now you've come along and made me open it all up, and I might, just might, be able to make it right and put it behind me." She paused, took a deep breath, and went on. "I'm thirty-six years old." Her voice began to rise. "My God, I've been living in a state of suspended animation. I want life to go on. Life *must* go on."

"Claudia, you may have buried Tom. Even tried to shut his memory out of your life. But his ghost still haunts me, and I don't know how to lay it to rest. I came here to do it, but I don't think I can."

"Why? What in God's name are you talking about?"

Joshua looked away from her.

"Try me," she challenged.

Joshua got up from the step and stood on the porch. He jammed his hands deep in the pockets of his jeans and looked down at Claudia. "I put Tom in the body bag."

Claudia stared at him. "I know you had to do some awful things, Josh. I can't even imagine . . ."

Joshua jerked a hand from his jeans and stabbed himself in the chest with a forefinger. " I killed Tom!" It was an elemental, anguished cry.

Claudia sat rigidly on the steps. Hands clenched. Uncomprehending. Startled by the torment and despair in Joshua's voice.

"I killed Tom," Joshua repeated dully. The vehemence in his tone had been replaced by numb resignation.

"How? What do you mean?"

Joshua paced restlessly back and forth on the porch and began to talk. The words came hesitantly at first, then spilled out in a rush. "I told you before about the last night of the attack. We were in the trenches waiting for the NVA assault. The remaining Americans were scattered all over the perimeter. I was alone on the east wall with a couple of squads of Nungs." Joshua glanced down at Claudia. "I told you that Tom's position got overrun and I went to help him." He paused. "That's not true. I got overrun and Tom came to help me."

Joshua's voice choked, and he stopped. Stopped pacing. Stopped talking. He stood on the porch in the gathering dusk and gazed into the distance. After a while he resumed talking, voice flat and expressionless.

"The NVA got through the wire. I emptied my M-16 clip, but they kept coming. They were dropping into the trench all around me. One of them started to bayonet me, and I knew I couldn't get out my pistol in time. Then a bullet hit him, and I was able to draw

my forty-five. The flare went out and I couldn't see. I shot everything that jumped into the trench. Someone landed in the trench
behind me. I turned and pulled the trigger." There was a long
pause. "It was Tom. He was on the northwest wall and had seen
I was in trouble. He had come across the compound to help me.
He saved my life, and I killed him."

Claudia wept silently, convulsed by sobs. Face buried in her
hands. Joshua stood apart from her and watched. He wanted to
reach out to her. To touch her. To speak to her. But the sense of
dissociation was too overwhelming. He was paralyzed. The words
that formed in his mind could not be spoken, and he was powerless
to perform the movements necessary to reach her. He watched her
cry, wretched and alone, in the gathering dark on the steps. After
a long time she stopped. She wiped her eyes with her hands,
brushed a sleeve across her cheeks and nose, and stood up. The
movement released Joshua from his paralysis. He stepped toward
her, reaching out a tentative hand.

"No," Claudia said. The single word was cold as ice, distant as the
moon, a disembodied sound detached from the woman herself. She
raised her hands in front of her, slowly moving them from side to
side as she shook her head.

"I'm so sorry," Joshua murmured.

"No," Claudia repeated.

"What am I going to do?" Joshua's voice was a pitiful whisper.

"No." Claudia backed down the steps.

"Claudia, please."

"No."

Joshua followed her down the steps. Claudia turned and stumbled across the yard, reached the wheat field, and kept going across
the dry stubble.

Suddenly the screen door crashed open and slammed back
against the house. The sound cracked like a whip. Joshua spun
around, heart hammering his rib cage apart. Todd stood just beyond the door. His face was streaked with tears and twisted with
misery. The flag Joshua had given him was crumpled in his hand.
He hurled it at Joshua. It struck him in the face and fluttered to the
ground. "Go away!" he sobbed.

"Todd—" Joshua began.

"You made me like you and you killed my father!"

Joshua placed a foot on the porch step. His face was taut. A steel wire stretched so tight that if touched, it would snap.

"I hate you," Todd moaned. "Go away and leave us alone."

Claudia parked her Fairlane in front of St. Mary's of the Plains. There was just enough light from the fading moon to cast a faint shadow of the steep-roofed, steepled church across the grounds. The angular shadow stretched obliquely to the windbreak of elms. She hurried in, paused just inside the nave at the laver, wet her fingers, quickly genuflected and crossed herself. She went down the aisle, almost running, and knocked on the door of the rectory. Wilson opened the door, a cigar clamped in his teeth. Before he could greet her, Claudia spoke, a little breathless.

"Charlie, has Joshua been here tonight?"

"No, why?"

"There was a terrible scene at the house and he left. I can't find him."

Wilson came out of the rectory, closing the door after him. He removed the cigar from his mouth. "What happened?" He motioned her over to a pew in front of the altar rail.

Claudia didn't sit. She poured out the story while they stood. Joshua's part in the death of Tom. Her numbed reaction. How she had finally returned to the house to find that Todd had overheard everything in his room above the porch. Todd's grief-stricken invective. Claudia's voice was strained with anxiety and thick with tears when she finished. "I waited for Josh, hoping he would come back, but he didn't. I'm worried about him, Charlie."

Wilson glanced at his watch. Spoke reassuringly. "It's not even ten yet, Claudia."

"I know, but I can't find him anywhere and I need to go home. Todd's there and I don't want to leave him alone. He's in a bad way."

"Where have you looked?" Wilson asked.

"I went to the motel first. He wasn't there."

"Maybe he checked out." ·

"No. I asked at the office. Old Mr. Lloyd said he hadn't. I made him let me in his room. His things are still there."

"Would he have left without them?"

"I don't know," Claudia shook her head. "Maybe."

"Where else have you looked?"

"I just drove around town looking for his Toyota, but I didn't see it."

"All right, Claudia, you go on home. I'll check around." Claudia hesitated. "Go on, I'll call you as soon as I know something." He put a hand on her shoulder, turned her toward the front exit, and gave her a gentle shove.

Charlie Wilson went back to the rectory. He changed to jeans and a jeans jacket, and pulled on a pair of dilapidated cowboy boots, the leather scuffed and down at the heels. He took the parish vehicle, a nine-passenger Chevy Suburban that spent most of its time locked in the garage attached to the rectory. He drove to the courthouse and for the second time that day found himself in the sheriff's office. A burly deputy sheriff appeared from the door beyond the desk. He had a glass of milk and a half-eaten sandwich in his hands.

"Evening, Father," the deputy said, "we don't have no mackerel snappers in jail tonight." His tone was cordial.

"Hello, Luther. This is not a professional call. I just wondered if you'd had any trouble around town tonight."

The deputy chewed a mouthful of sandwich and reflected a moment. He shook his big head. "Everything's quiet. George is in the black and white. He rousted a hitchhiker earlier with a stash of marijuana in his backpack." He jerked a thumb toward the door behind him. "He's gonna be in the Plains Hilton tonight."

"No fights, rowdies?"

"Nothing."

Wilson waved a hand and left. He walked across the street and down the block to the Billiard Parlor Bar. Mostly pickup trucks were parked outside, with a sprinkling of four-wheel-drive vehicles. But no Toyota. Inside, the smoke was so thick, with a green cast from the shaded lights over the pool tables, that it looked like everything was underwater. The crowd was cowboys and farm-hands, with a few custom cutters and teenagers from town. Raucous, but good-natured. Wilson scanned the place and then went to the bar and asked to use the phone. The bartender set it up on the bar and Wilson dialed the Bishop farm. Todd answered.

"Todd, this is Father Wilson. Is your mother home yet?"

"She just got in." His voice sounded like sleet against a window-pane.

There was a pause and the receiver hummed with rural static until Claudia came to the phone. "Have you found him, Charlie?"

"Not yet. Where is Vanlandingham staying?"

"At the RV park outside of town."

"Is his crew with him?"

"I think so."

"I'll get back to you."

Wilson drove the Suburban west on Main. Just beyond the city limits a gravel road was marked by a KOA campground sign. He turned left on the road and drove a quarter of a mile to a grove of cottonwoods. A small A-frame served as both office and living quarters for the attendant. It was nearly eleven. Wilson woke the attendant and inquired if Travis Rawlins had space in the campground. He did not. He got directions to Vanlandingham's slot and found a pickup with a camper on the back. He knocked. Knocked again. The third time he heard movement in the camper and a groggy voice asking him to hold his horses. The truncated aluminum door at the rear of the camper opened and Vanlandingham stood there in his B.V.D.'s, stooping, peering into the night.

Wilson stepped back. "Mr. Vanlandingham, I'm Charlie Wilson, the Catholic priest for the local parish, and I need to find Mr. Travis Rawlins."

Vanlandingham looked Wilson up and down, taking in the jeans and worn boots. "You don't look like no priest."

"No, sir, I'm sort of off duty."

"If Travis is in trouble, he don't work for me no more."

"I know that," Wilson said. "I just wanted to talk to him and I thought you might know where he was staying."

"Travis is about as religious as a razorback hog," Vanlandingham muttered. "Just a second." He disappeared back into the camper and returned a moment later with a clipboard. He ran a bony finger down a list. "Travis and three other men in my crew have a couple of rooms in town with a Mrs. Rose Cassiday. At 312 Avenue D." He looked up. "I don't know if he's still there, though."

"Thanks. That's all I need. I'm really sorry I had to wake you."

Wilson headed back to town feeling better. Mrs. Cassiday, bless her widowed Irish soul, was a Catholic. He drove to an older residential area on the southern edge of Plains. The homes were neat and well-kept, but so alike that they were almost indistinguishable. Squat rectangles with wood siding and verandalike front porches. There was a turquoise pickup and a GMC High Sierra with a heavy-duty trailer hitch parked in front of Rose Cassiday's house. Wilson pulled the Suburban up to the curb. He mounted the steps to the porch, boards creaking with his weight, and pressed the doorbell. He heard a chime inside strike three notes with sonorous tones. He waited a full minute, was almost ready to ring again, when he heard someone approach the door.

A voice cracked with age called out, "Who is it?"

"It's Father Wilson, Mrs. Cassiday, don't be alarmed. Nothing's wrong." The door opened and Wilson stepped back and motioned her out on the porch. Rose Cassiday, frail and desiccated, closed the door softly behind her. "I just need to ask you a question or two. Is Mr. Rawlins still staying with you?"

The old woman nodded gravely.

"I'm sorry to seem so mysterious, but it's a discreet matter." Wilson looked at Mrs. Cassiday with a half-smile. "Would you keep our visit a secret?"

"Oh, sure." Her brogue was still lustrous and lilting, although sixty years had elapsed since she had left Kilkenny County.

"Has Mr. Rawlins been in all evening?"

"He went out for supper," Mrs. Cassiday said somberly.

"Did the others go with him?"

"Yes."

"Did they come back to your house together?"

Mrs. Cassiday thought a moment, then nodded affirmatively.

"What time?"

"I don't know for certain." She rolled the *r* deliciously. "Before eight, I think."

Wilson nodded, relieved. Joshua was probably still at Claudia's farm, then. "Was there any trouble here after they came in?"

"None a'tall."

"They didn't have any company? No one came by?"

Mrs. Cassiday kept peering at Wilson with great seriousness, giving careful deliberation to his questions before answering. "No, Father Wilson. No one else has been here."

"Thank you, Mrs. Cassiday." Wilson laid a hand on her shoulder and guided her back to her door. "I'm so sorry to have waked you and caused you this trouble."

"Not a'tall, Father." She paused at the screen door. "There's been no trouble with my boarders, Father. I won't have any shenanigans in Sean Cassiday's house, God rest his soul." She crossed herself and opened the door.

Wilson left Rose Cassiday's, certain that Rawlins and Joshua had not seen each other that night. He cruised up and down the streets of Plains, but did not run across Joshua's Toyota. He stopped at the Wheatlands Motel and made Mr. Lloyd open Joshua's room again, but he wasn't there. Wilson was out of ideas. He returned to St. Mary's and parked the Suburban. He let himself in the rectory, went to his desk, and removed a cigar from the bottom drawer and lit it. He knew he should call Claudia, but his reluctance to call her with nothing good to report prompted him to make his night rounds first. Puffing the cigar, he passed on into the nave to make certain that everything was in order, checking the sanctuary, library, confessionals, choir loft, foyer, and restrooms. As he was returning to the rectory, trying to think of what he should say to Claudia, his eye was caught by the votive candle rack. A single candle had been lit and left to burn in solitary supplication. Wilson walked over to the rack and stared at the candle. He thought back to the first night Joshua had come to St. Mary's. He had asked Josh whom he lit the candles for, and he had replied, "Tom Bishop." Josh must have been here, Wilson thought. And it had been since Claudia's visit, or he would have heard the bell in the rectory.

Wilson hurried to the garage and backed out the Suburban for the second time that night. It was worth a try.

As Wilson drove up cemetery hill, he could see Joshua's Toyota parked in front of the wrought iron gate. Clouds had massed and obscured the moon, and the barren rise of ground, with its mix of stones and obelisks, appeared spectral and forbidding. He left the Suburban behind the Toyota and picked his way among the monuments until he reached the Bishop family plot. He had a moment of misgiving as he approached the plot, because Joshua was nowhere in sight. Then he saw him inside the picket fence, sitting on the ground with his arms resting on his knees as he leaned back against a corner post.

Joshua watched Wilson as he made his way across the Maple Grove Cemetery. He spoke first when he saw that Wilson had spotted him. "You lost?"

"No, you're found."

"I didn't know I was lost."

Wilson opened the gate to the plot and stepped inside the picket fence. A coiled extension spring pulled the gate closed behind him, the rusted hinges squeaking in protest. "Claudia was looking for you. She got worried when she couldn't find you."

Joshua didn't respond.

"She has good instincts," Wilson said. "Don't sell her short."

"How'd you find me?"

Wilson squatted on the warm night earth and leaned back against the pickets. "Just a hunch," he said. "When Claudia couldn't find you, she came to the rectory. She didn't want to leave Todd alone any longer, so I told her I'd check around. I hadn't had any luck and went back to St. Mary's. I saw your candle." Wilson looked over at Joshua. "The one you always light for Tom Bishop." He paused and shrugged. "You told me today that you came out here last night, and I know what happened at the farm this evening."

Joshua looked up. "Claudia told you what happened to Tom?"

"Yes. Of course it happened to you, too," Wilson added.

Neither man spoke for a while. They sat under the shadowed moon and felt the earth beneath them, and listened to the night sounds. The wind rustling in the dry grass. The crickets' chirping. A whippoorwill's melancholy call. And at least a mile away, a coyote's howl.

Joshua finally spoke. "She told you about Todd, too?"

"Yes."

"I didn't mean for him to overhear."

"It's just as well, Josh."

Joshua gave a dry, bitter laugh. "Just as well for whom?"

"For all of you." Wilson reflected a moment. "Too many secrets from too many people means too many burdens."

"If I'd wanted a chaplain I'd have stayed in the Army."

Wilson laughed quietly. "You're such a hard-ass, Josh. You haunt churches. You light candles. You carry guilt. You look for God. There's a religious thread woven into the fabric of your entire life. You can't unravel it without unraveling yourself. And that's as it should be. There's a religious dimension to life, Josh. Your religion just prevented God and real life from making connections."

"What makes you think you know so much about my religion?"

"It's my job." Wilson plucked a blade of buffalo grass, grown high and gone to seed between the shelter of the pickets. "When your religion consists of being right, Josh, not much good will come of it." He chewed the bitter stem between his front teeth. "You remember the first night we talked, when I surprised you in St. Mary's?"

"Yes."

"I told you then that every man needs a priest. It's true. It can be anyone, of course. A parent, brother, sister, friend, wife, casual acquaintance. A drunk in a bar." Wilson laughed again. "Failing all those, even, God forbid, a clergyman." He spit out a small fragment of the grass stem and looked at Joshua. "Claudia Bishop was a priest for you tonight." Wilson began to chew the stem again, gradually grinding it to pulp. "A priest hears the confession and gives absolution."

"I received no absolution from Claudia tonight," Joshua said bitterly.

Wilson nodded. "Give her time."

"She never wants to see me again, Charlie."

"She came looking for you, didn't she?" Wilson retorted sharply. "Anyway," he went on in a quieter vein, "at least you've made the confession." He paused. "There's a fine line between revealing a secret, and a confession." Wilson shifted his back against the picket fence, easing a cramp. "You've been burdened with a terrible secret, Josh. A secret that was too painful to tell and too shattering to live with. It has sapped your whole life ever since. Secrets are funny things. If we can't ever keep a secret, we're not a whole person. But if we can't ever tell a secret, we're not a whole person either."

Joshua was leaning against the fence, head thrown back against the corner post, eyes fixed on some distant constellation in the black sky.

"When we keep a secret," Wilson went on, "about ourselves I

mean, it's a way of affirming our individual freedom. When we tell
a secret about ourselves, freely, to a person of our choosing, it's an
even greater affirmation of our individual freedom. The person
who can't keep a secret is not free, but the person who can never
reveal one is not free either." Wilson had chewed the grass stem
down to a stub. He tossed the blades and shank of seeds away.
"There are men who need to unburden themselves, Josh, in order
to free themselves and to find themselves."

Joshua sat unmoving, eyes closed, for a long time. Sifting through
the thoughts expressed by Charlie Wilson. Turning them over in
his mind, like prisms held up to refract light, while he absorbed the
calm, reassuring presence of the priest. Joshua didn't open his eyes,
but spoke in a quiet, resolute voice.

"Father, I killed Tom Bishop." Joshua stopped. His confession
hung between them. Suddenly he jerked his head away from the
corner post. Stared at Wilson in shock. He opened his mouth to
speak, but made no sound.

"Go on," the priest said. It was a command.

"Killing Tom was an accident." Joshua's voice was hushed. "A
terrible accident, but the fact of it crushed me. But, there was
something else that I don't think I realized until just now. Or
perhaps I knew it deep down, but couldn't face it." He paused,
looked again at Wilson. "The killing was an accident," Joshua repeated, as though confirming it in his own mind. "Not telling it was
an act of cowardice. I let everyone believe it was the NVA."

The priest did not hesitate. He raised his hand to Joshua and
made the sign of the cross. "In the name of our Lord Jesus Christ,
who by His passion and resurrection reconciled the world to His
Father, and by the power of the Holy Spirit, I absolve you from
your sin and I reconcile you with the Church. Amen." He repeated
the sign of the cross. "Go in peace."

Joshua was quiet, absorbing the enormity of the moment. Wilson
respected his silence, as comfortable in his role as friend as he had
been in his role as priest. Finally Joshua turned to him. "What's
going to happen now, Charlie?"

Wilson looked carefully at Joshua. "The secret has been told. It's
out in the open." He paused. "Your secret was an abyss when you
buried it. I think it can be a bridge now that you've told it."

"What should I do?"

Wilson shifted his weight against the fence, easing the pressure of a picket that pressed into his back. "I've given you absolution, Josh. Now I'm going to give you a penance."

"I don't know the rosary."

"Stay and work it through with Claudia and Todd," Wilson went on. "You've been responsible for death, now be responsible for life."

"How?"

"We'll go see them tonight."

There was a long silence. Finally Joshua spoke. "You're a hell of a priest, Charlie."

Wilson smiled and nodded diffidently. After a moment's hesitation he said, "I'm not a bad detective, either." He told Joshua what he had found out about Rawlins.

Joshua mulled over the information the priest had uncovered. Then he chuckled. "Claudia told me Rawlins' silo wasn't quite full."

Wilson laughed quietly. Then he added a word of caution. "Don't take it too lightly, though. The guy could be dangerous."

Joshua and Wilson remained in the Bishop family plot a while longer, each lost in his own thoughts. Then Wilson stood up and lightly shook Joshua's shoulder. "Let's go see Claudia," he said.

Joshua followed the big Suburban's taillights all the way to the Bishop farm. Claudia met them at the front door. Her face was composed. She held the screen open without a word.

"Where's Todd?" Wilson asked.

"In his room. He went up as soon as he saw your headlights turn up the drive."

Wilson nodded. "Just as well." He stood in the middle of the living room, studying Joshua and Claudia. They stood like stones, a dozen feet apart. The priest turned around and surveyed the room. His eyes fell on Tom Bishop's portrait above the fireplace mantel. He shuffled over and picked it up, holding it with both hands in front of him as he contemplated it.

"I wish I'd known this man." Wilson's voice was vibrant and wistful. "You two are really lucky." He went to Joshua and put an arm around his shoulders. "You felt too much, Josh," he said softly.

He pulled Joshua along with him, drawing him reluctantly but inexorably toward Claudia. "You tried to bear it all." Wilson approached Claudia with Joshua in tow and placed his other arm around Claudia's shoulders. In his hand he held Tom Bishop's portrait. "Claudia," he said, "you felt too little. You wouldn't allow yourself to bear anything."

Wilson drew them together, encircled in his arms, pulling them close in an embrace. "Today there's been a shifting of the load." Joshua and Claudia stood there, awkward and hesitant, held tight in the grasp of the priest. "You can help each other," he challenged. "To withhold that grace will be a sin against life."

Joshua felt Claudia's hand come up and tentatively touch his arm. "I would like to try," she whispered.

Joshua slowly lifted his arms to reach out to both Claudia and Wilson. He nodded in agreement.

"It must have been horrible for you," Claudia murmured.

"I'm sorry, Claudia," Joshua said. "So very sorry."

"It was a terrible accident," Claudia wept softly. "I know that."

Wilson tightened his grip on Joshua. "And you know it," he said passionately. Then he added, "And Tom knew it, too."

Joshua felt the tears sting his eyes as he and Claudia clung to each other, Charlie Wilson a bridge between them.

CHAPTER TWELVE

The Harvest Street Dance celebration attracted a huge crowd. Joshua left the Wheatlands Motel a little before noon and walked to town to meet Claudia. Streets were glutted with trucks, tractors, and farm implements. State troopers were stationed at either end of the town with barricades, diverting traffic to keep Main Street clear of vehicles for the parade. The sidewalks were crowded with pedestrians. The buzz of conversation, catcalls, and laughter swirled around Joshua as he picked his way along.

When he reached the benches in front of the Main Street Café, he took a seat and waited for Claudia to find him. They had talked until the early morning hours. Wilson had gone back to the rectory to leave for Forty Hours Devotion at Great Bend. They had sat on the porch swing, tentatively reaching out to each other across the pain and loss and confusion. They had examined the configuration of their lives, tracing the shadows of their past and weighing the substance of their future. When they finally separated they had agreed to meet in front of the café.

Joshua saw Claudia before she saw him. She was on the opposite side of Main, talking with a young couple who had two small boys in tow. Joshua looked closer and shook his head. The boys each had on a pair of tiny cowboy boots. They reminded him of the picture of Claudia holding Todd. He was young and innocent then, Joshua thought. Now he's big and losing his innocence. He watched Claudia. She threw back her head and laughed. The sound was lost in the street noise, but he could see the spontaneity and joy. It made him ache with a bittersweet hunger for her. He stood up and started across the street.

Claudia saw him coming, said good-bye to the couple she was talking to, and turned to face him. She waited on the curb in her Gloria Vanderbilt's, open-necked white blouse, and boots. She held the wicker picnic basket, and there was an air of expectance about her. She smiled. All those even white teeth. "Isn't it a marvelous day," she said.

Joshua reached out and took the wicker basket from her. "Quite a do," he said, glancing around.

"I told you the Harvest Street Dance was a big thing. It's kind of a county fair and Fourth of July picnic all rolled into one."

"What do we do?"

"Find a place to watch the parade." They moseyed along Main. Claudia spoke to nearly everyone, calling them by name and exchanging pleasantries. They stopped a couple of blocks beyond the courthouse where they could find some space on the curb. The sidewalk filled up behind them. Children pushed between their legs and wormed their way to the front where they could stand on the blacktop and see.

Joshua leaned over to Claudia. "Where's Todd?"

Her face clouded. "He wouldn't come with me."

"Do you feel like you need to be at home with him?" Joshua asked. "We can cancel our plans for the day, and I can go out to the farm with you if you like."

"No. He was all right when I left. I told him if he felt like it to come in later and find us."

"I hope he does."

"I think he'll be okay," Claudia said. "There's some space now to handle Todd later. When Charlie found you last night and brought you back to the farm, that was the beginning."

Claudia and Joshua were interrupted by the whistles and cheers of the crowd. Applause echoed up and down the street. The parade had started. Leading the way were the Plains mayor and his wife. They were in a big white 1959 Cadillac convertible. Tail fins and all. They were seated on the body of the car behind the rear seat. Big Ed waved and hollered at the crowd, pointing sausagelike fingers and calling out to friends. Mrs. Big Ed sat primly beside her garrulous husband with the patient, martyred look of someone who had seen and heard it all before. Joshua joined the applause as the Cadillac passed. It had a personalized license plate: MOBY DK.

Behind the mayor was a huge Conestoga wagon drawn by two yoked oxen. It appeared to Joshua as if the brass historical marker he had seen on the edge of town the first night he arrived in Plains had come to life. A man with a full beard, dressed in homespun, drove the big covered wagon. Beside him on the seat were a woman and a boy in settler's garb. None of the three waved to the crowd. Their jaws were set, and it was as if they were alone, eyes fixed on some far horizon. The wagon rolled past, pots and pans clanking on its ribbed sides, with a wooden water barrel lashed to the tailboard, water sloshing over the top.

They were followed by a man riding a huge buffalo. He wore deerskin and carried a long muzzle-loading flintlock rifle. He was as seedy-looking as the shaggy brown beast he rode. Someone from the crowd called out, "Hey, George! Someday one of those animals of yours is gonna stomp your ass flatter'n a buffalo turd!" The man cackled. A high, maniacal laugh that seemed to skirt the fringes of sanity. He pointed the flintlock at the man in the crowd and pulled the trigger. It went off with a tremendous roar amid a cloud of black powder smoke. The crowd shrieked with delight and cheered as the man spurred the buffalo along.

Joshua leaned over toward Claudia. "Did you ever think that most of the men who first came west must have been a little nutty?"

Claudia laughed and applauded. "Old George would have fit right in."

Some floats rolled past. The 4-H had a flatbed trailer pulled by a big green John Deere tractor. It displayed the produce of Cimarron County. The Demolay float consisted of a Demolay banner stretched between two young men standing in the back of a pickup. They were sweating heavily in their blue serge suits, white shirts, and navy ties. They looked serious and dedicated.

At that moment the little girl in pigtails Joshua had watched skating in the park moved down the sidewalk pulling a milk crate in a wagon. The crate was filled with paper cups of iced Kool-Aid. Her nemesis, Billy, the boy with the cottonwood pods, worked the crowd for her—twenty-five cents a cup. Joshua selected the grape flavor, Claudia the lime.

When they turned back to the parade, a big flatbed truck inched by with the Plains Pairs and Squares Club. A speaker mounted over the cab blared out fiddle music. A caller stood on the truck bed with a bullhorn in his hand and stomped his foot in rhythm to the music while four couples do-si-doed and promenaded.

The presidents of the Rotary Club, the Lions Club, and the Optimist Club each rolled by in identical blue Chevrolet Impalas. A notation on the banners identifying the clubs informed the crowd that the vehicles were provided by the Winston Voit Chevrolet-Cadillac Dealership in Wichita. Apparently Winston Voit drove the lead Impala, because a heckler in the crowd called out, "Why didn't you let 'em use the Cadillacs, Winnie?"

Another long trailer approached. It held the Cimarron County Consolidated High School football team. The boys had bushel baskets filled with miniature rubber footballs, and they hurled them at the spectators. The bystanders cheered while someone bellowed, "Undefeated this year!" Someone else yelled, "Get Wichita!" The crowd roared approval. Claudia put two fingers in her mouth and emitted an ear-piercing whistle.

Joshua looked at her in admiration. "I never could do that," he said. They looked in vain for Todd. "Do you see him?" Joshua asked.

"No," Claudia replied, shaking her head, "but he'll come around."

Next came a gaggle of kids. Some rode bicycles and tricycles decorated with crepe paper. Others roller-skated. One girl blowing huge bubbles with purple bubble gum did incredible front walkovers while skating. Kids pulled their dogs or cats in wagons. Some of the pets jumped out and had to be chased down, while other children had their pets on leashes. One boy walked nonchalantly along with a skunk on a leash. He got lots of advice from the crowd. There was one dog cart with a well-behaved shepherd in the traces. Some kids pushed soapbox cars or pedaled along in toy cars and fire trucks. A few got tired and pulled over and quit. Some cried. Their parents came along and collected them.

The Plains fire truck rolled past. It was shiny and apple-green. The brass and chrome had been polished to mirror perfection. To the delight of the crowd, occasionally they would crank up the siren. The ladder men on the back tossed handfuls of candy to the people lining the parade route. Joshua joined the scramble to come up with his share. He retrieved two pieces. Kept the sour ball for himself and gave the marshmallow peanut to Claudia.

A procession of farm implements followed, some antique and some modern. Tractors, combines, drills, harrows. A mule dragged along a heavy wooden sod-busting plow. The single curved blade rode a few inches off the pavement on a board with coasters. The board was layered with dirt that had been sculpted into a furrow. A man in coveralls and straw hat trudged along behind the mule and geed and hawed whenever the mood struck him. The mule ignored the commands and plodded straight ahead.

It was followed by a score of mounted cavalry. They were dressed authentically in Union blue, campaign hats at a rakish angle. A number of the men sported impressive regimental mustaches. Sheathed sabers rattled from their belts. Remington repeating rifles were booted in saddle scabbards. The lead rider held a Second Cavalry guidon that snapped in the breeze. A cheer went up as they clattered by, which was followed immediately by a high-pitched series of rebel yells. Another dozen mounted riders trotted along Main Street. They were a motley mix of rowdies in black cutaway coats, greatcoats, waistcoats, homespun Mexican vests, and serapes. Pistols were tied low on their hips, and they carried rifles or wore crossed bandoliers of ammunition on their chests. Some wore cowboy hats, while others wore sombreros or Confederate forage caps. Some of the men fired their six-guns in the air and the horses skittered. The crowd gave them plenty of space.

"Quantrill's Raiders, right?" Joshua asked.

"That's right," Claudia replied.

Wheat trucks followed, the beds filled to overflowing with harvested grain. Some of it sifted to the pavement like golden rain as the trucks jostled over the blacktop. Lettered poster boards tacked to the sides identified the strain of wheat in each truck, as well as the production level. Eagle, dryland, 29 bushels per acre. Vona, irrigated, 52 bushels per acre. Newton, dryland, 34 bushels per acre. And so on. Each time a truck passed, the crowd stomped their feet and whistled and applauded.

Behind the loaded wheat trucks was an incredible sight. A mile-long column of combines, tractors, flatbeds, wheat trucks, pickups, four-wheelers, vans, and campers. A fusion of diesel fumes and grinding gears and air horns and shouts as several hundred men maneuvered the heavy equipment along the parade route. The gigantic caravan provoked an emotional transport among the citizens of Cimarron County. A peculiar mix of pride, delight, satisfaction, accomplishment, well-being, nostalgia, regret, and good-bye. The custom cutters would trek north, a mass exodus of men and machines that would find them in Canada in September.

As the last of the custom cutters passed by, the attention of the crowd was diverted by four sharp blasts on a whistle. The High School band broke into "Stars and Stripes Forever." The spontaneous applause quickly solidified into rhythmic hand-clapping in time to the march.

Close on the heels of the band was a color guard from the Kansas National Guard. The four men half stepped with parade-ground precision to the music. The two guardsmen in the middle held an American flag and a sky-blue Kansas state flag. A guardsman on one flank carried a thirty-four-star American flag, and the guardsman on the other flank carried the Stars and Bars of the Confederacy. The applause swelled and continued in volume for the next group of marchers, a contingent from the VFW and the American Legion. They marched along in ragged rhythm, waving at the crowd. Not a man among them appeared less than fifty years of age.

All in all, Joshua thought as he stood there applauding with the rest of the crowd, they looked rather pathetic. Old and pathetic. And a little bit foolish. But proud. Some of them wore the blue peaked cap of the VFW. Others wore their service caps. White Navy caps. Leather Army Air Force flight helmets. Marine Raider caps. Army dress hats. And here and there a pot helmet. Some had medals pinned to their shirts. A few carried tiny American flags. There was one emphysematous old man being pushed along in a wheelchair. He wore a pitted olive-drab helmet of the American Expeditionary Force and held a card across his chest that read, "Rainbow Division—1917." A scattering of the veterans held hand-lettered signs. "Guadalcanal." "Utah Beach." "Kasserine Pass." "The Big E." "Chosin Reservoir."

Joshua watched the procession. "And Thang Duc, too, dammit," he muttered aloud. Suddenly, on impulse, Joshua handed Claudia the basket and stepped off the curb. He turned to face the crowd that lined the curb six deep. "All right," Joshua called out, "there must be some grunts out there!"

The crowd stared at him, puzzled.

"Come on," Joshua yelled, "I want some grunts in this parade!"

The applause thinned. Then died out. The crowd stirred uneasily and watched Joshua with embarrassment. No one moved. The band was playing "She's My Sunflower from the Sunflower State."

"There's some men out there who've been in the shit!" Joshua called out. "Now get in this parade!" Joshua started moving along the street in the wake of the VFW and American Legion. The Highway Patrol car that was trailing the end of the parade slowed and gave him some room. "You," Joshua said, pointing at random at a man about thirty-five who stood on the curb. "What unit?"

The man looked blankly at him and shook his head.

Joshua pointed at another man. "How about it?"

"First of the Fifth. Hue."

"Get your ass out here, Marine." Joshua gave him a hard, ironic smile and stuck out his hand. "A-two-one-niner, Special Forces, II Corps." They shook hands.

Joshua turned back, cupped his hands to his mouth, and yelled at Claudia, "I'll meet you at the big well!" He and the Marine walked together along the street. Joshua felt a surge of exhilaration and reached out with both arms and motioned to the bystanders on either side of the street. "Okay, grunts! Front and center, come on now!"

A big man, burly gone to fat, pushed through the crowd to the curb and joined Joshua and the Marine. "Nineteenth MP Battalion, Tan Son Nhut!" he said. He shook Joshua's hand and there was a small ripple of applause.

Suddenly the Marine called to a man on the sidewalk. "Hey, Frank, get out here!"

The man hesitated a moment, then let go of his wife's hand and stepped into the street. "1st Infantry Division, Iron Triangle!" he said. The applause picked up.

A few yards further on, a short, square man with a thinning crew cut forced his way past the crowd and bounded into the street. He turned back to face the crowd, raised his hands over his head in the victorious stance of a fighter, and yelled, "Big Red One, Cantigny!" The applause swelled.

Then the momentum took over. Joshua just walked along in the middle of the street. Every ten yards or so another man would join the parade to the gathering applause and cheers of the crowd. Joshua listened to the outfits and the names and the comments. Some of it laid a frost on his soul.

"173rd Airborne Brigade, Dak To!"

"G-2, MACV, Saigon!"

"Vietnam was like making love to a gorilla. Even if it didn't kill you, it still got your gonads."

"Ten years ago I got blamed for going. Now I get blamed for losing."

"USS Ranger, Yankee Station, South China Sea!"

"25th Infantry, Pleiku!"

"How was it, man?"

"Oh, you know. We killed a mess of them and they killed a mess of us. Then we came home."

"101st Airborne, A Shau Valley!"

"It's been like ten thousand miles of bad road."

"Payback is a mother-fucker."

"Charlie Company, 1st Infantry, Fire Base Julie!"

"3rd Brigade of the 25th Infantry, Dau Tieng!"

"I didn't know you were in the Nam."

"Hell, my wife don't know it."

"2nd Battalion, 1st Marines, I Corps!"

"B-52 Navigator, Eighth Air Force, U-Tapao, Thailand!"

"You made some big holes, man."

"Hotel Company of the 26th." The man held up a clenched fist. "The Few, the Proud. Khe Sanh!"

"I hated them fuckin' hills."

"The heat! It was like one of George's buffaloes came and laid down on your face."

A spare woman with her hair pulled back in a bun gave a three-year-old boy she was holding to the lady next to her and joined the marchers. "Nurse, U.S. Army, 8th Field Hospital, Qui Nhon!"

"The Vietnamese, man. We was either killin' 'em, feedin' 'em, or fuckin' 'em."

"It was just me and God, baby."

"Black Lions, 2nd Battalion, 28th Infantry Regiment, Parrot's Beak!"

"I was a killer-ambusher. All alone at night three hundred meters beyond our wire. It was crazy but I kept goin' back out. Like

an alcoholic whose first drink makes somethin' click in his brain.
You know you're onto somethin'."

"I loved it. I hate to admit it, but I did. I really loved it."

"We did some things. We *did* some *things.* Nobody ever cared,
though." He spit and wiped the sweat from his forehead with the
back of his forearm. "Hell, I don't need a pat on the butt. But
nobody even *knows.*"

"First Air Cav!" The man's right leg was shorter than his left, and
he walked with a stiff knee. He took a quick extra hitch-along on
his gimp leg to keep pace. "Ia Drang Valley!"

"Piecemeal killin', just piecemeal killin'."

"Hide-and-seek. It was like chasin' a witch's tail."

"Most of the time I felt like some migrant killer."

"Big Red One, Bravo Company, Bandit Hill!"

"I dug it. Terror and survival. The ultimate high."

"The nights were beautiful. The incomin' and the outgoin'. Blue
and green and red. Scared the shit out of me."

"Felt like someone was drivin' over my chest with a John
Deere."

"There was enough 'Can you believe this fuckin' shit?' to hold
me till the day I die."

"Like makin' a stab wound in hell just to let some stuff out."

"Cobra pilot, 206th Assault Helicopter Company, Phu Loi!"

"Some of you bastards shot up my platoon."

"Can't guess right every time."

"River Patrol Group 44!" The man had a burn scar across his left
face that pulled the corner of his mouth down. "Mekong Delta!"

"I read somewhere it cost forty-two cents for the Vietnamese to
kill one American, and twenty-seven thousand dollars for the
Americans to kill one Vietnamese."

"There it is."

"Man, we sprayed the Orange. Motto was 'We Prevent Forests.'
But I think we prevented a lot more 'n that. Do I look a little yellow
to you? I think I prevented my liver. Fuckin' VA in Topeka says
I drink too much. Hell, I don't drink a six-pack a month."

"Fourth Infantry, I Corps!"

"When I came back through the Oakland Army Terminal, some
goddamn hippies told me the war was immoral. Dumb fuckers. It
wasn't immoral, it was *futile.*"

"Makes no difference how you slice it. It was either a failure in judgment or a failure of nerve. Either way, I got no respect for the government."

"Americal Division, II Corps!"

"When I wasn't hatin' them dinks, I felt sorry for 'em."

"Tough little fuckers."

"Only difference between us and them NVA grunts is that their leaders knew what they were doin'."

"U.S. Navy Light Attack Squadron 4, Binh Thuy!"

"We were right all along. Vietnam, Laos, Cambodia. They were fuckin' dominoes."

"If I had known what Washington was gonna do in 1974, I'd have gone to jail in 1970."

"You know, I think there was a point in history where America could have done somethin'." The man shrugged his shoulders. "But what the hell, we quit."

"Vietnam, baby. The great American snipe hunt."

Another woman joined them. She was blond, tall and lanky. "Nurse, 3rd Surgical Hospital, Binh Thuy!"

"Tanks, man. They had fuckin' tanks. We never had a chance."

A man on the curb reached into his wife's purse, took out her eye shadow, and smeared it across his forehead and cheeks. He stepped into the street. "Long Range Reconnaissance Patrol, 4th Division, Can Tho!"

"U.S. Navy, Seals, Mekong Delta!"

"I didn't know there were this many of us."

"Long fuckin' war, man."

"We went, we got the rug jerked out from under us, and when we came home our money wasn't worth nothin'."

"You got it, man. Every Vietnam vet was ultimately the victim of friendly fire."

"1st Infantry, Dian!" From the cuff of the man's sleeve a metal claw protruded.

"I hadn't been there a month when I knew we couldn't win. Not under our ground rules. I decided then just to get in my three-sixty-five and take the Freedom Bird back to the world."

"I'll tell you how we could have won. Nuked Cambodia, nuked Laos, and then took fifty-seven thousand men, the number we lost, linked hands all across South Vietnam and walked north to the

DMZ, and then nuked the North. Been home in a month."

"1st Infantry, Lai Khe!"

"Would you have rather fought 'em there or in Wichita?"

"I think we could have whipped 'em in Wichita."

They walked along the parade route engulfed in applause. There was an element of ecstasy and euphoria about it. As though they had pulled the pin on themselves, and in so doing had sucked it out of the crowd. It was an insular time warp. The parade they never had. There was no logic to it. All of a sudden the applause died out. They were on the edge of town opening up to a field of wheat stubble. The parade was breaking up. They all stood there, shifting their weight on their feet. Hands in pockets. Sometimes looking at one another. Sometimes avoiding it. Absorbing the consequence of the moment. Caught up in it. Coming down off of it.

"Shit!" a man said and burst into tears. The Lurp from the 4th Division, his wife's eye shadow smeared on his face like camouflage cover, said, "Hell, let's go back to the Billiard Parlor Bar and not take any prisoners." Everyone laughed. "Yeah," said the trooper from the First Air Cav, "we'll search and destroy the mother-fucker." The Marine who had first joined Joshua on the street turned to him and said, "I want to buy you a drink."

"Just one," Joshua agreed. "I got to meet a lady."

CHAPTER THIRTEEN

Joshua finished his Heineken, left the Billiard Parlor Bar, and crossed the street. The park was filled with people. He left the crowded brick sidewalk and moved across the lawn. He spotted Claudia on a park bench near the well. He skirted picnickers with their blankets spread out, people relaxing in folding lounge chairs under shade trees, old men at picnic tables playing forty-two, card tables where people sat playing carom, frisbee throwers, hula hoopers, horseshoe pitchers, a game of softball workup, and a dog trying to mount a bitch in heat, to the delight of some teenage boys, while a lady crammed into a pair of pedal pushers tried in vain to put a stop to it. Joshua walked past the rutting dogs, unable to suppress a smile. The city park in Plains, Kansas, he thought, a good place for lovers. He stopped in front of Claudia and slipped his hands in the hip pockets of his jeans.

Claudia looked up and smiled, shading her eyes with her hand. "I know you," she said. "You're the Pied Piper of Vietnam veterans." She moved the picnic basket to the edge of the park bench and scooted over to make a place for him. "How was the parade?"

"Interesting." Joshua didn't sit down, but placed a foot up on the bench and leaned forward with his elbows on his knee.

"You attracted quite a crowd."

Joshua shrugged self-consciously. "Well, maybe we needed a parade."

"In Plains, Kansas?"

"Good place for it." Joshua smiled. "Maybe the only place we could have one." He picked up the picnic basket and held out a hand. "I'm hungry. Where do you want to eat?"

Claudia took his hand as she stood up and looked around. "Over there." She pointed to a huge cottonwood beyond the hand-dug well. It was away from the crowd. When they reached the tree, Claudia opened the wicker basket and removed the same blanket they had picnicked on beside the Cimarron. They spread it out beside the cottonwood's massive trunk, and Joshua lay down. He stretched his long frame across the length of the blanket, not so much lying on the ground as giving himself to the warm earth. Claudia placed a platter between them and began to lay out wedges of cheese, cold cuts, hard-boiled eggs, sliced tomatoes, cucumbers, and assorted crackers. She glanced sideways at Joshua. "You look relaxed," she observed.

"It's been that kind of a day. The kind of a day you can lean into. Put your weight on. I haven't known that feeling for a long time."

"Sounds like a good feeling."

"A little strange, though."

Claudia laid out squares of gingerbread around the edge of the platter. "How strange?"

"I haven't put my full weight on anything for years. It's like the earth shifted under my feet twelve years ago and I've been off balance ever since." Joshua sat up and leaned against the trunk of the cottonwood, feeling the rough bark through his shirt. He glanced away from Claudia, a respite from her steady gaze. Finally he looked back and smiled.

Claudia studied his face. The guarded look was still there, especially in the shadowed, distant eyes. But the features were less taut, and the dislocation between eyes and smile was not as extreme as the afternoon she had first met him. Claudia reached out and touched his face. "Maybe Charlie's right," she said, "about sharing burdens and all." She removed a chilled bottle of wine from a wine caddy in the picnic basket. "We can get through life without friends or love, Josh, but it's a lonely way." She handed him the wine and a corkscrew.

Joshua held the bottle up and read the label. It was a Chardonnay, Robert Mondavi Vineyards, Vintage 1974. "Ripple Blanc." He grinned and extracted the cork with a sibilant pop.

Claudia produced two long-stemmed wineglasses. Joshua poured the Chardonnay and lifted his glass toward Claudia's in a toast. "To the less lonely way," he said.

"And to putting one's weight down," Claudia added as she inclined her glass toward his and drank.

They lowered their glasses and evaluated each other across three feet of blanket, twelve years, and two lifetimes. Claudia slowly rose up on her knees and leaned toward Joshua. Their mouths brushed. Her lips were full and cool and soft. Joshua felt the tip of her tongue graze his lips in a light caress. He parted his lips slightly and tasted the biting piquancy of the Chardonnay. They held the kiss with a wistful, gentle ardor. Then Joshua lifted a hand to the back of Claudia's head. He tangled his fingers in her hair and pressed her mouth firmly against his. Lips moved and tongues roved with an urgent need that ignited in a flash of passion, then steadied and slowed to an attenuated longing. They drew apart.

Joshua studied Claudia's face. He could see her pulse throbbing in her neck. Her eyes were moist. He reached out and brushed a tear from her cheek. "Maybe we should eat," he said, his voice husky. He topped off the wineglasses while Claudia got napkins from the picnic basket and placed the platter between them.

They ate for a while in silence, enjoying the moment and the hot, lazy afternoon. Finally Claudia spoke. "How do you feel about last night?"

"Like what?"

"All of it."

Joshua sipped the wine and let it lie on his palate a moment before he swallowed. "I have some regrets. There are ways I hate for you to know . . . to know what happened . . ." He struggled a moment, searching for a bland euphemism, then decided to say it and looked Claudia full in the face. "There are ways I hate for you to know that I killed Tom. I feel it diminishes me."

Claudia nodded in understanding. Her silence an invitation for communication.

"But in other ways," Joshua went on, "the fact that you know is a tremendous relief. Maybe life won't seem counterfeit anymore."

"Sometimes," Claudia mused, "we are given no solutions and no alternatives. Our only choice is how we're going to eat the pain." She paused as she reached for a wedge of cheese, then looked up at Joshua. "You lived with it for a long time. I don't know how you stood it."

"I've tried to keep my life compartmentalized. That way I could keep a tight grip on it. But there was always spillover. Tension. Flashbacks. Nightmares. Guilt. The shakes." Joshua paused as he came to a gradual realization. "You know," he said, "the parade today with all those veterans was almost like a Vietnam muster of units and places." He shook his head. "Incredible. And their comments. Jesus." His words trailed off into the vaporous heat of the afternoon as he reflected on it. "But it didn't trigger a single flashback. And I didn't get the shakes. Today I *remembered*, but I wasn't the victim of memory."

Claudia smiled. Then laughed. Threw back her head and laughed through tears.

Joshua picked up a square of gingerbread. Warm and moist and sticky. He placed the entire square in his mouth as he licked his fingers. "Charlie Wilson," he mumbled around the gingerbread, "said you were my priest. To hear my confession and give absolution."

"When did he say that?"

"Last night at the cemetery."

Claudia sipped her wine. "Someday I think I would like to go with you to Tom's grave."

The thought made Joshua's stomach turn. "For God's sake, why?"

"To share the memory, and to grieve together. To say some final benediction in each other's presence."

"Todd, too?"

"I hope it can happen."

"I've hurt him a great deal," Joshua said.

"He'll come around," Claudia said. "He has to learn that accidents happen. People make mistakes. Tragedies occur. Things are not always what they seem, good or bad. Maybe you can help Todd understand that."

"Maybe."

"You can, Josh. You're real, and you're here with us, and you're a good person. That counts for something."

Joshua didn't reply. He swirled the wine in his glass and stared into it.

"It counts for something with me," Claudia said quietly. She began to place the leftover food in Tupperware and pack it away in the picnic basket.

Joshua lay back on the blanket and experienced the heat of the afternoon. The warmth seeped into his flesh and fused with the wine to produce a lassitude that bordered on the peace Wilson had pronounced. He closed his eyes and drifted with the moment. . . . When he awoke, the late afternoon sun was slanting across the blanket in patterned leafy shadows. He looked around. Claudia was seated off to one side, leaning back against the trunk of the cotton-wood, watching him. She smiled. A private smile that acknowl-edged secrets already shared and hinted at secrets yet to be discov-ered.

"I thought you might sleep the afternoon away," Claudia said, her voice lazy and liquid in the heat.

"Why didn't you wake me?"

Claudia tilted her head back against the tree trunk. "It was so peaceful," she said, "I didn't want to interrupt it." She moved away from the trunk and crawled toward him on the blanket, moving slowly on hands and knees with feline grace, as though stalking him. She stopped over his face, eyes bright and eager, and dipped her head and gave him a quick kiss. "But now," she said, "we've got to see the exhibits and get ready for the dance. We're going to two-step till the fiddle breaks."

The wind died down by late afternoon, but the temperature barely declined from its midday high. It promised a hot, quiet night. Joshua and Claudia wandered through the park. On the back side of the park in a field of wheat that had been reduced to stubble, they watched a tractor-pulling contest. Huge blocks of concrete stacked on heavy wooden sleds were drawn through an intricate maze. Then the tractors were chained together back to back by their rear axles, and each driver tried to drag the other across a line. It was arm wrestling with 400-horsepower diesel biceps.

At the edge of the field was a grueling competition among wheat scoopers. A grain loader moved wheat from a truck bed to the ground. The auger device delivered fifty bushels per minute in a cascading pile at the feet of the contestant. A second grain loader, a few feet away, returned the wheat to the truck as the contestant scooped it from the pile accumulating at his feet to the loading funnel of the second grain loader. Each contestant was allowed exactly three minutes. It was deadly serious. A matter of pride. They worked with grim determination at a feverish pace. Joshua and Claudia watched a half-dozen competitors. Lean, powerful men. Stripped to the waist. Muscles rippling and sweat glistening in the afternoon sun. Travis Rawlins was one of the competitors. He moved an astonishing ninety-two bushels of wheat in his allotted three minutes. He turned to face Joshua and Claudia as he wiped his chest with his shirt. His taunting look was laced with resentment.

They drifted back into the park and circulated among the booths. They stopped at the booth where the aberrations of nature's vegetable kingdom were on display. Todd's watermelon didn't even place. A mind-boggling green bean that was six feet in length won the blue ribbon. A sunflower that measured thirty-two inches across its face placed second. And a squash that had engulfed a cucumber, devouring it, placed third.

When they reached Main Street, the fire truck was providing a cooling diversion for anyone willing to get wet. The nozzle on a hose had been adjusted to deliver a fine mist. Everyone from naked babies to fully clothed adults frolicked in the spray.

Joshua and Claudia meandered back into the park, soaking up the carefree mood. They kept an eye out for Todd, but he was nowhere to be seen. They found themselves at the barbecue pit where the wire mesh cages of snakes had been collected. Over five thousand snakes had been brought in. Some cages were placed around the area at random so people could gawk at the reptiles. Other cages were sequestered behind the barbecue pit so they could be "harvested" for the snake fry. And some had been tagged for judging in the various categories in the rattlesnake competition. The judging was in progress: the snakes were being measured and weighed, and the rattles counted. Big Ed was in charge and handled the snakes. He appeared fearless, grasping the rattlers behind their jaws with deft, sure movements that delighted and amazed the crowd. They gasped and applauded with a delicious sense of danger by proxy as they observed Big Ed's act. Joshua had the feeling that his principal mayoral duty was to let his constituents watch him handle the snakes.

A diamondback five feet nine and a half inches long won in the length category. A prairie rattler, shorter, but with a body almost as thick as Big Ed's arm, won in the weight division, topping the scales at twenty-nine and a quarter pounds. And a prairie rattler with fourteen rattles outdistanced all competitors for the number of rattles. A sidewinder, much smaller than the one Joshua and Todd had tried to take, won length among the few sidewinders rounded up.

The three Plains service-club presidents were busy at the barbecue pit cooking the rattlesnakes for the evening meal. Several men worked behind a fence partition at the rear of the pit, preparing the snakes for cooking. After they decapitated them, they cut them into six-inch sections. Then they filleted them, cleaned them, and passed them on to the cooks. The crowd filed past the barbecue pit, paper plates in hand, to get their rattlesnake steak, beans, salsa, and bread. The picnic tables in the park filled up, as well as the extra tables set up around the barbecue pit. Several tables were kept clear for those entered in the snake-eating contest. Sheer quantity was the goal, and judges monitored each table, meticulously weighing each contestant's portions.

"How about supper?" Claudia asked.

"What's it like?" Joshua asked, nodding at the rattlesnake fillets.

"Barbecued chicken."

"Think I'll pass it up," Joshua said.

"Then how about dessert?" They walked back across the park to the booths, where they purchased two slices of chocolate cake with burnt-sugar icing and two dishes of homemade ice cream.

They returned to their cottonwood tree and ate in the gathering dusk. They had a good view of the band shell, and as they ate they listened to the final competitors in the talent contest. A trio of girls sang an anemic, slightly off-key version of "Whispering Hope." A young man who was a credible juggler worked his way through a series of balls, clubs, and flaming torches while he delivered an atrocious comic monologue. A barbershop quartet sang a medley of Stephen Foster songs. And a teenage rock band slammed their way through a number using three chords, while they gyrated and screeched unintelligible lyrics.

The final contestant was a withered old man who played the saw. He wore faded overalls and the top from a pair of long-handled underwear for a shirt. Joshua wasn't sure if it was a costume or if that was the way he really dressed. The old man shuffled hesitantly to the front of the band shell, wiping his face with a crumpled blue bandanna. He sat in a straight-backed chair and carefully resined up his bow. This task completed, he placed the tip of the crosscut saw on a block of wood between his feet and tentatively drew the bow across the rear edge of the blade. He cocked his ear to the saw with thoughtful concentration and played a few notes, changing the pitch by applying pressure on the saw handle to vary the curve of the blade. A gentle tremor of his hand caused the saw to vibrate, and the blade sang with a wailing vibrato. Satisfied with what passed for tuning when playing the saw, he paused a moment, then played a movement of a Mozart violin concerto with brilliant precision.

Nearby listeners were astonished, and the forceful presence of the artist and his music impressed itself in ever-widening circles until almost everyone in the park was listening with rapt attention. He closed to enthusiastic applause. Shouts of "Encore!" echoed through the crowd, mingled with cries of personal admiration. "Attaboy, Thurman!" "Outasight!" "Go for it, Thurman!" "We dig it, Thurman!"

The old man seemed confounded at first by the outburst of applause and affection. He shifted his weight, ill at ease, then with embarrassed graciousness sat down again. He waited until the applause and cheering subsided, and then played "Amazing Grace." The notes of the familiar hymn rose and fell and reverberated through the park with a sonorous metallic moan. The melody floated on the warm evening air, quavering with a haunting beauty that cast a spell over the hushed audience. As the last notes died away, the crowd was silent. Reluctantly, quietly, they slowly resumed their activities.

Joshua and Claudia relaxed on the blanket beneath the cottonwood tree. They listened to the rising chorus of locusts as darkness fell. Then the strings of multicolored lights came on. The hues and haze gave the park a mystical, magic-lantern quality. A country-western band began to assemble beneath the concentric tiers of recessed lighting in the band shell. Joshua saw that Thurman, the virtuoso on the crosscut saw, played fiddle for the group. With a minimum of fuss the band got ready to play, and in a few minutes were wheeling through a rendition of the old bluegrass tune "Soldier's Joy." Joshua couldn't help but grin. They were good. The plywood dance floor in front of the band shell filled up with couples. They spun and twisted and whirled and stomped and hollered. Some were merely enthusiastic. Others wheeled through the intricate maneuvers of country swing with a smooth, effortless grace that raised kicker-dancing to an art form.

Joshua and Claudia listened to a few numbers, relishing the irresistible gaiety of the music and the style and expertise of the musicians. After a while they made their way onto the dance floor. They moved and swayed and touched and two-stepped, captivated by the music and the motion. Claudia taught Joshua the twenty-seven-step schottische. Joshua talked three other couples, one of them the Marine from Hue and his wife, into joining him and Claudia, and he taught them the Virginia reel. By ten o'clock they were happily exhausted, sweaty, and flushed with the quiet pleasure of unexpected joy in each other's presence.

They left the dance floor and found a booth where a motherly lady made them each a slush of sherbet and lemonade. They sipped their drinks beneath their cottonwood and listened to the band. The lead guitarist and the mandolin player sang "Silver Threads and Golden Needles" in a harmony so tight it could etch brass. Thurman played the "Orange Blossom Special" so well they should have retired his bow. Then the leader of the band announced that a special number had been rehearsed, and asked all the fiddle players to get their instruments and join the band. It appeared to Joshua that every fiddle player in Cimarron County trooped onstage. The leader introduced the number, "Smoke Along the Track," and said the breakdown would be done as a twenty-one-fiddle salute. He turned back to the band, and with "uh-one, uh-two, uh-three, uh-four" and a nod of his head, they ripped into the tune. The massed fiddles joined in with a strident flourish. A penetrating resonant horsehair-and-gut squeal that reduced the band to backup.

With a yell the crowd swarmed the dance floor, dug in their heels, and danced with abandon. A corner of the dance floor was taken over by about eight men. Joshua watched in fascination. The men shuffled, tapped, and stomped their feet in loose-jointed rhythm to the music, while at the same time they turned and wheeled and executed kicks and slapped their knees and feet with their hands. It was a blend of tap dance, soft shoe, buck-and-wing,

Irish jig, Highland fling, polka, jitterbug, and country swing. The moves were performed with the grace of a Bojangles, but the entire effect was exuberant rowdiness.

Joshua shook his head and looked at Claudia. "They're cloggers," she yelled above the music and the dance-floor racket. She pointed a finger at the men. "That's cloggin'!"

The fiddles and the band propelled "Smoke Along the Track" to a frenzied climax. The cloggers stomped into a long row, linked arms across their shoulders, and formed a cloggin' chorus line. The maneuver was so natural it seemed spontaneous, but it was so practiced it must have been choreographed. They finished the number with such rousing energy that the remainder of the dancers stopped to watch, clapping in rhythm and yelling encouragement. With a shout and thunderous applause the musical mayhem and dancing crashed to a close.

Big Ed made his way to the band shell and took over the microphone. He restored order as the band took a break and prepared to announce the winners of the various contests held throughout the day. The crowd in the park began to drift toward the band shell. The first award went to the boy who had won the rattlesnake-eating contest. He was a towheaded kid of about fourteen who looked well on his way to being the town's next Big Ed. He had consumed nine and a half pounds of rattlesnake meat.

Joshua and Claudia decided to call it a day. He would go back to the motel and pick up his Toyota, then go out to the farm. Maybe talk to Todd. They folded the blanket, tucked it in the picnic basket, and started across the park on one of the brick walkways. At the big well they found their way blocked by Travis Rawlins.

Rawlins stood determinedly in the middle of the walk. Joshua could tell he was a little beery, but he figured Rawlins could sweat Jack Daniels and not really feel it. Travis deliberately ignored Joshua, fixing his eyes on Claudia as he pushed his black Stetson back on his head. He shook a cigarette into his mouth from a Camel soft pack with studied insolence, and struck a wooden kitchen match with his thumbnail. As the match flared, he cupped the flame with both hands and lifted it to his cigarette, drawing deeply on it. Rawlins waved the match out and tossed it aside. "Could I have a dance, ma'am?" His drawl was as abrasive as a West Texas dust storm.

Claudia hesitated briefly, then said, "You and I have had our last dance, Travis."

"Not even one for old times' sake?"

Claudia reached up and swept the hair back from the side of her face. "I didn't have any old times with you. Just hard times."

Rawlins' gaze probed Claudia's body like fingers. "Let's start now and work on some old times."

"You've been turned down, Travis," Joshua said. "Let it drop now."

Rawlins looked at Joshua for the first time, his lips pressed together in a thin line. The rebuff from Claudia found a focus in his resentment of Joshua. "Well, well," he said, "if it ain't the man with the shakes." He swiveled his head and spat on the walk, missing Joshua's foot by a few inches. "I should have finished you off the other night."

"Quit acting like a schoolboy, Travis. This isn't recess with some scuffle in front of the girls. Let's step back."

"You'll think schoolboy. I'm about ready to tear you a new asshole."

Joshua held up a hand. "Don't push it, Travis," he said quietly. "You're all alone this time." They faced each other in silence as Travis calculated his chances. In the background Big Ed could be heard announcing the winners in the tractor-pulling contest. After a moment Joshua reached out for Claudia's hand. "We're going to go home now." His voice was quietly emphatic. "Good night, Travis."

Rawlins' right hand slashed out. Joshua deflected the blow with a raised forearm and ducked under it. Rawlins' momentum carried him halfway around and Joshua leaned back against the well, drew back a foot, placed it on Rawlins' backside, and gave him a vigorous shove. Rawlins lost his Stetson as he went sprawling across the grass. Joshua reached down and retrieved the hat, brushing it off lightly with his hand. Rawlins scrambled to his feet and faced Joshua. He crouched, fists clenched.

Joshua didn't take his eyes off Rawlins. "Make a wish, Claudia," he said.

"I wish this saddle sore would disappear from our lives."

Joshua deliberately held the Stetson out over the world's deepest hand-dug well, paused for a moment, and dropped it. After a seemingly endless wait, there was a muffled splash. Rawlins was immobilized, struck dumb by the unexpected disaster that had overtaken his hat.

"You son of a bitch," Rawlins finally spluttered. He began to edge toward Joshua, moving to keep him pinned against the well.

At that moment Big Ed's voice could be heard announcing the winners of the wheat-scooping contest. He was calling Rawlins' name. "Mr. Travis Rawlins," the loudspeakers boomed, "come to the band shell, please. Mr. Travis Rawlins. First place in the wheat-scooping competition. Report to the band shell to claim your blue ribbon and twenty-five dollars cash prize money, compliments of the Plains Jaycees." Rawlins hesitated. His name was announced again over the loudspeakers, and then someone else was calling to him. A man had come over from the crowd in front of the band shell. "Come on, Travis," he said, pulling at his arm. "You beat me again. Let's go pick up your six-pack change and I'll help you spend it."

Slowly Rawlins backed away. Before he turned to go he pointed a finger at Joshua. "You owe me," he said.

"You overcharged me for the Winchester."

"You ain't paid the half of it."

CHAPTER FOURTEEN

Joshua and Claudia sat together on the front porch swing. They sipped iced tea and made small talk, and hoped that by waiting Todd would relent and come downstairs so they could visit. He had gone upstairs to his room when he saw Joshua pull up in the drive behind the Fairlane. Joshua nudged the swing into motion with a shove from his foot. The springs emitted a euphonious creak that gentled the senses. Joshua drifted on the sound, buoyed by the hot night air, and watched the June bugs fling themselves monotonously against the lighted screens of the front window and door.

A vehicle stopped down on the section line road where it joined the drive. Its headlights cut a yellow wedge in the night that dimly lit the fence line and telephone poles. The dust raised by the vehicle drifted across the beam of light like a night fog. In a few minutes the vehicle began to move. It turned up the drive and came slowly toward the house.

"You expecting company?" Joshua asked.

"No. Jake Vanlandingham might come out, or maybe Jess Walters. But I think they would call first."

Joshua allowed the swing to creak to a halt and watched the vehicle approach. As it rounded a small curve in the drive the headlights cut across the porch, and the glare blinded him momentarily. When the pinpoints of light stopped dancing on his retinas, he saw Travis Rawlins' turquoise pickup. He got to his feet. "I should have known," he murmured, and moved across the porch to the steps.

Rawlins gunned the pickup down the drive along the side yard, cut past the Fairlane and the Toyota, and spun around in a gravel-spewing U-turn. He roared back along the side of the house, wheeled into the front yard, and slammed on his brakes. The truck ground to a shuddering stop, headlights converging on Joshua and Claudia. Joshua didn't look directly at the headlights, but shifted his eyes just off to the side, preserving what was left of his night vision. There was no movement in the cab of the truck, and as the moments dragged on, the silence seemed to project itself toward them like the headlights, ominous and threatening. Joshua sensed Claudia's presence behind him, then felt her hand on his back. "Go inside," he said.

"No." Her voice was so soft it was barely audible, but it cracked with the force of a velvet whip.

The doors of the truck slowly opened. J.W. and Norton unloaded on one side of the cab, Rawlins and Farrell on the other. They faced Joshua without speaking. As he looked at the four men who had worked him over in the motel parking lot, Joshua couldn't resist. "Didn't you men get enough the other night?" His grin was hard and mocking.

"We decided to come callin' on Claudia," Rawlins said. "We was hopin' you'd object."

Joshua swept his eyes over the three men with Rawlins. He knew Rawlins' quarrel meant nothing to them. They were just drinking and hell-raising buddies, rowdy and belligerent. This fight was as good as any for a Saturday night. His eyes cut back to Rawlins. "There's a lot more trouble here than any of us really want," he said. "Let's not hook into it. You go on back to town. We'll go inside." Joshua backed up, moving Claudia with him. They reached the screen and stepped inside.

"Ain't you gonna invite us in?" It was the big man, Norton. The man with the gut hanging over the Skoal belt buckle.

Joshua said nothing. He just leaned against the doorjamb inside the screen and watched them.

"Just one drink," Norton badgered.

"One drink with the lady," Farrell echoed stupidly. His voice was as thin and stringy as his gaunt frame.

"They ain't gonna be sociable, Farrell." It was J.W. The big, heavyset man moved around in front of the pickup. He heaved himself up on the hood between the headlights.

"That's okay, J.W.," Norton said. "We brought our own stores."

He leaned inside the cab and reached behind the seat. He brought out a fifth, unscrewed the cap, and lifted it to his lips. Norton wiped his mouth with the back of his beefy hand, then capped the bottle and spun it through the air to J.W. J.W. reached up and caught it, drank, and passed it on to Farrell. The fifth made the rounds. Rawlins took a short slug the first time, but declined as it went around again. Norton swaggered up on the porch, peered past Joshua at Claudia where she stood against the far wall of the living room, then settled into the porch swing. "Pass me the hair of the dawg, Farrell. This is soft, country livin'." He bounced up and down heavily in the swing, then set it in motion with a kick from his scruffy engineer boots. Farrell, as loose-joined as a scarecrow, mounted the steps to the porch. He drew on the fifth, then tossed it to Norton.

Joshua watched them, trying to gauge their mood and intentions. He thought about latching the screen but decided against it.

Farrell turned and stared across the porch at the truck. He lifted a spadelike hand and shielded his eyes from the glare of the head-lights. "Turn off them damn lights," he growled. Rawlins reached in the cab and switched them off. Farrell turned back and saun-tered along the porch railing, trailing his hands through the flowers in the planters.

"Hey, Farrell," Norton called out, "pluck some flowers for the lady."

Farrell grasped several flowers with both hands and ripped them out of the soil. "I'd rather fuck and plow her," he said as he turned back to Norton, the plants crushed in his fists. Both men sniggered. Joshua looked at Farrell. The big man stood in front of the screen door, grinning crazily. Each hand clutched several mangled plants, their roots trailing black dirt. He looked like some deranged gen-tleman caller. Just then Joshua heard Todd's footsteps on the stairs.

Todd came into the living room, glanced at his mother, and then moved over to the door. He stood at Joshua's shoulder. "What's going on?"

"What's the matter," Joshua asked quietly, "don't you hear so good from up there anymore?"

Todd looked sharply at Joshua. "I can hear okay. What are they doing?"

"They just want to hoo-rah us. Try and scare us a little."

Farrell turned away from the screen. "Hey, Travis, you hear that?" He dropped the plants on the porch and wiped his hands on his shirt. "He says we're just trying to scare 'em a little." He laughed. It was a high, thin whinny.

Rawlins didn't respond. J.W., still perched on the pickup like some bloated hood ornament, picked it up. "How about it, y'all scared?"

"We're not scared," Joshua said, "but we're not stupid either. So let's call it a night."

Rawlins pushed himself away from the truck and stalked toward the porch. "The night is young. I say when it's over."

Joshua didn't take his eyes off Rawlins as he moved onto the porch. "Call the sheriff, Claudia," Joshua said. "Get him out here." He heard her lift the phone off the hook. Rawlins stopped and leaned a shoulder against the post by the steps. The Camel pack and kitchen match appeared. He lit up and watched Joshua, eyes derisive, slitted against the smoke. Joshua heard Claudia jiggling the phone hook; then she hung up and came back in the living room. She stopped at the French doors.

"The phone's dead," Claudia said.

"They cut the line," Joshua said. "That's why they stopped on the section line road."

Rawlins flicked his cigarette at the screen door. The butt bounced off and the glowing ash exploded in a shower of sparks. "You got it," he snorted, and started toward the door.

Joshua leaped back and slammed the front door, turning the dead bolt. Rawlins flung open the screen and rattled the handle, then delivered a kick with the toe of his boot against the bottom of the door. The solid oak didn't give. He whirled and vaulted over the porch railing and raced around the side yard. Claudia saw him through the dining room windows and rushed to the kitchen. Heart pounding, she reached the door just as Rawlins bounded up on the stoop. He slammed against the door and turned the handle at the instant she threw the dead bolt. The door held. Rawlins stood there, chest heaving from the exertion. He stared at Claudia through the glass. He reached out his right hand and pressed his fingertips against the pane. Claudia slowly backed up, her hand raised to her throat. Rawlins curled his fingers and drew the nails down across the glass with a skittering screech. He stepped backward off the stoop and turned toward the front yard.

Joshua met Claudia in the dining room. "Are you all right?" he asked.

"Yes," she breathed, her voice shaking a little.

Joshua went back to the living room and peered out the window. The men were grouped in front of the pickup. The fifth of whiskey was making the rounds again. Rawlins broke away and moved onto the front porch. He looked at Joshua through the window. "You might as well come on out and take your whippin'. There's no gettin' away from it."

Joshua stared at him, expressionless.

"We can come in and get you, but we'd have to bust up the house. You don't want that, do you?"

Claudia came up behind Joshua. "Don't go out, Josh. Don't even think of it."

Rawlins leaned back against the porch railing. "You ain't goin' anywhere. You're outnumbered and cut off."

The phrase whipped through Joshua, fusing past and present. Rawlins didn't know. Rawlins could never know. The thought leveled him out, steadied him. Joshua smiled.

Rawlins suddenly snatched up a flowerpot and hurled it through the window. The glass shattered. Joshua ducked. "Turn off the lights!" he hissed. Claudia and Todd hurried through the house and in a moment it was completely dark. Joshua braced himself by the front window, but Rawlins disappeared off the porch. Joshua knelt and peered into the night. Rawlins and the others were nowhere in sight.

"Where are they?" Claudia called softly from the dining room.

"I don't know." Joshua crept into the dining room, the broken glass crunching under his feet. He moved to the windows and checked the side yard and the drive down toward the shed. The night was moonless. Everything was obscured in dark shadows. The Toyota and the Fairlane were barely visible in the drive.

"See anything?" Todd whispered.

"No." Joshua stood off to the side of the windows a moment longer, watching. "Let's turn on the yard lights."

"I'll get them," Todd said. He moved quietly into the kitchen, and a moment later the light over the shed and the one on the pole near the front drive came on.

Joshua positioned himself at the French doors and tried to keep an eye out both the front window and the dining room windows. The night was quiet. No one was visible in the lighted farmyard. It was as though Travis and the others had disappeared. "Todd," he said, "go look out back by the kitchen window."

Todd's voice came softly from the kitchen. "I can see someone down in the garden."

Joshua joined Todd at the window over the kitchen sink. He saw Norton walking back toward the shed, carrying about four feet of lath used to stake the tomato vines. Norton took a swipe at the naked light bulb over the door of the shed. He missed, but connected the second time and the light bulb exploded.

"Josh," Claudia called quietly, "in here."

Joshua returned to the dining room and joined Claudia where she had taken his place at the window. Rawlins was shinnying up the wooden light pole. When he reached the top he licked his fingers, quickly unscrewed the light bulb, and dropped it to the gravel drive.

"What do they want anyway?" Todd was at his elbow.

"I had hoped they just wanted to raise a little hell," Joshua replied. "But they're capable of more meanness than that."

"Like what?"

"Almost anything. Beat me up really good." Joshua looked at Todd. "Maybe more than that from your mother." His words hung in the air as they maintained their vigil at the edge of the windows.

"What do we do now?" Todd's voice was hushed.

"Wait. And listen." Joshua stationed Todd in the kitchen and he and Claudia sat down by the French doors. Joshua leaned back against the doorjamb, positioned where he could see both the front window and the dining room windows. The minutes dragged. Joshua could see nothing beyond the windows. He strained his ears to try and pick up some sound, some movement, some clue as to where the men were and what they were doing. He heard nothing except his own pulse pounding in his temples. Claudia slipped a hand into his. They waited.

Suddenly one of the dining room windows exploded in flying splinters of glass as a rock sailed through it. Claudia jumped involuntarily and stifled a cry. Joshua gripped her hand tighter. The rock struck the far dining room wall, thudded to the floor, and rolled under the oak table. In quick succession other windows were smashed, both upstairs and downstairs, and when the rock-throwing ended, not a pane of glass in the Bishop farmhouse had been left unbroken.

Todd came into the dining room. "Let's go out and take care of those guys," he said, his voice a mixture of anger and frustration.

Joshua moved over to the dining room windows and stared into the night, trying to sort out the shadows.

"Well," Todd pressed, "how about it?"

"That's what they want us to do."

"Then let's oblige them."

"There are four of them and two of us," Joshua said quietly. "Do you think we can take them all?"

"I've got a four-ten in my room," Todd said, "That should improve the odds."

Joshua looked over his shoulder at Todd. "No guns," he said emphatically. "We get a gun, then they get a gun." He left the sentence hanging.

"So?"

"You can't do it halfway. Are you prepared to kill them, or have them kill us?"

"Well, what do we do?"

"We keep quiet and hope they go away." Joshua looked around at the broken windows. His eyes stopped at the front door. Just below the shattered glass he could see the dead bolt. "Do you have any tape?" he asked.

"In the bathroom," Claudia said.

"Let me have it." He followed her to the half bath off the kitchen. She removed a roll of adhesive tape from the medicine cabinet and handed it to him. He crossed the kitchen to the door and placed strip after strip of tape over the knob for the dead bolt. Then he went to the living room and taped the knob to the dead bolt there as well. "This will give us enough time to stop them if we keep an eye on the doors." Joshua went back to the dining room and laid the tape on the table. "Do you have a ladder anywhere on the farm?" he asked.

"Just a short stepladder in the shed," Claudia replied.

Joshua thought a moment. "Well, even if they found it, they probably couldn't come through upstairs very easy. At least we'd hear them if they try it." He stared into the darkness beyond the broken window panes. "Todd," he said, "go upstairs and see if you can see anything from up there." Joshua returned to the living room. He scanned the front yard through the window for a while. Even the wheat stubble at the edge of the lawn lay in dark shadows. He thought he saw movement behind Rawlins' pickup for an instant, but as he concentrated on the vehicle he saw nothing further. He shifted back to the dining room, stared out the windows for a while, then passed on through to the kitchen. He stayed at the window over the sink a long time. As he leaned against the counter he felt the jagged edges of broken glass under his hands.

Suddenly there was a loud crash and the sound of splintering glass from the front of the house. Almost simultaneously Claudia screamed Joshua's name. Joshua whirled and raced into the living room. Todd clattered down the stairs in a stumbling rush and crowded in behind him. A planter had been hurled through the front window, smashing out more of the pane. It lay on its side in the middle of the floor in a litter of glass and dirt and mulch. Norton was halfway through the window, headfirst, trying to insinuate his big paunch past the remaining shards of glass. Joshua stepped quickly up to him and drove a knee into his face. There was a sickening crunch as his nose flattened, smeared across his face like a ripe plum. Norton shrieked and sagged down against the glass at the bottom of the frame. Joshua and Todd grabbed him by the shoulders and wrestled him up, dumping him back through the window onto the porch. J.W. and Farrell, crouched down by the front door, scrambled over beside him. They lifted him by the arms and dragged him off the porch. He could be heard moaning and swearing as they hauled him out behind the pickup.

"That takes care of one," Todd said, breathing heavily from the exertion and the excitement.

"He'll be back," Joshua said.

"His nose ought to at least slow him down."

"May just make him madder," Joshua said. They retreated back to the dining room.

"What now?" Claudia asked.

"I don't know," Joshua replied. He looked at Todd. "Could you see anything from upstairs?"

"Not really. It's just too dark."

Joshua nodded. "You watch from the kitchen. I'll be in here." As Todd took up his place in the kitchen, Joshua hunkered down beside the French doors, brushed some broken glass away, and resumed his position there. Several minutes passed, the silence broken only by the sound of a dog barking in the distance. Then he heard a door to the pickup open and slam shut. He scrambled to his feet and hurried to the front door. The pickup engine kicked over, choked down momentarily, and then whined as the driver raced the motor. The truck lurched backward as the driver switched on the headlights. It spun out on the grass and headed down the drive. Joshua couldn't tell who was driving or how many were in the truck. He watched it make a left at the section line road, a wide, skidding turn without stopping, then gather speed and head back toward town. Claudia and Todd joined him at the door.

"Have they gone?" Claudia asked.

"The truck left. I don't know how many were in it." They peered past the broken pane in the door, listening carefully. The yard seemed deserted.

"I think they've gone," Todd ventured.

"Perhaps. Too easy, though."

"Maybe they took the guy with the busted nose to the doctor," he added.

Joshua smiled, but there was no humor in it. "They're all heart." He returned to his place by the French doors. "Let's wait a while." Claudia joined him, and Todd went back to the kitchen. "We'll stay real quiet," Joshua said, "and see what happens." He looked at his watch. It was just after midnight. A long time till dawn, he thought.

They waited. The minutes dragged by. Five. Ten. Joshua heard a vehicle down on the section line road. It didn't slow down and he listened to it as it rattled on past and disappeared into the night. Fifteen minutes. He got up and went to the kitchen. "Anything?"

"No," Todd replied.

Joshua returned to the living room and stared out the window. After a little bit, he turned back to Claudia. "I'm going outside."

"Do you think you should?"

"Well, they might be gone. If not, we may as well find out now." He began to peel the tape away from the handle to the dead bolt. "Go get Todd," he said. A moment later Claudia and Todd were at his shoulder. He felt in his jeans for the keys to the Toyota. "I'll go out and look around. You wait here. If they're gone, we'll take the Toyota and go into town."

Joshua unlocked the dead bolt and opened the door. He waited a moment, watching and listening, then pushed open the screen and stepped onto the porch. A board creaked under his foot. He paused, then moved to the steps. The night was quiet. Hot and still. He could feel the sweat between his shoulder blades. He scanned the yard, the big cottonwood, the field of stubble beyond the lawn. The shadows blended and fused and melted away into an oblong black blur. There was no sign of Rawlins or his buddies. He eased down the steps carefully, one at a time, until he reached the grass. He glanced over his shoulder. Todd stood in the door holding open the screen, with Claudia beside him. Joshua moved along the front of the porch, staying close to the railing. When he reached the corner, he stopped and studied the side yard. He could see nothing all the way to the shed. He started across the yard, being careful as he passed the big cottonwood, but no one was there. He approached the Toyota, moving slowly, one cautious step at a time, eyes and ears straining. Something was wrong. He stopped a dozen feet from the Toyota. Waiting and listening. Puzzled. He took a few more steps toward the Land Cruiser. Then he could see what it was. The tires were flat. He turned his gaze to the Fairlane. Its tires were flat as well.

Suddenly the horn on the Toyota blared. The sound ripped the night like a shell and lodged in Joshua's chest, where it detonated, fragging him with adrenaline. The flush pumped him up until he felt like his nerves were on the outside of his skin. He stood poised, watching the Toyota. Someone slowly rose up from the passenger side, where he had been lying down, and opened the door. It was Norton. The overhead light in the Land Cruiser lit his features with a pallid glow. His face was grotesque. A swollen mass of purple bruises, with eyes glaring through puffy heliotrope lids.

"You thinkin' about goin' somewhere?" Norton's voice was a clotted gurgle.

"You look like a nightmare," Joshua said. "Go haunt somebody else."

Norton swung his engineer boots out of the Toyota and found the ground. He pushed his bulky frame out of the seat and slammed the door behind him. "Farrell!" he bellowed as he fumbled in his pocket. He pulled out his jackknife and peeled the blade from the bone handle.

Joshua felt the violent edge creep across his soul. It was familiar. Frightening. He backed up, glancing over his shoulder. He saw Farrell step from behind the rear of the farmhouse and move along the side yard, cutting him off from a quick retreat to the front porch. Farrell stood there waiting, gaunt and lean, grinning.

"Norton," Farrell croaked, "we don't have to wait on Travis and J.W."

Joshua decided he had better neutralize Norton and his knife. He started toward him. He could hear Farrell rush him from behind, but he concentrated on the knife. Norton lunged at him with an underhand thrust. Joshua spun away and delivered a numbing flat-hand chop to Norton's forearm. As he did so, he glanced up to find Farrell, and saw Todd come flying over the porch railing and slam into him from behind with a crushing body block.

Joshua turned back to Norton. He had switched the knife to his other hand, and slashed upward at Joshua's midsection. Joshua fell away from the blade and swung hard with his right hand, trying to connect with Norton's nose again. He missed, and backed up to where Todd stood over Farrell. Farrell, wind knocked out of him, was struggling to get to his knees. "Finish him off!" Joshua grunted. Todd looked at Joshua quizzically and stood there, fists clenched, waiting. Joshua kicked Farrell hard in the ribs, then turned back as Norton stalked them.

"Josh!" It was Claudia, calling from the front porch. He looked up. She was standing at the railing, pointing toward the section line road. "It's Travis!"

Joshua saw the lights of the truck as it turned up the drive. A moment later the high beam flashed on and the lights illuminated the yard. The pickup accelerated up the drive. "Come on, Todd," Joshua said. They retreated to the porch, keeping an eye on Norton and Farrell. The pickup roared into the front yard as Joshua and Todd bounded up the steps and into the house. Joshua slammed the front door and turned the dead bolt in time to see the pickup slither sideways to a stop on the grass. The headlights went off and Rawlins and J.W. piled out of the cab.

"Tape the dead bolt, Todd," Joshua said. "The tape's on the

dining table." He went to the window to see what was happening in the front yard. Rawlins and the three men were huddled in back of the pickup, talking in low tones. J.W. pulled a half-pint flask from his hip pocket, hit it hard, and passed it to Farrell. There was more talk and then Rawlins turned toward the truck bed and dropped the tailgate. J.W. and Farrell unloaded some things from the truck while Norton and Rawlins climbed in the cab. Rawlins didn't turn on the lights, but backed the truck slowly out of the front yard, pulled around the Toyota and the Fairlane, and drove down by the shed.

"Keep an eye out front," Joshua said to Todd. He moved through the dining room and into the kitchen, keeping the pickup under surveillance. He could see Rawlins and Norton unloading the truck, but couldn't make anything out of it in the dark. They started back up to the house, Rawlins moving toward the rear kitchen window while Norton headed for the side yard. Each man carried a box. As Rawlins gingerly placed the box on the ground just beyond the kitchen window, Joshua heard a sustained dry rattle. Cages! Joshua froze. "Todd!" he yelled. "What's happening out front?"

"They're bringing some boxes up to the porch!"

"It's the snakes!" Joshua watched Rawlins and Norton return to the truck and haul up two more cages. Claudia hurried in and joined him at the window. She placed a hand on his arm. He could feel it tremble. "Don't do it, Travis!" Joshua warned.

"Then come on out!" Rawlins hissed.

"Maybe we should do it, Josh," Claudia whispered.

Joshua was silent for a moment. "No."

"Whatever they do to us is better than being dead."

"We have a chance in here," Joshua said. He watched Rawlins and Norton return with more wire cages. "There's no telling, now, what they'll do. It's gone too far."

"But that's crazy." Claudia's voice was breathless.

"Rawlins is crazy." Joshua watched Rawlins set another cage down with the others. He backed away from the window, moving Claudia behind him into the dining room. "Todd," he called out. Todd turned away from the front window and Joshua picked up a dining room chair and tossed it to him. He turned back to Claudia and gripped her by the arms as he faced her. "Use a chair," he urged quietly, "and stop them at the windows."

Joshua snatched up a chair and hurried back to the kitchen. He watched through the window as Rawlins carefully picked up a cage and opened the top panel. Joshua stood poised, holding the chair by its back like a baseball bat. Rawlins hefted the cage to his shoulder, turned it on its side, and jammed it against the window. He shook it, trying to dump the rattlesnakes through the broken pane. Joshua swung the chair. Glass went flying as he struck the cage and drove it back on top of Rawlins. Rawlins ducked away from the cage as it tumbled to the grass; then he sprang back to it and quickly closed the top panel.

As Joshua watched Rawlins readying for a second attempt, he heard the rising sounds of struggle from the front of the house. Broken glass. Blows. Curses. Claudia frantically calling to him. He rushed into the dining room. J.W. and Norton were maneuvering at the dining room windows, leering in the dark, each with an open cage of rattlers. Claudia stood in front of the windows, holding a chair, trying to anticipate their threat and parry it. Joshua turned the dining room table up on edge and rammed it against the bank of windows. It blocked off the lower half, but the top half was still open. At the same time he heard the crash of glass from the kitchen and hurried back to the door. Rawlins had flung an entire cage of snakes through the window. The cage lay on its side in the middle of the kitchen floor. As Joshua eased toward the cage, hoping to be able to close the top panel, he could make out the movement of a snake as it slithered from the cage and slipped into the dark shadows along the baseboard under the kitchen cabinets. He slowly backed up to the door. Another snake appeared at the opening in the cage, its wedge-shaped head weaving back and forth. Joshua stopped, mesmerized. He watched six more rattlers find their way onto the kitchen floor. He could make out the shadows of some. Others simply disappeared into the darkness. He heard a rattle somewhere near the refrigerator.

The sharp sound of shattering glass broke the trance. He turned back to the dining room. A wire cage had landed in the dining room near Claudia. A rattler emerged, gliding swiftly across the oak floor to insinuate itself against a leg of the table. Claudia shrank back and joined Joshua at the door to the kitchen. Another cage hurtled through the upper half of the windows, sailed over the table, and crunched against the far wall. As it came to rest, three rattlesnakes slipped into the room almost simultaneously.

"Todd!" Joshua called sharply.

Todd glanced away from the front window, where he had successfully held Farrell at bay.

"In here!" Joshua commanded.

Still holding the chair, now missing two legs, Todd backed out of the living room. He eased through the dining room, keeping an eye out for the snakes in the dark, and joined Joshua and Claudia. They watched, helpless, as Farrell dumped his load of snakes through the front window. Rawlins emptied two more cages at the kitchen window. Some snakes stayed on the kitchen counter, coiling themselves among the automatic coffee maker and the mixer and the canister set. Others dropped to the floor, hitting the linoleum with a flat, slapping sound.

Joshua and Claudia and Todd huddled together in the corner of the dining room by the door to the kitchen. Rawlins stared at them. His face was just visible at the kitchen window, framed by the shards of glass still held in place by the caulking, malice etched in hard lines across his features. "That's enough!" he yelled. His face disappeared from the kitchen window.

"Josh," Claudia whispered, her voice strained, "what shall we do?"

"Don't move. Let's see what happens."

They felt the heat and the stillness of the night close in on them, as suffocating and pervasive as the presence of the rattlers. Joshua thought he could smell them. Rotten squash. But he concentrated on it and decided it was just his imagination. Or his own fear that he could smell. He could hear them, though. There were moments of absolute silence. Then they would move about in some restless serpentine migration, gliding across the floor and spilling over each other. Sometimes they couldn't see the snakes in the dark. Only hear a sustained rattle or a fang-bared hiss. At other times a sinuous form could be made out, twisted across the floor like a warped shadow. Once, in the obscure gloom of a corner, a writhing snarl of rattlers rose up like some medusan nightmare, then shrank back into the darkness.

Joshua licked his lips, his tongue dry and thick. He swallowed hard. "You know," he finally rasped, "I think Travis outsmarted himself. They're damn sure not going to come in here now. All we've got to do is wait this out till morning."

"What time is it?" Todd whispered.

Joshua looked at the phosphorescent glow of his wristwatch. "One-nineteen."

"We'll never make it."

"Sure we will."

They waited, trying not to move or make any noise. Muscles knotted in painful cramps, followed by spasms of involuntary twitching. They shifted their weight from one foot to the other, trying to ease the strain. Light-headedness crept toward a total blackout. Then the rattlers would move again in a sibilant shift.

"Why don't they stay still?" Joshua muttered.

"They're nocturnal," Todd replied.

"You're a big help."

"Joshua!" Claudia's voice was cracked with terror.

"What is it?" Joshua breathed, but he already knew.

"There's a snake crawling over my foot!"

Joshua reached out a hand in the dark, found hers, and gripped it. "Just stay still a moment," he said.

"It's around my ankle," Claudia said in a frozen voice.

"Todd," Joshua whispered, "will it strike if we move?"

"Not necessarily."

"Do you think there would be snakes on the stairs?"

"Probably not."

"All right, let's ease along the wall to the stairs. No sudden moves." They inched their way, slowly, cautiously.

"It's still there," Claudia whispered in a barely audible voice.

"Keep moving," Joshua said through clenched teeth. "Slow and easy." His foot brushed against a snake. He hesitated momentarily, then slid his foot along the floor. He pushed the snake ahead of him. Suddenly it moved. Uncoiling and gliding away. Then Joshua heard it rattle, a brittle buzz no more than a foot away. He stepped again, waiting for it to strike. Nothing happened. Another terrified step.

"There's snakes all along here, Josh," Todd whispered frantically.

"Keep moving."

Todd reached the stairs first. He carefully took the first step, then scurried halfway up the staircase. Claudia made it to the stairs, but didn't mount them. "The snake is still around my ankle, Josh." Her voice broke.

"Put the other foot on the first step," Joshua said. He steadied her with his hand as she stepped up. "Now let the other foot hang over the floor." He could barely make out Claudia's leg in the dark, dangling awkwardly in the air, as she balanced against the wall with one hand and gripped his with the other. The rattler was coiled about her ankle. The end of the shadow swayed rhythmically as the head oscillated back and forth. Joshua eased up onto the stairs behind Claudia. "Maybe it will drop off," he murmured. Sweat beaded on his forehead as he watched the snake.

"I'm too tired, Josh." Claudia's leg began to sink toward the floor.

"Todd," Joshua said, "get your shotgun and all the shells you have. Do it quick."

Todd hurried up the stairs.

"Hold on, Claudia," Joshua urged. She began to tremble from muscle fatigue and exhaustion. Her leg sank lower to the floor.

Todd could be heard banging around in his room. Then he was back, easing carefully down the stairs. "I've got it," he whispered.

"What's the action?" Joshua asked.

"Single shot, breech loading."

"Load it." Joshua could hear the breech break and then snap closed. He reached out and took the shotgun from Todd. "Is it on safety?"

"The safety's when you half cock the hammer."

"Give me a couple of extra shells," Joshua said. He took the shells and tucked them under his belt. "Now," he said, "take hold of your mom by the shoulders and hold her so she can keep her balance."

"I've got her."

Joshua let go of Claudia's hand and moved up the stairs, stopping just above them. "Can you reach the hall light switch?"

"Yes."

Joshua sat down on the stairs and braced a foot where he could rest his forearm on his knee. He swiveled the shotgun into position so he had a clear shot past Todd and Claudia, and sighted along the barrel toward Claudia's extended foot. He cocked the .410 and slid his finger into the trigger housing. "Claudia," he said quietly, "close your eyes and keep them closed. Hold still no matter what happens." Joshua took a deep breath, let it out halfway, and held it. "Now!" he grunted.

The light flashed on. A large gray diamondback was coiled around Claudia's ankle. It reared its head, fangs bared, poised to strike. Joshua pulled the trigger. The stairwell reverberated with the blast of the shotgun. The snake's head was shredded to a bloody pulp. Joshua scooted down beside Claudia. He grabbed the remains of the snake, twisted it free, and flung it into the dining room. Claudia clutched at him, sobbing and retching. He held her and looked down into the dining room. The floor was alive with writhing snakes. He felt his own gorge rise in his throat. He clung to Claudia.

A steady tapping finally insinuated itself into Joshua's consciousness. It was the sound of a fingernail striking glass. He looked up. Farrell, tapping a broken pane with a bony index finger, was staring at them through the dining room window. "Turn out the lights," Joshua said. Todd hit the switch and the hall went dark. Joshua helped Claudia up beside him on the stairs. He took one of her hands in his and held it till the trembling began to subside.

The tapping resumed at the dining room window. Repetitive. Incessant. And then, overriding it, Farrell crooned in a wailing, chilling singsong, "Guess where J.W. and Travis are?"

Todd shifted his weight and started to get up. Joshua reached out and placed a restraining hand on his shoulder. "Wait," he said.

"You can wait if you want to." Rawlins' drawl was pitched just above a whisper. "But we're through waitin'."

Joshua whirled and focused on the sound at the top of the stairs, but could see nothing in the dark. He fumbled at his belt and withdrew a shotgun shell, loaded the .410 and cocked it. "Hit the lights, Todd." The bulb came on and Joshua could see Rawlins and J.W. at the top of the stairs, one on either side, half hidden from view, staring down at him from around the corners of the upstairs hall.

"While you were busy there," Rawlins went on, "we just obliged ourselves of the window over your porch." He glared at Joshua. "Which will it be now? Us up here, or them snakes down there?" He nodded his head at the dining room floor below them.

Joshua cursed himself for forgetting about Todd's window over the porch. He leveled the .410 at Rawlins. "Very little difference from where I sit," he said.

Rawlins eased back behind the corner a bit more. "You think?" He took the toe of his boot and pushed a wire mesh cage from the hall to the head of the stairs. He tipped it over on its side. The top panel was open. A rattler appeared, head weaving its primeval dance, then slithered forward and settled onto the top step. A second and third snake joined the first. One was a four-footer, the other no more than eighteen inches in length. Then four more spilled onto the step.

Joshua raised the shotgun and fired. Two rattlers were decimated and flung back against the riser. He quickly broke the breach and inserted the other shell from his belt.

"You got an unlimited supply of ammunition?" Rawlins taunted.

"That's right."

"Good, 'cause we got an unlimited supply of snakes." Rawlins reached around the corner, partially shielding himself behind the wall. He had the lath Norton had used to swat out the light bulb over the shed. He wedged the tip of it into the heap of rattlesnakes on the top step, slipped it under the fat body of a three-footer, and flung it at Joshua. Joshua threw himself flat on the stairs as Claudia screamed his name. The rattler sailed over his head, glanced off the wall of the stairs, and landed in the middle of the dining room.

Joshua held a palm out flat to Todd. "Keep the shells coming," he ordered. Todd slapped a shell into his palm and Joshua fed it into the breech. He stood, took another step up the stairs to improve his firing angle, sighted on the snakes, and fired. He snapped open the breech and plucked out the spent shell at the same time he took another shell from Todd. He locked it in and again blasted the coiled tangle of snakes. Joshua reached out for another shell and loaded the shotgun as he surveyed the mangled nest of rattlers. There was an occasional shudder or twitch among the snarl of lacerated snakes, but nothing more.

"Let's go!" Joshua barked at Todd and started up the stairs.

Rawlins and J.W. bolted down the hall corridor into Todd's room. Joshua paused at the top step and probed the bloody rattlesnakes with the barrel of the shotgun. There was no movement. He vaulted over them, Todd close behind, and started after the two men. He slowed as he reached Todd's room, cocked the shotgun, and slid around the door with his back against the wall. Rawlins was already through the window and on the porch roof. Joshua caught J.W. with one leg extended carefully past the remaining pieces of broken glass, the other still on the floor. Joshua lifted the .410 to his shoulder and took aim. J.W. froze in the window and looked at Joshua. Fear obliterated his features. Joshua's finger tightened on the trigger, then he lowered the weapon and eased the hammer down to safety. "Get out," he said.

Rawlins ducked his head down to the window, a sneer distorting his face. "You pussy," he said contemptuously.

Joshua thumbed back the hammer and snapped the shotgun to his shoulder.

Rawlins disdainfully took J.W.'s hand and gave him an assist through the window. He and Rawlins retreated across the roof and clambered to the ground on the rose trellis.

Joshua leaned against the wall, not moving, body and mind slack. He raised his eyes. Tom Bishop stared back at him from the opposite wall. Tom Bishop with the Cimarron County High School Mustangs. Tom Bishop as a KU Jayhawker. Tom Bishop, almost as big as life, as a 49er running back. Tom Bishop. Tom Bishop. Tom Bishop. Joshua put the .410 on safety and held out a hand to Todd, who stood quietly, almost apologetically, at his elbow. "Give me all the shells," he said.

Todd dug deep in his jeans pocket and placed four shells in his palm.

"All of them."

"That is all of them. I didn't even have half a box."

"Great. Just great." Joshua slid the four shells inside his belt, then stepped past Todd and went back down the hall. He knelt at the top step. The wooden lath lay on the floor where Rawlins had dropped it in his rush to get out of the house. Joshua picked it up and used it to turn the wire cage right side up. It was empty. He handed Todd the lath, trudged down the stairs, and slumped wearily to the step beside Claudia. He looked up to see Norton, his face looking like he'd lost all fifteen rounds of a title fight, staring at them through the dining room window. "Turn off the lights," he muttered. Todd flipped the switch with the tip of the lath. They sat in silence for several moments.

Joshua wiped a hand down across his face. "I couldn't shoot them," he said. Claudia laid a hand on his arm. Joshua tapped the .410 with his index finger thoughtfully. "And the trouble is, Travis knows I can't."

"Will they try and come back through the upstairs?" Claudia asked.

"Probably," Joshua replied.

"What should we do?"

"We only have five shells," Joshua said, almost to himself. "If they really have more snakes like Travis said, we don't have enough shells to keep ahead of them. And if they fill the upstairs with them . . ." His voice trailed off.

"If you could shoot Travis and the others," Todd suggested tentatively, "you wouldn't have to kill them."

Joshua looked at Todd. "Your shells are bird shot. Unless I was close in, this popgun wouldn't really hurt them, let alone kill them. They'd just keep coming. I'd have to try and shoot them in the face." He paused and let the implications of that sink in. "With just five shells, it won't do any good to keep peppering them."

"Do you think we could go outside with the shotgun," Claudia asked, "and use it to get to Travis' pickup and get away?"

Joshua thought a moment. "He might not have left the keys in it. That means I'd have to try and force him to give them to us." He shook his head. "That would be hard. And if I did use the shotgun I'd only have one shot. It takes too much time to load this thing. They'd rush me." Joshua paused. "We need another place to hide and wait them out."

"There's no place in the house," Claudia said.

"What about the storm cellar?" Todd asked.

Joshua thought a moment. "It just might work."

"How would we get there?" Claudia asked. "The house is crawling with snakes."

Joshua patted the stock on the shotgun. "With this," he said. "Todd, can you reach the light switch on the dining room wall with that lath?"

Todd hefted the lath in his hands. "Probably."

"Okay, here's what we'll do. You turn on the dining room light. I'll clear out the snakes with the .410 and we'll move along the wall. If necessary maybe you can flip some away with the lath. We'll go to the kitchen, make sure we've got a path to the door to the cellar, then turn out the dining room light. We'll go down to the cellar in the dark and barricade ourselves in." Joshua stopped. "Any questions?"

Claudia and Todd shook their heads.

Suddenly Joshua held up his hand for silence. There was a rustle at the front porch. "Someone's going back up on the porch roof," he said. "Wait here." He raced up the stairs and down the hallway. He stopped just inside the door to Todd's room, cocked the .410, and waited. He heard someone creeping toward the window. Maybe two people. He decided to waste one shell. When they reached the window, he fired. The remaining glass shattered in a hail of buckshot. Joshua backed out of the room, hurried quietly down the hall, and joined Claudia and Todd on the stairs. "That will slow them up," he whispered. He broke the breech and inserted his second shell. "Let's get to the storm cellar. Hit the dining room light," he said to Todd.

Todd moved to the bottom of the stairs. Joshua gripped his hand to steady him as Todd pressed his belly against the wall, leaned around the corner, and reached for the light switch. Joshua could hear the lath sliding up and down along the wall as Todd swiped at the switch. On his fourth try the dining room light flashed on. Joshua hauled Todd back around the corner to the stairs. He could see Norton's face at the dining room window and quickly raised the .410 to his shoulder. Norton ducked away in panic. Joshua surveyed the dining room. Some thirty rattlesnakes nestled at various points around the floor, most of them along the walls. There was a nest of snakes coiled on the floor beneath the first step. He pointed down with a nod of his head. "Get rid of those first," he said to Todd. "Fast."

Todd jammed the tip of the lath into the mass of snakes and started flipping them away. One rose and struck the lath, driving it back with a thrust that nearly jarred it loose from his grip. He flipped another snake away and the remainder slithered out of reach.

Joshua stepped to the floor. A half-dozen rattlers were strung out along the wall to the kitchen door. He knelt in the hope he could scatter the shot down the length of the wall, and squeezed the trigger. Two snakes were dead along the wall. Several glided away.

One coiled, fangs bared, blocking their way. Joshua quickly re-loaded, using the next to last shell. He stepped out where he could look into the kitchen. It was shadowed from the dining room light, but there were no snakes just beyond the door.

"They's in the dining room, Travis!" It was Norton at the dining room window again.

Joshua whirled and aimed the shotgun at Norton. He dodged away. Joshua spun back and blasted the rattler, spattering it into the corner. "Let's go," he said as he inserted the last shell in the shotgun. "Stay close." He could hear a pair of boots upstairs. Some-one had decided to come through the window. He hurried to the door to the kitchen, Claudia and Todd right behind him, and squat-ted and stared along the baseboards on either side of the cellar door. Nothing. He looked around the corner toward the half bath. A rattler lay coiled by the doorjamb four feet away. It was a thin gray shadow, maybe sixteen inches in length. He looked down the other wall toward the refrigerator. A foot away two snakes lay twined together. Joshua could hear steps at the head of the stairs. He pointed the shotgun at the two rattlers and fired his last shell. "Hurry!" he whispered, and motioned Claudia and Todd into the kitchen toward the cellar door. They rushed to the door and waited. Joshua backed into the kitchen, keeping his eyes on the foot of the stairs.

"Josh!" Claudia's voice was a muffled shriek. "The snake!"

Joshua glanced down, heart hammering. The tiny rattler near the bathroom door was gliding swiftly toward him. He swung the shotgun by the barrel. The stock caught the rattler just as it coiled and struck. Its fangs glanced off the polished wood and then its neck was crushed beneath the stock, smashed to a pulp against the linoleum floor. Joshua, nerves jangling, reached out with the shot-gun and switched off the dining room light. He crossed the kitchen, fumbling for Claudia in the darkness. Todd pushed open the cellar door and started down the steep steps. Claudia took Joshua's hand and led him down. He stopped when he was through the door and quietly pressed it closed behind him. Then carefully negotiated the remaining steps, hand trailing along the rough stone of the cellar wall. When he reached the floor he paused. It was much darker than the house. The small window, dug into the ground on the rear wall, allowed almost no illumination. Claudia guided him across the cellar and then pulled him down beside her on the floor, where Todd sat against the workbench.

They waited in the dark, straining the senses for some clue as to the whereabouts of their assailants. They heard nothing. Not a whisper. Not a footfall. The minutes dragged. Joshua looked at his watch. It was only nineteen minutes past two. He held Claudia's hand. It felt small and cool and dry in his sweaty palm. They waited.

Rawlins' voice abruptly broke the silence. "Where the hell are they?" Claudia jumped involuntarily and clutched a hand at her throat. His voice seemed to come from right beside them.

"I don't know." It was J.W. He and Rawlins were standing right outside the cellar door.

"Well," Rawlins growled, "I'm done waitin' around. Let's find 'em." They moved off and there was a moment of silence; then Rawlins called out, "Farrell!"

"Yeah?" It was Farrell's nasal twang on the stairs in the dining room.

"Anything?"

"I ain't heard nothin' or seen nothin'."

"Well, they sure as hell ain't out here."

"Maybe they're in that bath off the kitchen." Norton's voice sounded as bloated and gummy as his face.

"How about I take a look?" Farrell drawled.

"You forget the house is full of snakes?" J.W. asked.

"Hell," Farrell muttered, "rattlers won't fuck with you unless you fuck with them."

"He's still got the shotgun," Norton warned.

"He won't use it," Rawlins sneered.

Joshua heard the floor creak above them. Measured footsteps through the dining room. Silence. "Bathroom door's open, Travis," Farrell called out. "They ain't in there." A pause. "I don't think they's in the kitchen, either. Awful dark in here, though. I think . . ." Farrell's voice broke off into a high-pitched wail. "He got me! Oh, God, he got me!"

"Farrell?" Rawlins yelled.

"He did it!" Farrell's voice was a terrified moan. "He hit me!"

"Where are you?"

"In the kitchen."

"Get back to the stairs."

"I can't," Farrell whimpered. "Oh, God, there's snakes all around me." Joshua heard a crash as Farrell stumbled blindly against the kitchen counter and knocked one of the canisters to the floor. A moment later he lurched against the door to the cellar and slumped to the floor. "Help me," he moaned pitiably. "Please help me."

"We can't get to you, Farrell," Rawlins said, his voice harsh. "Get to the stairs."

"I can't move. Oh, God, it hurts. My leg hurts."

"J.W.'s going in over the porch, Farrell," Rawlins called out. "He'll meet you at the stairs."

"I can't make it," Farrell cried in a panicky whimper. "I'm gonna die." His voice trailed off into a sustained moan; then he fell silent. "Travis!" he suddenly shrieked. "You got to help me!"

"We ain't comin' in there," Rawlins snarled. "Get back to the stairs. J.W.'s waitin' for you."

Farrell could be heard sobbing, "Please help me. J.W.?" It was a plaintive cry. "Norton? Somebody? Please."

Claudia gripped Joshua's arm. "What are we going to do?" she whispered.

"Nothing," Joshua replied flatly. They sat there, hunkered down beside each other in the dark, listening to Farrell's terrified, increasingly incoherent, helpless moaning.

"Josh," Claudia urged quietly, "we should help him."

"If we give ourselves away we've got no fallback position."

She glanced up above them where Farrell could be heard groaning and weeping. "It sounds like he's right at the door."

"We've got the snakebite kit down here in my tackle box," Todd offered.

"Jesus Christ," Joshua muttered, "those guys are trying to kill us." He shook himself free from Claudia's grip, scooted over and knelt by Todd. "The day we went hunting, you told me that a chickenshit way to hunt rattlers was with gasoline."

"That's right."

"Why?"

"Gasoline bothers them. You can flush them out of their dens easy."

"Will kerosene have the same effect?"

"Probably."

"Okay," Joshua said, "we'll use the kerosene you have down here for the Coleman lanterns to drive any snakes away. If it works, we'll pull Farrell down here with us." He turned to Claudia. "Help me find the kerosene."

Claudia filled an empty Mason jar she found among the shelves of canned goods with kerosene. Joshua took the jar and Todd joined him as he moved to the steps that led to the kitchen. They could hear Farrell retching and vomiting. Joshua started up the steps, moving cautiously in the dark. When he was almost to the top, he glanced back over his shoulder. Todd hadn't moved. "Come on," Joshua urged.

"I'm afraid." The words were a tormented whisper.

"So am I," Joshua said. His voice was sympathetic, quiet and soft. "Now let's go." He quietly turned the doorknob, swung the door back, took another step, and peered into the kitchen. Farrell was sprawled just beyond the door, moaning to himself. There were snakes along the wall to his left, and a large diamondback was stretched out right beside his big frame. Joshua looked to the right along the baseboard of the kitchen cabinets, but everything was hidden by shadows. He glanced back over his shoulder at Todd and inclined his head toward the kitchen, a gesture that implied "let's get it over with." He reached around the doorjamb to his right with the Mason jar and sloshed a little kerosene along the baseboard under the cabinets. There was a rasping hiss. Joshua shrank back as a three-footer roiled away from the cabinet toward the far side of the kitchen. Joshua splashed some kerosene to his left at the snakes coiled along the wall. The floor seethed with angry rattlers as they streamed away. Joshua took the last two steps up to the kitchen, and tossed a dollop of the kerosene at the diamondback beside Farrell. It rose in fury. Joshua flung the last of the kerosene at the rattler's head, and it slithered away.

Farrell roused himself, shuddering with a hoarse gurgle as the snakes churned around him. "Oh, God," he quavered. Then he saw Joshua's obscure form crouched above him in the dark of the kitchen. "Travis?" he burbled hysterically. "Oh, thank you, Travis." His nasal voice cracked with relief. "I'm obliged to you . . ." Farrell stopped short as he recognized Joshua.

"Keep quiet," Joshua urged softly. "We're going to get you out of here."

"What are you doing?" Farrell wailed in a strangled voice. "You're gonna kill me."

"If we were going to kill you, we'd have left you alone. Now shut up!"

"Farrell!" Rawlins' harsh drawl broke in from the dining room window. "What's going on in there?"

"I think that feller's with him," J.W. called from his place on the stairs.

"Can you see what's happening?" Rawlins asked.

"No."

"Well, dammit, take a look!"

"Are you crazy? Them snakes is all riled."

Joshua and Todd grabbed Farrell up between them and wrestled his long frame awkwardly down the steps. Farrell moaned and whimpered as they jostled him along. As Joshua maneuvered past the door, he pushed it closed behind him. When they reached the floor, Claudia met them and whispered, "I've cleared the top of the workbench." They stretched Farrell out on the long table. He began to babble incoherently, calling for Travis with fevered pleas for help. Joshua clamped a hand over Farrell's mouth and muffled his cries.

"Get the snakebite kit," Joshua whispered at Todd. Todd located the tackle box under the workbench and placed it beside Farrell. He rummaged among the contents until he found the kit. "Have you ever used it?" Joshua asked.

"No."

"Okay, come here and hold Farrell. Try and keep him quiet." Joshua took the kit from Todd and reached out in the darkness for Claudia. "We'll need some light," he said.

"We can light a Coleman lantern."

"Too bright. Just use matches."

Claudia fumbled for the matches on the shelf over the workbench. She leaned against Farrell's leg. He moaned loudly, shook free of Todd, and began to swear. Todd tried to hold him, but he flailed away belligerently with both arms and sent the tackle box with the snake-hunting gear crashing to the floor.

"They's in the storm cellar, Travis!" It was Norton's puffy voice just outside the cellar door.

Joshua looked at Claudia. "No act of kindness ever goes unpunished," he muttered.

Claudia couldn't help herself. She began to giggle.

"It's not funny," Todd said sharply.

"You've got to see the humor in every fight," Joshua said.

Suddenly there was a thunderous banging on the metal storm door. "Open up!" Rawlins bellowed.

"They're going to have lots of trouble getting in here," Joshua whispered with a confidence he didn't feel. "They sure as hell won't try and come through the house, not after what happened to Farrell." He turned back to the workbench. "Might as well see what we can do for him now that we have him down here. Let's light a Coleman."

Claudia found the matches and lit a lantern, adjusting the flame on the mantle to a steady white glow. She placed it on the shelf over Farrell. Joshua slid Farrell's jeans up to expose his legs. He was wearing work shoes without socks. His right calf was swollen, ballooned up half again its normal size. There was a scattering of livid purple blotches under the skin. Just above the shoe top, two fang marks could be seen. It looked like he had been stabbed twice with an ice pick.

There was a sudden jarring crash against the metal cellar door. Joshua jumped, startled. A succession of blows rained down on it. It was metal against metal. Maybe a shovel or an ax. But the door didn't give.

Joshua turned back to Farrell. "Let's hurry up and get this done." He broke open the snakebite kit. It contained two large suction cups, a rubber tourniquet, a surgical blade, and a set of directions. Somehow he had expected a lot more. Joshua turned the directions toward the Coleman and scanned them. "Rule number one," he muttered, "is to get the victim to a doctor as soon as possible." He laid the directions aside and picked up the tourniquet. "We may not help him much. It's been more than thirty minutes since he was bitten." Joshua placed the tourniquet around Farrell's calf four or five inches above the bite. He peeled the blade out of its sterile packaging and made an incision through each puncture wound. Farrell moaned, but it apparently didn't hurt much. Joshua wondered if that was a bad sign. He applied a suction cup over each incision and stepped back. "That's it," he said. "The great snake-bite cure." He checked the tourniquet to make sure it wasn't too tight, turning to observe the cellar door as another series of heavy blows rained down on it.

"Should we turn out the Coleman?" Claudia asked.

Joshua shrugged. "They know where we are. We might as well see what we're doing." Abruptly the banging on the cellar door stopped. Joshua moved over to the steps and listened a moment. He could hear someone shuffling around in the grass. "Travis," he called out.

"Yeah?"

"You ought to get your friend here to a doctor."

"You just open up and we'll do that."

"I've still got the shotgun, remember."

"Yeah, but you ain't got any shells," Rawlins drawled slyly. "If you had, you'd have used 'em when you went up to get Farrell."

Joshua turned back to the cellar, grimaced, and went over to the workbench. He looked at Farrell. He was sweaty. His features were ashen. He breathed with shallow fits and starts, moaning restlessly. Joshua could smell the alcohol on his breath. Hell, he thought, alcohol is supposed to be a cure for snakebite. If science won't save him, maybe the Jack Daniels will.

Claudia came up beside Joshua. She placed a hand on his arm. "Is he going to be all right?"

"How should I know?"

"Maybe we ought to let Travis in to get him so he could take him to a doctor."

"You mean the way he took Norton to a doctor?" Joshua shook his head. "Travis doesn't want to help him, Claudia. He wants to get us."

"It's madness!" Claudia looked around her helplessly. "All of it. How could it even happen?"

"Easy," Joshua said quietly.

"What do we do now?" she asked.

"Wait," Todd said, and sat down with his back against the shelves of home-canned produce.

Joshua nodded. He went to the Coleman lantern and turned it down to a dim glow. He sat down and leaned against the workbench where he could keep an eye on the cellar door. Claudia joined him, sitting down and clutching her knees to her chest. Long minutes passed. There was no sound from beyond the storm cellar. All that could be heard was Farrell's restless moaning and the soft hiss made by the Coleman lantern as the mantle burned but was never consumed. Joshua tried to imagine what Rawlins was up to. To try and be ready. One step ahead of him. He shook his head. Weariness overwhelmed him. He could think of nothing. Make no plans. His head sagged down on his chest. He waited. Time seemed to grind to a halt.

From the rear of the house they heard a slow metallic squeak. Like something needed to be oiled. Creaking. It came closer to the house. Joshua looked at Claudia, his question unspoken. Her eyes were wide. She pressed a hand to her throat and shook her head. The sound, a grating, high-pitched uneven squeal, was just outside the rear of the cellar. Near the window.

Todd jerked erect. "It's the grain loader!"

Suddenly the tiny window in the rear wall of the cellar shattered. The grain loader smashed through it like some monstrous spear. The end of the galvanized steel tube lodged in the center of the cellar just below the kitchen floor. A moment later they could hear the gears grinding on one of the wheat trucks as it backed up to the rear of the house. The gasoline engine on the grain loader coughed to life, and the auger bit within the tube began to spin with increasing speed. In a matter of seconds wheat spilled into the cellar in a pyramiding pile. And with it came a fine mist of wheat dust and chaff. Within moments the small confines of the cellar were filled with choking dust. It clogged eyes, noses, and mouths. Strangling and stifling. It seeped into pores like a smothering fog.

Joshua and Claudia and Todd backed away from the deluge of grain. It swept around them like a flood of quicksand, sucking at them. They sank into it, floundering, choking and coughing. Joshua waded through the thigh-high wheat to the workbench and removed a snake hook from the wall above it. He pushed his way to the steps that led to the kitchen and hauled himself free of the grain. He squinted into the boiling dust, drew the metal pipe back over his shoulder, and rammed it into the end of the grain loader where it spewed wheat into the cellar. The spinning auger blade deflected it, and it caromed off against the floor joists. Joshua pitched forward and plunged into the maelstrom of wheat. He came up choking and wheezing and retrieved the snake hook. Gasping for breath, he made his way back up the steps. He reared back with all his might and again tried to ram the snake hook into the end of the grain loader. This time there was the shearing, grating shriek of metal on metal, and the grain loader ground to a stop, jammed by the snake hook wedged between the auger and the steel casing. The engine choked down and died.

Joshua sagged to the steps, head between his knees, chest heaving. He coughed and gagged, trying to clear the muck from his throat and lungs. The dust gradually settled and his breathing eased. He surveyed the cellar. It was waist-deep in wheat. Claudia was half buried, wedged against the shelves of canned goods. She had her hands over her face and was trembling from exertion, still gasping for air. Todd stood on the workbench, face pressed into the subflooring in the hope of finding cleaner air, straddling Farrell, who was coated with dust like a mummy. Joshua dropped into the wheat and waded through it to Claudia. He reached out and touched her face, wiping the dust from her features. "Are you all right?" he choked.

She nodded. "How about you?"

"I could use a bath."

Todd crawled down from the workbench. He checked on Farrell and began to brush some of the dust from his face. Joshua pushed through the grain and joined him. He helped Farrell sit up and pounded on his back while he coughed and hacked. Farrell began to moan and whimper again and Joshua eased him back on the table.

"You've got real nice friends, Farrell," Joshua muttered. He loosened the tourniquet on Farrell's leg for a few moments, then reapplied it. Suddenly he froze. Inhaled deeply. The smell seemed to vaporize his muscles. For a moment he thought he would fall. He gripped the workbench and turned. A thin sluice of gasoline spilled from the end of the grain loader. The amber liquid splashed onto the wheat, seeping into it. He watched, horrified, as it percolated through the grain, saturating it. "Put out the lantern," Joshua ordered.

Todd reached to the Coleman on the workbench and damped

out the flame. They waited in the darkness, half buried in the wheat, scarcely breathing as they listened to the gasoline as it trickled through the grain loader. Suddenly it stopped. The silence and the smell of fumes threatened to unhinge the mind. A few moments later it began again.

"They're using the can by the pump," Todd whispered.

"Surely they wouldn't try to burn us out," Claudia gasped.

"The son of a bitch has gone berserk," Joshua said. In his mind's eye he could see the matches appear miraculously in Rawlins' leathery hand and burst into flame.

"He'll burn the house down," Todd said.

"He'll burn us down," Joshua muttered. He listened to the gasoline spilling onto the wheat. "We've got to put an end to it."

"How?" Claudia asked.

"I'll go out and try and stop them."

"I'm going, too," Todd said.

Joshua turned to look at Todd, a determined shadow at his shoulder. "Okay," he said. He waded over to Claudia. "Have you got some more empty Mason jars?"

"Yes."

"Find some."

Claudia rummaged through the shelves behind her in the darkness. "I can only find four."

"Good enough." Joshua took two of the jars, left one with Claudia, and handed the other one to Todd. "Let's get out of here." His voice was urgent.

"What about Farrell?" Todd asked.

"We can't take him with us. He'll have to hope we can get to his friends before they decide to torch the place." Joshua pushed across the cellar to the kitchen steps, pausing beneath the grain loader. He held his Mason jars under the trickle of gasoline and filled them. "Fill your jars up," he said as he struggled free of the wheat and started up the steps. He stopped near the top, placed one jar on a step at his feet, and turned around and pulled Claudia up behind him. When Todd joined them, he said, "We'll go straight through the kitchen and go upstairs."

"What if J.W. is still on the stairs?" Todd asked.

"Hope he is. That will be one less out back." Joshua pulled the door open and reached down and picked up the Mason jar of gasoline. He lifted it toward them like a toast. "Be quiet and be careful, but let's move!"

Joshua dashed some gasoline under the baseboard along the kitchen cabinets, sloshed some on the other side of the door along the wall toward the bathroom, and flung the rest of it in an arc into the kitchen. He could hear the hiss and rattle of the snakes as they slithered away. He stepped quickly into the kitchen and started toward the dining room door. Claudia and Todd followed, splashing gasoline blindly to either side as they hurried after Joshua. Joshua paused at the dining room door, slopped gasoline from his second Mason jar along the wall, then scattered the remainder toward the center of the dining room. The floor itself seemed to move away from him. He moved along the wall toward the stairs. There was a brittle rattle in front of him. A snake reared its head in the darkness, fangs bared. From behind Joshua, Claudia flung the last of her gasoline at the coiled rattler. It struck, an aborted lunge that fell short of Joshua's leg, then glided away.

Joshua plunged to the stairs, prepared to meet J.W. head on. The stairs were empty. He raced to the top, Claudia and Todd at his heels. He stopped in the hall, his breathing labored. "Stay here," he said to Claudia. "If you smell smoke or have any reason to think they've started a fire, get out. This old place will go up fast." Joshua started down the hall toward Todd's room, stopped, and turned back. "If you have to get out, get into the fields and try and make it to a neighbor. Don't come looking for us." He went down the hall and into Todd's room, shoes crunching on broken glass. A second later Todd joined him at the window over the porch.

Joshua stared out the window and listened a moment. Nothing. He turned to Todd. "There are no rules and no referees and no penalties. Do whatever you have to." Todd nodded slowly. Joshua stepped through the window and crept across the porch to the trellis. He swung down it and dropped quietly to the ground. He waited for Todd, then led the way down along the side of the house. He paused at the kitchen stoop and listened. Farrell's frightened ramblings and moanings could be heard filtering up through the cellar door. From the rear of the house came the muted chink and rustle of activity. Joshua skirted the cellar door, stopped at the corner of the house, and peered into the backyard.

A wheat truck was backed up to the house. The rear panel had been jerked out and the grain loader extended from the truck bed through the cellar window. Rawlins was up in the truck, pouring gasoline from the gas can into the grain loader. Norton and J.W. stood on the ground with their backs to Joshua, observing Rawlins' progress and offering advice in hushed tones.

Joshua motioned to Todd and rushed them. He slammed into Norton, trying to smash his face into the side of the truck. Norton half turned and slid away. Joshua only succeeded in sending him sprawling in the grass. Joshua spun around and sent a right cross to J.W.'s beefy jaw just as Todd hit him with a chest-high tackle and drove him against the truck. J.W. chopped down on Todd's head with his elbow and delivered a kick at Joshua, missing his groin and catching him on the thigh. Joshua stepped in close and stabbed the stiffened fingers of his right hand straight into J.W.'s throat.

Rawlins staggered across the wheat in the truck like a man wading in a mud bog. When he reached the edge, he leaned over and swung the gasoline can at Joshua's head. It struck him a glancing blow above the right eye. Joshua's knees buckled as blood poured from a jagged laceration. Norton hit him from behind, driving him to the ground and grasping him in a bear hug. Joshua lashed backward with his head, smashing into Norton's battered face. Norton shrieked and rolled away, hands clutched to his face. Joshua struggled to his knees, trying to clear his head, wiping the blood from his eyes. He glanced up and saw Todd and J.W. exchanging blows as they wrestled back and forth along the side of the truck, using it like a fighter would use the ropes in a ring.

Rawlins jerked his belt from his jeans and dropped on Joshua, driving his knees into his back and slamming him face down to the ground. He whipped the belt around his neck and twisted it, clamping down like a vise. Joshua clawed at the belt but felt his world going black. Rawlins tightened his grip and reared backward to avoid Joshua's grasping hands as he tried in vain to reach back and wrest the belt from Rawlins' grasp. "Take the belt," Rawlins grunted at Norton. Norton, still nursing his injured face, rolled to his feet and took the belt from Rawlins. The big man straddled Joshua's hips and hauled on the belt as Rawlins swung away. Rawlins stepped over to where J.W. and Todd grappled with each other. He kicked Todd's feet out from under him. Todd crashed to the ground and J.W. fell on him, throwing a muscular arm around his neck and driving his other fist into his face. Rawlins stepped back. "Take care of these two guys," he rasped, and turned on his heel and disappeared around the corner of the house.

Joshua wedged the fingers of both hands under the belt and eased the pressure on his throat. He sucked air into his lungs, deflating the balloon that threatened to explode inside his skull. Norton renewed his efforts to choke Joshua into unconsciousness, snuffling and wheezing through his bloated and bloody face. Joshua twisted his arm behind him and forced it up along the inside of Norton's thigh. Norton leaned into the belt and bucked against Joshua's probing hand. Joshua reached Norton's crotch, jammed his hand backward, and gripped his privates. A thin wail was forced from Norton's lips. He released the belt and slammed a fist against the back of Joshua's head as he jerked backward and wrenched free of Joshua's grip. Joshua rolled over, kicking and scrambling, broke free and stood up. As Norton struggled to his feet, Joshua moved in and gouged his eye with an extended thumb. Norton bellowed and flung a fist at Joshua's head. Joshua ducked into it and it slid harmlessly past. He slammed both palms against Norton's ears, and drove a knee upward into his belly. Norton sank to his knees. Joshua kicked him in the groin, doubling him over, then raised both hands high over his head like a club and sent them crashing against the back of Norton's skull. Norton sprawled facedown in the grass. Joshua sank to his knees beside him, gasping for breath, fighting off a dizzying exhaustion.

Claudia's shrill scream floated on the hot night air. Her cry for help washed against Joshua's senses. He roused himself and turned to find Todd and J.W. They were still on the ground, locked together in mute struggle. Todd had broken J.W.'s hammerlock, and they clawed and punched each other. Joshua moved in close and kicked J.W. in the ribs. J.W. grunted, turned away from Todd, and grabbed at Joshua's foot. Joshua sidestepped, raised his foot and sent it smashing down on J.W.'s outstretched hand, then stepped in and delivered another kick to his chest. This time J.W. caught Joshua's foot and tripped him. He lunged toward Joshua, but Todd flung himself on his back and drove him to the ground. Joshua scrambled up and kicked J.W. in the side of the head. He kicked again, and J.W. shuddered convulsively and lay quiet.

Another scream reached Joshua. Claudia was calling his name, but her voice was cut off in midcry. The silence was more chilling than her call for help.

"Hurry!" Joshua gasped to Todd as he grabbed J.W. by the shirt. "Give me a hand." They dragged J.W. over to where Norton knelt, vomiting in the grass. Joshua kicked Norton in the back and toppled him over into his own vomit. They worked swiftly, stretched the two men out on the ground back to back, and encircled their necks tightly with Rawlins' belt. Joshua rummaged in J.W.'s pocket, found his cigarette lighter, and tossed it to Todd. He glanced around, picked up the gasoline can Rawlins had clubbed him with, and emptied the contents over Norton's and J.W.'s prostrate forms. He knelt beside Norton and grabbed him by the hair, jerking his head up where he could see his face. "Can you hear me, you baboon's ass?" Joshua hissed.

Norton grunted an affirmative response.

"If you or J.W. move a muscle, Todd is going to flick your Bic permanently. Understand?"

Norton didn't respond.

Joshua shook him violently by the hair. *"Understand?"*

"Yes," Norton croaked.

Joshua stood and turned to Todd, his face twisted with fury. "If these bastards try anything, do it!" he said. "I mean it!" He wheeled and raced to the front of the house, and scrambled up the trellis. As he crossed the roof of the porch, he could hear muffled cries and the sounds of a struggle in Todd's room. He plunged through the window. A shard of glass raked his back but he was oblivious to it.

Rawlins sat astride Claudia on the floor. Her blouse was ripped open and a thin trickle of blood oozed from the corner of her mouth. Rawlins slapped her hard as he fended off her attempts to scratch his eyes out, and worked his hand into her jeans.

Joshua crouched low and charged. He slammed a shoulder into Rawlins' back, piling him into a heap against the far wall. Claudia scrambled away as Joshua rolled to his feet and turned to face Rawlins. Rawlins pushed himself up from the floor and stood with his back against the wall. They evaluated each other in silence across the shadowy room, neither moving. A pinched smile on his lips, Rawlins doubled his fists and edged toward Joshua. Joshua waited for him, then stepped in and flashed a right to Rawlins' left eye. Rawlins took the blow and countered with a left to Joshua's head. They moved toward each other cautiously. Joshua jabbed with his right, two swift successive blows to Rawlins' nose. Rawlins roundhoused Joshua with a right to the head that staggered him. They backed away.

Slowly Joshua pressed in on Rawlins, backing him toward the corner of the room. He threw a right. Rawlins blocked it with his forearm and counterpunched, catching Joshua on the chin. Joshua edged in closer, took another blow, and then charged, pinning Rawlins in the corner. He drove a fist into Rawlins' midsection and caught him with a quick, glancing uppercut before Rawlins grabbed him and wrapped his long, sinewy arms around his chest. Rawlins squeezed, tightening his grip with crushing, relentless force. Joshua reared back and smashed his forehead into Rawlins' face. He wrenched free and aimed a short jab at Rawlins' jaw. Rawlins took the punch and lunged forward, closing his fingers around Joshua's neck. Joshua felt Rawlins' thumbs gouging into his windpipe. He whipped a knee up between Rawlins' legs, then jammed his hands up inside Rawlins' forearms and broke his choke hold. He brought both hands back down in a vicious chop to either side of Rawlins' neck.

Rawlins sagged backwards against the wall. Joshua bored in with a series of punches to his face. Rawlins stumbled forward, trying to get a grip on Joshua's arms, but Joshua slammed a knee into his gut and drove him back against the wall again. He hit Rawlins with a slashing right cross, drew back and threw another quick right. Rawlins' knees buckled and he began to slump toward the floor. Joshua hit him again with his right fist while he twisted his left hand into Rawlins' shirt front and held him up. He kept smashing his fist into Rawlins' face, slowly driving him to the floor.

Suddenly Joshua was pushed aside. He turned and raised an arm in defense, fearful that Norton and J.W. had somehow gotten away from Todd. It was Claudia. She flung herself at Rawlins' face, nails extended like claws, slashing the skin. "Kill him!" she sobbed. "Kill him, kill him, kill him, kill him." Her words turned into a tormented, chanting moan. Joshua gripped her by the shoulders and pulled her away. Lifted her up. Steadied her on her feet. He turned her to him and held her until she calmed. He gazed at Rawlins' unconscious form. "It's over," he said.

Joshua looked up and found himself staring at Todd's bric-a-brac shelves. The fearful, familiar memorabilia of Tom Bishop's war. Of his war. It was all there, in front of his eyes. Two new items had been added. Tom Bishop's business card and the souvenir American flag. Joshua picked up the card and tilted it in the shadows so he could make it out. It seemed as marvelous now as the first time he had seen it.

Joshua stared back down at Travis Rawlins. He stooped and tucked the card in Rawlins' front shirt pocket. There with the Camel cigarettes, where he would find it the next time he lit up.

EPILOGUE

Joshua and Claudia and Todd climbed the low rise toward the Maple Grove Cemetery.

Summer storm clouds drifted away to the south. The base of the deep purple thunderheads was suffused with crimson, tinted by the sun as it sank below the distant horizon of the Cimarron River Valley. The river was a ribbon of green that meandered across the plain toward the Oklahoma panhandle. The endless wheat fields, now reduced to stubble, mirrored the burnt orange of the western sky. A late afternoon thunderstorm had passed through, and nature's violence of wind and rain and lightning had broken the hot spell.

Cooled by a breeze that smelled of wet, newly cut wheat, Joshua followed Claudia and Todd as they picked their way among the markers. They let themselves into the Bishop family plot as the last glint of sunlight reflected off the granite gravestones. Without a word, they went to work. Joshua realigned and oiled the hinges on the gate. Todd repaired the fence, reattaching fallen pickets and setting weather-loosened nails. Claudia braced a sagging corner post, pulled weeds, and cleared snags of tumbleweed and windblown litter.

Finally, they stood together at the foot of Tom's grave. The valley was obscured as the twilight deepened. The barren knoll seemed an isolated promontory cut off from the rest of the land. Joshua knelt and removed the flag from his pocket. He tucked a corner of the blue field under the brass marker and traced his fingers across Tom Bishop's name. "I know I have a debt that I can never repay," he said slowly. "Maybe that's why tributes are made."

Claudia knelt beside Joshua and placed a hand over his. "Last night, Josh, you paid that debt. You did," she said, with quiet emphasis. "Let it go now."

Joshua lifted his gaze from his friend's grave. Night had fallen, and scattered lights from the farmhouses dotted the limitless prairie.